Blood Rose

Also by Margie Orford

Like Clockwork
Daddy's Girl
Gallows Hill
Water Music

Blood Rose

A Clare Hart Thriller

MARGIE ORFORD

WITNESS
IMPULSE
An Imprint of HarperCollinsPublishers

This book was originally published by Oshun Books in 2007.

EPub Edition MAY 2014 ISBN: 9780062339072

Print Edition ISBN: 9780062339089

10 9 8 7 6 5 4 3 2 1

For my parents Jock and Rosie

Blood Rose

Blood Rose

Scorpio Rising ...

No MOON. THE *desert wind knifes down the gully, rattling the dry grass. Stars hang heavy above the dunes. To the east, the sky is clear. In the west, the retreating fog hovers over the sea. The vehicle crests the dune, its lights malignant twin moons. Car doors open, spilling a peal of laughter, music, the tang of tobacco.*

Later, the heft of a pistol in your hand. Perfect. Circled forefinger and thumb slide down to trace the blind eye. A fingertip dipped inside the barrel fans desire, warms your cold body. Pace back one step, two. He watches, the target. Hands bound. Breath held. Eyes riveted. Filled with the hope that you mean something else. Not this. Not you.

Your finger curled round the trigger anticipates the weight needed to fire. Uncurls, extends the ecstasy. Your eyes on the metal marker, an erect nipple on the barrel. Breathe out. Your breath mists the desert air. Breathe in. Breathe out as you beckon. Release. The force of it explodes through your arm, chest, head, groin and erases everything.

Turn and reach for a cigarette. The match flares into the night, filling again with calls and stars. The cigarette glows; the nicotine stills the choppy sea that is your blood. You yearn for what is coming.

Oh. His final breath tongues up your back. You turn to look. Wonder lingers in the unblinking eyes, almonds above the high cheekbones. The crumpled whorl of the ear is innocent of the blood marking the forehead. The open eyes glaze. You go home to sleep, tail lights red in the dark.

Scorpio's tail is poised over the numinous star at its base. Winking in the centre of the constellation, the star-eye mocks the dead face. The blood soaking into the sand summons the first wave of tiny scavengers. Insects, flies, bacteria marshal themselves for the onslaught.

Chapter One

THE SOUND SLICED open Clare Hart's Monday morning, dragging her out of a catacomb of sleep. She sat up, heart pounding, and pushed a tousle of hair from her face. It was her cellphone writhing on the bedside table. She reached for it, knocking over a glass of water. She shook the droplets off the phone and onto the sleeping cat. Fritz hissed and dug her claws into her mistress's bare thigh. Clare caught the tiny bead of blood on her nail before it trickled onto the sheet.

'Witch!' she hissed. The cat strutted out of the room, flicking her tail in regal affront.

'Dr Hart?' the phone crackled.

Clare pulled the duvet around her naked body. 'Who is this?' The reception was always bad in her bedroom.

'Captain Riedwaan Faizal. South African Police Service.'

Clare sat up, zero-to-panic alert. 'Where are you?' The other side of her bed was empty.

'I'm downstairs. Buzz me in.'

'You bastard!' Clare could not hide the relief in her tone.

'Tell that to my mother.'

'Where's my tea?'

'Come on, Clare. It's freezing out here and the security guard is getting suspicious.'

'You know the deal, Riedwaan. You get sex and a bed for the night; I get tea as I wake up.'

'I'm trying to break your habit. I've got you a cappuccino and hot croissant instead.'

Clare wrapped her gown around her body. 'Fair enough. Hang on.' She pushed the red button on the intercom, listening for the thud of Riedwaan's shoulder against the glass door. He came upstairs, bringing with him a blast of cold dawn air and two steaming coffees.

'Giovanni's. My favourite.' Clare took the coffees from him and led the way to the kitchen.

Riedwaan followed her down the passage. 'Maybe you should give me some keys. I could have brought you this in bed.' He tipped the croissants onto a plate and opened the microwave.

Clare opened the plastic coffee lid. 'Maybe.'

She snatched the *Cape Times* he had clamped under his arm and went back to bed. Clare had allowed her defences to be breached once, long ago. The consequences had been devastating. It would take more than breakfast in bed for her to lower her defences a second time.

But Riedwaan pinged the microwave optimistically a second time and put his coffee and the croissants onto a tray.

In the bedroom, Clare had propped herself up against the pillows. The soft fabric of her wrap fell open as she leaned over to get a croissant.

'I love this about you.'

'What?' asked Clare, her mouth full.

'That you wake up ravenous.' Riedwaan reached forward, cupping her breast on an upturned hand. The air seemed thin, as if there was only just enough oxygen, which he would have to use judiciously. He moved his hand down her body, onto her hip. Clare put her cup on the table and slid down the bed. She pulled him towards her, practised hands undoing buttons, seeking the satin warmth of the skin on his belly, his back.

'I'm glad you came back,' she whispered.

Riedwaan smiled down at her. 'I'll be back any time for a welcome like this.'

When he reached for his coffee again, it was cold …

'It's time to get up,' said Clare.

'Stay a bit.' Riedwaan tightened his arms around her. 'You're going away.'

'I've got things to do.' Clare slipped from his grasp and went to the adjoining bathroom.

Riedwaan listened to her hum as she splashed and opened and closed cupboards. 'Do you hum when I'm not here?' he asked.

The humming stopped. 'None of your business.'

He rolled over and looked out at the grey sea heaving itself against the rocks. He had meant to tell Clare last night about his wife's decision to return to South Africa.

When she came out of the bathroom, she was wearing a tracksuit. 'You coming?' She bent down to put on her running shoes.

'You must be joking.'

Clare reached under the duvet, her hands cold on Riedwaan's chest. 'I'm not. You need to do more exercise than occasionally getting it off with me.' She turned towards him at the door, sunlight catching her face and the trace of a smile.

'Clare, I wanted to—'

'What?' She raised an eyebrow.

But Riedwaan could not spoil the happiness he had coaxed from her. 'Your eggs, fried or scrambled?'

'Hardboiled would be apt, don't you think?' Then she was off, two steps at a time.

'Feed Fritz,' she yelled up the stairs. 'Then she won't attack you.' The door slammed and she was gone.

Chapter Two

ONE THOUSAND SIX hundred kilometres north, as the crow flies, Herman Shipanga lay waiting, the cold biting through his thin mattress. The houses hunkered together for protection from the wind that moaned across the exposed dunes of the Namib Desert, only breaking into its hyena-laugh when it slunk between the houses. The wind probed cracks in the bricks, places where doors and windows had shrunk from their frames; it sought out and found tender limbs uncovered in sleep.

At last it came: the siren's wail, tearing through Walvis Bay. Shipanga threw back the covers, his damaged hip protesting. He stepped over the huddle of children asleep on the floor, filled a bowl with water and went outside to wash. As he threw out the icy water, the siren wailed again. The fishmeal factory looming over the pinioned houses belched yellow smoke. Shipanga gagged at the stench.

His wife was up, stirring porridge on the two-plate. 'You should be used to it by now. The smell of money,' she said by way of a greeting as she handed him a bowl. He shovelled down the porridge without appetite.

He pulled his jacket on over his blue overalls. The children stirred, puppies burrowing back into the warmth of each other's bodies. He bent down to stroke the smooth forehead of his youngest before leaving.

Outside, he broke into a steady trot, footsteps echoing down the empty streets. The viscous fog parted for him. A dustbin, a chained bike, a woman walking her dog materialised just in time for him to avoid colliding with them. He took a short cut through the alley running between the sandy yards. It spewed him out at the back of the school. Walvis Bay Combined School was perched on the edge of the town. Here, the shifting red sand shored against the perimeter fence as if looking for a way in. Shipanga slipped through a gap in the fence and fetched a rake from his caretaker's shed.

He made his way to the youngest children's playground and closed the tall wooden gate behind him. The jungle gym reared up in the mist. The swings hung mute beneath their frames. Vacant, except for the last one.

The child's knees were drawn close to his chest. He was leaning, with adolescent nonchalance, against the chain looped around the yellow swing.

'What are you doing?' Shipanga called.

The boy did not answer. These swaggering older boys always taunted Shipanga, mimicking with pen marks on their own pocked cheeks the ritual scars on his face. The triple verticals were the last trace of the home Shipanga had left to seek his fortune in this sunless port.

A cat's paw of wind buffeted the swing, but still the boy remained silent. Anger welled hot and painful in Shipanga's chest. He grabbed the chain, turning the boy to face him.

The startled insects paused only for a moment before returning to their busy feasting. Where the forehead should have been, a third eye leered.

Shipanga's rage gave way to horror. He backed away, his eyes riveted by the swing's cargo. When he reached the gate, he turned and ran towards a pair of lights raking over the parking lot.

'Mr Erasmus,' he gasped, his chest raw with exertion and shock.

'What?' The headmaster was unlocking the boot of his car. He did not bother to look up.

'Someone's there.' Shipanga put his calloused hand on the man's arm. 'On the swings.'

'Speak to Darlene Ruyters. She'll deal with it.' Erasmus took his briefcase out of the boot.

'It's a child, sir.' Shipanga blocked the man's path, anger returning. 'Another boy.'

'The same as the others?' asked Erasmus, looking at the caretaker now.

Shipanga nodded. Erasmus walked towards the enclosed play area, opening the gate to reveal the figure twisting on the bright-yellow swing.

'Who brought him here?' Sweat beaded Erasmus's forehead.

'I don't know.'

'The first one in town,' Erasmus said, flicking open his cellphone. Calling an ambulance sustained the illusion of hope. 'Go and wait for the police, Herman. I'll watch him. And don't let anybody through the gates.'

Shipanga walked towards the gate, the corpse's staring eyes prickling his back with dread. The leaden sky was silvering the truck approaching the gate. George Meyer, always first, rolled down his window. 'What is it?' asked Meyer.

'An accident,' Shipanga explained. 'In the playground. We're waiting to see what the police say, Mr Meyer.'

'Thank you,' said Meyer. He shot a sidelong glance at the small red-haired boy sitting next to him. Oscar was craning his neck forward to see what was wrong. Mrs Ruyters was Oscar's teacher. Her car was there. That part was right. Herman Shipanga stopping them at the gate wasn't, even though his familiar smile was a comforting white flash in his face.

A shiny new Mercedes Benz skidded to a halt behind them. Herman Shipanga stepped forward as a man hurled himself from the driver's seat and planted his hand on the caretaker's chest. Shipanga cracked his knuckles and stood his ground. Twenty years on fishing trawlers gave him the edge over a manicured man who spent his days in a heated office.

'Why is this car blocking my path?' demanded the man.

'No school today, Mr Goagab,' Shipanga said. 'You must wait here, please. There was an accident at the—'

'I must speak to Mr Erasmus.' Goagab pulled out his phone. Before he could dial, Erasmus appeared, attracted by the noise.

'Explain this, Erasmus,' Goagab shouted. 'Why can't I drop off my sons? I demand an explanation.'

'I'm sorry, Mr Goagab, but you'll have to wait. Everyone will have to wait. The police are on their way. They'll decide.'

Erasmus was relieved to see a blue light glowing in the distant mist. A pair of cars pulled up. Two men got out of a white 4x4. Elias Karamata was dark, shaven-headed and compact, just the hint of a beer belly pushing at his crisp khaki shirt. Kevin van Wyk was lithe and precise. In the right light, he could pass for a movie star.

'Who's in command?' asked Erasmus, looking from one to the other.

A woman heaved herself out of the other car, a clapped-out bakkie. 'I am,' she said. 'Captain Tamar Damases.'

Erasmus suppressed a sigh and took her hand. It was smooth to the touch. 'Thank you for being so quick. You know Mr Goagab?' he asked.

'I do. Good morning, Calvin.'

'What about my meeting? I've got to get to the mayor,' bellowed Goagab.

Tamar Damases's jaw set hard under her soft skin. 'You'll wait here. Either in your car or outside. You choose.'

'I'll report you to Mayor D'Almeida, Captain Damases,' said Goagab.

'Would you?' she said. 'I'm sure that he'll appreciate the time to tell the media that we've a third dead child to bury within the same number of weeks.'

Goagab looked apoplectic, but when Karamata folded his muscular arms and stepped forward, he retreated, his sons scrabbling after him into his car.

'Now,' said Captain Damases, turning to Erasmus, 'where's the body?'

THE HEADMASTER OPENED the gate to the kindergarten playground. The high wooden paling shielded only three sides of the area. The fourth side was an open stretch of sand that sloped down to the barbed-wire perimeter fence. A red jungle gym, blue roundabout, a wall painted with rabbits and squirrels in aprons and hats. The yellow swings. A gust of wind twisted the body. The chain creaked, dismembering the silence.

'Oh.' Tamar Damases's voice was soft with pain.

'Strange fruit,' murmured Van Wyk. Tamar looked at him, surprised. She would not have marked him as a jazz man.

'Shall I send the scene-of-crime officers here when they come, Captain Damases?' asked Erasmus.

'You've been watching too much American TV,' said Tamar with the ghost of a smile. 'This is Walvis Bay. Scene-of-crime officer? That's me. Police photographer? That's me. Forensics? That's me. Ballistics? That's me, too.'

Erasmus stared at her blankly and she softened her tone: 'Would you call the mortuary and see which pathologist is on post-mortem duty? It should be Dr Kotze. Get her to send a van round.'

'I'll leave you to it then.' Erasmus hurried off, relieved to have a task.

'Get some crime-scene tape, would you, Sergeant van Wyk?' Authority crackled in Tamar Damases's voice. 'Cordon off the area. I want to limit access to the crime scene. Both the previous investigations were compromised because everyone was everywhere.'

'Pity you weren't here to take charge, Captain.' Van Wyk didn't bother to hide the sarcasm in his tone. 'Must be difficult to do a good job' – he ran his eyes over her full belly – 'the state you're in.'

Tamar watched him go, relieved to be alone with the body. The wind was picking up now from the south, chilly and mean. She zipped her jacket up to her chin and turned to examine the dead boy. Looking at him on the swing, his back to her, he could be just another child carrying on some game for that moment too long. If he could climb out of the swing, if they could stand back to back, she and the boy, as growing children love to do, they would have been evenly matched.

When she moved towards the swing, marking her path, the boy's eyes seemed to follow her progress like one of those trick portraits, beckoning her towards him. Tamar obeyed, her feet as small as a child's, picking through the stony litter, recording each detail on her camera. The sand at the base of the swing was slightly disturbed, punctuated by a series of neat, tapered holes. She inserted an index finger into one. It was about two inches deep.

The swing that cradled the body faced due north. It was the only one at an angle. It was also the highest off the ground, the most difficult to reach. If Tamar had to hazard a guess, she would say it had been chosen for the view, but the sullen fog had its back hunched low and she could see nothing of the desert. She turned her attention and her camera to record the macabre display before walking down to the edge of the playground.

There were several gaps in the fence. She bent down, her camera steadied by her elbows on her knees. Tamar was comfortable squatting like this. She had learned to do this alongside her grandmother; the old lady explaining to the sharp-eyed child how to read the hidden signs that told if an animal had moved through an area, if a person had stopped to think or eat, or if a woman had been there to do her secret business. Hurrying. Ambling. Hunting. Hiding. There were signs for all actions if you knew how to look.

The jungle gym was livid against the fingers of grey mist. The fog flattened everything, bleaching detail from the landscape. Tamar straightened up, waiting for the fog to thin and for an anaemic sun to cast its short-lived shadows. When it did so, she could just make out the marks. They were so faint as to be almost absent: blades of grass broken and angled in the same direction, an impression on the salt-encrusted sand as faint as a palm print on glass. She increased the contrast reading on her camera and snapped pictures until the sun withdrew. She unclipped the loop of yellow tape from her belt, fingering the service pistol nestled below her rounded belly en route. She stepped backwards into her own footsteps and taped off the area, finishing as her phone rang.

'Helena,' she answered. There was no need to check the caller identity.

'What is it?' asked Helena Kotze. 'Another weekend stabbing?' Working in a port had hardened the young doctor's heart and sharpened her eye.

'I almost wish it was,' said Tamar. 'It's another dead boy.'

'Same as the others?'

'Looks like it,' said Tamar, her voice catching. 'A boy again. Young. Maybe fourteen. This time in a swing at the school in 11th Street. Looks like a bullet that's punctured the forehead. Ligatures on both wrists. Wrapped in a dirty sheet.'

'Was he killed there?' asked Helena.

'No. No blood to speak of. Nothing on the ground. Smells as if he's been dead a couple of days, too.'

'I'm in the middle of surgery. I can't come for another hour or so. Can you do the preliminaries?'

'I'm about to,' said Tamar. 'Your guys are here. I'll speak to you later.'

Tamar looked up at the two mortuary technicians skulking at the gate. The two Willems, she liked to call them. 'How are you, boys?' she greeted them.

'Cool. You?' mumbled the taller Willem. His skin was raw from a rushed shave.

'I'm okay,' said Tamar. She shook out two evidence bags.

'Who's that?' asked the other Willem.

'Don't know yet,' said Tamar. 'We'll only get an ID later.'

The two Willems stuck their hands in their pockets, hunching their shoulders like a pair of bedraggled crows. 'Why so sad?' asked Tamar.

They shrugged. The taller Willem lit a cigarette. Tamar knew their disconsolateness wasn't for the dead boy. The pair moonlighted for Human & Pitt, the most enterprising of the flourishing undertaking franchises in Walvis Bay. The funeral director paid them one hundred upfront for the first call to a fresh body, provided it brought in business. A three-day-dead body that nobody had reported missing was not worth getting into a suit for first thing on a Monday morning.

They watched listlessly as Tamar walked back to the boy and steadied the swing between the uprights and her knee. The stench of decay haloed the body. Another day and it would have been unbearable. Tamar took a deep breath and bagged the hands bound with nylon rope. The boy's shoes were covered with fine sand. She bagged those too. She looked at the wound in the middle of his forehead. It was seething with larvae. Two, maybe three, days in the life cycle of the blowfly, Tamar guessed.

Trusses held his arms locked around his knees, but the shroud had loosened. There was a large area of bloodied flesh where the boy's oversized shirt gaped. Tamar probed the writhing mass of feeding larvae, her nausea dissipating as she worked. She checked the boy's pockets. She did not trust the pair at the gate. If there was anything of worth on the body, it would be gone by the time the corpse got to a hospital gurney.

One trouser pocket held nothing but a black pebble. Tamar held it in her hand. She could see why the boy would have picked it up. It was symmetrical, smooth. There was some change in the other pocket and a greasy till slip for twenty-four Namibian dollars. This she dropped into a separate bag. In the other pocket was a pencil stub. There was an initial, looked like a K, inked into one ridge of the pencil. Could be his initials; could be something he picked out of a rubbish bin.

Tamar stood up and signalled to the two men. Like acolytes, they stepped forward with the stretcher, placed the frail body on it and covered it with a sheet. Tamar opened the wooden gate and walked with them as they carried their small burden to the van where Karamata and Van Wyk were keeping the curious at bay. The two Willems put the stretcher down to open the doors.

'The same thing?' asked Karamata.

'Looks like it to me,' said Tamar. 'Have a look. See what you think.'

Karamata knelt down beside the dead boy and pulled the sheet back. He pushed the grimy shroud aside and traced the boy's decaying cheek.

'You know the boy?' asked Tamar, prompted by the burly man's tenderness.

'He played soccer with my sons.' There was a sheen in Karamata's dark eyes when he stood up. 'Be careful with him,' he said as the two technicians picked the body up. The taller Willem sneered, but his swagger stopped at the hips and he picked up the boy without jolting him.

'His name?' Tamar asked.

'Everyone called him Kaiser,' Karamata replied.

Tamar nodded. The pencil with the K was his then.

The bang of the mortuary van's doors seemed to release the crowd of onlookers. They pulled out cellphones to tell those who had been unlucky enough to miss the excitement what had happened: that there was another body; another boy was dead, another of those street children who wheedled money at every traffic light these days.

'His surname?' asked Tamar.

'Apollis,' said Van Wyk. 'He has a sister. Sylvia. A whore, like he was. That'll be why he's in the van.'

'You knew him too?' asked Tamar.

Van Wyk spat out the match he had been using to clean his teeth. 'It's a small town, Captain.'

Captain Tamar Damases watched the vehicle bump down the road. Twice before this had happened and she had been unable to do a thing. Boys caught, killed, displayed, buried.

The violent secrets encrypted on their bodies turned Tamar's mind to Dr Clare Hart.

Chapter Three

RIEDWAAN FAIZAL PUSHED back the covers and went to the window, wrapping a towel around his waist. After a couple of minutes, Clare appeared in the distance, taking the curve of the Sea Point Boulevard in her stride. At this distance, in the thin September sunlight, she was a stranger to him, despite his intimate knowledge of her, gleaned in secret and hoarded. He watched her until she had disappeared, then he pushed his hands back through his hair. It had caused him a lot of trouble at high school, the way it grew straight up. He was always being sent to the headmaster to prove that he hadn't gelled it. That was long ago now. Two decades, give or take a year or so. Now it showed careless streaks of grey in places.

Riedwaan wandered through Clare's flat, picking up her things, putting them down, running a finger along the alphabetically arranged spines of her books. Mainly hardbacks. Above the television were a couple of shelves of Clare's documentaries, VHS copies of her broadcast investigative pieces, and an award for a film she'd done on human trafficking in the Congo. Putting the world to rights, that's what her investigative work was about, her beliefs giving her the courage to go where there were no nets to catch her if she fell. It fitted with her profiling work, her conviction that she could find the source of evil and eliminate it. Riedwaan was less sure about that.

He rifled through the heap of classical and acoustic CDs. 'How much Moby can one person listen to?' he asked Fritz. The cat flattened her ears and hissed in reply.

In Clare's bathroom, he opened one of the small pots of cream and held it to his nose. The jar carried the scent of her: tender, secret. Riedwaan put it down. He had done this so often in the homes of strangers. It had become second nature to look through the everyday artefacts of a woman's life after her broken body had been found, searching for reasons why that woman stepped out for that minute and never returned to finish half-used jars of expensive cream or to serve the meal cooking in the oven.

Clare was tired – he knew it – wrung out by the last case they had worked on together, profiling a killer whose refinements of cruelty had turned the stomachs of men who considered themselves inured to depravity. She needed to visit her reclusive twin, Constance. She needed to be alone, away. But Riedwaan didn't want her to leave him. He liked to live with the woman he slept with. The patterns of a long marriage like his, even if it was broken, ran deep.

He looked at himself in the mirror. He could get away without shaving. He showered and dressed, repressing the anxiety riffing down his spine. He fed Fritz. Clare would be back in half an hour. He went to watch for her. The sitting room was sparse, the way she liked it. The wooden floor a pale expanse that merged with the waves hurling themselves against the boulevard. He sat down on her sofa and picked up the pile of books she had been busy with before he had arrived the previous evening. There was a book on desert plants, the pollen of a forgotten cutting staining the index. A history of the Richtersveld, the harsh area around the Orange River. A novel about an early and murderous journey into that desert: Coetzee's *Dusklands*. She had made notes in her guide to southern African seabirds. He snapped it shut, amused at the thought of Clare with binoculars around her neck, bird list in her hand.

In the kitchen, Fritz glared as Riedwaan waited for the kettle to boil. He took his coffee through to the spare room. Clare's suitcase was open on the bed, half-packed. Clothes lay in methodical order, waiting to be placed in the suitcase. He picked up a dress, ran the silky black material through his hands and held it to his face. She must have worn it recently, because his touch released the feral tang of her sweat that lay just beneath the perfume she always wore. Jealousy surged through him. Who had she gone out with in that dress? Who had made her sweat?

He put it down and picked up a bra and a matching pair of panties – expensive, silky, low on the hip. Who were these for? Riedwaan could hear her mocking voice: for me is what she'd say. She was right, but her self-containment made him feel adolescent. He folded the dress again. He folded the bra and put it back. Her panties he slipped into his pocket. A memento for while she was away.

In the kitchen, Riedwaan put tomatoes on to grill and eggs to boil. He watched the last city lights go off. Cape Town in the light of the morning looked to him like a stripper past her prime. The lines were good, the breasts firm, but it was silicone and make-up that gave the nights their charge.

The front door opened. Riedwaan's hand curled around the filleting knife on the sink. 'Clare,' he called.

'You missed the best part of the day.'

Riedwaan looked at the knife in his hand in surprise. He passed a drying cloth over it and reached for a ripe melon.

Clare came in dripping, cheeks scarlet.

'I'm not going to kiss you.' She evaded him. 'I'm sweaty and disgusting.'

'Just how I like you.' Riedwaan sliced the spanspek. He didn't think much of fruit, but Clare loved it.

She picked up a slice and bit into it. 'Perfect.' She opened the window and put the skin on the sill for the birds waiting there. 'Come and talk to me in the shower.' She stripped, dropping her sweaty clothes into the washing machine.

'In a minute,' said Riedwaan, watching her disappear naked down the passage.

Clare stood under the shower. She loved the jet of water hot on her face, washing the sweat away. It took with it, though, the imprint of Riedwaan's warm skin on hers. She was going to miss him, being away for a month. She massaged shampoo into her blonde hair, working it down to the ends that hung below her waist. Damn. She had meant to have it trimmed before she left.

'You distract me with your clothes off.' Clare had not heard Riedwaan come into the bathroom. 'Especially when you look guilty like that. You thinking dirty thoughts?'

'I'm not telling.' Clare reached for the soap and scrubbed her shoulders.

'I can do that for you.' Riedwaan watched her deft hands lathering her body.

'You've seen all this before.'

'I'm not going to see it for weeks,' he pleaded.

Clare rinsed her hair. It coiled over her shoulder like a snake, the water making it almost as dark as Riedwaan's. She switched off the tap and stepped out of the shower.

'I didn't know you were interested in birds.' Riedwaan did not take his eyes off her. Dripping wet, she was as easy with herself naked as she was clothed.

'Well, I am. My father taught us. He would slam on the brakes in the middle of the highway, do a U-turn and hurtle back to identify some tiny ball of brown feathers. I decided that if I was going to die, at least I should know what I was dying for.'

'Why didn't you tell me?' Riedwaan asked.

Clare caught the look on his face and laughed. 'You never asked.' She put on cream, smoothing out her arched brows. She reached for her red kimono and tied the cord tight, emphasising the curve of her hips.

'I'll come find you in Namaqualand. You can show a city boy what there is to like about all those flowers and birds.'

The thought of him at her sister's farm bobbed bright as a lure, hiding the hook that lay beneath.

'I'd love that.' The need in her voice caught them both by surprise.

Riedwaan opened the door, letting in a blast of cold air. He reached for the words to tell her that things were more complicated than this morning routine. That Shazia was coming back. His wife. Instead, he pulled Clare towards him.

'Not now,' she said. 'It's freezing with the door open and I want my breakfast.' She kissed him on the mouth and slipped out of his arms. 'I'm going to get dressed.'

Chapter Four

ON THE DESOLATE southwest coast of Africa, Mara Thomson turned between the houses to take the short cut to school. A year ago, she had arrived as a volunteer teacher in Namibia with hope and two suitcases. The summer heat had buckled her knees as she stepped off the plane in the capital, Windhoek. The light had seared her eyes, but her heart had soared and she had walked across the blazing tarmac as if she was coming home. She had expected acacia trees etched against an orange sky. Instead, she was assigned to Walvis Bay. She cried herself to sleep for a week; then she'd decided to make a life for herself amongst the grime and the fog. A life that she was going to miss, now that she was leaving.

Mara jumped off her bike and wheeled it up the narrow alley, wondering why the dogs were barking. Elias Karamata was standing guard at a breech in the fence that was looped with chevronned tape. Black and yellow, nature's danger signal.

'Morning, Mara,' Elias Karamata greeted the girl. Skinny and brown, in her hoodie and jeans, she looked like one of the boys she coached rather than a volunteer teacher.

'What's wrong, then?' asked Mara, the clipped vowels marking her as foreign. English.

'Kaiser Apollis,' said Karamata, a gentle hand covering her arm. 'He was found dead in the playground.' He felt Mara tremble. At nineteen, she was still a wide-eyed child herself. 'Go around the other way.'

Mara walked around to the main entrance of the school, glad that she had her bike to lean on. Her legs were shaking.

'Where are you going, Miss Thomson?'

Mara had not seen Sergeant van Wyk until he had peeled himself off the wall and blocked her path.

'I volunteer here,' she said.

'I'm sure you do. ID.'

Mara handed it to him, even though he knew full well who she was.

Van Wyk looked her passport over. 'Only two weeks left on your visa.'

'Since when did you do immigration?' she shot back.

'The dead boy.' Van Wyk's eyes were cold. 'He's wearing one of your soccer shirts.' Mara paled. 'Interesting coincidence.'

'I know what you did to him. To Kaiser,' said Mara. 'I reported you.'

'Oh, I know you did.' Van Wyk was dismissive. 'Didn't get you or your little friend very far either, did it?'

Mara made for the entrance. That's when Van Wyk moved, trapping her body against the frame of the door. His breath was hot with intimate menace. 'I hear that you've been picking boys up in the clubs.' His fist, hard and hidden from view, came to rest on the soft mound between her legs. 'A step up from a rubbish dump, but sailors are a dangerous game, don't you think?'

'Why won't you leave me alone?' whispered Mara.

Van Wyk's thin lips twisted into a smile. 'It was you who started—'

'Sergeant,' Karamata interrupted. He was standing at the wall, his arms crossed. 'The staff are waiting to be interviewed.'

Van Wyk dropped his hand, and Mara pushed past him, tears in her eyes.

'I was just checking on Miss Thomson's movements,' Van Wyk said to Karamata as they walked back to the playground.

Tamar was sealing the last evidence bag, noting the time and date on each one. Karamata handed her the list of people who had been at school before they had arrived. 'Who've you got here, Elias?' she asked.

'Calvin Goagab, of course, and his sons,' said Karamata.

'Really made my day, seeing him so early in the morning.' Tamar grimaced. 'Who else?'

'Erasmus, the headmaster. Herman Shipanga you met, the caretaker who found the body. Darlene Ruyters, the Grade 1 teacher. She was in at six-thirty, but says she saw nothing. The only other person here was George Meyer. He drops his stepson Oscar early. Darlene Ruyters is his teacher and she keeps an eye on him until school starts.'

'Oscar's mother?' asked Tamar. 'Wasn't she killed in that car accident six months ago?'

'That's her,' said Karamata. He held the door open for Tamar. The school staff fell silent as she stepped into the stuffy staffroom. The preliminaries were soon over: statements, times for interviews, arrangements to close the school, the staff dismissed for the day.

Tamar drove back to the station, glad that she could lock her office door behind her. She let her head drop into her hands, allowing the first tears to splash onto the desk. It didn't help to dam them all. When she decided it was enough, she made tea while she waited for her photographs to download. She wrapped her hands around the hot mug and stared at the images of the dead child on her screen. Again, she thought of Clare Hart.

She found Riedwaan Faizal's number and dialled. 'Captain Faizal? Tamar Damases here, Walvis Bay police.'

'Tamar, it's been a while,' said Riedwaan. 'You've got a body if you're calling me.'

'A dead boy in a school playground. Looks like the third in a series,' said Tamar. 'I'm going to need your profiler friend Dr Hart.'

'We'll need to pass it via the official channels,' said Riedwaan. 'But if you can get it past Supe Phiri I'll persuade Clare.'

'You're on first-name terms now?'

'You could put it like that,' said Riedwaan, with a smile.

CLARE CLOSED HER suitcase and went into the kitchen. Jeans and a white T-shirt. No make-up yet, her damp hair in a twist on top of her head. Riedwaan was leaning against the counter, the paper spread out in front of him. Her stomach grumbled as she kissed him.

'I'm hungry,' she said.

'You look nice.' Riedwaan drew her against him.

Clare dampened down the lick of desire that flared between his hands. She would lose the rhythm of her day if she let her body distract her.

'We'll be late,' she said, prising herself loose. She sat down and helped herself to breakfast. 'Who were you talking to?'

'Phiri.'

'So where's the body?'

Riedwaan felt in his pocket for cigarettes.

'Don't smoke. It's too early,' said Clare.

Riedwaan shrugged and started stacking the dishwasher. She watched the muscles on his back flex under his shirt as she finished eating.

'Very domestic,' she said. 'Maybe I should just stay here with you. Play housey-housey.' She handed him her empty plate and slipped her arms around him.

Riedwaan laughed. 'Ja, right.'

'The other call?' She had him, trapped between her and the dishwasher. 'When I was in the shower?'

'Captain Tamar Damases. From Namibia,' said Riedwaan. Clare didn't miss a thing. Why did he always forget that about her? 'She came to your lectures last year on serial killers.'

Clare's right eyebrow shot up.

'Pretty. Soft voice. Tiny waist,' said Riedwaan.

'No wonder you remember her,' said Clare. 'Just your type.'

'*Was* my type. You're my type now. Skin, bone and attitude.'

'So there *is* a body.'

'It's Monday morning,' said Riedwaan. 'There's always a body.'

Chapter Five

'HELLO?' CLARE'S PHONE was ringing as she opened her front door, laden with shopping bags.

'Dr Hart? Please hold for Superintendent Phiri.'

'Okay, I'm holding.' She put down her bags, wondering if she had heard wrong.

'Dr Hart?' She hadn't. The clipped formality could belong to only one man. 'This is Phiri here. How are you?'

'I'm well.' Clare buried her surprise in pleasantries. 'How nice to hear from you. How are you?'

'Very busy, but well.' Phiri took his cue from her. 'I hope I haven't got you at a bad time?'

'Not at all.' Clare could no longer ignore the growing knot of anxiety. 'Has something happened to Riedwaan?' she asked.

Phiri laughed. The low, melodious sound didn't fit with Clare's picture of him: precise moustache, stiff and exact in his uniform. 'He's fine,' Phiri said. 'Looks as if someone's been looking after him.'

Clare blushed. She was glad there was no one except Fritz to see.

'I have a situation that needs ... lateral thinking. And tact –
something I couldn't get from Faizal for love or money. He suggested that I speak to you.'

Clare was taken aback. Phiri had always been reluctant to use
her services as a profiler. He had a policeman's distrust of civilians
and a man's scepticism about giving a woman authority.

'How can I help you?'

'I'd like to discuss it with you in person. In an hour. My office
at twelve.'

Clare put down the receiver, took her shopping to the kitchen
and packed it away.

Two weeks ago, Riedwaan had stayed the whole night with her,
slipping into domesticity as if it were a second skin. It was not so
easy for Clare. Doubling her shopping seemed easier than talking
about boundaries and space and her secret pleasure at being held
in the morning, but Phiri's call warranted a few questions.

Riedwaan picked up on the fourth ring.

'I'm meant to be going on holiday,' said Clare. 'Do you want to
tell me what's going on?'

'I'm coming to the meeting, too. I'll meet you outside the nut
house.'

AT FIVE TO twelve, Riedwaan pulled up outside the newly built Psychological Crimes Unit. It had been dubbed the nut house before the
first brick was laid, and the name had stuck, much to Phiri's chagrin.

Clare wrinkled her nose. 'You smell horrible.'

Riedwaan ground his cigarette under his heel. 'That's a nice
way to greet someone who just got you a job,' he said, reaching
his hand under her thick hair. Clare arched her neck. 'Are your
hackles always raised?' he asked.

'Only when I'm suspicious,' Clare laughed. 'Explain. Phiri's my new best friend?'

'Let's just say he sees you as a way out of a tricky political corner.' Riedwaan followed her up the marble stairs of the unit.

'Since when was I the answer to someone's political problems? Or you for that matter?'

'Captain Tamar Damases,' said Riedwaan.

'Who called this morning?'

'That's the one.'

'I don't trust you, Riedwaan. There's something going on that you're not telling me.'

'She called. Out of the blue. She was looking for you, not me.' Riedwaan knocked on Phiri's door before Clare could interrogate him further.

The senior superintendent gave the impression of a man in uniform, despite his civilian clothes. Phiri was lean to the point of thinness. He moved with the agility of the champion athlete he had been as a young man, desperate to escape the legacy of grinding poverty that illegitimacy had bequeathed him.

'Thank you for coming, Dr Hart, Faizal. Can I offer you some coffee?'

Clare declined. Phiri's coffee was notoriously strong and he only ever served it as he drank it – with three sugars and powdered milk.

'You'll have some, Faizal.' It was not a question. It had taken Riedwaan twenty years with the police to learn which battles were worth fighting. This was not one of them and he accepted the cup without demur.

Phiri opened the Manila folder in front of him. 'I have an unusual request to make, Dr Hart,' he said, steepling his fingers over the single page of spidery notes, the careful handwriting of a man who had started school at twelve.

'You know about the policing cross-border cooperation agreement signed between the South African government and some of our neighbours?'

'Yes,' said Clare. 'It was signed in April as I remember.'

'Correct,' said Phiri. 'Extremely tricky negotiations, as you can imagine. Very often what South Africa offers regionally is seen as interference, domination even, rather than cooperation.' Phiri looked pained at the thought.

'The agreement focuses on terrorism and weapons of mass destruction and car hijacking syndicates, doesn't it?' asked Clare.

'That and the upsurge of armed gangs. We know that increasing numbers of soldiers from our ... how shall I put it ... less affluent neighbours are moonlighting as hired guns in South Africa for cash-in-transit heists and armed bank robberies. So the South African Police Service is providing expert assistance to our neighbours' developing police forces.'

Clare looked from Phiri to Riedwaan. Riedwaan had just ventured his first sip of coffee and had a stricken look on his face. He was not going to be of any help.

'That's not my field of expertise at all,' she said. 'I specialise in head cases: psychological crimes, sexual murders in particular.'

'I know,' said Phiri, impatient at having his presentation speeded up. 'That's why I've called on you. One of the subclauses – 6.6 of the agreement if you want to read it – deals with unusual violent crimes. The current terminology for predatory sex crimes, serial rape or murder and unusual crimes against children.'

'It excludes the more usual murders or assaults of children,' Riedwaan added, 'committed by their very own loving parents, teachers, relatives and—'

Phiri cleared his throat. 'Thank you, Faizal. It was the best that could be produced in a short period. At least we've something to work with.'

'I do apologise, sir,' said Riedwaan with just sufficient sincerity to pacify his boss.

'As I was saying, Dr Hart,' said Phiri, turning back to Clare, 'section 6.6 deals with unusual violent crimes. As you know, few of our neighbours have either the manpower or the scientific expertise to investigate crimes such as these. We've had our first request for assistance of this nature. I'm very keen that we're successful with this particular case. It'll go some way in showing that the agreement's worth something and that we can provide a service beyond our borders.'

'So what happened where?' asked Clare. 'And why me?'

'We've had a request from the Namibian police, from Captain Tamar Damases of their Sexual Violence and Murder Unit. Faizal said she was keen that we ask you.'

'Ask me what exactly?' asked Clare.

'That you go up to assist with an investigation. She thinks they need a profiler.' Phiri picked up his rose-speckled cup and sipped and put it back on its saucer. The clatter was loud in the silence. He was the only policeman Clare knew who drank from a cup and saucer. His mother had given the set to him when he had been made a senior superintendent. She did not think it fitting that her only son should drink from the chipped assortment of mugs the rest of the force used.

'I'm flattered that you asked me,' Clare said into the silence that stretched between them. 'But surely it'd be easier if someone employed by the police went up. Captain Faizal, for example.' She looked at Riedwaan. He pretended to drink his coffee and avoided her gaze.

'Dr Hart, the protocol is new, the bureaucracy not quite in place and the Namibians are territorial. What Captain Faizal suggested was that you go and work with the investigation. We send him up next week when we have all the formalities sorted out.'

'Where would I be based?' asked Clare.

'Walvis Bay,' Faizal interrupted Phiri's answer. There was a note of apology in his voice. As there should be. Clare had spent two godforsaken months there working on a documentary. The hot desert wind had whipped red sand off the dunes and ruined her camera.

'Faizal tells me that you know the place,' said Phiri.

Clare wondered what else Riedwaan had told the superintendent. 'I know it a bit,' she said.

'Will you consider it?'

Clare shifted in her seat, repressing an uninvited flash of memory: stars hanging low as lamps in the sky, the desert's nocturnal creatures calling, and her yielding to a man who had taken measure of her loneliness and her desire. She had given herself to him for a week, then flown home, edited her film and ignored his phone calls until they stopped.

'Tell me more about the case,' she said.

'A dead child. Bizarre killing. The body displayed in a schoolyard. Bullet to the head, but ritual marks and other peculiarities on the corpse. Reminiscent of at least one other. Maybe more. Interested?'

Clare was intrigued and Phiri could see it. He knew how to play her and she wondered how much of that was thanks to Riedwaan. 'I am,' she confessed, despite her misgivings at being the subject of discussion. 'But I need some more detail.'

'Faizal has all the notes. He'll brief you,' said Phiri with a tone of finality. 'There are the crime-scene photographs. No autopsy yet. They're holding that up until you get there. A few preliminary interviews. She's smart, this Damases. Organised.' He picked up Riedwaan's abandoned cup and put it on the tray on the counter behind him. He closed the file in front of him and stood up. The meeting was over.

Clare stood too. 'Thank you, Superintendent Phiri.'

'I watched you work the last time, Dr Hart. You were very … effective. Let me know what you decide and what you need. You'll be working under Faizal.' He straightened the immaculately arrayed files on his desk. 'Not a position I'd have chosen. But not everyone has the same taste I suppose.'

No secrets in the force, thought Clare. Everyone knew that Phiri, at fifty, still lived with his mother and that she made his lunch every day.

So, no reason that they wouldn't know that Riedwaan had been staying with her, although the breach in her hard-won privacy – secrecy, her sisters call it – rankled.

She followed Riedwaan to what he called his office. More a corner of chaos which his colleagues avoided like a domestic incident on a Saturday night.

'You've got some explaining to do, Riedwaan,' she said, closing the door. 'I don't for one minute imagine that Phiri thought this little scheme up by himself.'

'It's nearly lunch time. I need something to eat before we discuss this.' Riedwaan picked up a file with Tamar Damases's notes. 'You going to feed me?'

Chapter Six

'WHAT HAS CAPTAIN Damases got so far?' asked Clare, carrying a tray of fresh bread, carpaccio and a salad onto her balcony.

'Three dead boys. All in and around Walvis Bay. This boy, they found this morning.' Riedwaan turned over the top page of the faxed docket. 'And two others: Nicanor Jones and Fritz Woestyn. All found about a week apart.'

Clare stroked her cat, winding in and out between her ankles. 'And?'

'Same age, same cause of death. Vulnerable kids, easy targets. No one to report them missing. All the weird stuff with the binding, the risky display on the swing. It just said serial to her. She thought, rightly I imagine, that if she gets someone up there now there's a better chance of cracking it before another body washes up.'

'Sounds like a textbook case,' said Clare. She rolled a piece of paper-thin fillet between her fingers and ate it. 'What's the new boy's name?'

'Waiting for a positive ID, but they have him as Kaiser Apollis. Looks fourteen, could be sixteen. Been living on the street like the other two victims. Aids orphan, apparently. There's a sister around somewhere, but no interview yet. That's scheduled for the day after tomorrow. With you,' said Riedwaan. 'Here, have a look at Captain Damases's photographs.'

He pushed away their plates and spread out the pictures on the table. His phone rang. Not his usual ring tone, but one a little girl had recorded before she left for Canada with her mother. The child's voice, sweet and plaintive, called him: 'Daddy, Daddy, it's me.'

'Yasmin?' asked Clare.

'Yup.' Riedwaan looked at his watch. 'My biweekly fatherhood ration.' He stood up, phone already to his ear. 'Hello, baby girl. How's Canada?' Clare heard him say as he closed the door so that he could speak privately to the seven-year-old daughter he had not seen for almost a year.

Clare turned her attention to the images in front of her. They were eerie; the body huddled like any child escaping on the finite flight of a swing. The image nudged a buried memory. The tug of that weightless second at the top of the arc before the free fall of return; the solemn face of Clare's twin sister, watching her swing up higher, higher, higher. Away from her. Until Constance could stand it no longer and caught the swing, tumbling Clare out, dissolving Clare's rage with tears. Their father had removed the swing after that. To keep Clare safe, is how he had explained it. Clare and her older sister Julia had seethed, knowing that the real reason was to keep Constance calm. Clare felt for the forgotten scar on her elbow. The smooth ridge of skin was still there.

'You look like you've seen a ghost.' Clare had not heard Riedwaan return. He put his hand on her arm, drawing her back into the present.

'This tyre swing. We had one when we were children. I loved it. It made me feel free.' She turned to face him. 'How are things with Yasmin?'

'Fine,' said Riedwaan. 'She's fine.'

'Shazia?'

A shadow crossed Riedwaan's face at the mention of his estranged wife. He shrugged and did not meet Clare's gaze. 'The same.' He picked up the crime-scene pictures. 'What do you think of this?'

'So spiteful to kill a child on a swing,' said Clare, leaving the painful subject of Riedwaan's broken family.

'It looks like he was killed elsewhere; no blood in situ.' Riedwaan's attention was focused back on the soluble problem in front of him. 'He was dead a good couple of days before he was dumped at the school. Maybe kept out beyond the fog belt, in the heat. The body was starting to smell bad,' said Riedwaan, scanning through the faxed notes.

'Why in a playground?' mused Clare.

'That's the thing with nuts. It makes no sense unless you get inside their heads. Why put him on show a couple of days after he's dead? What were they doing together all that time?'

'The other two, were they also found near schools?'

'No. Tamar has linked them because they were all head-shot wounds, same calibre gun. Intermediate range and similar victim profile. Ligatures or remnants of ligatures. And the timing, too – looks to her like there's a pattern. A killing, then a cooling-off period.'

'You think you have me stitched up then?' Clare asked. The image of the dead boy had sapped the tentative spring sun of warmth, but she could not be sure that he was the source of her unease. She packed away the photographs and ushered Riedwaan to the front door.

'Come on, Clare. You're not going to say no. I'll be there next week, when Phiri gets the paperwork done.' Riedwaan, as usual, was reluctant to leave.

'I must phone Constance first,' said Clare, distracted. On the far side of the bay was a ribbon of white beach and beyond that the mountains, softened by distance. Clare imagined the road she would have taken up to Namaqualand, to see her twin. She felt the old tug deep within her. 'Tell her I'm not coming.'

'You and your twin,' Riedwaan sighed. 'I watch you, but don't ask me how your minds work.'

'It's one mind,' said Clare, 'divided in two.'

She closed the front door behind him and walked through her apartment, picking up clothes, CDs and books that Riedwaan had discarded. Before she realised what she was doing, she had bundled his things into a bag. She dropped it at the front door, feeling lighter. The thought of a working journey felt good, right; this holiday idea, going to stay in the middle of nowhere with Constance, had not. Two birds with one stone, you could say. Clare took a deep breath, releasing the tension in her neck, and went to phone her twin.

As she dialled she pictured Constance as if she were with her. The hip-length curtain of dark hair; the shoulder blades and angular hips jutting against the seamless white she always wore over her scarred body. Clare let the phone ring three times. She put it down. Redialled. Another three rings. She hated these subterfuges, this pandering to a neurosis so deep it had worked into the marrow of her sister's existence. And her own, she thought, irritation and hopeless love welling up together.

'Constance,' said Clare, envisaging her twin in the dim farm-house of their childhood.

'Are you all right?' Her twin's voice had the same soughing as wind in pine trees. You had to lean in to her to hear her. Which meant that when she spoke, which was rarely, everyone stopped, leaned in close, listened.

'I'm fine,' said Clare.

'You aren't coming.' Constance laughed, a silvery peal. 'I've been waiting for you to call.'

'I'm sorry, Constance. Something came up. A work thing. I have to go.'

'The dead boys.' Constance said it simply, a statement of fact.

'How did you know?' Clare's skin crawled.

'Television. We pick up the Namibian broadcasts here some-times. I saw a snippet about a boy on a swing in a school in a desert. I thought, she'll go to him, instead of coming here to me.' The mocking, musical laugh again. 'I thought, he's waiting there for Clare.'

Chapter Seven

EARLY THE NEXT morning, Riedwaan picked up the picture on Clare's hall table. The mom-dad-me-and-my-dog drawing, a gift to her from her little niece. He was overwhelmed with longing for his own child. Yasmin. His daughter. The undoing of his heart and his career. When she had been kidnapped, the husk of his desiccated marriage had blown apart, and he had signed the emigration papers that allowed Shazia to take Yasmin to Canada. Yasmin used to draw him pictures like the one before him now, but the drawings she sent from her new country were less exuberant. She had told him proudly that she could colour inside the lines now. Shazia would like that: getting Yasmin to stay within the lines. Riedwaan unlocked Clare's front door. That's what he liked about Clare, her disregard for limits.

It was cold on the street, and his breath misted and hung on the dawn air as he hefted Clare's suitcase into his old Mazda. The boot was temperamental and had been since a drunk in a Porsche had rear-ended him. As he slammed the boot, he felt cold metal against his carotid artery, warm breath on the back of his neck.

Fury whipped him around, his fingers gripping the wrist, twisting hard. It felt wrong. Plump. Soft.

'Still fast, Captain.' A giggle, not a grunt. 'That Bo-Kaap skollie in you.'

'Rita.' Riedwaan dropped her wrist, angry, out of breath. 'You'll get shot doing that.'

She laughed again. 'You trained me, Captain. But I'm younger and faster, so watch your back. Is Clare upstairs?'

'She's there. Go up, it's open.'

Sergeant Rita Mkhize sauntered to the front gate. Riedwaan knew, without rancour, that she would out-captain him soon. That was how things worked now.

'I'm here, Clare,' Rita called through the intercom. 'Sorry to be late.'

Clare met her halfway down the stairs. 'Here are the keys. Fritz's food is where it always is. The vet's number is on the fridge. I made a bed for you in the spare room.' She gave Rita the keys and a thick envelope. 'Those are the things that Fritz likes. I thought it might be useful. Don't tell Riedwaan about it.'

'It's our secret, but you'll owe me big time,' said Rita, keeping a straight face. She handed Clare a much thinner folder.

'I've put together everything that Captain Damases sent for you.'

'Brilliant, Rita,' said Clare, flicking through the file. 'Use my car if you want to.'

'I'll walk,' said Rita, picking up the cat and following Clare to the gate. 'The station's three blocks. It'll be a pleasure not being shot at coming to work. I've had enough of this taxi war.'

'Thanks for taking care of Fritz for me,' said Clare. 'She's not as fierce as she looks.'

'Don't believe her. Look at this.' Riedwaan showed Rita a scabbed scratch on the back of his hand.

'He teased her,' said Clare.

'I'm sure he did,' said Rita, stroking the cat purring in her arms. 'Don't let him tease you.'

'Get in,' said Riedwaan. Aeroplanes always made him irritable. Clare let her hair swing forward to hide her smile as she slammed the door shut. 'It's international, so you need some time.'

Clare put her hand on Riedwaan's knee, moving it up his thigh. 'I'm going to miss you,' she said, her breath warm in his ear.

'Hey, let me drive,' he said, smiling. 'You'll make me have an accident if you do that.'

Riedwaan drove along the elevated highway that cordoned off the city from the harbour. The lanes were already clogged, and overloaded taxis weaved between the cars as they raced into the city. Clare checked her face in the mottled mirror dangling from the sun visor.

'Have you got a comb in here?' she asked, opening the cubbyhole.

Riedwaan stretched across to close it. 'Leave that,' he said, swerving to avoid two schoolboys dashing across the highway.

A torch, a bar of mint chocolate, bills, letters, a map and a comb spilled onto the floor.

'Are you planning to live in your car while I'm away?' Clare asked. She bent down to pick up the scattered papers. 'When last did you do any admin? Rates. Water. Electricity. Telkom. Insurance.' She smoothed out the papers on her lap. She bent down to retrieve the last one, swearing as she bumped her head on the dashboard. A scrap of lilac paper fell out from between the stapled sheets. The childish script caught her eye, and she read, almost without thinking:

*Hey Dad this is Yasmin. Can't wait 2CU2. Mom got me new
shoos. It is cold here when it is hot where you live. They look
nice on my feet and we put paint on our nails. Red color.*

CU soon. I ♥ u daddy.

Ps the tooth fairy gave me six dollars.

CLARE LOOKED AT Riedwaan. His profile had set. A muscle on
the underside of his jaw jumped. She smoothed the piece of white
paper that had held Yasmin's handmade card and stared down at
the unfamiliar handwriting. This time she read deliberately:

Riedwaan

*It looks like we will both come. I'm not sure if this is the best
thing for me (or for you), but I think we have to try to work out
how to move on. We arrive on the 13th. Friday. I'm not sure
if it will be lucky or unlucky. Your mother has all the details.
I hope this works. I'm tired of waiting. I need a decision*

Shazia

CLARE FOLDED THE letter and put it back into the cubbyhole. The
comb lay forgotten on her lap. She opened the window, the air
cooling her hot face.

'You weren't meant to read those,' said Riedwaan.

'You didn't tell me she was coming.'

'I did tell you Yasmin might come.' Riedwaan knew he was
clutching at straws.

Clare turned to him, anger flaring from the spark of hurt. 'I'm
glad that you'll see your daughter,' she said, teeth clenched, voice
low. 'But you didn't tell me they were *both* coming.'

'I only knew for sure a few days ago.'

A truck hurtled past on the inside lane, hooting. Riedwaan swerved again.

'A few days?' said Clare. 'And you didn't think to tell me?'

'I thought you'd be angry.'

'I *am* angry.'

Riedwaan took the off-ramp to the airport. 'Shazia and I have a child together. We've been married for twelve years. I have to talk to her to sort things out.'

'I know.' Clare looked out of the window, dashing the tears from her eyes with the back of her hand. 'But you should've told me.'

'You'd still have been upset,' said Riedwaan.

'I'd have been able to make a choice then.'

'Let me explain.'

'No! You had your chance. Just drop me and go.'

There was a steel edge to Clare's voice. The armour she used to protect herself from feeling too much moved along familiar grooves to protect the vulnerability she had risked with Riedwaan. His separation was too recent and his ties to his family were too strong. It was her fault for letting him insinuate himself into her life, her heart. She was as angry with herself for letting it happen as she was with him for doing it.

Riedwaan ignored her and parked the Mazda. 'Talk to me, Clare.' He switched off the ignition and turned to face her.

'About what?'

'About all of this.'

'Why didn't you think of that before, genius?' Clare opened the door.

Riedwaan got out too, waving away the porter. 'I can explain.'

'You've had weeks to explain,' said Clare. 'Yesterday, when Yasmin called. Perfect opportunity to explain. Not telling me is worse than lying to me.'

'It's complicated.' Riedwaan put his hands on her arms.

'It *was* complicated,' said Clare, shrugging him off. 'Now it's simple.'

'It's hard to talk to you about this, Clare,' said Riedwaan. 'It's hard for me to tell you anything. I don't know what you think. What you feel. What you want.'

The blinds came down over the hurt in Clare's eyes. 'There's a bag of your things at the front door,' she said. 'Fetch it from Rita.'

'Clare, I'm so sorry.'

'It'll be simpler professionally.'

'I'll call you,' said Riedwaan.

'About the case. *This* subject is closed.' Clare touched his cheek, back in control, fingers cool, more dismissive than a slammed door. She strode towards the international departures terminal and into the embrace of the automatic doors.

'Fuck it,' Riedwaan said and went back to his car.

He threaded through the cars offloading passengers at domestic departures and joined the sluggish flow of traffic making its way into town.

'Fuck it,' he said again as the traffic gridlocked on the Eastern Boulevard.

Chapter Eight

CLARE HANDED OVER her ticket and passport, submitting to the pat-down when the security machine beeped.

'Your bra,' smiled the woman who searched her. 'The underwire always sets this thing off. But what can you do? We all need a bit of lift.'

'Don't we just,' said Clare.

The morning mist was still wreathed across the Cape Flats, stranding Table Mountain and the leafy suburbs that clung to its base, but as the plane headed north, trees, fields, roads, towns, then villages, fell away and the land became drier, stripped of any vegetation except the hardiest plants. Clare opened the file that Rita Mkhize had put together. Precise notes in convent-school cursive. A plastic sleeve for expenses and petty-cash slips. A list of contact numbers. Empty file dividers for the post-mortem report, forensic analysis, ballistics report, and Clare's profile. Anticipation tingled up her spine.

Tamar Damases had e-mailed an aerial photograph of Walvis Bay. It showed a marshy river delta south of the port. Extending northwards was a slender sand peninsula that protected the lagoon and the harbour. At the tip of this encircling arm was Pelican Point, around which the calmed Atlantic tides swirled into the bay. The little town squatted behind the harbour. It was a bleak place, pushed closer to oblivion by the collapsing fishing industry. The town had ceased to grow as planned, so the school where the body had been found was right on the edge of the town, a bulwark against the red dunes that marched northwards until the dry Kuiseb River halted them.

A lonely place to live and an even lonelier place to die.

Clare looked at the photographs Tamar had taken of the dead boy. Kaiser Apollis might have been fourteen, but he was so undernourished that it was hard to view him as anything but the child he had been. The thin arms were clasped around the angled knees, the arms and legs shielding the stilled heart. Slender ankles disappeared into too-large takkies. Even in the grainy low-res prints, Clare could make out Nike's expensive swoosh. The forehead rested on the knees, and the back of his skull was missing. The autopsy was scheduled for the next day. Then the pathologist's knife would peel open any secrets hidden in the body of this dead child.

Clare closed the file and rested her forehead against the window as the plane started its descent. To the west, the surf-white beach corralled the red dunes. Beyond it stretched the restless Atlantic. The sun, angled low, revealed the Namib Desert's wind-sculpted dunes, dotted with tiny impoverished settlements. Every now and then, Clare glimpsed a flash of a corrugated-iron roof or the flurry of a flock of goats browsing on the acacias growing along the subterranean Kuiseb River bank – evidence of sparse human habitation. Walvis Bay, blanketed in fog, was invisible.

Clare let her thoughts drift back to Riedwaan. Her anger had burnt itself out, but it had left cold ash in its wake instead of calm. She missed him with an acuteness that hurt. Who would have thought?

'THIRTY DAYS.' THE bulky customs official dropped Clare's immigration form into an untidy box at her feet. An unexpected smile dimpled her round cheeks as she handed back the stamped passport. 'Captain Damases told us to expect you.'

Tamar was waiting at the arrivals terminal when Clare exited. Her heart-shaped face was as beautiful as Clare remembered, but the tiny waist was hidden by a pregnancy that seemed ominously close to term.

Tamar's green eyes lit up with recognition. 'Let me help you.' She reached for Clare's suitcase.

'You're not carrying anything,' Clare protested. 'You look as if I should drive you straight to hospital.'

'It's just because I'm so short that I look huge,' laughed Tamar. 'I'm glad you could come.'

Tamar led Clare to a white Isuzu double cab. An officer was leaning against it, smoking. His black shirt stretched tight across a muscular chest. His hair was cropped close, giving his handsome face a hard look.

'Sergeant Kevin van Wyk,' said Tamar, 'this is Dr Clare Hart.'

'Welcome.' The man shook Clare's hand but made no move to help her load her suitcase.

As they exited the airport, Van Wyk turned the radio up just loud enough to make conversation an effort. Clare took Tamar Damases's cue and watched the desert slip past in silence, wondering how much had changed since her previous visit.

Two years ago, the factories perched like hungry cormorants around the harbour had gorged on bulging catches. Clare had filmed vessel after vessel offloading their silver harvests. Namibia's suited elite, circling like sharks, had allocated ever-bigger quotas to themselves, buying farms and BMWs hand over profligate fist, ignoring the scientists and their warnings. Now the fish had all but vanished and an eerie lassitude pervaded the town. The bounty that had followed the retreat of the South African army, itself leaving a gaping hole in the town's coffers, was gone.

Walvis Bay still wasn't much to look at. The town huddled around the harbour, ready to suck what it could from passing ships. The Walvis Bay police station faced a black coal-heap that waited to be loaded onto increasingly intermittent trains from the uranium mines deep in the desert. The gaunt cranes were sinister against the leaden sky. A seagull startled when Clare slammed her car door, its cry harsh on the raw air.

'Not as nice a view as you have in Cape Town, Dr Hart,' said Van Wyk, his gaze a lazy trawl across her body as she walked ahead of him. The fine hairs on Clare's neck rose.

The station was a low, featureless building with grenade mesh on all the windows. Someone must have thought that swimming-pool blue would make it more cheerful, but the coal dust had settled on every available surface. Two outlandishly pink pots marked the entrance, but all that flowered in them were cigarette butts. A few lipstick-stained, most not.

A stocky man was putting out a cigarette as they walked up the steps.

'Sergeant Elias Karamata, this is Dr Hart,' said Tamar. 'Elias is also working with us on the case.'

'Welcome to Namibia, Doctor.'

'Please call me Clare,' she said. Karamata looked like a prize-fighter – bull neck, broad shoulders – but his handshake was gentle, his smile warm. 'It's good to be back.'

'You've been here before?' asked Karamata, pleased.

'A couple of years ago,' said Clare, filling in a visitor's form. 'I made a documentary about the fishing industry.'

'All that corruption business is cleared up now.'

'Elias would be better off working for the Walvis Bay Tourism Board,' Tamar interjected. 'He spends his spare time trying to persuade me that it's heaven on earth.'

'People cry twice in Walvis Bay, Captain,' said Karamata, shaking his head. 'Once when they get here, once when they leave. You'll grow to love it too.'

Clare followed Tamar down the dim passage. Right at the end, a tattered sign saying 'Sexual Violence & Murder' was sticky-taped to the door.

'Welcome to S 'n' M.' Tamar gave the door a practised kick and it swung open, revealing a surprisingly spacious office. There were four new desks, each with a plastic-covered computer.

'This is where Van Wyk and Elias work,' Tamar said. 'You can use that computer by the window.'

'It looks brand new,' said Clare.

'It is,' said Tamar. 'I got Elias after the marine-poaching unit was closed down, because there's nothing left to poach. Van Wyk was transferred from the vice squad.'

'Why was he moved?'

'Gender-based violence is the government's flavour of the month, so in theory it was a promotion.'

'Someone should let him know,' said Clare.

Tamar led the way to her own office. It was private and painted a sunny yellow. One corner of the room was covered with children's pictures. There were toys and two red beanbags next to the blue sofa, and a low table was covered with paper and crayons.

'The kiddies' safe corner,' she explained. Her soft mouth hard as she picked up a drawing and handed it to Clare. It was of a child's idealised house – red door, cat on the window sill, yellow sun smiling in the corner, smoke curling from the chimney. The family stood on green grass. A little girl, her head haloed with ribbons, with panda eyes. A mummy with bruises to match. A suited daddy with bunched fists, his groin scored out with black crayon. Someone had written 'Joy' at the bottom of the page.

'Her name,' said Tamar. 'I went to her funeral last week. Her stepfather beat her to death. Said she was cheeky.'

'How old was she?' asked Clare.

'Six.' Tamar's voice wavered.

On the wall were framed photographs of a laughing boy of eleven and a dimpled little girl dressed in Barbie pink.

'She's pretty,' said Clare. 'Your kids?'

'My sister's. She passed away, so they live with me now.'

'I'm sorry,' said Clare.

'They're sweet kids.' Tamar patted her belly. 'This one'll be born into an instant family. You've got no children?'

'Not for me,' said Clare. 'I'm an aunt though. My older sister has two girls.'

Tamar put on the kettle. 'Some tea?'

'Please. Rooibos?' asked Clare.

'The only thing for lady detectives,' Tamar said with a grin, handing her a cup. 'Here's a schedule.' She pulled out a sheet of paper with a list of names and dates. 'The city manager wants to meet you.'

'That's fine,' said Clare, 'but why does he want to see me?'

'You're a novelty and this murder has been a shock. Usually the only murders we get are the odd prostitute floating in the harbour or a drunken sailor stabbed in a shebeen.'

'Or little girls like Joy,' murmured Clare.

'Or little girls like Joy, yes.' Tamar's cup clattered in its saucer. 'My decision to bring in outside help hasn't been unanimously welcomed,' she said. 'Serial killers don't quite fit in with Walvis Bay's new vision of itself as a tourist Mecca.'

'Is this a bit of a political minefield for you?'

'That,' said Tamar,' is an understatement. Important people have been jumpy since the fishing collapsed. They've pinned all their hopes on tourism, and dead boys don't attract many tourists.'

'I'm going to need a bit of specialised sightseeing.' Clare turned her attention back to the schedule.

'Elias will be taking you tomorrow,' said Tamar. 'He was born and bred here, one of the few, so he knows this place like the back of his hand. He even speaks the language the Topnaars speak.'

'Topnaars?' Clare frowned. 'Are they those desert people?' She vaguely remembered them from her previous stay.

'That's right. They live in the Kuiseb River and know the desert really well. You probably saw their huts when you came in to land this morning.'

'I did,' said Clare. 'White goats all over the dunes. Looked like snow for a second.'

'That's them,' said Tamar. She put her teacup aside. 'I need to eat something before our meeting with the big boys; otherwise I'll unravel.'

Chapter Nine

'THE VENUS BAKERY. This is the best place to eat,' said Tamar, parking under a palm tree on the other side of town. A group of boys uncurled themselves from its base.

'I'll watch your car,' said the tallest boy.

The bakery was on a corner, the walls painted a festive blue. Succulent cakes and pies were on display behind the glass counters of the self-service area, behind which were several tables, most full with a satisfied-looking lunch crowd.

'Why aren't you at school, Lazarus?'

'Sorry, Miss.' The boy looked down at his shoes, his shoulders bowed in well-practised contrition until Tamar walked past him. Then he moved his hustle over to the next car, pushing a smaller boy out of the way when he saw that they were tourists. He was wearing a grubby white shirt with a silver fish emblazoned on it.

'Pesca-Marina Fishing's still going?' Clare recalled the fishing company from her documentary.

'It is. One of the few. The company sponsors anything and everything. They're trying to clear their name of fishing this coast to death. Calvin Goagab, the city manager, who you'll meet later, has shares in it. They only do specialised fishing now, export added-value products.'

'What does that mean?' asked Clare, following Tamar to a table in the corner.

'It means packaged fish to the rest of us,' said Tamar with a smile. She ordered rolls and coffee, which arrived promptly.

'This is good,' said Clare. She hadn't realised how hungry she was. 'What's the meeting about then, if there's nothing to report yet?'

'The mayor established a community policing forum to deal with family violence. After this body was found in the playground, Calvin Goagab called me in to see how we were going to tackle it. I told him then that I'd approached your new cross-border unit for help and that you were coming. He said he wanted to meet you.'

'Sounds fair enough,' said Clare.

'Goagab is a difficult man and he seems to have taken it as a personal insult that the dead boy made him late. It's best just to let him say what he has to say. He's not thrilled that our arrangement with the police was a fait accompli.'

Clare and Tamar walked the two blocks to the municipal building.

'Somebody had delusions of grandeur,' said Clare when she caught sight of the concrete bunker that reared up in an extravagant wilderness of lawn. The building dwarfed the few citizens scurrying up its steps, disputed bills clutched in fists.

'Army money,' said Tamar. 'South Africa's two fingers to the desert.'

Once inside, it took Clare a few seconds to adjust to the dim light of the cavernous entrance hall. Tamar pushed open the carved double doors to the executive wing, where their footsteps were absorbed by the pile of a garish carpet.

'Hello, Anna,' Tamar greeted an exquisite young woman who looked out of place behind the vast desk. 'We're here to see Mr Goagab.'

'Do you have an appointment, Miss Damases?' the girl asked, glossing her full lips.

'It's Captain Damases, my dear. And it was you who arranged the meeting.' There was enough irony in Tamar's voice to penetrate even Anna's self-absorption. The girl scrolled a crimson fingernail down the desk diary, before uncrossing her legs and leading Clare and Tamar down the passage.

'Damases and the doctor from Cape Town,' she said, flinging open the door to the mayor's conference room. Cigar smoke undulated on the overheated air. Gilt chairs with spindly legs and red cushions were arranged around a shimmering table. The velvet swagged across the windows was held in place with thick gold tassels, which would have been more at home in a bordello. The effect was both ludicrous and oddly sinister.

'Ladies, you're welcome.' The man closest to them stood up, his charcoal suit tailored within an inch of its life. 'I'm Calvin Goagab. CEO of cleansing. You are Dr Hart?'

'I am.' Clare held his gaze. 'It's good to meet you.'

'This is His Worship, the Mayor, Mr D'Almeida.' Clare thought Goagab was going to bow, or make her curtsey, but he managed to restrain himself.

'Call me Fidel,' said the mayor. 'Calvin likes all this protocol, but I'm a simple man. Sit down, Tamar. In your condition, you must not strain yourself. Sit. Sit, Dr Hart. Anna, bring the ladies tea.' The secretary closed the door a notch below a slam.

'You're a runner, no?' D'Almeida was a compact man of about fifty, with iron-grey hair that set off his olive skin. He took Clare's measure appreciatively.

'I do run,' she said.

'Well, you must run by our lagoon then. You can watch the flamingos.' He turned to Tamar. 'She's staying in the cottage? I hope you'll be comfortable.'

Anna brought in a tray and set it down. She slopped tea into four cups before flouncing from the room. The mayor turned to Calvin Goagab. 'You wanted to have this meeting, Calvin. Please go ahead with what you wanted to say.'

Tamar, Clare and D'Almeida all turned to Goagab expectantly. 'I just wanted to welcome Dr Hart.' Goagab put his fingers together. They were slender, manicured. His sleeve slipped back to reveal an ornate Rolex watch. 'And to make sure that she understands that she is working for Captain Damases and the Namibian Police at all times.'

'Calvin is sensitive about South African imperialism,' D'Almeida explained. 'Trying to make up for the time he spent in closer-than-intended proximity to the South African army. Independence rather took him by surprise.'

Goagab flushed. He did not like to be reminded of his two menial years shunting trains in the desert for the army.

'I understand,' said Clare. 'I'll be doing preliminary work here while Captain Riedwaan Faizal's paperwork is sorted out. He'll be joining me when that's done. Then you'll have a direct police counterpart here. My own expertise is more specialised.'

'A profiler, yes.' Goagab stared up at the ceiling. 'I'm sure that it is a difficult skill to bring across cultures. I'm sure you'll find that this ... unpleasantness will have the usual explanation.

We've many foreigners who come to our port who have' – again
he ferreted for a word – 'needs. Unusual needs. We had a case
before Captain Damases was posted here. A girl was found dead,
but she'd been seen frequenting nightclubs where such services
are for sale. I'd be careful of jumping to conclusions.'

'I'm not that way inclined, Mr Goagab.'

Tamar concentrated on her tea. Goagab started to speak again:
'Of course, I didn't mean—'

'Thank you, Calvin.' D'Almeida silenced him. 'I'm sure
that Dr Hart will bear that in mind during her investigation.'
D'Almeida stood up and Clare took the cue and rose to her feet.
The mayor walked the two women to the door. 'I'm sorry we have
so little time,' he said. 'But we've a land claim to deal with. Some
of the rag-and-bone people from the Kuiseb.'

'The Topnaars?' asked Clare.

'Ah, I see you know something about this place.' D'Almeida's
grip on her arm was just short of painful. 'Yes, them: pastoral
nomads following an ancient way of life if you're a romantic foreigner; poverty-stricken squatters who drink their pension money
away and litter the desert, if you're from Walvis Bay. The one man
who knows everything about where their so-called ancestral
lands are won't speak'.

'Spyt?' asked Tamar.

D'Almeida nodded. 'The problem pre-dates us, unfortunately.
The South African military has more than just the war to answer
for. This is some confused claim about sacred sites. Apparently
the ghosts of the dead must walk the land because of what went
on here in the past.'

'Walvis Bay is a busy place for ghosts at the moment,' said
Clare.

'These murders, yes.' D'Almeida waved a dismissive hand. 'People in the town are getting anxious. The rumours are getting increasingly exotic, as you can imagine. We must deal with them, of course.'

'With tourism, image is everything,' Goagab added. 'And we depend on it now that the fish are gone.'

'That, and of course the fact that we've a series of unpleasant crimes on our hands, Calvin. Not just a PR problem. I trust you won't forget that.' D'Almeida made sure that he had the last word. 'Please, Dr Hart, let us know what you need to make your investigation work.' He inclined his head towards her. 'And I do hope to see you running.'

Chapter Ten

'I'LL GET ELIAS and Van Wyk,' said Tamar when she and Clare got back to the station. 'Then we can get started on our display.'

Tamar, Clare and Karamata made their way to the special ops room. Evidently, Van Wyk had more important matters to attend to, declining Tamar's invitation to join them without even looking up from his computer screen.

There was a roll of maps and a neat stack of autopsy photographs on the trestle table in the middle of the room. Stacked alongside were three murder dockets, sheets of coloured paper, scissors, blue tac, drawing pins and marker pens.

'We'll work backwards,' said Tamar. 'Let's start with Kaiser Apollis.' She wrote his name large in red.

'Monday's Child …' Clare pinned up the photographs of the boy drifting on the swing.

'Was fair of face,' Tamar finished. 'We'll have to wait for the autopsy before we can finish him.'

'There's a police file for him,' said Clare, checking through her documents.

'He was caught trespassing a month or so ago,' said Karamata.

'He was beaten?' Clare asked, glancing through the scrawled report.

'He worked the docks when he had to,' said Karamata. 'Van Wyk handled the case. The volunteer teacher, Mara Thomson, accused Van Wyk of beating Kaiser but it could just as easily have been the Russians on the old Soviet ships.'

'What are they doing here?' asked Clare.

'They've been rusting here since perestroika,' said Karamata. 'They don't dock because they don't want to pay harbour fees. They can't go home, because the state that owned them disintegrated with Gorbachev.'

'They like rough stuff,' Tamar continued. 'And they pay, but you've got to be desperate to go out there. The bar girls have stopped going after they beat up one of them for fun and threw her into the water. Some guy working on the *Alhantra* pulled her out.'

'Alive?' Clare asked.

'Just. Gretchen was lucky to survive. She worked at Der Blaue Engel, the most expensive of the sailors' bars. The "Gentleman's Club" is a new one in Walvis Bay. God knows where the money's coming from, but the local politicians and businessmen lap it up.'

'Gretchen von Trotha,' Karamata picked up the story. 'Unfortunate surname. Von Trotha was the German general who gave the extermination order for the Hereros a hundred years ago. My great-grandfather survived, so it's just luck that I'm here today.'

'Did she lay a charge?' asked Clare.

'Not likely in her line of work,' said Tamar. 'And she wouldn't know any better. She's been selling her body since she was thirteen. Van Wyk told me she's working the clubs again.'

'Van Wyk keeps tabs on things,' Clare noted, picking up the second slim file. 'Nicanor Jones.' She checked the date that he was found. 'A Wednesday's Child. Full of woe,' she said, shuffling through the photographs. An eyeless face leered up at her, a small neat hole blown clean through the skull, filigreed flesh peeling back from the snowy bone underneath.

'Looks like something got to his hands.' Clare pointed to a close-up of his hands. The palms were scored with callouses, freshly healed. The second finger of the left hand ended in a nail-less stump.

'A trophy collection.' Tamar pulled the autopsy report out of the folder. 'That was post-mortem. The gunshot was ante-mortem.' She shook her head. 'Only a pathologist would define life as being pre-death.'

'If death's your main business then it is, I suppose,' smiled Clare. 'Where was he found?'

'Right near the dump. It's on the edge of the Kuiseb River. It's on the aerial map there.' Tamar showed her. The dry river with its fringe of hardy plants held back the dune marching north. The Kuiseb curved along an ancient faultline until it dissipated into the salt flats on the cusp of the lagoon.

'How did you find him?' asked Clare.

'An anonymous tip-off,' said Tamar. 'Two Wednesdays ago. The call came through to the switchboard operator and she told Elias. He went out and looked until he found the body.'

'Do you know who called?' Clare asked.

'The operator said it was a foreign woman,' Karamata told her. 'But Namibians speak more versions of English than I can count.'

'And a boy's voice could be mistaken for a woman's,' Clare suggested. 'Who else but another homeless kid would have seen him out there? I can't imagine these kids want any police attention themselves.'

'No, they don't,' said Tamar. 'But they're very frightened. Those who can have moved back to whatever families they have.'

'Nicanor Jones had no family, by the looks of it,' said Clare, reading his file. 'Who's the last boy?'

'Fritz Woestyn. He was found three weeks ago, last Saturday.' Tamar handed her a sheaf of photographs.

'Saturday's Child,' said Clare, 'works hard for his living.'

'Woestyn, his name. It means desert,' said Tamar. 'And that's where he was found by some municipal workers doing a pipeline inspection.'

'On a Saturday?' asked Clare, disbelieving.

'Water's more precious than gold here. The foreman identified him. He'd seen him scavenging.'

'Peculiar that there was anything to find,' said Karamata. 'A hyena, even jackals make quick work of anything dead.' Fritz Woestyn stared up at Clare from the autopsy photograph. She looked over the small evidence boxes. Each contained the remnants of the boys' lives – shoes, some bloodied clothes, a note found in a pocket – making the displays look like small, morbid shrines.

'Easy targets, street children; many different reasons to do them in and no one around to report them missing.' Clare paced up and down in front of the boxes. 'You don't think it could be some kind of unofficial clean-up operation? Out at the dump where there are plenty of homeless kids scavenging. The school, too' – she checked Tamar's notes – 'where it looks like this Mara Thomson was running some soccer thing for homeless kids. That might make sense of the killer's desire to display them: that the bodies are a kind of threat. That's what happened to street kids in Rio.'

'It crossed my mind,' admitted Tamar. 'But with those Rio kill-ings, you always had two or three together, kids sleeping in door-ways in a city of ten million. You're not going to get away with that in a town of forty thousand people.'

'Have you done a search for a similar pattern in other ports?' asked Clare.

'I did. Nothing came up on any of the databases I have access to,' said Tamar. 'Rita Mkhize did a search in South Africa too. Nothing.'

'Nasty, brutish and very short, these lives,' said Clare. 'Unless the killer's left town, there'll be another body before too long.'

'I have to get home,' said Tamar, stretching her arms up to loosen her shoulder muscles. 'Let me drop you off at your cottage.'

Clare picked up her bag and the three files. 'I'll go over these again tonight.'

TAMAR DROVE ALONGSIDE the deserted harbour. It was fenced off from the road by twenty feet of razor wire. The barbs were fes-tooned with grimy plastic bags: Africa's national flower.

Tamar stopped outside a secluded series of stone cottages, all of them closed up. Shadows were deep beneath the palms trees and narrow service alleys. 'Lagoon-Side Cottages' said a sign hanging from the bleached whale-ribs that arched up over the entrance.

'The view is great on the few days when the fog lifts,' said Tamar.

'You don't like this weather?' Clare asked, taking her suitcase out of the car.

'I hate it,' said Tamar. 'I grew up in the sun, so this cold worms its way into my bones.'

'How did you get posted here?' asked Clare.

'It was my choice.' Tamar fished in her bag for keys. 'My sister needed help before she died, and there's plenty of scope for promotion in the police force.'

'Your husband?'

Tamar ran her hand over her swollen belly. 'There's only me for this little one.' Her tone invited no further questions.

'I'd like to see where Kaiser Apollis was found before the autopsy tomorrow morning,' said Clare, switching tack effortlessly.

'You have to see everything yourself?'

'Photographs flatten things. I've looked at your pictures, but there's something about being where the body was found.'

Tamar opened the door of the cottage. 'I hope you aren't superstitious. It's number 13; that's how the police got it cheap. No one ever wants to rent it.'

'Did you think I might be?' asked Clare.

'From your lectures,' said Tamar. She unlocked the French doors onto a small stoep. The sea air was welcome in the stuffy room.

Clare was glad to put her suitcase down. It had been a long day. 'I usually get accused of being too scientific,' she said.

'There was one thing you said that stayed with me.'

'What was that?'

'You said that when you go to a crime scene you like to sit there a while alone or with the body. That sometimes a feeling of what happened washed over you like a warm breeze. That spooked me.' Tamar was quiet for a second. 'You weren't talking about the feeling of the victim. You were talking about the killer. What you feel is what the killer leaves behind. His heart, that's what you find. When I saw that body in the school playground it raised the hairs on the back of my neck. I had that feeling, Clare. The one you described.'

'I wouldn't put that down in the case file, if I were you,' Clare laughed.

'I won't.' Tamar looked tired, older than her thirty-two years. 'Stranger killings are the hardest to solve,' she said.

'Hard to be a stranger in a town this size,' said Clare. 'Hard to keep a secret, I'd imagine.'

'You'd be surprised how many secrets there are.' Tamar opened the fridge. 'I put some wine in for you. And some milk and bread.'

'Very thoughtful,' said Clare, walking outside with her.

'I'll see you at 7.00 am, then?'

Clare nodded and watched Tamar ease her bulk into the front seat of the vehicle. Within moments, the mist had swallowed her car. She was heading due east. Clare guessed that she lived in Narraville, a windswept township that had uplifted itself into a suburb. There had been a few nice gardens there, if she remembered correctly. Roses flowered in some of them, despite the desert.

Chapter Eleven

OUT OF HABIT, Clare locked the front door to the cottage. It didn't take long to put away her tracksuit, T-shirts and jeans. She hung up her black dress and put a framed photograph next to the bed. Three little girls next to a childhood swimming pool laughed up at her. Two identical in frilled white swimming costumes: Clare and Constance. The third stood in the middle: Julia, older, breasts budding in her yellow bikini top, her arms around her twin sisters. Clare always carried the photo with her.

She opened the sliding doors and stepped onto the sheltered stoep. The lawn sloped away towards the boulevard that circled a tempting five kilometres around the lagoon. Clare reckoned she still had another hour of light. She was tired, her limbs sluggish, but the nausea from the small plane lingered. She needed a run.

It was a release dropping the weight of the day with her clothes and replacing them with her tracksuit.

The lagoon stretched towards the horizon, burnished a deep copper by the setting sun. A swathe of flamingos took off in a startled flurry of pink. They whirled out to sea before banking to fly inland, stragglers trailing like the tails of a kite. A boy of about seven hurtled past Clare on his bicycle, his hair set aflame by the setting sun. He waved shyly before turning in to the yard of a dilapidated double-storey house.

The wind was picking up, carrying the ice of the Benguela current with it. The last kite-boarders were peeling off their wetsuits and packing up their equipment. Clare was glad of her hood. The thick grey fabric cocooned her, the rhythmic thud of her feet on the ground as familiar now as her own heartbeat. For the first time since she had opened that Pandora's box in Riedwaan's car, her mood lifted. She ran faster, pushing the thought of him from her mind, burying it beneath the task that lay ahead of her.

Some problems are better buried. The boy on the swing, for instance; he would have been less trouble if he had been buried. To the killer, at any rate. Clare wondered what lesson had been intended.

She reached the end of the paved boulevard, but she wasn't ready to go back to the empty cottage yet. She kept on, running past the arc of streetlights and towards the salt marshes. Beyond them, if she remembered correctly, lay the Kuiseb Delta, an area of treacherous tributaries and restless sand blowing off the dunes. She repressed an atavistic fear of the dark and pressed on into the wind, losing herself in the comforting rhythm of her loping stride. A truck materialised without warning, forcing her off the road.

'Hey!' she yelled after it, fright making her furious. She stopped, leaning forward, trying to get her heart to slow down. The vehicle accelerated into the thickening fog, flashing its hazard lights in apology. It was time to go back.

Clare turned towards town, the wind at her back now, the chatter of the sea birds feeding in the shallow water to her left. She rounded a dune, planted with a copse of dusty tamarisks. The trees cut out the sound of the lagoon, but here the wind carried the faint, percussive echo of unfamiliar footsteps. The sound of it goosefleshed Clare's arms and made her stomach feel hollow. She picked up her pace, certain now that she could also hear the sound of breath rasping in lungs unused to running.

Just before she broke free of the trees, a wiry arm snaked round her, yanking her backwards. The other arm twisted into her hoodie, snapping her neck back. Clare kicked hard backwards. There was a sharp gasp of pain as her foot reached a shin, but the arms around her body did not lessen their hold. Her hood had pulled tight across her throat. She could smell him, the feral tang of adrenaline and wood smoke on his skin. Clare pulled forward, but that made it more difficult to breathe, so she leaned her weight in to her attacker, using the momentary slackness in his arms to twist loose. They both fell onto the damp sand, Clare beneath him. She calculated the distance to the lights beyond the trees. Three hundred metres. The takeaway restaurant she had passed earlier would still be open. She needed fifteen seconds, twenty at the most. She looked at her attacker, trying to see if he had a weapon. There was no glint of steel in the dim light. No knife out. No gun. Clare took a deep breath and fought again to slow her heart rate.

'I'm sorry, Miss.' The voice was light, almost girlish. Not what Clare had expected. So was his body, lighter than hers, now that she thought about it. 'But I need to talk to you,' the voice said.

Clare's heart was still hammering against her ribs. She took a breath, trying to slow it down. He wouldn't be the first man to attack a woman and say he just wanted to talk. But it gave her a gap. 'Let me sit up,' she said, the steadiness of her voice hiding her panic.

The figure of a young boy came into focus. 'Don't run away,' he pleaded.

'I won't,' said Clare, although the unwashed smell of him turned her stomach. She moved slowly so as not to startle him. Still no knife that she could see. She realised now that she was sitting up that she was taller than him.

'I saw you outside the bakery today.' Clare's heart was returning to normal. 'Lazarus. That's your name.'

The boy nodded, pleased that she had remembered.

Clare stood up cautiously. The boy rose with her. He came up to her shoulder. 'What do you want?' she asked. 'I've got nothing on me.'

'I'm scared,' said the boy.

'You're scared,' said Clare.

'Nobody helps us. Sometimes we die,' said Lazarus, 'but then it's just a drunk person who didn't mean to kill us dead.'

'Is that what happened with Kaiser?' Clare asked gently.

A car pulled in to the lot outside the takeaway, the shards of light from its beams raking through the trees, the glare catching the boy's face. He looked very vulnerable, very young.

'Kaiser, he went to stay with his sister.' The boy blurted the words out. 'He thought he'd be safe with her.'

'That's the last you saw of him?'

The boy nodded. 'Friday morning. He went to town.'

'What happened to him?' asked Clare.

The boy shifted his weight. 'I don't know. No one saw him. He never came back.'

'Lazarus, I'm going to start walking now,' said Clare, moving slowly so as not to alarm him. 'Do you want something to eat?'

'You go home, Miss,' Lazarus said, glancing nervously in the direction of the car. 'I'll be in trouble if someone sees me with you. We go to jail if we bother the tourists.' He looked down at his scuffed shoes. 'Mr Goagab said so.'

'Okay,' said Clare. She checked instinctively for her keys and her phone. They were both still in her pocket. Clare looked Lazarus in the eye. 'Was there anything specific you wanted to tell me?'

His gaze slid away. He shook his head.

'Okay,' said Clare again. 'But you find me if you hear anything. Just don't knock me down again.'

'There are people who won't like you if you help us. Be careful, Miss.'

'Who won't like it?' asked Clare. She looked at Lazarus, but it was too dark to read his expression.

'I don't know,' he shrugged. 'There are so many people who think we're just trouble.'

'Is that what happened with Kaiser?' Clare asked a second time. Another car turned in to the parking lot. Clare put her hand up to shield her eyes. When she turned to Lazarus for an explanation, he had blended into the darkness cascading in from the desert. Like a ghost. The thought made her shiver.

She was glad she had left the lights on in her room; the yellow light made it seem like a haven amidst the unlit cottages. She let herself in, locking the door behind her before taking a shower.

When she was dry and dressed, she poured herself a glass of wine and made toast. Then she fanned the dockets around her on the bed and set to work. Monday's Child: Kaiser Apollis. Nicanor Jones: Wednesday's Child. Fritz Woestyn: Saturday's Child. She was becoming accustomed to the unfamiliar names, but she had to reach behind the violence of their deaths to conjure an image of what they had been alive. She picked up a news clipping about the homeless soccer team. The key to the dead was in the living. To find their killer, Clare would have to resuscitate, if only for a moment, the laughing boys they had been, taking a shot at the goal posts at the end of a dusty soccer pitch.

Chapter Twelve

It took Clare three cups of coffee to get going the following morning. Tamar arrived early to take her to the school. The streets were still empty, and wide – wide enough for an ox-wagon to turn. A hundred years ago, they would have been the only form of transport into the waterless interior. The dusty streets would have been the only way inland for the ingredients of civilisation – tea, coffee, sugar, alcohol, and later guns – and the route out for colonial spoils – copper, uranium, gold and diamonds. The only reason anyone would live here, Clare thought, is to take a cut of whatever passes through.

It was five past seven when Tamar stopped before the school's locked gate. The caretaker eyed them warily, but waved when he recognised Tamar.

'Herman Shipanga,' Tamar said to Clare. 'He found the body.'

'When will the school re-open?' Clare asked.

'Maybe Thursday; otherwise next week. The headmaster Erasmus took it badly. I was surprised. He was such a tough guy when he was in the army.'

'South African?'

'Ja, he took Namibian citizenship and stayed on after they pulled out in '94.'

'Did many people do that?'

'A few. Some said they loved this place. For others it was a good way of avoiding Bishop Tutu and his Truth and Reconciliation Commission. Us up north of the Orange River, we decided to just brush our little atrocities under the carpet.'

Tamar parked beneath a wind-ravaged palm tree. 'Come this way. A path runs behind the school. This is how the boy got in.'

'You think he was alive then?'

'No, sorry. I'm sure not,' said Tamar. 'I meant the body, which Helena Kotze will confirm during the autopsy later.'

Clare picked her way down the path. It was strewn with chip packets and empty bottles. In places, used condoms had been snagged by the barbed-wire fences.

'Prostitutes bring their clients here?' she asked.

'They do, but we don't do anything unless there's a complaint,' said Tamar. 'I've checked with the regulars. Nobody saw anything.'

'You think that's the truth?'

'That I can't say.' Tamar stopped when the playground came into sight.

The houses had their backs to the alley. In the yards, dogs barked, chained to wires staked into the ground. Damp clothes hung on sagging lines. In the yard opposite the flapping strip of crime-scene tape, a faded-looking woman hung up her last item of washing and hitched the empty basket to her hip. A pudgy toddler tried to push his scooter through the sand.

'Hello,' greeted Clare, stopping at the fence.

'What you want?' The woman's tone was belligerent.

'These dogs always bark like this?' Clare asked.

'Only for strangers.' The woman fished out a cigarette from her pocket.

'Did you hear anything on Sunday night, Monday morning very early?'

'She asked me already.' The woman jerked her cigarette towards Tamar. 'I was watching TV.' She blew a smoke ring. 'Then I was asleep.'

'It's important, anything unusual,' said Clare. 'A boy was murdered.'

'Ja, the third one. You tell the police to do their job, so that our kids are safe instead of bothering innocent people.' With that, the woman turned and went indoors, yelling at her child to follow her.

'Who uses this alley?' Clare asked Tamar.

'People taking a short cut to the school,' answered Tamar. 'The rag-and-bone men used to come through here with their donkey carts.'

'Not any more?'

'Not as much,' said Tamar. 'Most of the recycling is done at the municipal site. The Topnaar carts were banned from coming into town. Hygiene reasons apparently, according to our CEO of cleansing. But they still come from time to time.'

'My friend Goagab?' asked Clare.

'The very one.'

The playground stood at the top of a gentle incline. A new wooden fence sequestered the youngest children's area. It had been decorated with a garish mural, the laughing Disney characters mocking in the childless silence.

'That's the swing?' Clare pointed to the last tyre hanging from the yellow frame.

Tamar nodded. 'And this is the gap in the fence where he got in.'

They walked together through the desolate playground. The bright-yellow paint had flaked off the links of the chain from which the seat was suspended. Clare sat down on the inverted tyre. The smell of the rubber, the metal sharp against the back of her legs, tipped her down a tunnel of memory again. It took her breath away, the immediacy of it. Herself a solemn six-year-old, swinging in the hot school playground, bare legs pushing time behind her, brown arms bending into the future. Willing herself older so that she could get away. Watched by Constance, her twin, whose face mirrored hers except in what it concealed, watching her, willing her to stay. Constance, a thought fox sniffing out Clare's most secret desires to be the only one, whole in and of herself.

Clare stopped, aware that Tamar was looking at her. She steadied the swing and hopped off.

'It's got the best view,' said Tamar. 'That swing.'

'You tried it?' asked Clare, looking out at the expanse of sand circled by the dark arm of the Kuiseb River to the south.

'I wanted to get a sense of him. Of his death. To see if there was anything left of the violence of it.'

'And was there?'

Tamar blushed and shook her head. 'There were some indentations in the sand, though,' she remembered. 'Like someone had poked it with a thin stick. Maybe a cane.'

Clare nodded and went over to the classroom block. A single window overlooked the playground. She peered into the dim classroom. The rows of miniature red desks and cheery yellow chairs were empty. A pile of marking lay abandoned on the teacher's desk. The writing on the board caught her eye: Mrs Ruyters, Grade 1, Monday's date.

'Ruyters,' said Clare. 'That rings a bell.'

'She's on your list for interviewing. She was here early, before Herman Shipanga arrived,' said Tamar, looking at her watch. 'Shall we get going? I need to get some coffee and pastries on the way. I can't do pregnancy on an empty stomach. Post-mortems neither.'

THE VENUS BAKERY was bustling with early-morning trade when Tamar pulled up on the opposite side of the road. At the stop street ahead, a familiar figure peered into the windows of cars caught by the traffic light.

'That's the boy I met last night,' said Clare, feeling the bruise on the side of her arm. 'I'll need to talk to him again.'

'Lazarus,' said Tamar. 'Lazarus Beukes. He's sharp. Been living on the streets most of his life. He'll spin you whatever story he thinks you want to hear.'

'You wouldn't believe him?' asked Clare.

'Put it this way,' said Tamar, 'Lazarus rarely lets the truth interfere with a good story.'

To the left of the bakery entrance, a wiry girl, her hair a wild black halo, chained her bike to a blue column. Lazarus approached her, trying to sell her a tatty-looking newspaper, his bony shoulders sharp against his worn jersey.

'That's Mara Thomson. The English volunteer.' Tamar pointed to the girl as she entered the store.

'They look so alike,' said Clare as they crossed the road. 'Funny to think they grew up six thousand miles apart.'

'Two rolls with cheese, please,' Mara was saying when they entered the bakery.

The woman behind the counter pulled two buttered rolls out of a tray, slapped the cheese onto them and wrapped them in plastic.

She pushed them across the counter to Mara. 'You shouldn't talk to these street boys.' Disdain curled her thin upper lip. 'Six Nam dollars.'

'They're good kids,' said Mara, 'living a bad life.'

'It's easy for you foreigners to feel sorry for them, but we have to live with them. Aids orphans are just trouble.' The woman counted out Mara's change. 'Look at that one who got himself killed. And the other two they found in the desert. What do they think that'll do for our tourism?'

'I'm sure they'd have avoided being shot,' Tamar interjected tartly, 'if they'd known what their murders would do to your business.'

'Hello, Captain,' said Mara, her relief at being rescued palpable.

'Morning, Mara. This is Dr Hart,' said Tamar. 'She's here from Cape Town, working with me.'

'Yeah, well, I'm glad somebody's bothered,' said Mara, shaking Clare's hand. 'Nice to meet you.'

'And you,' said Clare. 'You knew Kaiser? And the other boys, I understand?'

'Kaiser plays ... played in the soccer team I coach. So did Fritz and Nicanor, on and off,' said Mara, moving towards the door, out of earshot of the sour-faced shop assistant. 'Fritz Woestyn's death, that was part of the odds they play with anyway,' she went on. 'There've been murders before this. Nicanor Jones's death made them scared. This last one ...' Mara's voice trailed off.

'I'll need to talk to you,' said Clare. 'About the boys.'

'All right,' said Mara. 'I rent a room in that double-storey on the lagoon. George Meyer's house, if you need to ask for directions.'

'I've seen it,' said Clare. 'A little redhead on a bike went in there.'

'That's Oscar,' said Mara. 'I'll be back after soccer practice this afternoon.' She nodded goodbye and walked outside. Clare watched her give a roll to Lazarus.

'No meat?' he asked, pulling off the wrapping and dropping it to the floor.

'How about a thank you?' said Mara, picking up the discarded wrapping.

'Thanks,' he said, throwing the cheese roll into the bin as Mara turned the corner.

'Her visa's almost expired.' Clare had not heard Tamar come outside. 'She's got to go home, whether she wants to or not.'

'And does she?' asked Clare.

'I don't think so,' said Tamar. 'She's fallen for a beautiful young Spaniard called Juan Carlos. I doubt she can think straight at the moment.'

Chapter Thirteen

THE WALVIS BAY private hospital was a drab building. The mortuary, housed in a weather-beaten prefab round the back, was the grim heart of the establishment. A young woman in hospital greens opened the door when Tamar knocked.

'Welcome.' She stood aside for Clare and Tamar. The lemony scent of her hair held the institutional smell of disinfectant and instant coffee at bay.

'You must be Dr Hart.' The hand she offered Clare was broad and capable, the square nails cut short.

'Call me Clare. I feel like a fraud around proper doctors. You're Dr Kotze?'

'Helena, please,' the woman said. She turned to Tamar, looking her over. 'How are you?'

'Fine. Here's some breakfast for you.' Tamar gave Helena a pastry.

'Thanks. It's good to meet you, Dr Hart. I've read some of your work.'

'And your old professor, Piet Mouton, was singing your praises.' Clare returned the compliment.

'I'm just sorry I wasn't here to do those other two boys,' Helena said. 'A medical intern did the autopsies on Fritz Woestyn and Nicanor Jones. They're about as much use as a politician's election promises. Those boys were buried and the intern went back to Cuba, so a lot rests on this post-mortem.'

Helena gave Clare and Tamar gloves and gowns, ushering them into a cubicle off the entrance hall. Clare pulled the shapeless green gown over her clothes and tucked her long hair into the disposable hairnet. Helena opened a door, releasing the smell of the morgue. The ammonia was biting, but it was no match for the cloying stench of decay. Thick plastic curtains thwacked against metal when Helena Kotze wheeled in the metal trolley.

Kaiser Apollis's scrawny body was curled under the white shroud Clare had seen in the photographs. Helena pulled back the cover to reveal the child's head and face. The back of his head was missing and there was a small, neat hole in his forehead, the caked blood erasing the delicacy of his features. The three women circled him.

'A single gunshot wound to the forehead,' Helena said, more for her tape recorder than for Clare and Tamar. 'Probably a pistol. Nasty exit wound at the back, so no bullet for ballistics. Cause of death, I'd say. Put the call through to Piet Mouton, won't you Clare? The red button switches it to speakerphone.' She pointed to a machine near the window.

Clare busied herself, relieved to have something to do. She was also glad to have Mouton orchestrating this, even if it was remote. His experienced eyes missed nothing.

'Dr Hart,' bellowed Mouton, right on cue. 'You girls ready?'

'We're here, Piet. Me, Dr Helena Kotze and Captain Tamar Damases of Nampol.'

'Where's that useless bastard Faizal? He leave you in the lurch in the desert?'

Clare kept her voice light. 'Looks like it.'

'Tell him from me that absence makes the maiden wander. Doc Kotze, what you got there?'

'You've got the photos?' Helena asked.

'Yes, of course I have the photos. They jammed my e-mail all morning. Photos help me bugger-all. Forensics is science in court. On the slab, it's intuition and luck. Put me in your head and let me see through your eyes.'

Helena took a deep breath. 'Body of a child. Male. Looks twelve. Sixteen next week, according to his ID book. Weight: forty-two kilos. IDed as Kaiser Apollis. Bullet to the head. Close range. Body placed in a rubber swing. Blue and white nylon ligatures around both wrists. My guess is washing line.' Helena moved closer to the still form on the gurney and looked at the rope that had held the child's wrists together. 'A clean cut. Looks like—'

'Cut with what?' interjected Mouton.

'Looks like it was a pair of pliers,' Clare finished for Helena. 'Something rough.'

'Body folded into a foetal position,' Helena continued. 'Arms wrapped around the legs when discovered. Wrapped in an old piece of cloth. All held together with riempie. Riempie also used to attach the child to the swing where he was found.'

Helena untied the leather strips holding the shroud loosely in position. Kaiser Apollis looked as though he could have been asleep. His limbs had flopped wide, palms up. She pulled the shroud from underneath him and spread it out. There were no bloodstains. His life had seeped away before he had been swaddled in the cloth.

Helena continued: 'The top joint of the ring finger is missing.' Tamar brought her camera up close to the mutilated digit.

'The only finger with a dual nerve supply,' Mouton noted. 'Double the nerves; double the pain. No wonder it's the wedding finger.'

'An unlikely bridegroom.' Clare picked up the boy's hand and spread out the fingers. 'Some bleeding. If it was done post-mortem then not too long after he died.'

'Dr Kotze,' said Mouton, his disembodied voice startling them. 'What's your time of death?'

'The body was cold when it was found,' said Helena. 'But I'd say at least thirty-six, maybe forty-eight hours before we got to it. There was only a little stiffness left. Weekends are generally our murder nights anyway. So Friday.'

'Any other wounds? From the photographs it looked like his chest was a mess.'

'Yes,' said Helena. 'Considerable post-mortem cutting. Surface wounds on the chest and abdomen. Not much oozing. Done quite some time post-mortem. We'll wash it off and have a closer look.'

Helena and Tamar laid the slender boy out on the trolley, his hip bones twin peaks under the bloodstained white shirt. 'The Desert Rats' was emblazoned across the front of the grubby shirt.

'Mara Thomson's soccer team,' said Tamar.

Helena removed his clothes. He had no underwear on under his jeans. His feet were too small for the shiny new Nikes.

'Expensive shoes for a homeless child,' Clare commented. She bagged and tagged the clothes and shoes.

'Fake,' Helena explained. 'Chinese Nikes. Thirty Namibian dollars. That's what? About four US dollars. Try China Waltons in the middle of town. That's where everyone gets them.'

Helena looked away from the still face, androgynous in death, and put her hand on a dirty knee. 'Old scars on the knees and elbows. Uncircumcised. No tattoos. A leather necklace with a beaded pouch at the end.'

'It's for protection.' Tamar reached forward. She untied it and dropped it with the clothes. 'He'd have worn it since he was a baby. Whoever gave him that loved him.'

'Didn't do him any good in the end,' said Helena. 'Will you help me turn him, Clare?'

Clare nodded reluctantly. The naked boy was insubstantial. When they laid him on his stomach, his heels flopped outwards, leaving the feet pigeon-toed. Helena leaned forward, oblivious. She pressed a forefinger against the naked buttocks. 'The discolouration on the back of the legs is quite marked. Buttocks, back, thighs, calves. The blood looks like it's pooled.'

'What's that telling you?' barked Mouton.

'That he lay on his back for some time before he was trussed up for his trip to town.' Helena ran her finger over the boy's matted hair. His drying blood had trapped fine sand. She held a glass strip beneath the locks and tapped a bit of sand onto it, holding it up to the light. It glinted. 'See that? It's mica. Fool's gold. You don't get that at the coast. At the coast the sand's darker, purple even.' Helena put the glass aside.

Clare's eyes traced down the lattice of scars on his back. 'Kaiser Apollis took a few beatings in his life. I'd like to hear what Van Wyk says about his weekend stay in the cells.'

Helena turned on the tap, and warm water spurted out of the garden hose she had rigged up. She and Clare turned Kaiser onto his back. The water ran pink, clearing the boy's face of the crust of blood. Bone and skin filigreed over the hole the bullet had punched into his forehead.

'The killer was close when he fired. Look at this.' Helena pointed to the boy's forehead. Fanned out around the entrance wound was an intricate stippling. 'It's called tattooing. You see this if the victim is shot at close range. Between ten centimetres and two metres. Further away than that you don't see it.'

'What's it from?' Clare asked.

'The propellant and gas that travels with the bullet as it leaves the muzzle embeds itself into the tissue, like a tattoo,' Helena explained. She moved the hose down, rinsing blood from the boy's neck and chest. She turned the water down and washed the wound on his chest. Marks were deliberately scored into the flesh with a few deft, deep strokes.

'It looks like a 3,' said Helena.

'There had better not be a number 4. There was a cutting like this on Nicanor Jones too,' said Tamar. 'He had a 2 on his chest.'

'Did Fritz Woestyn have a 1?' Clare asked.

'Nothing. The finger joint was missing. Head shot the same, same type of gun, but not this mutilation,' said Tamar.

'How was this done?' Clare turned back to Kaiser Apollis.

'Non-serrated knife, I'd say,' guessed Helena. 'Very sharp. A fisherman's knife, something sturdy like that. Look here.' She pointed to the chest. 'It's nicked the ribs in places. But there isn't much blood here, so definitely done some time post-mortem.'

Helena washed the rest of the frail body, hands gentling the healed lash wounds on his back and buttocks. She examined his feet, pulling apart the toes. The tender flesh between them was still pink, the last vestige of a truncated childhood. There was sand and salt crusted around his toes, as if he had dug them into sand and then let a wave run over them.

'It looks like he walked in sand before he put his shoes on,' she said, taking a scrape of the soil. 'I could see if this sand is the same as the sand in his hair.'

'You studying soil to go with your gunshots?' Tamar asked.

'My boyfriend's a geologist. He thinks the best way of getting me to give him a blow job is to tell me in graphic detail about all the soil types of the Namib.'

'Does it work?' asked Clare.

'Put it this way, it keeps him quiet.'

'Have you thought about giving him something to eat?' asked Tamar.

'Gross,' said Helena, shocked. 'I hate cooking.'

'Ladies, I have work to do. Call me when you're done, Dr Kotze.' Mouton cut the connection, leaving a disapproving silence in the cold room.

'Oops!' Helena gave Clare and Tamar a grin. 'I'm going to start with the cutting now. It's a bit gory. Organs, brain and splatter. I'll do you lung slices too. If he vomited before he died, we might be able to see what his last meal was. If you two want to get on, I'll finish up here.'

'We've got an interview with Kaiser's sister anyway,' Tamar said. 'Clare, Lazarus told you that Kaiser had been going to her a lot lately. Maybe she can tell us why.'

Chapter Fourteen

THE CRISP AIR outside the mortuary was a relief. Kaiser Apollis's secrets would be scalpeled from him. The nestled organs separated. Liver, heart, lungs laid out in stainless-steel dishes to be weighed and tested. Clare doubted that this bloody grubbing would reveal much. The truth of his death lay in the dark maze of someone else's mind. This was her labyrinth; she an Ariadne armed with nothing but the slender thread of instinct.

A firm foot on the accelerator had taken Clare and Tamar past the warehouses and low-cost houses that sprawled north of the town. The wind lashed the washing, Mondrian blocks of blue, green, yellow and red, pegged to the fence defending the last row of cramped houses. The dunes seemed to sidle closer with each gust. A thin girl was sweeping the apron of cement at her front door. She had the same heart-shaped face and delicate build as the dead boy Kaiser. On her high cheekbone was a bruise, butterfly-winged around the almond-shaped eye. Tied to her back was a baby, perhaps a day or two older than the bruise.

'Captain Damases,' the girl whispered as soon as they were in earshot.

'Hello, Sylvia,' said Tamar. 'This is Dr Hart.' Tamar unlatched the gate and they stepped into the neat yard. A scrawny dog yapped. Sylvia raised a threatening hand. The dog cowered and was silent. She looked back at the two women, dazed. Tamar put a gentle hand on the girl's arm. 'Shall we go inside?'

'Sorry.' Sylvia jumped. The house was empty, but the air was laden with a fug of sleep, cheap coffee and sadness. A snowy television spluttered into the gloom. It was hard to move among the over-sized furniture. Sylvia switched off the TV and the radio, and silence crackled into the chilly little house.

'How are you?' Tamar touched the girl's swollen cheek.

Sylvia dropped her eyes. Two fat tears appeared, rolled down her cheeks and splashed onto her milk-swollen breasts. That was it.

'The baby?' The swaddled infant mewled. Sylvia retied the blanket and he puckered his rosebud mouth and went back to sleep. 'What's his name?' asked Tamar.

'Wilhelm. For his father.' Then a surge of defiance glowed in Sylvia's eyes. 'I call him Kaiser.'

'For your brother?' asked Tamar.

'For my brother.' Sylvia looked down, the unblemished side of her face illuminated by the morning light. She would be beautiful without the bruises.

'The boys at the dump say that Kaiser didn't always stay with them?' Tamar inflected the sentence into a question.

Sylvia's face had the look of a secretive child who refuses to tell tales. Her eyes flicked at the kitchen table. Tucked beneath the overhang of Formica was a thin blue mattress rolled tightly around a grey dog-blanket.

'Your brother slept here sometimes?'

'When my boyfriend worked night shift. He didn't like Kaiser to be here ...' Her voice trailed off. Clare wondered how long the infant's plump cheek would stay unmarked.

'Did you know your brother's friends?'

'We were always alone,' Sylvia said. 'Then Wilhelm took me to live here.'

'When was that?' Clare asked.

'Two years ago.' There was shame in the girl's voice. 'I had nothing to eat.'

'How old were you then?'

Sylvia shrugged. 'Maybe thirteen. I'm not sure.'

Clare supposed that at thirteen a regular fist from a man you knew was better than a knife in the guts from a man you didn't.

'And Kaiser? Where did he go?' asked Clare.

'He was with me sometimes. Sometimes on the street. I gave him money when I had some.'

'When last did you see him, Sylvia?' Tamar asked.

The girl slumped. She looked for an uncanny instant like the crone she would be at thirty. If she lived that long. 'My baby's father changed his shift,' she said. 'Kaiser had to go for good.'

'Try to remember when,' Clare pressed. Patience would get them what they wanted.

'Last week he stopped working night shift. When I came back from the hospital with the baby he told me that Kaiser had to go.'

Her hand touched the bruise on her face. That explained the timing: the bruise was younger than the baby, but only by twenty-four hours.

Sylvia took a deep breath. 'I left him a note.' She raised her head, the brief spark in her eyes snuffed. 'I never saw him again.'

Her voice was so quiet that Clare could hear the tiny panting breaths of the baby sleeping on its back.

'And Wilhelm?' asked Tamar. 'Where was he on Friday night?'

'No,' Sylvia said, 'he was with me all night.'

'Do you mind if we look round?' Clare asked.

Sylvia shook her head. She sat down and opened her blouse. The baby's mouth parted, clean and pink. A fat little hand kneaded her soft flesh. Sylvia cupped her hand over the child's fragile head. Tamar put on the kettle to make tea, asking Sylvia about the birth, the breastfeeding. The soothing talk of mothers.

Tuning out Tamar's gentle murmur, Clare unwound the worn bedroll. The faded Superman pyjamas brought her up short with the realisation of how recently the dead boy had been a child. She slipped her fingers inside the frayed blue cuffs. His skinny wrists and ankles would have protruded from them as he grew into his malnourished and delayed adolescence. She picked up the top and held it to her nose, breathing in the lingering, wood-smoky smell of him.

Someone had stood close enough to the boy to breathe in the same essence, to feel his warm, frightened breath on their hands. They had stood that close and then discharged a bullet into the unlined forehead. Tears prickled hot in Clare's eyes.

'What else was his?' she asked Sylvia.

The girl pointed to the window sill: a jagged scrap of mirror, a yellow comb, a jar of Vaseline. A blue bowl stood on the drying rack. The boy would have filled it, perhaps catching a glimpse of his small, peaked face before plunging his hands into the cold water to rub the accumulation of the night's sleep from his eyes. Outside, he would have heard mothers calling their children for breakfast, as Clare could hear now. Inside, the house was quiet, just the click of the baby's throat as it suckled, oblivious of the harsh life that awaited it.

Clare opened the Vaseline jar. Kaiser would have opened it one last time to dip his finger in for a final gob of pale jelly. He might have rubbed the grease into his cheeks. The cupboards would have been empty as they were now, and the child's belly would clench around the water he drank for breakfast. Kaiser's cheeks would have glowed brown in the morning light, creeping over the desert as he stepped into the cold. At least with his cheeks shining, his teachers wouldn't get angry with him for looking hungry.

Clare looked into the shard of mirror. It fragmented her face. She could see her mouth or eyes, a cheek or the chin. Her picture of the dead boy was the same, fragmented. A shattered face. A flayed chest. A delicately turned foot in a white Nike, a full bottom lip. A discarded child she had never met and into whose begging hands she probably wouldn't have dropped fifty cents.

Clare imagined the last afternoon the boy had come home, turning left at the bent fig tree that grew outside the shebeen where his sister's boyfriend drank before he beat her on Fridays. When he saw his sister's note, the boy might have wished that he could not read, but he would have read the lines on his sister's face anyway. The message was clear in black and blue. He would have just turned around and gone back to town. He'd have scoured the dustbins outside the fast-food restaurants.

The voice would have startled him and he'd have looked up to find the driver of a car asking him if he was hungry. Did he nod? Or was he too proud? His eyes would have flared wide at the proffered banknote.

'Get me a Coke. Something for yourself,' the driver would have said. 'Get in.' As the fog thickened, the boy had done just that. Nobody would have seen the car glide into the mist.

'Shall we go and watch the sea?' the driver might have asked. Or the desert. Or the lagoon.

The boy would have nodded. Why not?

At the edge of the lagoon, the tide would be rising, water rushing in over the exposed mud and around the pink legs of the stilted flamingos, necks down, looking for food. The birds would have raised their heads in unison at the sudden retort of a car door slamming. The car would've traced the curve of the lagoon towards the fog-blanketed salt flats, the boy watching the fingers on the steering wheel.

'You got a family?'

Perhaps the boy had thought about the wooden cross that marked his mother's resting place, or of his sister's battered face, before shaking his head.

'You busy now?'

The boy shook his head again.

'Would you like a drive?'

The boy had obviously thought that he would. They knew that much. Clare wondered if he had known it was going to be his last. If he had sought out what was coming, even welcomed it …

'Clare, we should go.' Tamar's voice drew Clare back into the small, stuffy house. Tamar was holding the baby, and Sylvia held a Mickey Mouse rucksack in her hands.

'He left his school bag. Take it,' she said. 'Maybe it'll help you.'

CLARE LOOKED BACK at the house as they reached the end of the street. Sylvia was standing at the gate where they had left her, the wind wrapping her skirt around her thin legs. Clare opened the bag. There was a pencil case, a dog-eared *Harry Potter* in Afrikaans, and a diary. She rippled through the pages: homework assignments at the beginning of the year with longer and longer gaps between them. One hundred Namibian dollars fell out. Clare put her finger in the place where it had been secreted. August. A month earlier when all three boys were still alive.

'A lot of money not to spend.' Clare tucked it back into the book as Tamar turned into the station parking lot.

'I'm going to take a walk,' said Clare. 'I need some fresh air.'

She headed towards the water, the wide sweep of it a relief after the confined space of the mortuary and Sylvia's cramped house. The sun, gilding the drab buildings along the shore, was as warm as a hand on her skin. She missed having Riedwaan as a sounding board for the ideas whirling in her head. All she had to do was swallow some pride and phone him to discuss the case.

She swallowed and dialled, but his cellphone went straight to voicemail. She called his office. It rang for some time and went through to the switchboard.

'Special Investigations Unit. Can I help you?'

'Clare Hart here. Put me through to Captain Faizal.'

'He's not in. He took a personal day.'

Clare knew the reservist. She was a bosomy law student with a uniform fetish.

'A personal day,' she said. 'That must be a first in the SAPS. You've been reading too many magazines.'

'Something about his wife and daughter, I'd call it personal.'

That silenced Clare.

'You want to leave a message, Dr Hart?'

'No.'

'I'll tell him you called then?'

Gabriella. That was her name, Clare remembered.

'Don't bother, Gabriella.'

Clare's stomach growled, reminding her that it had been a long morning and she needed lunch. On her way back to the police station, she stopped at the bakery and ordered rolls and coffee to take away.

'Twelve-fifty,' said the cashier, the same thin-lipped woman who had given Mara the third degree the day before. 'You're the expert from South Africa.'

'I'm from Cape Town.' Clare searched through the unfamiliar notes in her purse.

'A waste of money. One dies, and they spend how many thousands of our tax money to bring you here.' A vein pulsed in the woman's temple. 'Where are you staying?'

Clare was so taken aback that she answered: 'On the lagoon.'

'I knew it. In a town with no money and no work.'

Clare picked up her lunch and went outside, shaken by the woman's venom. She stepped off the pavement, right in front of a big Ford truck.

The driver slammed on his brakes and she jumped back. Her heart skipped a beat when she recognised him: Ragnar Johansson. She hadn't calculated on his still being in Walvis Bay.

'Hey, Clare.' Ice-blue eyes in a weathered face. Ragnar Johansson put out a vein-roped hand to restrain the Labrador whining next to him. 'I was wondering if you'd call.'

'It didn't take you long to find me.' Clare pushed her hair out of her eyes, playing for time.

'Not in a town as small as this,' said Ragnar.

'I wasn't sure if you'd want to.'

'Well, I found you,' he smiled. 'I'll tell you later if it's what I wanted.'

'How've you been?'

'Good.'

'Iceland?' she hazarded.

'Didn't work out. Cape Town?'

'It's been fine.'

'You alone?'

Clare looked away and nodded.

'You want a lift?'

'No, thank you.'

He put out his hand and touched her cheek. 'It'd be good to catch up.'

'It would.' It seemed churlish to step away from his forgotten touch.

'Dinner?'

'Okay.'

'I'll pick you up at eight-thirty tonight.'

'I'm staying at the Lagoon-Side Cottages.'

'I know.'

The light changed and Ragnar drove off. He and his wet dog huddled together on the front seat. Both grinning. Clare's face felt hot where he had touched it. She rubbed her cheek, then licked her finger. It tasted salty. Like blood.

Chapter Fifteen

TAMAR DAMASES HAD arranged a vehicle for Clare's interview with Shipanga. Clare signed for it, picked up the keys, and within five minutes was guiding the 4x4 along the wide avenue that led to Kuisebmond, the township where the caretaker lived. The quiet streets of the town gave way to a warren of lanes, and she slowed to avoid the darting children and mangy, slinking dogs. The cracked pavements were crowded with stalls selling single cigarettes and plastic bags holding an onion and two potatoes. Women squatted by low fires, tending fragrant vetkoek and frying pig trotters. Men with glazed eyes and the concentrated precision of the permanently drunk watched Clare drive past the dark shebeens, before turning back to the pool tables.

The address Tamar had given Clare didn't mean much in the thicket of houses. She hazarded a guess and turned down a newly laid road that took her away from the larger houses and into a maze of narrow paths. Tin shacks and tarpaulins had been replaced with brick boxes. Green, red, pink, yellow, brown: brightly coloured, poorly built. The Smartie houses. A flock of chubby-legged urchins ran alongside the car. Clare parked. An entourage of children clustered around their minder, a girl of nine or ten, staring at Clare getting out of the enormous car.

'Where does Herman Shipanga live?' Clare asked the girl.

The fat baby on the girl's hip gave a terrified wail and buried its face into her neck.

'Come,' the girl beamed. Clare followed her through backyards where washing snapped and forlorn patches of mielies somehow grew.

'There.' The girl pointed at a yellow house. The little boys backed up against her skinny legs. A few plugged their thumbs into their mouths and watched, solemn-eyed, as Clare knocked on the door. She could hear the radio blaring inside. It sounded like a church service, but the language was unfamiliar.

The door cracked open a few inches. A man, wiry and shorter than Clare, looked out from the gloom. His hair was sprinkled with grey; cheekbones high and wide; dark eyes, kind.

'Herman Shipanga?'

The man nodded, wary. The air that escaped was stale, laden with the smell of too many bodies in too small a place.

Clare held out her temporary police ID. Shipanga opened the door wider and took it. 'I'm Clare Hart. I'm investigating the death of Kaiser Apollis.' The man's eyes flickered with fear, anger, sadness; Clare couldn't say which. 'I wanted to ask you about him. About how you found him.'

Shipanga did not respond. Clare repeated the question in Afrikaans. Her train of urchins scuffled closer.

'One minute.' Shipanga answered in English. He closed the door, and the radio stopped. Then he opened the door again and set down two Coke crates in front of the house. 'Sit, asseblief.'

Clare obeyed.

'*Voetsek!*' Shipanga raised his hand at the children and they scattered like gulls to settle at a safer distance.

'English?' Clare asked.

Shipanga looked down and spread out his hands.

She switched back to Afrikaans: 'You found the boy?'

Shipanga nodded. He ran his hands over his eyes, as if trying to erase the image.

'I read your statement,' said Clare. 'But I wanted to hear from you what you saw on Monday, from beginning to end.'

Shipanga did not take his eyes off her face. The beginning? His fingers sought the ridged scars on his cheekbones. Precise incisions that had been filled with ash so that he would be forever marked as someone who belonged. But that had been forty years ago. The close-knit structures of family and clan up north had fractured and then broken apart. The force of that implosion had landed him here on this tract of bleak sand. It had kept him in the heaving bowels of a factory ship until it had crushed him beneath falling crates of filleted fish. Then it had spat him out again to find woman's work, sweeping and cleaning toilets, dragging his injured leg behind him until he had come face to face with the dead child in the swing. The end? Hard to say. Shipanga looked down at his shoes.

'We used to find them like that,' he said at last. 'Outside the villages.'

Clare waited, watching as Shipanga gathered memories, sought words in a language that did not belong to either of them.

Shipanga looked at Clare, frustration clear in his eyes. The words were inadequate for what he wanted to tell her, the shock of a buried past colliding with the present. 'I found him,' he said.

'The bullets to the head. Like the executions when the army was here, in the north ...' His voice trailed off.

The absence of war, thought Clare, did not result in the presence of peace. The elemental force of it, the trauma, shaped a man in unnatural ways, much as the wind along this Skeleton Coast bent the alien trees.

'You found him,' prompted Clare. 'Tell me how you found him.'

Shipanga straightened the seam in his trousers. Someone had ironed them with care. 'I ate early. I left after the first siren. Before six. I went straight to the school. Got my rake to clean.'

'Which way did you go in?'

'I went in the back. I take a short cut down the path between the houses.'

'Don't the dogs go crazy?' asked Clare.

'I always go there,' said Shipanga. 'They're used to me.'

'Did you see anybody?'

Shipanga shook his head. 'My wife was here, my kids. At the school, on the way there, the fog was too thick. I saw nobody. Nobody saw me.' He paused, thought about the implications.

'No one was at school before you?'

'Just Mrs Ruyters. Her car was there. I didn't see her.'

'Did you expect her to be there?' Clare asked.

'She's always first.'

'You always start with the kindergarten playground?'

'Always. Some of the children come early. Mrs Ruyters likes it to be ready for them.' Shipanga picked at his fraying cuff. 'When I saw him there,' he continued, 'I thought it was one of the older children teasing. Then the wind turned him and I saw the flies on his face.'

'Did you touch him?'

'I told Sergeant van Wyk,' said Shipanga, 'I ran for help. The headmaster was there and he called the police. I didn't see the boy again. My job was to stop anyone coming into the school.'

'Who came?'

'There were only a few,' said Shipanga. 'Mr Meyer, of course. He's always early. The little boy, Oscar. He sometimes helps me or he goes to Mrs Ruyters.'

'The other early people?'

'They all went away when they saw the police vans and the ambulance. Only Calvin Goagab caused trouble.' Shipanga's mouth twisted, as if the name was bitter on his tongue. 'He wanted to drop his sons at school.'

'Is he often early?' Clare asked.

'He does what he wants. He's a powerful man. He works for the mayor now. He has a smart house. He forgets that he came from here.' Shipanga gestured to the grimy dilapidation around him. The silent, staring children shrank out of sight again.

'Does anyone else use that back entrance?' Clare changed tack. Tamar had told her about Goagab. She needed more.

Shipanga shrugged. 'Sometimes the children. The ones who come from the other side of town. Mara Thomson sometimes. She comes by bike.'

Clare was about to get up, but Shipanga put his hand on her arm, restraining her.

'It was a warning, the boy. Like a warning from the spirits. This is a bad place. I told you we used to see them left dead to warn us, telling us to keep our heads down, not see things, to leave. That boy was a warning. Like the old ones we had during the war.'

'Who was the warning for?' Clare asked.

Shipanga shook his head. 'There are many ghosts in this desert. The desert sees everything. All our secrets.' He paused, waiting for a distant siren wail to cease. 'It keeps secrets only as long as it feels like it. Then the sand moves and there are all the skeletons. It is a message.'

'And what was the message?'

'That I must go home to my village,' said Shipanga. 'I mustn't die here.' He traced a curved line in the sand: the river on whose verdant banks he had spent his boyhood.

Clare stood up to go. Shipanga looked up at her. 'Did you speak to Miss Mara?'

'Not yet,' said Clare.

'Miss Mara knew that boy well. He was in her team. The other boys, too, the dead ones.'

To the left of the house, a woman turned the corner, laden with old plastic shopping bags. She stopped when she saw Clare, her brow furrowed with concern. 'Herman?' she said as she approached.

Shipanga stood up. 'This is my wife. Magdalena, this is the police doctor.' Clare took the woman's plump hand. It was as soft and worn as an old glove. Magdalena looked at her husband.

'He can't sleep,' she said to Clare. 'Since he found the dead boy, he keeps us all awake with his nightmares or with walking about. He says the boy was there to call him home.'

'What do you think?' asked Clare.

Magdalena shook her head. 'I was born in the city. I see no ghosts. There are sailors here, truck drivers, and foreigners from everywhere. It's one of them. Whoever did it is gone.' She sat down beside her husband. 'Gone, Herman.'

Shipanga leant against the sturdy body of his wife, the strength drained from him. 'You'll excuse us.' Magdalena pulled him to his feet, limp as a rag doll. Clare watched the little house swallow them. The radio crackled back to life.

The children drifted away when she returned to her car. She sat for a minute, wishing she still smoked. The caretaker had given her nothing new, nothing concrete.

The hand tapping on her window snapped her into the present. It was Shipanga again. 'I found this,' he said, reaching for Clare's hand and placing a tangle of gossamer threads in her palm. It was a cast, a compact ball of insect remains; wings, shimmering and transparent, some still attached to fragments of insect bodies.

'What is it?'

'It's from insects, after they've been eaten. You only find these ones in the desert.' Shipanga pointed to a red-streaked pair of wings, longer than the others. 'They come out if it rains.'

'Termites?'

Shipanga nodded.

'Why are you giving me this?' The tangled limbs moved in the breeze, their husky weightlessness horrible in Clare's hand.

Shipanga stepped back from the car window as Clare tipped the little corpses into the cubbyhole. 'After they took the boy away,' he said, 'I went back to the swing. I found it stuck in the tyre where his head had been.'

Chapter Sixteen

KARAMATA WAS FINISHING his coffee in Tamar's office when Clare got back to the police station. 'Are you ready to see the sights?' he asked. He was scheduled to take Clare to the dump site where Nicanor Jones was found.

'I'm ready. Are you coming, Tamar?' asked Clare.

Tamar shook her head. 'I am still going through all the ship logs to see if there's any pattern with which ships were in and these murders.' She leant back on her yellow couch. She looked so slight, despite her pregnancy.

'Find anything yet?'

'Not much. The Russian ships, of course. The *Alhantra*'s been in all the time. Ragnar Johansson's the skipper. You know him, I think.'

'I do,' said Clare. 'From the last time I was here.' She couldn't read Tamar's expression.

'There've been a couple of others, but there's no consistency,' said Tamar. 'I need to do a few more checks. I'll catch you later.'

Clare picked up her files and followed Karamata to the Land Cruiser. He opened the door for her, before heaving himself into the driver's seat.

Karamata took the road past the lagoon, but soon turned off onto a dusty track. Clare opened Nicanor Jones's file. A class photograph, taken several years earlier, was stuck in the front. A little boy with shiny eyes and a wide mouth smiled up at her, frozen in his last recording of an official moment. In the next picture, his eyes were hollows and the white cheekbones shone through. There was one of his torso. It was bloody, the skin on the bony chest torn away. Clare looked away.

'Not pretty,' said Karamata.

'No,' said Clare.

Karamata turned right, into pure sand. The wheels held and the Land Cruiser topped the dune. Hidden below at the foot of the dune lay a scavenger's paradise.

'That is where I found him.' Karamata pointed to the rusting razor wire looped along the edge of the dump. He pulled out a panoramic shot and held it up. The composition foregrounded the boy's limp body, giving perspective to the vast expanse of the sand.

From their vantage point, Clare could see the road that led back to town, the lagoon and the harbour beyond it. 'On this side of the fence?' she asked.

'Yes. He had been tied to that pole.' Karamata pointed to a sturdy log that held the swags of razor wire in place.

'Whoever dumped him didn't come through the dump then. If he'd gone through that wire, alive or dead, it would've lacerated him. Whoever dumped him must've come across the sand. You didn't see any tracks?'

'I didn't,' said Karamata. 'But the wind had been blowing, so anything would've been covered with sand.'

It was as sparse a crime scene as the schoolyard, according to the docket. 'He wasn't killed here, was he?'

'No,' said Karamata. 'He'd been dead five days when he was found.'

Clare pictured the shrine she and Tamar had made to the child full of woe, Wednesday's Child. That made the time of death Friday, the same as Kaiser Apollis. She looked at the autopsy pictures again. The mutilation was the work of human hands. So where was he? Why keep his body away from scavengers? When was he put here?

Clare looked over the unforgiving sand and rock. It made no sense, the risky display, the complications of transporting a corpse several days dead, the exhibition in a public place. Or was it intended that children see it? A warning of sorts, like Shipanga had said.

'The body must've been in full view of where the waste-pickers sleep,' she observed.

'They say they saw nothing and heard nothing,' said Karamata. 'They certainly said nothing.'

A blue dump truck moved along the black ribbon of tar. It lumbered past a windowless brick building then onto a weighbridge. A man with a clipboard took note of the number plates and weight before waving the truck on.

'George Meyer. The boss.' Karamata cut the engine. 'That's his incinerator.' The chimney, dark against the grey sky, spiralled smoke into the still air. It drifted towards the town.

'So much easier to just burn a body,' Clare said, half to herself.

'You'd think so,' said Karamata, 'but you'd have to get it past George first. He's very German about his record-keeping!'

'His movements have been checked, I suppose?'

'We spoke to him,' said Karamata. 'He was at home all weekend. Him and that funny little boy of his, Oscar.'

The truck stopped in the middle of the dump site. Scrawny supplicants emerged from the heaps of waste and swarmed around the vehicle, heads bowed, hands lifted. The driver jumped out and walked over to the foreman standing to the side, sjambok at the ready. The waste-pickers worked with practised efficiency, filling sacks with discarded affluence.

'The other economy,' Karamata noted. 'At the moment it's the only one that's stable.'

'The fishing is over?'

'Finish and *klaar*. Not even jobs left for pals.'

'You didn't put money in fishing?' Clare asked.

'Not me,' he laughed. 'I didn't have the right surname or the right connections. I suppose I should be glad about that now.'

Karamata started the engine, and the vehicle pitched forward down the vertiginous dune. He pulled onto a track that led to the dump and parked outside the entrance to the building.

'Let's say hello to George Meyer,' he said. 'A courtesy.' He pushed open the screen door and Clare followed him down the immaculate passage. The third door was open.

'Mr Meyer?' Karamata ducked slightly as he stepped inside the office. His bulky form dwarfed the furniture.

George Meyer was at his desk. The little redhead Clare had seen cycling along the lagoon was sitting at a small table. The boy's eyes widened in recognition when he saw her.

'Sergeant Karamata. Madam.' George Meyer stood up and smoothed down his hair, nodding at Clare.

'This is Dr Hart,' said Karamata. 'Dr Hart and I want to talk to the boys who live on the dump.'

'Sign in, please.' Meyer pushed a ledger towards Karamata. 'New policy since that body was found here. The boys are afraid. This makes them feel safer.'

'And are they?' asked Clare.

'I doubt it,' said Meyer. 'Whoever's killing them wouldn't start out here on the dump.'

'Why not?' asked Clare.

'Well, everyone here would recognise a stranger, wouldn't they?'

'They would,' said Clare, 'if it was a stranger.' She went over to look at what the child was drawing while Karamata took care of the formalities. Oscar had covered the page with drawings. Flowering people, winged trees, dolphins. The eerie whimsy was so at odds with this rough place.

'Those are beautiful.' Clare smiled at the boy, but the child looked down at his freckled hands, twisting them in his lap. 'What's your name?' She bent down beside him.

'This is Oscar,' Meyer answered for the child. 'He's been mute since his mother died six months ago.'

The pieces clicked into place: Meyer, Virginia Meyer. Clare remembered a book she'd read the last time she was in Walvis Bay. She turned back to the child. 'Your mother studied the Kuiseb plants, didn't she? She worked with the desert people, trying to understand how they use them.'

The boy's eyes lit up, confirming Clare's question.

'She was my wife.' George Meyer looked down as he spoke. 'Before that, she and Oscar lived in the Kuiseb for many years.' He held out his hand, and the child sidled over, but Meyer did not draw the child into the shelter of his arms. The two of them stood, side by side, watching Clare and Karamata get back in the vehicle.

'Unusual colouring Oscar has,' she said as they drove away.

'He takes after his mother,' said Karamata. 'Virginia was like Moses's burning bush with all her red hair. And such a white skin, no good for this country.'

'She wasn't from here?'

'She was American. She came here to work at the desert research centre. Then her visa ran out and she found George somewhere and married him. I think for her it was like collecting a rather dull specimen. A husband was something she needed. Oscar is what she wanted. The two of them were always alone out in the Kuiseb, her trying to preserve things, stop any kind of development. That's where she died, in a car crash.'

'George Meyer's not his father?'

'No. That child has no one now she's gone. No one came from America to claim him, so he stayed here with the stepfather.'

Karamata stopped the car. The rubbish truck they had seen from the dune stood empty, everything of value winnowed from the rotting black mass lying around it. The truck driver waved as he headed back to town. A group of boys had left off scavenging and were watching them. The foreman came towards them, caressing his palm with his whip, a flock of ragged children at his heels.

'You looking for work, Karamata?' asked the thickset man.

'Good afternoon, Mr Vermeulen. This is Dr Hart from South Africa. She is working with us on the murder of the boy here, and the one at the school.'

'*Nee, fok*, Karamata. Foreign experts for a couple of dead street kids.' He glared at Clare, his muscled neck bulging. 'Don't you have enough corpses of your own down south?'

'Nice to meet you, Mr Vermeulen.' Clare extended her hand; Vermeulen wiped his palms on his overalls and held her fingers for a moment.

'These poor little fuckers, their mothers throw them away.' Vermeulen caught the child closest to him, a boy of five or six, by the scruff of the neck.

'Who's your mother, hey?' The boy giggled and Vermeulen tossed him aside. 'He never even knew. He's lived on the streets since he was three. When he gets a bit sicker, then maybe those nuns will come and get him. They'll take him to their place out there.' He gestured eastwards with an arm as thick as a pole. 'So what you want here now?'

'I'm not a social worker,' said Clare. 'But I might be able to help find who's killing these boys.'

'Ag, you can believe what you want, lady,' Vermeulen sighed. 'It's nice of you to try to help. Not many do.'

'Where do these boys sleep?' Clare looked around the site; it was hardly an orphan's haven.

'A few go sleep in town,' said Vermeulen. 'The rest sleep here at the dump. You want to see?'

'Sure,' said Clare.

'Lazarus!' he bellowed. A scrawny boy was pushed to the front of the group.

'We've met, I think,' said Clare. Lazarus gave her a shifty smile.

'Why weren't you at school?' Vermeulen demanded. 'You know how I had to *gatkruip* that headmaster to get him to take you back?'

'School's a waste of time.' Lazarus was careful to stay out of Vermeulen's reach.

'This is our Einstein,' said Vermeulen. 'Knows everything, cocky bugger, which is lucky because the school won't take him back again this time. Take the doctor and show her where you sleep.'

Clare and Karamata followed Lazarus into an enclosure behind the truck. An old tarpaulin served as a roof, and a nest of mattresses was arranged underneath, neat bundles of clothes at the top of each one.

'That was Fritz Woestyn's bed,' said Lazarus. 'And Kaiser's.' Clare looked down at the yellowed sponge mattress. There was a photograph next to the bed.

'That's our soccer team.' Lazarus came and stood next to her. His breath was rank. 'We were in the newspaper for the Homeless World Cup,' he said. 'See, there's Kaiser and there's me. There's Fritz and the other boys. Mara took it. She gave us all a copy. Look, here's mine.' He dived onto the last mattress and pulled out an identical shot.

Clare took it and turned it over. There was an inscription on the back. *From Mara*, it said. *For my boys. Remember to always believe.*

'When was that?' she asked.

'I don't know.' Lazarus shifted from one foot to the other. 'I suppose about four weeks ago. We went away for a weekend and she took it then. It was when she got us our new uniforms. Look, it says "The Desert Rats".' He pointed to the photograph.

It must have been cold when it was taken, because the boys were huddled together. They all wore the same shirt that Kaiser Apollis had been wearing when he was killed.

'Cool shirts,' said Clare.

'Pesca-Marina Fishing sponsored them. Look, it says so here on the back.' He whipped up his sweatshirt and turned around to show Clare the logo, pleased to have a witness to the small joys of his life.

'Can I keep this?' Clare asked.

'Keep Kaiser's picture,' said Lazarus, handing it to her. 'He won't need it. Maybe in Cape Town you can get us some more sponsorship, find us a new coach.'

'What about Mara?' asked Clare, slipping the picture into her pocket.

'She's going back to England.'

'When?' asked Clare.

'I don't know,' said Lazarus. 'But they all do. What's there to stay here for?'

There was no answer to that. 'Is she still coaching you?'

'Ja, we have a practice later. But it's not the same any more.'

'The boys who were killed, you knew them all,' said Clare.

'None of us live long, Miss. They went quick. You try going like him.' Lazarus pointed to the darkest corner of the makeshift tent. There was a small mound of blankets. 'He's afraid to go to the nuns. If the sisters come for you, then you know you're over and out.' Lazarus gave a bleak laugh. 'It's not much of a team any more. Three dead.'

'Who do you think did it?' Clare asked.

'Someone they went with, that's what everyone's saying,' said Lazarus, watching the other boys kicking a makeshift soccer ball on the level patch of gravel that was their pitch.

'You got any names?' asked Clare. 'Anyone in particular?'

Lazarus looked at her briefly, but the focus of his attention had shifted. 'A sailor? Maybe one of the old men who live alone here in town. A lawyer from Windhoek? It happens like that to us boys.'

'Is there anyone ...' – but Lazarus was gone, dribbling the ball expertly towards the goal posts – 'regular?' Clare finished the question.

'Too much glue,' said Karamata, watching Lazarus score.

'Or too afraid,' said Clare as Lazarus careened across the field, arms extended in the universal language of football victory. 'I want to ask him some more questions.'

'Another time,' said Karamata, checking his watch. 'We've got to get going now, if you want to get to the next crime scene before dark.'

Clare followed him reluctantly back to the car. She waved at Lazarus. He lifted one hand in salute, watching them drive away.

KARAMATA DROVE TOWARDS the Kuiseb River, a sinuous line of green that parted the vast ocean of the Namib. A group of oryx made their way in single file, their measured pace only emphasising the stillness. The road they took snaked through stands of dusty tamarisks. Their branches whipped against the windscreen as Karamata picked up speed.

'Topnaars,' he said, pointing at the donkey cart rattling home, feathering golden dust into the sunset. Clare could hear the crack of a whip above trotting hooves, the shouts of the driver urging his tired animals home.

'You know this place well,' she observed.

'Like the back of my hand,' said Karamata. 'I grew up around here.'

Old flood-marks had scoured a wall out of the sand. Debris from upriver was stranded high above the dry bed. The road petered out into a sandy track, pocked and scarred with the previous year's rains. The mud had dried and cracked as it had retreated from the relentless sun.

Karamata cut the engine. 'Fritz Woestyn. This is where he was found.' He pointed towards a bleak stretch of sand. The ridge of an old railway was visible in places where the water had churned and frothed in the riverbed, desperate to reach the sea.

'Who found him?'

'Pipeline maintenance. There was a leak and they came out to check. They found Fritz staring up at the sky with a hole in his head. Van Wyk was on duty. He came out.'

'Saturday's Child. Where exactly?'

'Under that big tree.' Karamata pointed to a spreading acacia.

'Tied up?'

'Curled up in a piece of cloth. His hands had been tied, but the rope had been cut through, like with Kaiser.' Clare knelt down in front of the tree, photograph in hand. She traced the area where his head had lolled sideward. The bark was rough, pitted with age and heat.

'You got the autopsy photographs there?' she asked.

Karamata handed her the gory close-ups. Bare feet, calloused hands. She flicked through until she came to the close-ups of the bullet wounds. The bloom on his forehead was clear, the petals of crusted blood and bone delicate around the dark centre. The back of the child's head was intact.

'No exit wound?' asked Clare. 'So the bullet was still in the brain. I haven't seen anything for ballistics. The autopsy?' Clare knew what the answer would be; Helena Kotze had said that it had been cursory. So cursory that a bullet in the brain went undetected.

'Not detailed,' said Karamata. 'Just enough to give a cause of death. Gunshot wound, easy. He was buried three days after he was found.'

'Why?' Clare tried to hide her frustration.

'The head of cleansing ordered that the city pay for all the paupers' funerals.'

'Calvin Goagab?'

'That's him,' said Karamata.

'Generous.'

'The state morgue is always full these days. Families can't afford to bury their loved ones, and then the cooling systems broke down. The mayor is a practical man, so he went along with Goagab's request to clear the backlog and get everyone buried. It had been ordered before the murder. Fritz Woestyn just happened to benefit from it.'

'Captain Damases went along with it?' asked Clare.

'She was on sick leave,' said Karamata. 'Complications with her pregnancy. The case was with Van Wyk.'

'Burying murder victims,' said Clare, standing up. 'It's a novel way of getting rid of a caseload.'

'I don't know if this stuff seems worthwhile to him,' said Karamata, opening a packet of biltong.

'Murder?'

'Street children. There are so many now. He says it's just Aids orphans; that they're going to die anyway. A lot of people think like that.'

'Do you?'

'I'm a policeman,' said Karamata. 'I don't think about it. I do my job. To me a life is a life. I was like those boys once. Just a piece of rubbish.' His eyes were so dark it was impossible to read any expression in them. 'And now look.'

Chapter Seventeen

THE SUN, ALL day a hot, unseeing eye behind the fog, was sinking towards the sea when Tamar Damases switched off her computer and stood up, arching her back. She couldn't find any pattern in the dates on which the ships had docked in Walvis Bay Harbour and when her three boys – how she was starting to think of them, her three dead boys – disappeared.

Her own baby kicked, one tiny protesting foot bulging the tight drum of her belly. She put her hand there, feeling the foetus glide away from her touch, safe in its dark, secret world. From the parking lot outside came snatches of shouted conversations, arrangements to have a beer, talk about a soccer practice, the night shift arriving. It was time for Tamar to steel herself for her own long night-shift.

She straightened her desk and rinsed the teacups, ready for tomorrow. She had never liked the thought of the night peering in at the windows, so she closed the curtains. She picked up her handbag and the groceries she had bought at lunch time. The hard-earned package from the chemist was tucked deep in her jacket pocket. It cost her a substantial chunk of her salary. She felt for it again, like an anxious passenger checking their passport, their ticket, just to make sure.

Tamar locked her office door behind her. Karamata was out in the Namib with Clare. There was no sign of Van Wyk. She went through to the special ops room where a light was burning. There was a scarlet pashmina tossed over the back of Clare's chair. Tamar picked it up and folded it before sitting down.

She considered the boys from Clare's perspective: Monday's Child. Wednesday's Child. And Saturday's. Three ephemeral children who had slipped into the river of life with barely a splash. Who would have sunk without a trace if Tamar had not reached out for their spectral hands. She held out her own hands now, in front of the desk lamp. They cast a startling silhouette across the display. Tamar read Clare's notes. First about place, of the crime scenes virtually devoid of physical evidence. They would be; the bodies had been moved and deliberately displayed.

She thought of the bodies, of the boys they had been, wondering about this killer who managed to pick up his victims without witness, without leaving a ripple of anxiety. In such a small town, why did no one notice someone away for hours and days on end? Unless it was someone who was working shifts. Someone who could be all over the place, no questions asked. On the ships, in the factories, in the bars, a truck driver passing back and forth, ferrying goods. The silhouette of a killer, just the shadow of a man on a blank wall. Malevolent, shifting, shape-shifting, like a Javanese shadow-puppet theatre. Tamar thought of this figure moving unseen through the fog and she shivered. Who? Why? And where? The questions beat an urgent rhythm.

A siren wailed, insistent as a hungry baby. It was time to get on to her next shift.

TAMAR FOUND HER niece leaning against the wall outside her day-care centre.

'What are you doing out here, Angela?' she asked.

'The other children ...' The little girl's eyes glittered with tears.

Tamar put the sobbing child into the back seat of her car and strapped her in, feeling once again for the package of ARVs in her pocket. Her talisman. She drove home fast, relief flooding her when she realised that Tupac, her nephew, only eleven, had already cooked the macaroni.

She held Angela in her arms and coaxed five, then six, then seven, slow, painful spoons of buttered pasta into the child's mouth. The boy hovered on the kitchen steps, staring into the darkness. When Tamar thought it was enough, she took her precious package from her pocket and counted out the pills into a Mickey Mouse saucer which Tupac had put out.

Angela pressed her lips together and closed her eyes, but the tears seeped out anyway. They made her feel so sick, the pills. Tupac knelt down beside her, his thin brown hands cupping her face.

'Please, Angela,' he said. 'You're a dancer. You can do anything.'

Nothing.

'Take them for me.' Desperation edged his voice. 'I'll tell you a story later.'

Angela opened her eyes. 'About Mommy?'

Tupac was quick. He popped a tablet in and held her mouth closed. 'About her and the day you had your first dance class,' said Tupac.

Angela swallowed. Tamar breathed.

'Here. Just three more.'

'Tell me about what she said about me.'

Tupac popped the pills into her mouth, like coins into a slot machine. Tamar was not religious, but she was praying that the expensive drugs would repel the virus that had prowled Angela's blood since her birth, the virus that had wrested the life from her plump, laughing, fecund sister five years ago.

She put the little girl to bed and helped her arrange her princess puppet. The child had given her a doek, so that the shadow looked like her mother leaning over the bed, always just about to kiss her.

Tupac lay down next to his sister.

'They wouldn't play with me today,' Angela told him. 'The other children, they say I'm dirty and that I'll make them sick. Will you get them?'

'I'll get them.' Tupac had defended his baby sister since their mother had died the previous year. 'But first let me tell you a story.'

Tamar closed the door on his once-upon-a-time. It was always the same story: a little girl and a mother who didn't really die, who just went away somewhere for a while, who was coming back.

She went to lie on her bed, too tired to eat or change. It was quiet on the edge of the desert when the children stopped murmuring. From far away came the cry of a jackal; further away the answering call of its mate. Tamar folded her fingers over her belly.

Her child might be fatherless, but it was safe.

Chapter Eighteen

RAGNAR JOHANSSON WAS hesitating between two blue shirts. Clare Hart, she made him worry which near-identical shade would be best. He chose the darker of the two, walked over to his apartment window and did up the buttons, looking out at the emptied street. The night had settled in, but he could still make out the cranes offloading the trawlers that had berthed that afternoon. The girls would be busy already. It was eight-thirty and cold out, but Ragnar Johansson decided to walk. He liked the fog. It blocked out the flat desert lines of Walvis Bay, let him pretend that he was somewhere else, not immured here at the arse end of the world, no better off than when he arrived. The security gate rattled shut behind him as he strode towards the lagoon.

Clare was easy to find in the deserted holiday complex. Hers was the only cottage spilling light onto the worn grass, as she had not closed her curtains. Ragnar stopped beyond the pool of light to watch her through the open window. She had her back to him and he could see the curve of her waist, the slim hips in faded jeans. She slipped her hands under her hair and twisted her hair up, exposing the nape of her neck. She pinned up the thick coil, then turned and looked out into the blackness. Wary as a gazelle. Ragnar lit a cigarette, ignoring a tug of desire. When he had finished smoking, he went across the dark garden and knocked. She opened the door, standing aside so that he could enter.

'Hello, Clare.'

'How are you?' She closed the door behind him.

'You look beautiful,' said Ragnar.

'You were watching me.'

'How did you guess?' Ragnar kissed her cheek. 'Same perfume.'

'No. 19.' Clare picked up her jacket and they walked along the water's edge, immediately falling into step. They had been easy together, physically. She let him take her arm, glad to put the day behind her.

'What happened to your boat?' she asked.

'Money's tight. Had to sell it.' Ragnar could taste the bitterness of failure on his tongue.

'I didn't know,' said Clare, walking up the steps to the Raft.

The restaurant was built on stilts against which the lagoon's dark water lapped. It was usually frequented by tourists or locals celebrating rare special occasions. Tonight, the candlelit tables were mostly empty.

'You didn't stay in touch, did you?' said Ragnar.

'I never said I would.'

A waitress showed them to a window table, the lights rippling on the lagoon beneath them. The lighthouse at Pelican Point pulsed on the horizon.

'What are you doing now?' Clare asked. 'I can't imagine you without your boat.'

'Lots of kite-boarding, a little consulting for the mayor and his team. I just got a new ship to skipper, the *Alhantra*,' said Ragnar. 'And a licence for orange roughy. Very popular in the US and in Spain. Expensive, so worth fishing. Tonight can be a celebration, if you like. That and seeing you again.'

The waitress brought the wine and bread. Ragnar poured.

'It didn't take you long to track me down,' said Clare.

'A single woman under two hundred and fifty pounds is always news in Walvis Bay.'

'Come on,' she said. 'Who told you? I can't believe that your nearly running me over was a coincidence.'

'Actually, that was,' said Ragnar. 'But Calvin Goagab had told me you were here. I saw him yesterday afternoon. After you'd been there. There's official concern about this incident, about what it'll do to tourism here.'

'What about official concern about finding who hung a child's body in a playground?' Clare bristled.

'Oh, there is, but this is a port.' Ragnar leant towards her. 'Goagab's saying that what they found in that playground was just a quick midnight transaction gone wrong. Whoever did it was back on board ship before the body was discovered.'

'And the others?'

'Unrelated probably,' said Ragnar. 'Captain Damases is inclined to jump to conclusions.'

The waitress arrived with their food, before Clare could respond.

'You did well with that documentary.' Ragnar noted the flare of anger in her eyes and changed the direction of the conversation.

'It worked,' said Clare.

'You made some people uncomfortable.'

'Good,' said Clare. 'I meant to.'

'Some quite influential people, Clare. People lost money. A lot of money. Goagab was one of them.'

'You too?' asked Clare.

'That's not what I lost when you left.' He took her hand, turning it over and running his thumb over the vein pulsing in her wrist.

'Let's not go there, Ragnar,' said Clare, withdrawing her hand to pick up her wine glass. The nights they had spent alone together up the Skeleton Coast ... she would had to have been an ice queen to resist him.

Ragnar let it go, and they ate their meals without further conflict. They talked of people Clare had met on her last visit: who'd made money; who hadn't. The bill arrived and Clare reached for her purse.

'Let me get this.' Ragnar put his hand over hers. 'If you owe me I'll be sure of having dinner with you again.'

'I'm finessed then,' Clare smiled.

'Shall we get a brandy?' asked Ragnar as they stepped outside into the cold wind.

'Where were you thinking?' Clare was tired, but she wasn't quite ready to go back to her lonely bed.

'Der Blaue Engel.'

'Where is it?' The name was familiar. Clare tried to place it.

'It's a club down near the harbour.' He saw Clare hesitate. 'Think of it as anthropology.'

Ragnar put his arm around Clare's shoulders and they walked back towards the harbour. Clare remembered where she'd heard the name. From the story about the lap dancer who'd come off worse for wear after a visit to one of the rusting trawlers anchored outside the harbour.

'Gretchen von Trotha,' said Clare, 'doesn't she dance there?'

'How do you know her?' Ragnar asked with obvious surprise.

'I don't,' said Clare. 'Elias Karamata, one of the cops who's working on this case, told me that she'd been beaten and thrown off a Russian ship. The name stuck.'

'Someone fished her out, a South African,' said Ragnar. 'Ironically, he had a Russian name. Gretchen owes her life to that man.'

Clare could feel the dull thump of the bass long before she could hear any music. The club's logo was a naked pole-dancing angel, complete with wings and a halo.

'That must drive the fundamentalists nuts.'

'It does,' said Ragnar. 'Sundays, there are always pickets by the Christian Mission ladies, lying in wait for their husbands, I suppose.'

Inside, the air was thick with smoke. Around the pool table, girls were leaning along their cues to the advantage of their cleavages. A few couples were dancing, and waiting women nursed Coca-Colas at the bar. A group of drunken Russians working their way through a bottle of vodka at the bar looked Clare over then returned to their drink. Only two tables were occupied.

'That's him.' Ragnar pointed to one table where a man sat alone. 'The guy who pulled Gretchen out of the water.' The man's shirt was moulded over his lean belly, long legs stretched out, the steel caps glinting at the end of his dusty suede boots. A cigarette dangled from one tanned hand. He had tilted his chair back and his face was hidden in the shadows.

'Is he trying to play Clint Eastwood?' asked Clare.

'I don't suggest you ask him,' said Ragnar. 'He's not much of a joker.'

Clare recognised some of the occupants at the other table, groaning with champagne bottles, near the stage. D'Almeida had his secretary, the beautiful Anna, on his arm. He raised a glass to Clare. Opposite him sat Goagab, in conspicuous Armani. Two heavy-set men in their forties were with them. One of the men held a delicate girl on his knee, a smile plastered over her discomfiture. The other one ran lazy eyes over Clare, his tongue flicking across his moist, parted lips.

'Politicians?' asked Clare.

'Businessmen. Politicians. One and the same in this part of the world. My new bosses,' said Ragnar. 'They own the *Alhantra*. They're celebrating the licence too.'

'You want to join them?'

'Not now that I have you to myself.' His hand brushed hers. It was disconcerting, the intimate roughness of his skin.

'What will you have?' he smiled.

'A brandy, please.'

The bar was filling up as men drifted in singly and in compact, eager groups. Chinese, Spanish, Senegalese, South African, freshly showered, hair slicked, eyes darting towards the women unpeeling themselves from bar stools, the pool table.

'When's the show?' Ragnar asked the barman pouring their drinks.

'Ten minutes, maybe fifteen.' The barman pushed across a brochure that showed a young woman – maybe twenty-five – coiled around a pole.

Five minutes later, the lights flickered, then stayed off. A prerecorded drum roll drowned out Clare's objections. The velvet curtains opened, and a nubile blonde stepped into the spectral light, her body voluptuous beneath the transparent layers of blue chiffon, the scar beneath her left eye a slender crescent bleached white by the spotlight. Her eyes, shadowed by dark, arched brows, revealed nothing.

'Der Blaue Engel?' asked Clare.

'That's her. Gretchen von Trotha. Not yet in all her glory. Then she's quite something,' said Ragnar. 'Another?'

'One more,' said Clare. 'Then home?' Her interest was piqued.

'Nicolai,' called Ragnar. The barman filled Clare's glass, his eyes on her face. 'Enjoying the show?' he asked.

'It works for the audience,' she said.

Gretchen moved effortlessly, disdain infusing her movements with an erotic menace. The rowdy groups of men sat transfixed. She peeled off first one garment then another, until she stood naked except for her tattooed wings, a tinsel halo and the wisp of silk between her thighs.

A movement to Clare's right drew her attention to D'Almeida's table. A fat politician was snapping his fingers at the barman. Nicolai bent low for the man's order. He looked up at Gretchen and nodded. A whispered word from Nicolai and she left the safety of the stage. The fat man leant back in his seat and beckoned her into the space between his splayed knees. She stepped closer, nipples glinting in the dim light as he tucked money into the thigh-high boot gripping her soft flesh. Her skin was milky; her limbs were smooth and firm. The shaved pubis lasciviously childlike as she twirled out of his grip and made her way to the lean man sitting alone at the table in the corner.

The man took a note and slipped it into her halo before standing up and sauntering out. Gretchen removed the rolled-up note and looked at it as she walked back to the stage, ignoring the beseeching, empty hands that reached after her.

'I think I've had enough lap dancing for tonight,' said Clare. 'Let's go.'

IT WAS COLD out. Clare pulled her collar up and her beanie down as they walked towards the unlit cottages.

'If I didn't know better, you could pass for a boy,' said Ragnar.

'Maybe I should be careful then,' she said, unlocking the door. 'Walvis Bay is not the safest town to be a boy in.'

'You should be careful anyway, Clare.'

'You're the second person to tell me that.' She turned to face him, remembering Lazarus's clumsy attempt. 'Is that a warning or a threat?'

'A warning.' Ragnar's hand was cold on her cheek. He slid a finger down her neck, finding the warm skin under her collar. 'From a friend.'

'I'll keep it in mind.'

Clare stepped away from his caress and into the cottage, ignoring his wry look as she said a swift goodnight and locked the front door. But as Ragnar's footsteps died away and the stifling silence draped the night again, she did wonder if she'd made the right call.

Chapter Nineteen

CLARE WOKE THE next morning, her limbs leaden and her head aching, but she pushed back the covers and pulled on her running clothes. She washed down two aspirin with a glass of water. The wind had come up in the night, and the unfamiliar sounds meant that her sleep had been fitful.

The bracing air and the morning light cleared her mind and she found her stride, running faster until the paved boulevard petered out into sand. There had been a high tide; straggles of seaweed lay across the path. A flock of startled flamingos took off ahead of her. Clare scanned the path to see what had disturbed them. It was Goagab in a black velvet tracksuit, complete with gold chain, approaching her.

'Dr Hart,' he called. Clare came to a reluctant halt. 'You're up early. I trust Johansson let you get to sleep at a reasonable hour.'

'He did.' To her annoyance, Clare found herself blushing at his innuendo.

'I've got a PR nightmare on my hands with this case.' Goagab turned around and walked alongside her. 'I trust you're making progress.'

'Some,' said Clare. 'The groundwork: talking to people who knew Kaiser Apollis and the other two boys. The autopsy's done, but we'll need to wait for the forensic reports from Cape Town.'

'Any suspects yet?' asked Goagab, stopping beside his silver Mercedes sports car. 'We need an arrest soon to justify the expense of foreign expertise.'

'It's only been a couple of days,' said Clare. 'And the first two victims were buried without proper autopsies, on your orders. That makes for sparse evidence.'

'I understand,' said Goagab, without missing a beat. 'But there's pressure, I'm sure you can see that. I'd appreciate it if you let me know as soon as possible what shape our killer is taking.' He opened the car door, reached into the cubbyhole and gave her a card. 'If you need anything, here's my private number.'

'What do you imagine I'd need?' Clare turned the white square over in her hand.

'It helps to have as many friends as possible in a strange town,' said Goagab, sliding into his car. He pressed a button, and the window closed. For a second, Clare stared at her own pale reflection, then she slipped the card into her jacket pocket and ran back, but the unexpected meeting had put her off her stride.

By seven-thirty Clare was showered, dressed and breakfasted, her scattered thoughts in order again. She had time to see Mara Thomson before she met Tamar at the police station. She locked up, taking her small bag of rubbish out with her and dropping it into the bin standing in the narrow strip of sand between her cottage and the next one. She froze, ignoring the gulls scrapping over a stolen fish head, riveted by tracks in the sand.

A single set of human footprints stopped at her bedroom window. Clare followed them to the entrance to the service alley, but the night wind had erased any marks except her own. She followed the prints back, stepping carefully so as not to disturb anything. Whoever it had been had stood there for a while. The sand was compressed, as the watcher had scuffed about to keep warm. Or get a better view. She had opened her curtains the night before, hoping that the moon would break through the fog for a while. How long had he stood there?

What had he wanted? She searched through the disturbed dreams she had had the previous night to see if one of them had been triggered by the proximity of a stranger. There were bars on the windows, but her bed was close. He could have put his hand through an opening and held it over her face, feeling her breath soft and trusting with sleep on his skin. Her throat closed at the thought of it.

Clare squatted down next to the footprints. Whoever had stood there had been wearing some kind of trainer, but, even in this sheltered spot, the dawn wind had blown a cover of sand over any detail. Clare could not even tell what size they were. There were a few old cigarette butts lying against the fence, but that would have woken her, surely, if he had smoked. She stood up and looked in at her own window, as a stranger had, at her dishevelled bed, at the book on the bedside table, at yesterday's lace underwear abandoned on the floor.

Her breath came in a gasp, misting the glass and bringing to life the crude outline of a heart. He had stood here, breathing open-mouthed against the glass, looking in at her as she had slept, tracing with a lingering fingertip. She breathed out again, harder this time, to see if he had finished his drawing. He had. A sailor's tattoo, it was scored through with a jagged arrow, and blood was pooled below the heart.

Chapter Twenty

MARA THOMSON PICKED up the photographs propped against her clock. Her team of homeless boys in their brand-new football kit, holding up a silver cup in triumph. The other picture was worn at the edges: Mara and her mum in the park next to the London council estate that she had survived by learning to be invisible. She pressed the photographs between her hands, bookending her journey to the point where she sat now – with Kaiser Apollis's dead body bobbing on the periphery of her thoughts. It drove her to the kitchen in search of tea and company.

Oscar was at the kitchen table alone, uneaten cornflakes congealing in his plastic bowl.

'You're up early.' Mara smiled at him.

A door slammed upstairs and the boy's delicate throat constricted around the food. Oscar looked up. Mara did too, imagining George Meyer stepping from his other lodger's bedroom into the chill passageway upstairs, closing the door on the woman inside: Gretchen, who always paid what she owed, exuding contempt for her landlord, for his lonely dribble of pleasure.

'Go on,' said Mara, breaking the spell, 'eat your breakfast.'

Oscar, conditioned to obedience, picked up the spoon. The mournful wail of a ship's siren came from the harbour.

'The *Alhantra*,' said Mara, putting on the kettle.

Mara had taken Oscar on board once and he had seen Juan Carlos kiss her when they thought he wasn't watching. But the boy was always watching, so he had seen Juan Carlos, Mara's boyfriend, slip into her room in the middle of the night, and away again just before dawn.

George Meyer came into the kitchen, buttoning up his jacket. He greeted Mara and poured coffee, drinking in silence.

'Come, Oscar,' he said, putting down his mug and looking at his watch. Oscar reached out a tentative hand, but George thought he was reaching for his lunch and handed the boy two slices of cling-filmed white bread. The two of them stepped into the trails of fog hanging low over the desolate yard, the washing limp on the line, just as Clare Hart opened the gate.

'Good morning, Dr Hart,' said Meyer. 'Can I help you?'

'I'm here to see Mara Thomson,' said Clare. 'Is she in?'

'In the kitchen,' said Meyer, opening the door to his truck. 'Get in, Oscar. You're coming with me today. You can draw some more plant specimens for me. Your mother would've liked that.'

Oscar climbed in and placed his bag at his feet. He let his forehead rest against the cold glass. It could have been a nod.

THE DOORBELL CHIMED, interrupting the tangled drift of Mara Thomson's thoughts. She had been half-expecting Dr Hart, but seeing her on the doorstep gave her heart a little jolt.

'Please, come in.' She opened the door for Clare and led her down a dingy passage off the kitchen to her bedroom.

'Sit here,' said Mara, offering Clare the only chair and sitting on the unmade bed. A splash of sunlight framed her face, setting her apart from her anonymous bedroom. The only place that revealed any personality was the crowded table next to her bed.

'Lazarus told me you were at the dump,' said Mara.

Clare nodded, picking up a photograph. 'You?' she asked.

Mara nodded. 'That was taken just before I came to Namibia. Me and my mum.'

You had to have a charitable eye to see the blood that linked them. Where Mara was all tawny shades and wild hair, her mother was pale, her lips as prim and pressed as her blue suit. But it was there, in both their narrow faces, the wide-set eyes.

'My father was Jamaican,' Mara explained. 'But I never knew him. He was killed in a fight before I was born. So it was just me and my mum. It was hard for her when I left.'

'And for you?' Clare asked.

Mara sighed. 'I expected a village of light and heat and throbbing cicadas. Instead, I got Walvis Bay. Somebody had to,' she said, with a wry smile.

'That bad?' asked Clare.

'Oh, it's been okay. Till all this. I threw myself into my work, answered the kids' questions, read to them and organised a soccer team. My mum clipped out the sports pages from the Sunday papers and taped soccer games and films. *Bend It like Beckham* was a real hit. It all worked,' said Mara. '*I* worked and that was a first.'

There was a framed photograph of Mara with her arms entwined around a dark-haired man. 'Your boyfriend?' asked Clare.

'Juan Carlos.' Mara leant back against the wall. 'You want me to tell you about Kaiser?' she asked. 'The others?'

'Let's start with Kaiser,' Clare suggested.

'What don't you know?' asked Mara.

Clare thought of his body on the mortuary table. No secrets there. She knew how much he weighed; that he still had a couple of milk teeth; that he had been violently sodomised, but that he had healed; that his back was covered in scars; that someone had stood so close to him that their breath had mingled. Someone had looked the bound child in the eye, cocked his gun, pulled a trigger and shot him in the face.

'Tell me what he was like,' said Clare. 'What he did, where he went, who he hung out with, where he slept, what he ate.'

'What he ate?' repeated Mara, fiddling with the frayed hem of her hoodie. 'He ate what he could scavenge. Meat, if he could find it.'

Clare thought of Lazarus throwing away the roll Mara had bought him, her hurt and disappointment clear in the set of her narrow shoulders. 'Who were his friends?' she prompted.

'Lazarus, I suppose,' said Mara. 'Fritz Woestyn, too. They played soccer together, slept in a heap at the dump like stray dogs.'

'What did he talk about?'

'To me?' asked Mara, looking Clare straight in the eye. 'Not much. I know he loved his sister Sylvia and that he liked to draw.' She was quiet. Around them, the silence of the house was overwhelming.

'Tell me, Mara,' said Clare softly, 'what he dreamed.'

Mara slitted her eyes. 'How will his dreams get you to the truth of who did this to him, to the others?'

'Dreams take us to places we don't anticipate sometimes,' said Clare.

'He wanted to live. That can be quite an ambitious dream in a place like this.' The silence was taut, a tightrope between them.

'He wanted to go to school.' One tentative foot on the rope of her story. 'He wanted to draw.' Another. Mara looked at Clare as if she were searching for something. 'He wanted a mother. That's about it, as far as Kaiser's dreams went,' she said. 'Since I've been here so many kids I know have been sick, have died. It's Aids. That's why most of them are on the street in the first place. And if they didn't get the virus from their parents, then they soon catch it from their clients.' Mara's shoulders slumped.

'When did you see him last?'

'Friday afternoon,' Mara said with certainty. 'We always have practice and he never missed. I didn't see him at the Sunday practice. Weekends are different. The boys are less' – she pulled the cord of her sweatshirt – 'steady. Let me put it like that.'

'Did you ask where he was?'

'I was going to,' Mara replied, 'and then they found him, so I didn't need to.'

'The others?' asked Clare. 'Fritz Woestyn and Nicanor Jones?'

'I knew them,' said Mara. 'They played in my team.'

'What happened with Sergeant van Wyk and Kaiser?' asked Clare.

'I was stupid,' said Mara. 'Stupid and naïve. It was before Fritz Woestyn was found, so I wasn't worried. Just irritated that he didn't come to a weekend game. I asked and one of the boys told me he was in the cells, so I went to look for him.'

'Where was he?'

'By the time I found him he'd been dropped back at the dump,' said Mara. 'He'd been beaten. Badly. I tried to lay a child abuse charge.'

'What happened?'

'Sod all,' said Mara. 'Kaiser wouldn't say anything. I knew he'd been picked up near the harbour. Whoring maybe. I know that Van Wyk took him back to the cells and beat the shit out of him, but Kaiser wouldn't say nothing. I had to leave it …' Mara hesitated. 'You know Van Wyk used to be with the vice squad?'

Clare nodded.

'There've been rumours that he offers protection to the girls working the docks. You know, like … they have no choice but to accept it in return for a cut of their fee.'

'You think Van Wyk's running boys, too?' asked Clare.

'I don't know,' said Mara. 'I don't know if it's even true about the girls. I only know that Kaiser was with him and that afterwards he could barely walk. Van Wyk said he found Kaiser like that and picked him up to protect him.'

'That was the end of it?'

'Pretty much,' said Mara. 'Kaiser wouldn't say anything. Nothing more I could do.' Tears of frustration welled in her eyes. 'That's all I can tell you. Pathetic, right? To see someone every day and to know nothing about them.'

Clare stood up and opened the door. It was the end of the interview. They walked back to the kitchen where a woman in a blue dressing gown was stirring sugar into her coffee. A blonde plait snaked over one shoulder.

'Gretchen,' said Mara, disconcerted. 'You're up early. This is Dr Hart.'

'Hello,' said Clare.

Gretchen lit a cigarette. 'You're making progress, Doctor?' she asked. 'With these little boys?'

'I hope so,' said Clare.

'Good,' said Gretchen. 'So sad, what happened.' She sipped her coffee, her blue eyes fixed on Clare without a glimmer of recognition. She wouldn't have seen Clare at the bar of Der Blaue Engel the previous night. All she would have seen was a blur beyond the stage lights.

Chapter Twenty-one

CAPTAIN DAMASES REPLACED the receiver when Clare walked into the office. 'You have a bad night?' asked Clare. There were dark circles under Tamar's eyes.

'Angela wasn't well. That was her nanny to say she was sleeping at last.' Tamar rubbed her temples. It was only eight in the morning, but she felt as if she'd been working for hours already. 'You look like you had a rough night too.'

'Just a late one,' said Clare. 'I'm not twenty-five any more so it shows if I don't get my beauty sleep.' She poured herself a cup of coffee. 'I hope Angela's on the mend.'

'Kids,' said Tamar, 'they bounce back so fast. I'm taking them into the desert this afternoon. Why don't you join us, see something other than Walvis Bay?'

'I'd like that,' said Clare, checking her schedule. 'I've got some admin to do before I see Darlene Ruyters, and I'm hoping that Helena Kotze's going to drop off her preliminary histology report.'

'Did you see Mara Thomson, by the way?'

'I did,' said Clare. 'She told me about that incident with Van Wyk and Kaiser Apollis, about why she tried to lay a charge against Van Wyk. I think we should talk to him again.'

Tamar stood up, acting on Clare's request. 'We'll try,' she said, opening her office door.

Van Wyk was sitting at his desk. He minimised the window on his computer screen when Tamar and Clare walked in.

Tamar did not greet him. 'Tell me again about what happened with Kaiser, that incident for which there don't seem to be any records.'

Van Wyk looked up and sat back in his chair. 'He was caught in the harbour,' he said wearily. 'Happens all the time.'

'What was he doing?' asked Tamar.

'Looking for shit,' said Van Wyk, his voice thick with insolence. 'And he got it, from whoever it was who'd paid him to take it. The harbour master called me. Apollis had been pimping himself. I picked him up and put him in the cells for the weekend for his own protection.'

'That's all?' Clare spoke for the first time.

'It was.' Van Wyk faced her, as contained and venomous as a cobra. 'Until Mara Thomson laid an abuse complaint. She claims I assaulted him in prison. Apollis denied that anything happened. He was glad to get out of jail without any charges.'

'It wasn't because he refused to pay you for working on your area?' asked Clare.

'You've got quite an imagination, Dr Hart,' spat Van Wyk. 'I'm sure that you can use it to picture what prison would be like for a pretty boy like Apollis. I did him a favour. Now, if you ladies will excuse me, I have things to do.' Van Wyk shut down his computer, pivoted on his heel and walked out of the office.

'I'm sorry,' said Clare, watching Van Wyk churn the gravel in the parking lot. 'That little piece of quiet diplomacy would've done Riedwaan Faizal proud.' Clare followed Tamar back to her office.

'Someone had to say it,' said Tamar, sitting down, 'and my life will be easier because you did it. I'm not sure that it'll make yours easier, though.' She pulled a folder on her desk towards her.

'What've you got there?' asked Clare.

'Ships' logs.' Tamar opened the file. 'Sailors' visits, harbour reports around the times these boys went missing.'

Clare skimmed through the papers. 'Still no pattern?'

'Not yet,' said Tamar. 'But I'm going to follow up on a few things that don't fit.'

Chapter Twenty-two

CLARE SAT AT her desk, trying to think of what to say to Riedwaan as she waited for her computer to boot up. She checked her mail: chit-chat from her sister Julia, one from Rita Mkhize saying Fritz was absolutely fine, two from Riedwaan. Clare opened the first e-mail. It was full of official attachments written in incomprehensible bureaucratese. She filed them to read later. The second e-mail had nothing in the subject line. Clare opened it, her mouth suddenly dry.

Clare, it read. *I fucked up. Talk to me. R.*

She smiled. She couldn't help it. The message was so like the man. Direct. For Riedwaan, emotion meant action. He had wanted her, needed her, when they first met. So he'd taken her, simple as that. And she had acquiesced, intrigued by the novelty of having her emotional defences so easily breached, and charmed by the simplicity of Riedwaan's desire for her.

That moment of curiosity had set her adrift in treacherous waters, and now here she was: snagged on the reef of her own vulnerability, with only herself to blame.

She took a deep breath and with one sure stroke deleted Riedwaan's message. Then she e-mailed a terse case update, copying in Phiri to neutralise any intimacy Riedwaan might have read into her 'best wishes' at the end.

By nine-thirty, she was walking fast down 2nd Avenue, ignoring the thin, chained dogs barking in each sandy yard. Number 53 had its back to the red dunes, and although the façade was ravaged, the paint blistered and the gutters sagged, the windows were clear. Clare rang the doorbell and waited.

'Darlene Ruyters?' The woman framed in the doorway was fortyish and too thin. The exposed ankles and neck too fragile. She pulled her fraying cardigan tight around her body. 'I'm Clare Hart.'

'How can I help you?' asked Darlene. She opened the door, feeling in her pocket for her cigarettes.

'I wanted to ask you about the murdered boy in the playground,' said Clare.

Darlene held the door open and Clare stepped into the dim hallway. A pot plant wilted over a pile of post on the small entrance table.

'Kaiser Apollis.' Darlene walked through to the kitchen, her gait uneven. 'Tea?'

'Please,' said Clare, looking around the tidy room. A pair of trainers stood at the back door, a box of brushes and shoe polish open next to them.

Darlene put on the kettle, and set out cups and sugar on a tray.

'Are you from Windhoek?' asked Darlene. She picked up the tray.

'Cape Town,' said Clare.

'My home town. I miss it. All that green.' Darlene led the way to a meticulously neat lounge and gestured for Clare to sit.

'What brought you to Walvis Bay?'

'The army,' said Darlene. 'My husband was posted here. He was a major in a special operations unit.'

'And now?' Clare looked at the floral-print sofas and porcelain ornaments.

'Oh, that was a long time ago,' Darlene said, 'He was handsome then. Forty. I was twenty-two and in love. What did I know? I followed him. Ten years later when Nelson Mandela gave Walvis Bay back to Namibia, he left me with nothing. I've been alone ever since.'

'You stayed?'

'I was used to it by then. My marriage was over. I'd started teaching. I liked it, liked the kids. So I took back my maiden name and started a new life.'

'That's how you knew Kaiser Apollis?'

'This is a small town.'

'You taught him?'

'A long time ago. Grade 1. He was such a sweet little boy. Desperate for affection.'

'Tell me about him,' asked Clare.

'Usual things. His father lost his job. Then he disappeared. Kaiser came to school dirty, then there were the bruises. His mother drank and worked the sailors' clubs.'

'What happened to her?'

'She died. Aids, I suppose. Although here it's just called a short illness.'

'When did you see him last, Darlene?'

Darlene swirled the tea leaves in her cup, as if hoping they would give her the right answer. 'He came to school. Last Wednesday.'

'What for?' asked Clare.

'I don't know. I hadn't seen him for months. He looked so' – she shook her head – 'alone. So I asked him if he wanted to come and help me.'

'Was he there to see you?'

'I didn't ask him. I assumed he was. He used to help me get ready for my art classes on Thursday. He loved doing that. He had talent too. Real talent. Maybe if he had been born into a different life, who knows?' She trailed off, as if exhausted by her speculation.

'What did he do for you?'

'He helped me with the desks, got the paint ready. I'm doing a recycling project with my Grade 1s. Kaiser helped me cut things up. Prepare. He ate a sandwich I gave him.'

'Did he talk to you?'

'No, not really. He just liked to be busy.'

'How long was he with you?'

'An hour I suppose. Maybe more. He mixed the paints, then he said he was going to go. I gave him some money and he left.'

'He didn't say where he was going?'

'No. And I didn't ask.'

'How much money did you give him?'

'How much?' Darlene asked. 'I can't remember. Maybe ten Nam dollars in small change.'

'Is that why he came to see you?'

'Maybe.' Darlene shrugged. 'Like I said, we didn't talk much. He never begged. He hated it. He was a proud boy. I always gave him money for the odd jobs he did for me.'

'Were you surprised that it was him on the swing?'

'Herman Shipanga found him.'

'Shipanga doesn't wear high heels.' Clare's voice was uncompromising.

'No, he doesn't,' Darlene whispered. Her hands twisted around each other of their own volition. It was so hard to keep the sequence of things straight. She had been walking through the kindergarten playground when she heard the creak of the weighted swing, set in motion by a gust of wind that skittered papers across her path.

'Neither does Inspector Damases,' said Clare. 'There were holes in the sand leading up to the swings. I'm sure they would match the shoes you wore on Monday. The ones you cleaned.'

Darlene remembered walking towards the single occupied swing, transfixed, her ulcer stabbing. She had crouched down and thought about closing the lids of the accusing eyes staring at her. Her fingernail had trailed over the shoulder and the twinned curve of his buttocks beneath the stained shroud.

'Not surprised. Shocked, yes. Horrified, yes. But not surprised.' Darlene returned to the original question.

She did not know how long she had crouched there, but her legs had cramped. When she stood up, the fog had lifted, and there along the fence trotted a dark, blue-clad figure, so she had picked up her basket and gone down the passage to her empty classroom.

'Why didn't you call someone?' Clare asked.

'Herman Shipanga found him. I knew he would. He called the police. I knew he would. What did it matter that I saw him first?' Darlene pulled a crumpled cigarette out of her pocket and fumbled about for a light.

'Is this what you're looking for?' asked Clare, picking up a battered Zippo from the floor. It had a topless mermaid engraved on it. Darlene lit her cigarette, and put the incongruous lighter on the tea tray.

'They don't care if he's dead or not, anyway. He was just street rubbish to them,' she said.

'Who doesn't care?' asked Clare.

'The police. The municipality. You ask them. They don't care about this dead boy or Nicanor Jones and Fritz Woestyn. They threw them into a grave to save themselves any trouble. There are so many orphans now that in their hearts people are glad when they're eliminated. They just hope it's the one who might've smashed their car window.'

'You care.' Clare's voice was gentle.

'That's why they came to me, those boys. I didn't judge them, or want anything from them. They were like my children. They wanted me when they needed something.'

'What did Kaiser need?'

'I don't know,' said Darlene. 'I just don't know. Maybe nothing. Maybe he just wanted some company. Maybe he wanted to tell me something but he was too shy. I don't know.'

'You said you were shocked to find him, but not surprised.' Clare's voice rose, questioning.

Darlene shrugged. 'There was something about him when I saw him last. Like he had crossed some line. His sister tried to look after him when their mother died. How does that work, a child-headed household? Bullshit. There is no household. Those kids just sit there, waiting to be picked off.' She took a deep, angry drag of her filterless cigarette. It made her cough. 'Sorry,' she said, waving the smoke away with her hand.

'After it happened,' Darlene continued. 'When I found him, it seemed as if he'd come to say goodbye. As if he knew what was going to happen. He looked so at peace, even with the wound.'

'That's because he'd been dead a while,' said Clare. 'All the muscles relax. That irons the expression from the face. Hence the peaceful look.'

Darlene recoiled and Clare regretted being so blunt. She stood up. 'You've been helpful.'

Darlene opened the front door and stepped onto the stoep. Clare was glad to escape the dank house. The fog had thinned, revealing the soft-swelling dunes.

'It's so beautiful, the desert,' said Clare, captivated.

Darlene's laugh was bitter. 'A jumble of women's tits. That's how my husband described it. He said it turned him on, the way it just lay there, waiting to be taken.'

Darlene's hands shook as she put another cigarette between her lips. The sleeve of her cardigan fell back. There was a bracelet of bruises around her wrist. Clare put out her hand and circled Darlene's thin arm.

'What happened?' she asked.

'I'm just clumsy.' Darlene snatched her hand back and pulled down her sleeve. She went back inside, closing the door behind her.

Clare expelled the stale, bitter air she had breathed in the house. She walked back, thinking about Darlene Ruyters and ignoring the cascade of twitching curtains that followed her progress. The learned cowering of a woman once battered runs deep and cold, habituating her to secrecy. It lasts long after bones knit and bruises fade. Those bruises, fingered around a resisting wrist, were fresh, a few days old.

On a woman who lived alone.

Chapter Twenty-three

'IT'S SO OBVIOUS to suspect a sailor,' said Tamar. She stood at the window, her hands wrapped around a steaming cup of coffee.

Clare had gone back to the station to meet with Tamar and Karamata, who had spent the morning interviewing the captains and crews of ships that had been docked when Kaiser disappeared. Most of the captains had given their crew a few hours off on Friday night, and the men had gone to town in groups. Alibis all around.

The window behind Tamar gave Clare a framed view of the harbour. A skeletal ship, long abandoned, rocked on the breakers. Black cormorants perched along the gunwales, silent as waiting widows.

'We've had enough murders because of drunk, lonely sailors fighting over women,' Tamar continued, 'but this case points the other way.'

'Inland?' asked Clare.

'On land at any rate,' said Karamata. He was pushing his muscular arms into a leather jacket. 'I'll catch you later. I've got a community policing forum meeting with the Christian Mission ladies.'

'Good luck,' said Tamar with feeling.

'They love me.' Karamata winked at her. 'It's single mothers like you that they pray for.'

Tamar rolled her eyes. 'Thanks for doing this, Elias.'

Clare poured herself some tea when he was gone. 'On land,' she repeated pensively.

'Whoever is doing this knows this desert, knows how to make things disappear in it,' said Tamar.

Clare's phone rang. She looked at the caller identity before answering. The little bubble of delight put a lilt in her voice. 'Riedwaan.'

'You picked up.' He sounded pleased with himself. 'You're missing me.'

Bastard, she thought. 'I'm putting this on loudspeaker,' she said.

'Hello, Captain Damases,' said Riedwaan. 'Dr Hart, tell me what you've got.' Clare couldn't decide if hearing his voice, disembodied by the speakerphone, clipped and neutral because of Tamar's presence, was disconcerting or sexy. She settled for disconcerting and sexy as she winnowed through the interviews, feeding him the scraps of information – evidence seemed too grandiose a word – she had gleaned.

'You're not exactly ready to do a line-up, are you?' Riedwaan said when she was finished.

'Not yet.'

'She's only been here three days,' said Tamar.

'I know, I know. I was joking.' Riedwaan paused. Clare could picture him rubbing his temples, searching for the right words. 'You'll look after her, Tamar?'

'I am.' Tamar smiled at Clare. 'But she seems quite capable of doing it herself. I'm going to leave you to finish this, Clare. I've got some things to see to. I'll see you at two? At the Venus.'

Clare nodded and switched the phone off conference as Tamar left.

'It looks like you've got a textbook series,' said Riedwaan.

'Looks like it.'

'You're not convinced?'

'Like you say,' said Clare. 'A textbook. The problem with textbooks is that the cases are exemplary rather than true.'

'Well, give me what you do have.'

'Three victims, same profile,' said Clare, summarising her notes for Riedwaan. 'The killer's used the same method for all of them. Ligatures. Head-shot wound. Missing joint on the ring finger. Two with their chests mutilated. Nicanor Jones as Number 2. Kaiser Apollis, Number 3. Fritz Woestyn, the first one with nothing on his chest, but the rest all the same.'

'What else links them?'

'All the boys are small for their age, feminine looking. They were shot at such close range. There's a kind of intimacy to that, I suppose, a complete absence of empathy and a need for total control. I kept thinking that this killer needs his victims to witness what is being done to them. They have to watch you as you kill them.'

'The crime scenes?' asked Riedwaan.

'Not much. Though it seems whoever did it wanted the bodies to be found.'

'Any other street kids missing?'

'None reported, which is hardly surprising. Nobody reported these boys missing,' said Clare.

'All homeless?'

'Most of the time, yes. Apollis stayed with his sister sometimes. The rest of the time, he lived with the others out at the dump. There's some kind of a shelter there.'

'Who's running it?'

'The guy in charge of waste management,' said Clare. 'George Meyer.'

'Wasn't he first at the school where Kaiser Apollis was found?'

'He was. Him and his son.'

'I'd question his altruism a bit,' said Riedwaan. 'How old is the son?'

'About seven,' said Clare. 'Grade 1.'

'That rules them out as a team, I suppose. Although stranger things have happened.'

'I talked to the homeless kids while I was out there. The second boy, Nicanor Jones, his body was found there.'

'Inside the dump?' asked Riedwaan.

'Propped up outside.'

'Have you got a perpetrator profile yet?'

'The basics,' said Clare. 'I'd say the killer must have a vehicle, something that doesn't stand out too much. He probably lives alone; otherwise his absences would be noticed. But everyone works shifts here, so that isn't a definite. One thing's for sure: these bodies are kept inside somewhere for a couple of days and then displayed.'

'Why inside?' probed Riedwaan.

'No predator marks. None of the boys was killed where he was found either. So they're shot somewhere, then kept, then moved and displayed where they'll be found.'

'Homosexual predator?'

'Hard to say. Could be. Homosexuality is illegal here, so I'd imagine that he's either deeply closeted or is some kind of mission killer. There's some evidence that Kaiser Apollis worked as a rent boy. I'd be surprised if the others didn't.'

'Sexual assault?'

'Nothing overt, but whoever he is he's organised. Arrogant, too, to risk displaying these kids.'

'Sounds charming,' said Riedwaan. 'You're going to have to bring your stuff down for the forensic tests. It can't be couriered.'

'Not before Friday,' said Clare. 'I'll catch an early flight.'

'I'll organise things for you, then,' said Riedwaan. 'And I'll pick you up from the airport.'

'I don't think that's the best idea.' Clare kept her tone businesslike.

'I wanted to talk to you about what happened before you left, about what I didn't say.'

'I got your e-mail,' said Clare.

Riedwaan must have got up to close his office door; the silence on the phone was absolute. He broke it. 'Are you not going to talk about us?'

'It's a bit late.'

'Okay, I should've told you. I'm sorry I didn't. How many times must I say this? It's my family, my daughter. How the fuck must I know how to handle this and them and you?'

'Just deal with them and leave me out of it,' Clare said. 'It's better that way.'

'Clare, I have to see you.' Riedwaan's voice was coaxing, as warm as a touch.

Clare inhaled and closed her eyes. 'We are going to see each other ... professionally.'

'Fine,' said Riedwaan. 'I'll see you professionally then.'

Chapter Twenty-four

RIEDWAAN FAIZAL REPLACED the receiver, the click loud in the silence. He opened a window, letting in a rush of cool Cape Town air. He had meant to tell Clare. He had practised it in his car that morning: 'Their trip was cancelled. The trip was cancelled.'

'Their trip was cancelled.' He said it aloud again. Nonchalant. That was the trick, or, 'Shazia and Yasmin, they had to cancel, so …'

So what? Even he could see where that line of defence would go.

'I'm not coming,' his wife had said when she'd called the night before at home, when he was already two whiskies down. 'I want a divorce. You want a divorce. I can't afford to come back now, so I've changed the tickets. Yasmin will come to see you at the end of the year. If you can organise some leave. Oh, and I should tell you I've met someone.' Shazia had paused then, and in that suspended transatlantic moment, the memory of her pliancy, her eagerness as a young bride, was so immediate, he smelled for a moment the subtle, cinnamon scent of her skin.

'I'm getting married again,' she had told him.

'I'm pleased for you,' Riedwaan had said through gritted teeth, and she'd cut the conversation.

Riedwaan had tried to phone Clare after he got Shazia's call. It would have been easier if she had picked up then. It would have come out just as it was, unfiltered. But she hadn't, he thought, as he watched Superintendent Phiri park. The man reversed back and forth until his double cab was so precisely aligned that you could work out a geometry theorem with it. As his boss stepped over the scattered debris and disappeared around the building, Riedwaan's thoughts drifted back to his wife. His soon-to-be officially ex-wife. Some primitive part of his brain wanted to find the man who was sleeping with Shazia and brain him, even as he had felt the relief that came with resolution flood through him.

He poured himself a cup of coffee, his third, and put his hand into his pocket, looking for his cigarettes. His hand closed around the fax Yasmin had sent him: *Sorry Daddy, from my tears because we not comming to see u yet. Maybe in December. For my birthday.* The smudges of ink from her tears had been circled.

Riedwaan lit a cigarette and pressed his hands to his eyes, recalling the horror of his daughter's kidnapping. It was Yasmin's abduction that had brought him to Clare. She had profiled the men who had snatched his daughter and together they had found her.

He and Clare. They made a good team. Professionally.

'Why the long face?' Rita Mkhize sauntered in, saving Riedwaan from his tangled thoughts.

'Woman trouble.'

'No such thing,' said Rita. 'Man trouble, yes. Woman trouble, no.'

'Oh, really,' said Riedwaan. 'Then explain to me why Clare's not speaking to me.'

'Apart from the minor detail that you forgot to tell her that your wife was coming to stay?'

'She's cancelled her trip.'

'So she cancels and you phone Clare to say that all the problems are solved because Shazia's staying in Canada?'

'Well ...' Riedwaan scrabbled about for a better light to cast himself in. There wasn't one. 'If you put it that way.'

'And Clare's still furious?'

'Yes.'

'You can't think why?'

'Because I didn't tell her,' he ventured.

'Oh my God.' Rita slapped her palm to her forehead. 'A doctorate in the female psyche coming your way.'

'So what do you suggest I do?'

'Grovel,' said Rita. 'That's always a good start. If you let me watch I'll put in a good word for you.'

'I know I'm not the brightest, but Clare clams up. She's like an oyster. Bang! You get near her and she closes up on you.'

'Well,' said Rita. 'Hang around. A piece of dirt like you, maybe she opens up again. My advice is to slip right in. With any luck she'll turn you into a pearl.'

'Why do women always side with each other?' asked Riedwaan. 'What did you come in here for anyway? Just to give me a hard time?'

'Phiri's looking for you. He asked me to tell you to join him for coffee.'

'That's all I need, his poison,' Riedwaan muttered as he walked down the passage.

'THERE YOU ARE, Faizal,' said Phiri as Riedwaan entered his office. 'There's an envelope for you on the table.'

Riedwaan opened it and flicked through the contents. Phiri was a stickler for paperwork and he had a reputation for turning it to his advantage. The file was full of the countless forms an officer needed before he could move. He checked: every single requisite signature was in place.

'Thank you, sir.'

'You're going next week?' Phiri straightened things on his desk.

'Sunday.'

'Close the door, Faizal.'

Riedwaan did so, praying that there would be no coffee.

'I signed that lot off yesterday.' Phiri pointed to the file. 'And it's been logged by Miss La Grange.'

'I'm surprised that Susannah processed me so fast.'

Susannah la Grange was Phiri's gimlet-eyed secretary. She shared Phiri's fanatical devotion to order; she was also devoted to the man himself. She was Riedwaan's nemesis, returning his sloppy leave forms and expense accounting with metronymic regularity.

'Your paperwork shows no sign of improvement, Faizal.' Phiri looked him in the eye for the first time. 'But I asked Miss La Grange to expedite it, not something I intend to make a habit.'

'Thank you, sir,' Riedwaan said again, wondering where this was headed.

'I had a call this morning,' said Phiri, 'asking me to let things … drift for a while.'

'You mean someone asked you to kill the investigation?' Riedwaan did not like the idea of Clare so far from home with her back-up pulled away from her. 'Why?'

'I'd be hard-pressed to say it was as definite as that. Perhaps drift was not quite the right word.'

'Who called and what did they want?'

'It was … indirect.' Phiri steepled his fingers in his ecclesiastical manner. 'A whisper in a diplomatic ear over cocktails, a private call to me.'

'Clare is up there, already working on it.'

'Faizal, Faizal. I know she is. Relax and stop thinking about hitting me. It's not God's answer to everything.'

Riedwaan uncurled his fists and put his hands behind his back. He tried the deep breathing that the last cop shrink had taught him. It worked. He stopped wanting to punch Phiri and tried listening to him instead. 'What was the concern?' he asked.

'My little bird told me that it'd be better if the Namibian police handled this on their own.'

'A serial killer?' Riedwaan laughed. 'Apart from Captain Damases, most of Nampol wouldn't know one if he came at them with a meat cleaver.'

'Faizal, that's most uncomradely. That's not what we need right now.'

'What does Captain Damases say?'

'I spoke to her this morning. She told me things were progressing as well as could be expected for such a complex case.'

'So who's complaining?'

'Hard to say. It's all been unofficial, circuitous,' said Phiri. 'There seems to be some military interest in the case.'

'Military?' said Riedwaan, surprised.

'Rooibank, where one of the bodies was found, is on the border of an old military site that has a sensitive land claim on it. Some desert nomads, I understand. The Namibians are concerned that all this attention will stir up dormant issues like what happened in Botswana with the San.'

'This sounds ridiculous,' said Riedwaan. 'Have you told Clare?'

'It's not ridiculous, Faizal. It's politics. But so far, I've told no one.' Phiri controlled his irritation but with visible effort. 'When are you going up?'

'Clare's coming to Cape Town this weekend with the physical evidence. I was thinking of leaving on Sunday and going up by bike.'

'Good. Better than flying, under the circumstances.' Phiri walked to the door, but he did not open it. 'You might want to keep out of the station for the next couple of days. Not that you'd break the record for regular attendance, Faizal.'

'Why might I want to do that, sir?' Riedwaan asked with exaggerated politeness.

'If you're not here, Faizal, I can't cancel your trip.' Phiri's eyes gave nothing away. 'If it comes to that, of course.'

'Clare?' Riedwaan started, not sure how to articulate the unease he was feeling.

'She'll be fine. She knows how to look after herself, I'm sure,' said Phiri.

Riedwaan stopped at the door. 'This military angle ... What is it? Something new?'

'No, no,' said Phiri. 'It's just that this is a volatile region, awash with new money and old grudges.'

Chapter Twenty-five

HELENA KOTZE DROPPED off her preliminary report with Clare when she was back at the station. Clare scanned through it, most of Helena's findings confirming things she already knew. There was nothing revealing from the geologist boyfriend either, though some of the sand on the boy's shoes was from surprisingly far inland. There were still a couple of things that Clare could confirm once ballistics and forensics in Cape Town had had a look. She flipped through to the histology report, hoping that it would give her something new. The carpaccio-thin slices of lung lining that Helena had stared at through her microscope had shown a residue of deep-fried batter and cayenne pepper. Fast food, spicy chicken, so probably Portuguese. It wasn't much to go on, but it was a start. It made sense of the till slip Tamar had found in Kaiser's pocket. Clare turned the receipt over, wondering if the boy had known it was going to be his last meal. Twenty-four Namibian dollars was expensive for a destitute child.

Clare spread out a tourist map of Walvis Bay. The list of food outlets was unimpressive. She eliminated the restaurants, as she did the township's fish-and-chip shops and shebeens. They never gave receipts. That left five establishments, two of which were Portuguese takeaways.

The closest one was the Madeira, right at the entrance to the docks. It caught the trade from the harbour and from the factories that spewed out their workers at lunch times. A few men in blue overalls sat outside eating fish and vinegary chips with their fingers as Clare pulled up. Inside, a young woman with braided hair was texting with one hand, cigarette dangling from the other. Clare ordered a Coke from the pasty girl serving. The girl dragged herself off her stool and brought Clare her drink.

'Three-fifty.'

'Could I have a slip?' Clare asked.

The girl rolled her eyes. 'The people who eat here don't have expense accounts,' she said, pocketing the money Clare had given her for the drink.

In the centre of town, the streets had emptied of adults, filling instead with groups of raucous children heading home, white shirts grimy after a day of school. The Lisboa Inn was quiet. An old man was reading the takeaway menu. Clare approached the counter and asked for chicken peri-peri.

'Sorry, Miss. Just fish or Russians.' The pink sausages glistened in a greasy tray. Behind him, a score of splayed carcasses basted in the rotisserie oven. 'Electricity went this morning. Chicken's ready in half an hour.'

'No fried chicken?'

'No.' The cashier folded his hands across his belly, ending the conversation. His eyes moved to the man who had stepped up next to Clare. 'Yes?' he asked.

'Two Russians.' The Spanish cadences of the customer's accent lilted his English. He clicked his rosary beads as he recited the rest of his order. 'Onion rings, chips, two Cokes.' The man turned to face Clare. 'Try Lover's Hill.' His features were sculpted, his skin fine beneath the sunburn. 'They do the best chicken there. Spicy. Hot.'

'I'll try it then,' said Clare, trying to place the man's face.

'At the end of the Lagoon, you find it there. Sit and watch the flamingos while you eat.' He flashed her a smile and turned to collect his order.

'Thanks.' Clare left the gloom of the café, blinded by the sun that had fought off the sea mist outside.

'Hello, Dr Hart.' Mara's hand on Clare's arm was strong for such a skinny girl.

'Hello, Mara,' said Clare. 'What are you doing here?'

'Juan Carlos got some shore leave. We're just getting something to eat.'

'Your handsome boyfriend?' Clare asked. 'I think I just spoke to him inside.'

The young Spaniard strolled over to them. 'You two know each other?'

'Yes,' said Mara. 'This is Dr Hart. This is Juan Carlos. Dr Hart is here to investigate the murders. Kaiser and the other boys. You'll let me know when you find who it is?' Mara's eyes glistened at the mention of Kaiser's name.

'I'm sure it'll be all over the news when we do,' said Clare.

'You better be quick,' said Juan Carlos. He circled his fingers around Mara's slender throat and dropped a kiss onto her mouth. 'She's leaving me soon. If she wasn't so beautiful I might have to do something about it.' Mara blushed to the roots of her hair.

'When are you leaving?' Clare asked.

'Next week.' Mara looked down at her hands. 'My visa runs out. Come to my farewell if you're still around. On Saturday night.'

'It's better you don't talk about her leaving in front of me.' Juan Carlos wrapped his hand around Mara's waist and pulled her close to him. He slipped an intimate hand under her shirt as they walked off. Clare walked along the lagoon towards the café on Lover's Hill, aware of how acutely she missed Riedwaan. The takeaway was empty except for a woman at the till, and the cook leaning against the counter, reading the football results.

'Can I help you?' The woman did not take her eyes off the television screen.

'Chicken peri-peri,' said Clare.

'Antonio! Chicken 'n' chips,' the woman bellowed. 'Anything to drink?'

'Nothing, thanks.'

The woman took Clare's money and gave her a slip. 'Give that to Antonio.' The cashier turned back, riveted by her soap opera.

Clare handed her slip to the cook. He checked it and gave it back to her.

'Our best, the chicken peri-peri,' he said, picking up a piece of chicken and coating it with crumbs and spice. It sizzled when he threw it into the vat of bubbling oil. The thick potato wedges crisped golden. Clare could imagine a hungry boy's stomach contracting at the smell.

The sound of a car engine drew her attention, a Land Rover hurtling past.

'The desert road,' said Antonio. 'They drive so fast. So many accidents, especially if they drink.'

'It happens often?'

'These Namibians. They drink to drive; they kill each other every day like this.'

'You're not from here?'

'Not me, I'm from Angola,' said Antonio. 'I come here for work. In my country, there's nothing. Used to be war; now there is just nothing.' He wrapped Clare's order in paper and put it into a bag, tucking napkins and tomato sauce into the side. '*Bon apetito*.'

'Thanks.' Clare pulled a series of photographs out of her bag. 'I was wondering,' she asked, 'did any of these boys ever come here?'

Antonio looked at one of the photographs. 'Funny face, he's got,' he said. 'Like a frog.'

'You know him?'

'He was a soccer fan. What's his name?'

'Fritz Woestyn,' said Clare.

'He supported Brazil.' Antonio grinned, opening his white chef's jacket to reveal a yellow and green T-shirt. 'Like me.'

'How did you know him?' asked Clare.

'He slept there sometimes.' Antonio pointed to a padlocked glass door behind him. It was so covered with salt and grime that Clare hadn't noticed it. The kitchen vent was above the doorway. It would have been a warm refuge for a cold child at night. 'I gave him food sometimes.'

'When last did you see him?'

'One month ago, maybe. The owner put spikes there to keep them away. He didn't come to sleep here after that. Maybe you find him at the shelter at the dump.'

'And these boys?' Clare put the pictures of the other two boys on the counter.

'I never see them,' said Antonio. 'Who are they?'

'This was Nicanor Jones,' said Clare. 'This was Kaiser Apollis.'

'Why you ask me?' asked Antonio, anxiety in his eyes.

'Maybe one of them was here,' said Clare. 'With someone.'

Antonio shook his head. 'I don't remember.'

'Think about it.' Clare wrote down her name and cell number on a serviette. 'Call me if you do. This one loved Portuguese chicken.' She pointed to the picture of Kaiser. 'It was the last thing he ate,' she said as she walked towards the door.

Antonio picked up the napkin and folded it, watching Clare step out of the way of an accelerating 4x4 as she crossed the road. Antonio put down the forgotten serviette. Another car had flicked its lights, the roar of its engine disappearing into a quiet, star-spangled night with the child's familiar face in the window.

He wiped his hands on his apron and pushed open the swing doors. 'Wait!' he shouted to Clare. 'Let me look again. I think maybe I see one of them.'

Clare spun around and crossed the road again. 'Which one?' she asked when she reached the door. She took the photographs out of her bag again and held them out for him.

Antonio looked through the photographs again. 'This one,' he said.

'Kaiser Apollis?'

Antonio nodded.

'When? When did you see him?' Clare asked.

Antonio was weighing up whether he could trust her or not. 'I think it was Friday night. One week ago,' he said. 'He came in last. Was only me here, and I'm already closing up. He had money, new money, in his hand, a rich person's money. He asks me for chicken and chips. I make it for him, give him a Coke and then he went.'

'Where?' asked Clare.

'He walked back to town; I saw him. I see him walking, yes. Then I lock up and I also walk home.'

Clare let out her breath. She hadn't realised that she had been holding it. Back to town, that made no sense. The straw she had been grasping at was slipping away from her.

'Then I see the car. It's waiting for him.'

'What car? Where?'

'A car pull to one side of the road.'

'Did you know it? See any number plates?'

'It looks like all the cars here. White double cab.'

'Did you see the driver at all?'

Antonio shook his head. 'That is all I see. This boy.' He tapped the photograph of Kaiser. 'He talked to the driver, then he got in the back and they drive away, into the desert.'

'Thanks.' Clare was smiling at him. 'If you remember anything else, anything at all, you give me a call.'

He went back inside and watched Clare walk down towards the lagoon. She sat down on a bench and took out a notepad, her parcel of food unopened beside her. The boy had ordered the same meal, but the sound of the café door opening interrupted Antonio's thoughts.

'Gretchen.' The cashier greeted the blonde stripper without moving her eyes from the television. 'What you want?'

'Give me what she had,' said Gretchen, pointing outside to Clare.

'Antonio!' the cashier boomed. 'Another chicken 'n' chips.'

Chapter Twenty-six

IT WAS THREE o'clock by the time Clare went to meet Tamar outside the bakery. From beneath the shade of a palm tree, a knot of boys untangled themselves, offering to guard Clare's car, wash her window, sell her an old newspaper.

'Where's Lazarus?' Clare asked one of them, exchanging fifty cents for yesterday's news.

'He went to the docks,' said the child.

'Tell him I want to talk to him,' said Clare. The boy looked around furtively. 'It's nothing bad,' she added. She slipped ten Namibian dollars into his hand. 'Tell him to find Dr Hart.' The boy nodded, sidling away before a bigger boy could twist the money out of his fingers. Clare went inside to buy the last cake, a sticky chocolate confection.

It was hot on the desert side of town, the morning's mist a ragged memory suspended above the ocean. Clare drank some water and watched the street children hustle. Tourists looked furtive, then handed over handfuls of coins. Locals walked on, oblivious. Clare pulled her notebook from her bag and read her notes. The desert revealed its secrets, everyone kept telling her, but when it was ready and in its own way. Someone has been very determined that the three bodies were found. That part was easy. Why they were so determined was less easy. The seduction, the trust quickly established, quickly broken. The bullet, the knife flashing across a chest. The severing of the fingertips. That small, nail-tipped joint from the ring finger lying, oozing, in the palm of a killer's hand. Everything about it said mission killer to her, cleansing the streets of rubbish, mending what had been broken by illegitimacy, poverty and delinquency, but the detail refused to crystallise into a coherent whole. The ghost, the killer, glided away from her when she reached for him.

'Come with us.' Tamar's voice at her window made Clare jump. 'It's half an hour, the drive. We don't need two cars.'

Clare got out and locked the car, balancing the cake box on the bonnet. 'Dessert,' she explained. 'I think your niece will like it.'

TAMAR STOPPED THE vehicle near a copse of acacias huddled against the cliffs. The children exploded from the car, dashing across the hot sand to the shadow of the trees, shrieking as if they had driven five hundred kilometres instead of fifty. Only a dark line marked the flow of underground water. Clare turned her back on the sprawled plain with its encrypted alphabet. Everything left a trace on this vast Rosetta stone of a desert.

She and Tamar set down their laden basket on the cement picnic table. It was cool, shaded, where they were. Water welled to the surface at the crook of this elbow of river. The children shouted, splashing in delight because there was enough water to swim in. Another day, perhaps two, and it would be gone, as the river retreated underground, leaving nothing but cracked earth and insect and rodent corpses trapped in the mud. Clare flicked some eggshells and a curl of orange peel off the table, shook out the tablecloth and settled it over the rough round surface.

'I'm glad we could come,' said Tamar. She settled herself onto a cement bench, cradling her belly between crossed knees. 'I've been promising to take them on a picnic for weeks, but this business has taken all my time.'

'It's nice to catch my breath before I catch my plane,' Clare commented. The children splashed, slick as otters in the water, and Clare sipped her lemonade. 'It doesn't feel real out here.'

The breeze came up off the desert, hot and short-lived. When it dropped, the mantle of air settled again. Clare leant back against the tree. She was tired and the heat made her sleepy. Tamar unpacked the picnic basket, setting out mounds of white bread.

'Here,' she said. 'Butter these.'

Clare took the knife. It sliced through the margarine, separating into an ooze of bilious yellow oil. Tamar sliced cheese, waving away the clumsy flies flustering towards the exposed food. Slices of anaemic tomato wilted under plastic wrap.

'How are you finding Walvis Bay the second time around?' Tamar asked as Clare buttered the bread.

'Quieter. Like half the town left in the middle of the night. Its soul seems to have gone.'

'But it grows on one, despite itself and against one's better judgement.'

Clare looked at the dunes, auburn tresses of sand rippling next to the black parting of the Kuiseb River. 'I suppose it does,' she said.

'Your profile? How do you feel about it?'

'I still feel like I'm missing something.' Clare put the last buttered slices of bread on the plate. 'Like a conversation I can hear through a door but that's just too low to distinguish the words.

I get the emotion, the tone, a sense of a dialogue, but the words elude me. Maybe being outside of all this will clear my head.'

'Phiri called before we left. Captain Faizal should be here early next week. It's all sorted.'

Riedwaan's name lay between them. A challenge or an offering of sympathy, Clare wasn't sure. She wondered what Tamar knew, if anything. Not that there was much left to know.

'Aunty, Aunty, come and look!' The children burst from the undergrowth, a flutter of shrieks and pigtails and wide-eyed horror. Tamar's hand went straight for the pistol tucked inside her trousers, nestled next to the foetus, free-floating in its watery cave. A breeze curled off the dunes and around Clare's neck, lifting the downy hairs.

'What is it, Angela?' said Tamar.

'Come see, come see.' The child was hysterical, hopping from one pink-sandalled foot to the other. Further up the river bed, the children had discovered a tunnel in the scrub that had grown up over three seasons of good rain. Clare had to bend as Angela and Tupac wove through the bush. The pathway twisted and turned, as disorientating as a maze. Some of the branches had been cut back to clear a path. The cloying stench of death filled the air. Clare's blood ran cold as she thought of who might have been there before them.

The little girl stepped into a sun-dappled clearing. A semicircle of stones faced a small cave in the sheer, black cliff face. In front of it was a makeshift altar; the stumps of a few candles leant drunkenly, melted by the heat. A small body hung limp, a shrivelled fruit among the profusion of white blossoms at the entrance to the clearing. Clare stepped forward to touch the corpse's ginger fur. The skin was starting to slough off, leaving grotesque strips of exposed flesh. Flies clustered where its life had bubbled away.

'Tupac, take your sister back to the picnic place,' said Tamar.

Angela clung to her aunt, tears glistening on her plump cheeks. 'Who do it? Who do it to the kitty, Aunty Tamar?'

Tamar squatted down beside her distraught niece and drew her into the circle of her arms. The child buried her head in Tamar's shoulder.

Clare walked around the semi-circle. Faded Coke tins and discarded cigarette butts littered the place, the milder brands bearing telltale lipstick stains. She picked one up. A menthol ultra-thin. A teenager's nicotine starter pack.

'I'm going to take her back to the car,' said Tamar, gripping Angela firmly by the hand. 'Will you check here, Clare? Come on, Tupac, you too.'

The undergrowth closed on Tamar and the children, leaving Clare alone. On the other side of the makeshift altar lay a brandy bottle and a red G-string. Clare took a tissue out of her pocket and picked up the wisp of stained underwear. It was dim inside the cave. Once her eyes had adjusted, though, Clare could make out the graffiti: Chesney and Minki. The girl's name had been scored through when LaToyah had replaced Minki in Chesney's affections. There wasn't much else – a couple more empty bottles, a bottleneck with the remnants of a filter in it, a filthy old mattress. Unimaginative, small-town Satanism. A lizard bobbed on tensed elbows, liquid black on the sun-ravaged rocks, watching Clare duck into the tunnel of undergrowth.

'You get a lot of this Satanic stuff?' she asked Tamar when she got back to the picnic site.

Tamar had her niece on her lap. Tupac was sitting close to her too. He sidled away when Clare reappeared, an eleven-year-old sensitive about his image. Clare sat down opposite them.

'There've been a few incidents: bored teenagers wearing black nail polish and experimenting with group sex. Nothing too serious.'

'Crucifying cats is something else. The men I go for often start their careers torturing small animals.'

'I want to go home, Aunty.' Tamar stroked the hair out of Angela's eyes and popped a piece of bread into her mouth.

Clare packed up the picnic. 'Do you know anyone called Minki?' she asked.

Tamar shook her head.

'LaToyah?'

'Dime a dozen in Narraville, LaToyahs,' said Tamar. 'Three in my street.'

'And Chesney?'

'I know him,' said Tupac. It was the first time he had said a word. 'Chesney used to go to my school, but then he left to go to the school in town, the one where you found that dead boy in the swing.'

The two women looked at each other over the children's heads.

'I'll talk to him,' said Tamar quietly, strapping Angela into her seat. They were all silent as they drove back to town through the gathering dusk.

Chapter Twenty-seven

MUSIC BLASTED THROUGH the girl's iPod as the bike hurtled through the desert. She snaked her arms under the driver's leathers, and he accelerated, pluming dust behind the bike. It shimmered across the sinking sun as they passed the rusted no-entry sign. 'Danger/Gevaar' said the next one. The girl hopped off the bike and opened the gate. In among the trees were the remnants of three huts and a car wreck.

'Who lives here?' she asked, climbing back on the bike.

'Nobody now,' said her companion. 'Some Topnaars used to, but the South African army kicked them out twenty years ago.'

The man hadn't been this way in what ... ten years, twelve? He hadn't even thought of the place since his unit had given up, rolling south in their Bedfords when Walvis Bay was handed back to the Namibians. For their sins, he thought. What anyone wanted in this godforsaken dump was beyond him.

'When're you going to stop?' the girl whined. It would be dark soon and she wanted a fire and a joint. The man was enjoying the feeling of a girl's tits pressing into his back. It made him feel young again, like the soldier he had once been and not the overweight husband he had become.

'Where's the fucking road gone? It should be here.' Instead of a track leading to a hut under a gum tree, there was a bank of sand, pocked with branches and other long-stranded flood debris.

'That flood, a few years ago, it shifted the course of the river. It must've blocked Memory Lane,' said the girl matter-of-factly. 'Let's stay here. The desert's all the same, anyway.'

The man parked the bike under a canopy of gnarled acacia, thinking of the girls he and some of the others in his unit used to pick up and bring out here. Army mattresses, they had called them. A couple of days in the desert made them docile, amenable. Not like this wild thing with the same name as his wife's fancy perfume.

The girl had logs and kindling assembled before he had the panniers unpacked. She put a match to the grass and blew, showering red sparks across the satin sky. She leant back and offered the man a drag of her deftly rolled joint – another thing girls seemed to have learned to do in the last twenty years. He traded his hip flask for the joint.

The girl tilted her head back and he traced down her throat as she drank, stopping at the hollow between her collarbones where her breath fluttered below his thumb. She put his hand to her mouth, flicking her tongue along his fingers, clicking the piercing in the centre of her tongue against his wedding ring. Then his knee was between her thighs and he was spreading her legs and mounting her. He was finished before he'd really begun. The girl sighed, turning away to light a cigarette. He tried to kiss her, but she brushed him aside.

'I'm hungry,' she said, rummaging for food in the bag next to her, propped up on one elbow. She considered brushing her teeth, but the man had fallen asleep beside her, his arms around her stomach. She covered them both instead and lay, watching the stars wink, bright as lanterns in the branches of their tree canopy.

When the girl woke, it was dark. No moon. No wind either. She guessed it was two o'clock. Maybe three. The silence filled her ears, her lungs, making it difficult to breathe. She snuggled back into the man's arms, but the pressure of her bladder would not relent, so she wormed her way out from under the covers and felt around for the torch and her shoes. She picked her way towards a denser patch of darkness on the edge of their campsite.

When she flicked on her torch, nosing the light ahead of her into the trees, he was waiting for her. Grinning.

The girl's scream ricocheted into the night.

Chapter Twenty-eight

KEENING. HIGH AND wild. It feathered fear up Clare's spine. She sat up, putting her hands to her temples and trying to order her thoughts in the wake of the nightmare. She had been running, faster and faster. Her feet had been bare and bleeding, the flesh ribboned by the broken shells littering a beach. Spectral hands plucked at her legs, pulling her down towards the lagoon, wrapping around her throat. Clare looked around her room and orientated herself. She had been asleep. It was just a dream.

She was reaching for the water next to her bed when the terrible keening started again. Of course. Her cellphone.

'What?' Manners would be pushing it at three in the morning.

'Dr Hart? I woke you?' She tried to place the voice. 'It's Van Wyk.'

Of course it was. The receding dread of her dream circled back.

'What?' she said again.

'Another body. I'll pick you up.'

'Where? Who?'

'From your cottage,' said Van Wyk. 'I'll pick you up.'

'I meant where was the body found? Who is it?'

'Out in the Kuiseb, the old military site past the delta. Couple of bikers found him. I wouldn't be disturbing your beauty sleep if he didn't fit your bill.'

'How long have I got?' Clare needed coffee.

'Ten minutes.' Van Wyk hung up.

Clare made coffee and drank it while she dressed. Jeans, anorak. It would be cold out. She was finishing a second cup when Van Wyk pulled up in the double cab. He handed her a packet of rusks and a flask. Clare bit off a piece of the rough, dried biscuit.

'Thanks.' She hadn't thought that she would be hungry.

'My mother makes them.'

Clare hadn't thought of Van Wyk with a family either. If her brain had been functioning better, she might have ventured a question about them. Instead, she kept quiet, watching the streets slip past.

Tamar was waiting for them, her house dark except for the light in the kitchen. 'Is Elias out there already?' she asked, getting into the back of the vehicle.

'He took the call, Captain,' Van Wyk said. 'So he went straight out.'

'Is an ambulance on its way?'

'Karamata said there's no need,' said Van Wyk, skirting the sleeping town. 'It would be impossible to get one out there, anyway.'

The road forked at the salt mine, which gleamed white under the floodlights. Van Wyk turned into the dark cleft of the delta. He drove fast along the twisting track, never hesitating about which tributary road to take, which to speed past. He veered left, heading for a dense thicket of trees. The track narrowed and the tamarisk trees cut out the starlight. Van Wyk braked. Ahead of them was a gate, the only breach in an endless garland of barbed wire. Clare could just make out the sign: 'Danger/Gevaar'.

'What is this place?' she asked.

'It's part of an old military site,' said Tamar. 'The whole delta used to be the army's. This place has been off-limits so long that everyone forgot about it.'

'Not those little lovebirds,' said Van Wyk. He switched on the hunting lights, serried like evil eyes on the roof of the truck, flooding the clearing with white light.

A whippet-thin girl was hunched over her knees, a jacket wrapped tight across her back. Her eyes sparked with defiance. Fifteen, thought Clare. Sixteen, if you wanted to believe it. A man stood near his motorbike. His wedding ring glinted as he took a deep drag of his cigarette. Ponytail, pushing forty. The proverbial rabbit in the headlights. Wife and children blown for the brief thrill of a nubile body in his hands. The dead boy was slumped against a tree on the edge of the circle of light. A still from a horror movie until Karamata stepped out of the shadows, unfreezing the frame.

'Elias,' said Tamar, getting out of the vehicle, 'phone Helena Kotze and tell her I need her here this time. This one we'll autopsy tonight.'

'Has he been moved?' asked Clare, approaching the body cautiously.

Karamata shook his head.

Tamar handed Clare a pair of latex gloves, then pulled on her own pair before lowering herself next to the dead boy. A child drooped in jest against a tree at the end of a game. He had been secured with riempie, the same strips of cured leather that had kept the shroud around Kaiser Apollis's corpse.

'Same shroud for this one.' Tamar lifted away the gauzy fabric and shone her torch into the boy's ruined face, revealing a mouth wide open in amazement and a forehead that was nothing but shards of bone and burnt flesh.

'Lazarus,' gasped Clare, the shock of recognition a body blow.

'Lazarus Beukes,' said Tamar. 'He's got a record for petty thieving so long you could knit a jersey out of it.'

'What's his story?' Clare wished that she had heard it earlier.

'He had a mother who loved him when she was sober enough to remember he existed,' Tamar said, 'but she disappeared a few years ago. He's lived at the dump ever since.'

Tamar circled the body, resisting the urge to close the lids on the dulling eyes, to wipe away the fluid seeping from his forehead, eyes and slack mouth. The cold eye of her camera flashed on Lazarus's shattered face. The rope, a nylon washing line around the wrists, had been knotted, so that it would pull tighter as the victim struggled. It had been cut through in the middle, and the boy's hands lay between his knees, bloody tracks scored deep into both wrists. Clare envisaged the moment Lazarus had realised it wasn't a game, when he had fought for his life.

'Have a look at that rope,' she said. Tamar lifted the jaunty blue and white nylon. The ends around the wrists were cut clean through.

'This is frayed,' said Tamar, pointing to the longer piece that would have held his hands tight behind his back. 'Cut with a different knife. The same as Kaiser Apollis.'

'Two weapons,' said Clare. 'Two places. Two people? Or just one crime in two parts?'

'There's no blood here,' said Tamar. 'This isn't where he was shot, so there're your two places.' She put her hand against the boy's skin. It was cold, his body flaccid. She tried to move one of his fingers. He was starting to stiffen.

'It doesn't look like he's been dead long enough for rigor to reverse,' said Clare. 'There are no visible signs of decomposition. Looks like he was shot yesterday evening.'

A week since Kaiser Apollis had climbed into a vehicle and been driven into the desert to be displayed on a Monday. Now there was this one, Friday's Child. Loving and giving. Clare checked his left hand. The ring finger ended in a bloody stump. 'The signature,' she said. 'He's taken his trophy again.'

Tamar pointed to the pullover. 'This'll be the second signature,' she said, pushing back the bloody fabric, revealing ribs concaving into the stomach suspended between delicate hips. The flesh, as smooth as a girl's, had been ribboned by a series of sure, deep knife strokes. Tamar dropped the fabric.

'One with nothing, a 2, a 3 and now a 5,' said Clare.

'Please, God, there isn't a fourth victim waiting to be found,' said Tamar, supporting her lower back as she stood up. She turned to Karamata. 'You looked for a gun?' she asked.

'I did,' he said. 'I checked both their hands for residue. Nothing. It would last four hours on the hands of a live person after they'd fired.'

'Unless they washed their hands,' said Clare.

'I checked,' said Karamata. 'No sign that anyone washed their hands.'

'Knives?' asked Clare.

'Just this.' Karamata held up a small penknife. 'It had scraps of biltong on the blade, nothing else.'

'Who found him?' asked Tamar, walking over to the forlorn couple.

'Me.' It was the girl. 'I called the police too.'

'Your name?' Tamar pulled out a notepad.

'I'm Chanel,' the girl replied. 'That's Clinton.'

Tamar turned to the man. 'Why didn't you phone?'

'He was afraid to,' said Chanel, giving the man a look of withering post-coital clarity. 'He wanted to leave, but the bike's not working.'

Van Wyk walked over to the bike. 'This isn't going anywhere,' he said. 'Someone cut your fuel pipe. You're lucky you didn't end up with brain splattered across the desert like him.' He gestured to Lazarus's body.

The girl shuddered and Tamar put a blanket around her shoulders. Still a child under the smudged make-up, her face was drawn, foxy with fear and cold.

'What were you doing out here?' asked Tamar. 'This is a restricted area.'

'He wanted to come out here.' Chanel pointed to the ashen man.

'Why here?' Tamar addressed Clinton.

'Old times' sake.'

'Why here and why now?' Clare persisted.

'No reason really.' Clinton looked besieged.

'So let me get this straight: you just decided on the spur of the moment to bring an under-aged girl to a restricted military site?' asked Clare conversationally.

Clinton shrugged, a failed attempt at cockiness. 'I saw an old army connection the other day and it made me think about this place. We used to come here in the old days. Then Chanel wanted to go somewhere, and I thought, why not here? Seeing as we can't go anywhere together in town.'

'Who's your connection?' asked Clare.

'I don't even remember his name any more. Something foreign. Polish. Russian maybe, I don't know. It was years ago. He was an officer in some unit that used to work out here. I was just a troepie. I saw him there in the strip club, sitting alone, as cool as ever in his cowboy boots, and it reminded me of this place,' said Clinton, his shoulders sagging in defeat. 'It seems fucking stupid now.'

'How do you know him?' Tamar asked Chanel.

'I babysit for his wife,' the girl replied. 'Mrs Nel's going to kill me. So's my mother.'

'Tell me what happened,' said Tamar.

'Can I have a cigarette?' Chanel asked.

Clare tossed her a box of cigarettes. The girl lit one, hands shaking. Then she told them: they'd gone to sleep, she'd woken up, needed a pee, gone over to the trees, and there was the boy, staring at her like some sick joke.

'Did you look around before you went to sleep?' asked Clare.

'Not really,' said Chanel. 'It was getting dark when we arrived.'

'No other cars?' asked Tamar.

'We saw no one,' said Clinton. 'Heard nothing either.'

'And you?' Clare asked the girl.

'Just those geckos that call at night. Listen …' She held up her hand. 'You can hear them now.'

Clare listened: the chill, moaning laugh of a jackal, then there it was in the distance. Tjak. Tjak. Tjak. The knocking sound that solitary reptiles make to claim their territory, to attract a mate.

'Go and wait in the car,' Tamar said to Chanel. The girl was shaking now. Cold and shock. 'There should be some coffee there to warm you up.'

When Van Wyk cut the lights, the starlight washed over the scene, soft-focusing the horror. A bat swooped low along the ground, hunting. The wind rattled through the trees, then died away, leaving a silence so absolute Clare felt it as a pressure in her ears.

Like she was losing altitude too fast.

Chapter Twenty-nine

HELENA KOTZE KICKED her motorbike into life, the sound like a volley of machine-gun fire down the quiet street. Typical that the call had come once the pulse of the clubs and bars had ebbed, allowing her to plunge into the deep sleep she craved. She did not want to think of what was waiting for her on the indifferent desert sand. She did think, as she curved around the belly of the lagoon, that she was following the path the killer had taken. There was no other way into the delta. The trees closed in on her when she turned east.

She rolled the bike into the amphitheatre of dunes. Tamar and Dr Hart stood beside the body trussed against the tree. Van Wyk sat smoking inside the double cab. A blanket-swaddled girl leant against the window. Karamata and a middle-aged man stood near a motorbike.

'Helena, glad you're here,' said Tamar. 'Let's get started.'

Helena set down her sturdy bag on the sand.

'You've got your crime-scene kit there?' Efficiency smoothed out the edge in Tamar's voice.

Helena nodded. 'You got all the pictures you need?'

'I think so.'

'Close-ups of the gunshot wounds?'

'See if these are good enough.' Tamar scrolled through the pictures on her digital camera.

'Looks fine.' Helena palpated the boy's unresisting flesh.

'Time of death?' Clare asked.

Helena took out an instrument that looked like a sharpened bicycle spoke. 'I'm going to do a sub-hepatic probe. Taking a rectal temp can damage the tissue, making it hard to prove sexual assault later.'

Helena found the correct place just beneath the boy's chest. She pushed firmly downwards, puncturing the skin and driving the metal deep into the recesses of his body below the liver. She jotted down some notes about air movement and the number of clothing layers the boy was wearing. 'I need to get the weather report to check against body temp.'

'Would that shot have killed him instantly?' asked Clare.

'In a child, yes,' said Helena. 'Looks like whoever shot this boy was taller than him, or ...' Helena stood up and clasped her hands as if she were holding a gun. She softened her knees and angled her hands towards Lazarus. 'Or the victim was sitting or lying down.' She turned to face Clare and Tamar. 'Like it looks he was.'

'The gun?' asked Clare.

'Pistol shot again,' Helena said. 'Nice and clean and efficient. Punctured forehead. I'd say it's the same guy.' Helena took the boy's mutilated hand in hers. 'Your bridegroom has left his mark again.'

'I saw,' said Clare. 'Pre- or post-mortem?'

'Very little blood here,' said Helena. 'Between ten and thirty minutes post-mortem, it'll be bloodless unless a blunt instrument is used. Then you could get damage to the blood vessels. It'll cause a welling of blood and obscure the fact that it took place post-mortem. It's bloodless, just a little oozing. I'd say the two end joints of his finger were removed with a pair of pliers. And soon after he died.'

Helena pushed back the boy's shirt and shone her torch on the ravaged chest. The knife had cut through the skin. 'Looks like he used a non-serrated knife to cut the boy here. And quite a while after death. So a non-serrated knife for the chest and a pair of pliers or something else for the finger.'

'A strange calling card,' said Tamar.

'A warning, perhaps. To sinners,' said Clare.

The ebony night had thinned to pewter, giving form to the ghostly outlines of branches. Tamar moved off between the trees, following an invisible thread through a maze of bent grasses and shifted stones. The faint marks were familiar.

'He came this way,' she said. 'Carrying the boy. It's the same pattern as the school. Same print.' Clare followed Tamar over the stony ground along the river's edge. There was a thin track snaking through the sand, the ancient tracery of animals migrating in single file in search of water or food. Something you'd miss in the crushing light of day.

Tamar followed until she reached a pile of animal droppings. 'He would've gone back that way,' she said, 'but there's not much point in going on.' A flock of goats was moving down the river-bed. They had churned up the sand with their sharp little hooves. A couple of them stopped browsing and looked up at Clare and Tamar. They would obliterate any trail more efficiently than water.

'I'll send some men out later. See what they can find,' Tamar said, as they headed back to where Helena crouched by the boy.

She had spread a tarpaulin sheet on the ground and lain down Lazarus to examine him. She was moving her competent, gentle hands across the boy's supine body, under his clothes. She had made swabs and was combing the body for a killer's DNA, which might have confettied onto the boy.

'Let's get him out of here,' said Tamar. 'I want to autopsy him as soon as possible.' Karamata and Van Wyk stepped forward and lifted the body as one would lift a child who had fallen asleep. Tamar closed the lids, shutting Lazarus's dead eyes.

'The body?' asked Clare.

'Back seat,' said Tamar. 'With me.'

The police vehicles, Van Wyk and Tamar in the double cab and Karamata on his quad bike, disappeared over the dune. The hunting bats, flying low over the ground, returned to roost in the large Ana tree where Lazarus had been tied.

'I need to make a call,' Clare said to Helena. 'Can you hang on a minute?'

'Sure,' said Helena. 'Let them get ahead or we'll sit in their dust.'

Clare climbed halfway up a rise, hoping she would get cellphone reception. Nothing. She stood in the scrub, like any other predator, and scanned the dunes. A thickening of the darkness on the opposite dune caught her eye, thudding her heart against her ribs again. The shadow moved, lengthening down the swell of the dune. Then it stopped and Clare heard the eerie chuckle of a brown hyena, a rare and persecuted animal. She exhaled, and watched the animal lope, swift and sure, into the scrub. Its presence meant that people rarely passed through here. It also meant that no body would last long. Half an hour alone, and the soft bits – stomach, buttocks, face – would be gone. The small bones would be ground away, the long bones cracked open for their sweet, nutritious marrow.

The killer must have kept the dead boy somewhere. He had been able to predict where a sleepy girl would go to relieve herself. He had displayed the body just there, so that her torchlight would find his face leering at her. Clare scanned the empty gulley, the motionless trees. He had to know this place. Like the back of his hand. The phrase echoed through Clare's mind as she moved out of the shelter of the trees, climbing to the lip of the dune. One bar. She crossed her fingers for the satellite to be around long enough for her to make her call.

'Faizal,' mumbled Riedwaan. Half asleep. Warm. Naked in bed. Clare pictured him, one sinewy arm over his eyes to keep the morning at bay. The unexpected ache of longing was a knife-twist.

'Riedwaan.' Despite herself, she listened for the muffled sounds of somebody else. 'It's Clare.'

'Baby.' Worry clear as a bell in his voice. 'What's wrong?'

'What did you just call me?' she asked.

'I called you baby. It's … fuck, it's five o'clock in the morning, Clare. Get off your feminist high horse. What's happened?'

'Another boy, Riedwaan.' Clare put her hand to her mouth. 'I spoke to him two days ago. Now he's dead.'

'What is it now? Three? Four?'

'Four. Four bodies. But this one had a 5 carved on his chest. I'm scared it means there's another one out there that no one's found.'

'Where are you?'

'Out in the Kuiseb Delta. Some old military site.'

'Military?' Riedwaan was awake now, his ambiguous conversation with Phiri making his hair stand on end. 'What are you doing there?'

'A couple of bikers found the body,' said Clare. 'Well, a married man and an under-aged babysitter. It must've seemed like the ideal place. It's the middle of nowhere. Someone cut the bike's fuel pipe so they had no choice but to call for help.'

'Is there any connection between that place and the school? The other places where the bodies were dumped?'

'If there is, I'm not seeing it yet,' said Clare. 'Other than whoever is dumping these kids intends them to be found.'

Need and opportunity, she thought: malevolent twin moons that guided the ebb and flow of her killer's mind.

'You have to find some way of connecting these boys and the dump sites,' said Riedwaan. 'If the choice is purely opportunistic, then what does this guy do that allows him to be in the right place at the right time? Then you've got a chance of finding where he's shooting them.'

'Riedwaan, do you know how big this place is? It's like looking for a needle in a haystack.' The desert rolled away from Clare, ashen in the starlight.

'That's your job, Doc,' said Riedwaan. 'Unless this killer is a spook, someone's going to see him sometime.'

'It feels like I'm chasing a ghost sometimes,' said Clare, watching a moth alight on a cluster of creamy blossoms.

'What's the plan now?' asked Riedwaan.

'Captain Damases went back with the body. We'll do the autopsy immediately. I'm going back now with the pathologist.'

'Clare.' Riedwaan's tone softened. Not now, thought Clare. Not here. 'I wanted to tell you ...'

Clare broke off a flower-laden branch from the tree she was standing under. She didn't recognise the species, but the plants that grew in deserts were unique, each evolving to fit some tiny niche. The fragile blossoms smelt of honey, a subtle fragrance as out of place in this harsh place as the delicate, pollen-laden moth that fluttered in the moonlight. She waited.

'It's not what you're thinking. I just—' he started, but the satellite moved, cutting him off.

Clare wiped her hands on her jeans. Her palms left a swirl of Van Gogh yellow against the blue. She looked at the pollen smudge. It clung to her jeans, her hands, her watch strap. It would travel with her no matter how much she tried to rub it off. She thought of the dead boys and the unchartered paths they had followed to their deaths. All the signs they might have left – footprints, hair, skin particles – had been erased by the desert wind and the tenacious insects that fought for survival. Clare looked again at the pollen clinging to her, determined to journey with her on the off-chance that it would brush against a receptive female plant. She felt her pulse quicken as her idea coalesced. If Lazarus had brushed against a tree or a flowering shrub in the Kuiseb Delta, surely the traces of these plants would have adhered to the tiny crevices in his skin or the folds in his clothes. Adrenaline surged through Clare as she thought of the invisible code encrypted on the dead boy. On the others, too: Kaiser, Nicanor, Fritz.

'Clare.' Helena's voice cut through her thoughts. 'Shall we head back? I'll need to get to work on that boy if you're going to have anything to take to Cape Town with you later.'

Clare went to join her, picking a branch of every flowering tree she passed. 'I need to find someone who knows about plants.'

'Tertius Myburgh's your man then,' said Helena, giving her a strange look. 'Plant nut, works at the desert research institute in Swakopmund. Tell him I sent you.'

Helena's bike roared back to life and Clare got on behind her, cradling her bouquet in front of her. They bumped down the track and turned onto the gravel road that would take them back to Walvis Bay. The bike's lights flashed over objects, pulling them towards Clare: an old car wreck, a gnarled tree and a donkey cart clip-clopping along, the driver hunched against the cold, a sleepy huddle of children on the back, lulled by the regular thwack of the leather on the donkey's withers.

Helena parked in the hospital parking lot. Clare needed a hot shower and coffee, but neither of those was going to happen any time soon.

Tamar was waiting for them. 'Lazarus's inside already,' she said, leading the way up the steps of the morgue. 'Elias has gone over to the dump to try to trace his movements.'

'And Van Wyk?' asked Clare.

'At the station with Clinton and Chanel getting statements. His wife and her mother were waiting for them when we arrived,' said Tamar. 'They'd figured it out already.'

'Ouch!' said Clare.

In the antechamber, the three women pulled gowns over their dusty clothes before following Helena into her makeshift mortuary. The sheet draped across Lazarus peaked over his nose, his hands folded across his lacerated chest, over his too-large adolescent feet. In the dim light it looked like the marble tomb of a medieval crusader; then Helena flicked on the lights and he was a dead boy on a dented metal gurney again.

'Okay,' Helena said. 'Shall we start?' She drew back the sheet to reveal Lazarus Beukes, his gangly legs straightened, arms folded, eyes closed.

The scab on his knee was easier to look at than the neat cross bang in the middle of his forehead. Clare turned away, holding her hand up in front of her face. The gun here, ten centimetres from his forehead. Close enough to see each calibration of expression, but calm, contained, without the aggression of the barrel rammed against the flesh, twisting it. For the boy it was all the same, the end. The bullet tunnelling through the brain to lodge against the cradling skull at the back of his head.

Helena worked methodically, undressing and packaging the boy's clothes, recording her initial observations, her soothing tone in stark contrast to the unsettling details she was describing. The amputated tip of the Apollo finger, the 5 scored into the bony chest, the old scars, the new ones, the mapping of a rough and abbreviated life.

'Yes!' said Helena, turning Lazarus over. 'There's no exit wound here.' It took a second for the implication of what she was saying to sink in.

'Are you going to open his head up?' Clare asked, not sure how much time she had to get to Tertius Myburgh before her plane left.

'I am,' said Helena. 'Hang on, Clare. Five minutes and you're free.'

Clare felt the bile rising in her throat as Helena picked up the instruments that would tease the last secrets from Lazarus Beukes's brain. She went over to the window and rubbed one pane clean. With intense concentration she watched the day-shift nurses arrive, ten large women spilling out of the minibus taxi. The doors of the hospital closed on them, silencing their ribald banter. Clare wished the night staff would start their exit procession so that they would distract her from the quiet sawing going on behind her.

There was a low whistle from Helena, followed by a tiny clink. A gasp from Tamar. Then another clink. Clare cursed herself for feeling faint. Helena picked up the bullet in the metal dish with tweezers, rinsing the blood and scraps of brain that clung to the lead. She dropped it into an evidence bag and handed it to Clare. Small, spent, malignant in her hand. Her skin tingled.

'A bullet.' Helena's tired face was triumphant. 'And here's another. Two bullets, one behind the other. Means that the first bullet lodged in the tip of the barrel and was forced out simultaneously with the next shot. So when your killer fired again, Lazarus got two for the price of one.'

Chapter Thirty

FOUR PAIRS OF shoes rested on the back seat next to the labelled bundles of clothes packaged in brown paper, as neat as gifts. Clare's desert bouquet was in the boot. She drove through Swakopmund, a quaint holiday town, thirty kilometres north of Walvis Bay. Its coffee shops displayed dripping slices of Black Forest cake, and its snow-roofed German colonial houses seemed outlandish in the desert. But the street children were the same: wheedling, coaxing or pickpocketing money from flustered, sunburnt tourists. Clare turned towards the copper-domed aquarium, tarnished a Florentine green by the sea air. It was sequestered at the end of the road parallel to the beach.

It was early still and no one was about. Clare had made her way around the back of the building to find the air-conditioned shipping container. She pushed her way into the gloomy interior. The dim, dusty windows and the narrowness of the space gave it the air of a mausoleum. A young man was hunched over a microscope. Long hair curtained his face.

'Dr Myburgh?'

The man turned. His face was narrow, ascetic. He held out a pale, eager hand. 'Dr Hart?' His voice was soft, the hand that enveloped hers warm and dry. 'Tertius Myburgh.'

'I hope I'm not disturbing your work.'

Myburgh smiled and gestured to the phials and jars on his shelves. 'My companions are very quiet, so I'm quite happy with the occasional interruption. Helena Kotze said you'd be coming. What can I do for you?'

Clare put the parcels of shoes and clothes and the posy of desert plants on a trestle table. 'I'm helping with the investigation into the murder of four boys in Walvis Bay,' she said. 'The ones Helena autopsied.'

'Those Aids orphans?'

'A couple of them were, yes. Homeless children.'

'How can I help?' Myburgh looked puzzled.

'Their bodies have been dumped all over the place,' said Clare. 'At a school, on the Walvis Bay pipeline, at the dump. The latest in the Kuiseb Delta. None of them were killed where they were displayed.'

'Ah, you want me to tell you where they've been?' asked Myburgh, fingering the pale blossoms on the table.

'Can you?'

'I can try.' Myburgh's eyes gleamed at the challenge. 'Pollens are unique and they're tenacious. If they brushed a flowering plant, it's going to stick somewhere. Shoes, laces, hoodie ties. Pollen is the most conservative part of the plant. Mutations are rare. That's why we can pinpoint it so accurately. If there's a mutation it's like a red flag, pointing you in the direction of the correct species.'

'How long will it take?' Clare asked.

'This can wait.' Myburgh gestured at the leaves, seed pods and dissected buds arranged on his table. 'But it'll take a day or so.

Plants are like people. It's the little differences that make them unique. What distinguishes one type of pollen from another will be just the tiniest mutation, the smallest difference. With a killer I suppose it's the same: you look for that one calibration of difference that distinguishes him from me ... or you.'

'Those tiny discrepancies,' said Clare, 'that's what I look for.'

'My mother always told me you could judge a man by his shoes,' said Myburgh. 'When you have a suspect, bring me his shoes. They'll tell me where he's been. Take this in the meantime. It's the plant list I've been working on, and here are the corresponding pollens.' He handed her a pile of paper.

'These are beautiful,' said Clare, looking at the magnified photographs of the desert pollens. 'How long have you worked on this?'

'About two years, but most of the groundwork was done by an American ethno-botanist,' said Myburgh.

'He's no longer involved?'

'She,' said Myburgh. 'Virginia Meyer. She was killed in a car accident last year.'

'Oh yes,' said Clare. 'I've heard of her, and I've met her son Oscar. One of the bodies was found at his school. Outside his classroom, in fact.'

'Strange little boy, he is,' said Myburgh. 'He used to do field-work with her. Him and an old Topnaar man called Spyt, who was Virginia's guide. Knows the desert like you and I know our own faces. If you want to know anything about anything in the Namib – plants, stones, animals – he's your man.'

'Where is he now?' asked Clare.

'Spyt?' said Myburgh. 'He could be anywhere. He's even more of a recluse since the accident. He was devoted to Virginia and he loved Oscar.' He paused. 'I suppose Oscar was too young to see how odd Spyt is. All he knew was the magic places Spyt could find in the middle of nowhere.'

Myburgh walked Clare back to her car. 'Give me your cell number. I'll call you as soon as I have something.'

Clare wrote down her number for him. 'There was one more thing I wanted to know,' she said. 'Maybe you can tell me.' She stretched over to open the cubbyhole. The insect husks that Herman Shipanga had found tumbled onto her hand. She was revolted again by the scratchiness of the little ball of carcasses.

'What's that?' asked Myburgh.

'Something else's dinner,' said Clare. 'I was hoping you could tell me more about it.' She handed it to him.

Myburgh peered at the orb. 'Moth wings,' he said. 'And long-horned grasshoppers. Some termites. Where did you find this?'

'The school caretaker found it in the swing where Kaiser Apollis was found.'

'Impossible,' said Myburgh, looking at the insects again. 'You won't find these at the coast. Inland, yes. I'd say this comes from where Egyptian bats have been feeding. They don't need full darkness, so they roost in large trees in the delta; otherwise caves or other shelters.'

'So you'd find them in the Kuiseb?' asked Clare. The importance of what Myburgh was telling her banished her exhaustion.

'Yes,' said Myburgh, 'but they're rare. There's not enough food to sustain more than a few colonies, and the curious thing about bats is that they keep returning to established feeding sites with their prey. Find that, then you know where these little mummies came from.'

Chapter Thirty-one

THE FLIGHT FROM Walvis Bay circled Table Mountain, which stood in isolated splendour above the squalor of the Cape Flats. Clare was first off the plane. She slid her passport across the counter, her mind shuttling between everything she had to do in Cape Town and the fragmented picture she had of events in Walvis Bay.

'This way please, Doctor.' The immigration officer pulled down the grille in front of his booth. He had Clare's passport clasped in his hand.

'What is it?' All she needed now was officiousness about smuggling body parts across international borders.

'Come with me.' He opened a door marked 'Customs', standing aside so that she could enter. Riedwaan was leaning against the wall, his shirt white against his throat.

'Thanks.' Riedwaan was speaking to the customs official, but his eyes were on Clare.

'Any time, Captain.'

'Can I have a look at those?' said Riedwaan. Clare put her assortment of packages on the scuffed table and folded her arms.

'You need anything else, Captain Faizal?' the official asked. Riedwaan shook his head, and the man left, closing the door behind him. Riedwaan picked up the box of samples Helena Kotze had packed for Piet Mouton.

'What are you doing?' Clare hissed.

'I'm here to see you. Like you said. Officially.' Riedwaan opened the door. 'Shall we go?'

'Where are we going?' asked Clare. 'Officially.'

'Security exit. It's much quicker.'

'Riedwaan,' said Clare with an incredulous laugh, 'you know I have appointments.'

'I know. I'm driving you, officially.' He turned to look at her. 'Don't look at me like that. Orders from Phiri.'

'Well,' she snapped, 'I don't really have a choice then, do I?'

'Doesn't look like it to me.' He was relieved that she didn't phone Phiri to check.

Getting her this far was easier than Riedwaan had thought. She got into his old Mazda and he inched through the chaos at domestic arrivals. He turned east along the N2, heading away from Cape Town. So far, so good. He suspected that getting her to talk – or to listen – might be harder.

'Where did your friend at customs spring from?' Clare asked.

'An old friend from my narc squad days. He owed me a favour.'

'I can just imagine.'

'Aren't you going to ask me about my family?' asked Riedwaan.

'After you've practically kidnapped me, does it matter what I do or don't ask?'

'It matters to me,' Riedwaan said. 'Yasmin is my daughter. I love her. And you … Look Clare, I'm sorry about that back there.' He gestured at the space between them. 'All this …' He gave up.

Clare stared at the shabby houses blurring past her window. Her autonomy had been so hard-won; loosening the bonds of her damaged identical twin Constance had left her determined to resist the lure of losing herself again in another person.

'Aren't you going to say anything?' asked Riedwaan, exasperated with her silence.

'You've missed the turning.'

'For fuck's sake.' Riedwaan did a U-turn, bumping over the traffic island. He accelerated across three lanes and took the turn-off to Bellville.

'It's red,' said Clare. Riedwaan braked at the traffic lights. 'There is the tiny issue of your wife, Riedwaan.'

'Why's it so difficult to tell you anything?' he asked, running his hands through his shock of hair.

'What you *didn't* tell me is what matters. You never gave me the chance to decide about things. You just ducked behind the luck that I was going to Namibia. A most convenient coincidence, seeing as you organised me to go there.'

Riedwaan parked in a visitor's bay at the large teaching hospital in Cape Town's northern suburbs. He turned towards Clare, but she spoke before he could say anything: 'We have to work together on this case, Riedwaan. It's just easier if you sort your family situation out yourself.' Clare needed air. She opened the door.

Riedwaan got out too. 'What're you so afraid of, Clare? With people, things are messy. That's how life is.'

'I'm not up to a philosophy lesson, especially if it's just a rehash of what some cheap cop shrink tells you when you drink too much.' Clare picked up her box, holding it like a shield across her chest. 'Let's just stick to the case, shall we?' Easier terrain that, the mechanics of death.

'Explain your case then. Tell me something I don't know.' Riedwaan took the box from her hands. His skin was warm where their hands touched.

Clare snatched her hand away. 'Leave it.' She sounded adolescent, even to herself. 'Let me get this to Mouton.' She marched over to the hospital's forensic pathology entrance.

The rotund security guard at the entrance beamed at her. 'You don't need to sign in if you're with Captain Faizal,' he said. 'He's responsible for you.'

'That'll be a first.' Clare could not help herself.

'The doc's waiting for you, Captain. In the morgue.' The guard waved Riedwaan and Clare towards the lift.

'All I need,' muttered Clare, standing aside as a group of chattering students rushed past. She followed Riedwaan down the corridor. He opened the last door, revealing Dr Piet Mouton bending over his large stomach, his hands careful as he worked on the yielding body laid out in front of him.

'Sorry about this.' Mouton spoke without looking up. 'I'm almost done. Move my tape recorder a bit closer, Faizal man.'

Riedwaan pushed the trolley with Mouton's notes and small black recorder closer to the gurney. Clare made herself look at the naked body on the slab – an elderly woman, ribs pulled open.

Mouton lifted the heart and laid it in a dish. 'Car crashes. I hate them,' he said. 'Make an Irish stew out of anybody, the way people drive. BMW jumped a barrier on the N1. Speedometer at 190 when it jammed.'

Whatever it was Mouton was doing made a horrible sound. Clare looked up at the vaulted windows, light-headed. 'She was driving?' she asked.

'You must be joking. She was just on her way to see her grand-children. The fucker in the BM is fine, just worrying about his insurance and trying to stall a blood alcohol test. You know what it stands for, Faizal? BMW?'

Riedwaan shook his head.

'*Bankrot Maar Windgat*,' said Mouton in disgust. 'So, Dr Hart.' He had always refused to call her Clare. 'Post-mortems are not a spectator sport yet. I presume you want something?'

'Riedwaan told you?' Clare had moved to the window. The sun streaming in did nothing to counter the air conditioning, but she was glad of it; the cold stifled the smell of chemicals and bodily wastes.

'He did.' Mouton went to rinse his hands. He pulled off his gown, releasing his belly from his tight scrubs. 'I don't know who they make these things for. Midgets, I suppose,' he muttered. 'So this Namibian serial killer. You had another victim?'

'Same thing,' said Clare. 'Single gunshot to the forehead, body displayed where it would be found. Outside again, and some time after death. No scavenger marks, so someone was keeping him somewhere.'

Mouton ushered them out of the mortuary and into his adjoining office. He opened a cake tin and offered them each a slice of succulent apple cake. Riedwaan accepted but Clare refused.

She took a sip of the tea that Mouton passed her. It was luke-warm and tasted as if it had been brewing since lunch. She put her cup down.

'We wanted you to look at these.' Clare handed him the four autopsy reports. 'In all the cases there's been a delay between the death and finding the body. I want to find out where they were kept before being displayed.'

'You got a keeper?' Mouton looked up from the reports.

'Seems like it,' said Clare. 'It would help me if I could work out where he was keeping these boys and why. What he was doing with them before he shoots them. And why he waits afterwards.'

'Gunshot wounds. Desert corpse. Mutilation. It's like Namibia when it was still South West Africa, South Africa's Wild West,' said Mouton.

'I'll take a look.'

Riedwaan drove fast, rejoining the cars speeding towards Cape Town. The vivid red sky set off the mass of Table Mountain and Devil's Peak to perfection. Clare felt a pang for the simplicity of the Namibian landscape, composed of horizontals: sea, sand, sky. The Sea Point Boulevard seemed too crowded, the rough swell too boisterous. She wouldn't really feel at home until she had finished her business in Walvis Bay. With Riedwaan, a mountain of unspoken unfinished business lay between them in addition to the silence that had filled the car on the drive back to her apartment.

'Rita asked me to give you these,' said Riedwaan. Clare took the keys he held out. She got out of the car and picked up her scattered belongings from the back seat.

'Give me that,' said Riedwaan, pointing to Clare's evidence box for ballistics. 'I'll drop it with Shorty de Lange. He said he'd look at it for you.' Riedwaan took it from her, his hand brushing against hers. 'You look exhausted.'

'I'm finished,' Clare confessed, before disappearing up the stairs. She picked up an ecstatic Fritz at the door and stopped herself from turning around to watch Riedwaan drive away.

Inside, she ran herself a bath and lay in it, letting the hot water soothe her. She listened to the waves beating against the boulevard, drowning the sound of the evening traffic and the noise in her own head. Her thoughts drifted to Mouton and his plump hands conjuring the secrets from the dead. 'A keeper' he had called this killer.

'Finders were keepers. And losers were weepers,' she said to herself as she towelled her body. She didn't aim to be one of those.

Clare took her supper onto her balcony and watched the filling moon rise up over Devil's Peak, but she didn't see it. Instead, she saw red sand bleeding to ash in the moonlight. The lights of a plane flying over the city transformed, in her mind's eye, into a vehicle, headlights dipping as it summitted her imaginary dunes. The lights vanished, and Clare imagined distant doors opening, slamming shut. A hand on a boy's skinny nape. Comforting in the emptiness. The fingers tightening. The food in his belly a nauseating lump. No struggle in the end.

She put her half-eaten meal aside and went through to her study. From the top of the bookshelf, she pulled down a couple of files with articles on profiling. She flicked through them, reading again about the progression of sadistic complexity that was, in Clare's mind, the hallmark of organised serial killers: the repeated attempts to recreate a fantasy, the perfect blueprint of which existed only in the mind of the killer. The fantasy behind these desert killings, so organised, so similar in outward appearance, had something cursory, something improvised about it which irked. The symmetry of the killings, the trophy-taking, the mutilation of the chest were textbook signs of a copycat killer. But her thoughts chased their own tails, so when the phone rang at nine she pounced on it. It was Mouton.

'What you got, Piet?' she asked.

Mouton got straight to the point. 'Helena Kotze did a good job on Lazarus Beukes and Apollis. The other two are a first-class bugger-up. Looks like they were done by some idiot who wouldn't be able to dissect a frog.'

'I'm not going to contradict that,' Clare said with feeling. 'Can you tell me anything about where they were kept?'

'If they were shot out in the desert?' asked Mouton.

'That's what I'm assuming,' Clare said.

'Then I'd say these boys were kept inside, somewhere where the temperature was even. I checked on the weather,' said Mouton. 'There were some pretty hot inland temperatures around when these boys were missing. Some isolated showers too.'

'That'd explain the termites,' interrupted Clare. 'Sorry, Piet, go on, I was just thinking aloud.'

'You think away, Dr Hart,' continued Mouton. 'Now, if they'd been outside, and someone had been there to keep the predators off them, they would've burnt in that sun.'

'So where should I look?' said Clare.

'A well-insulated house – definitely not one of those tin pondoks. Possibly a deep cave. Somewhere where the temperature would've been constant.'

'That's it?'

'That's it,' he said. 'I hope it helps.'

Clare put down the receiver and walked to the kitchen in a daze. She made tea and took it into the lounge. She put on a CD. She had missed Moby while she was away. 'Where were they?' Clare asked Fritz.

But the cat just purred and curled up like a comma against her back. Clare spread out the photographs of the four bodies and shattered skulls on the coffee table. She stood up, spilling the cat to the floor, and fetched her phone. 'I need to discuss the case with Riedwaan,' she told her baleful cat as she dialled, believing herself.

'Faizal.'

Her heart gave a leap when she heard his voice. 'It's Clare.'

'I know it's you.' Riedwaan was guarded.

'I needed to talk to you ... about the case,' said Clare, watching the sea tumble against the rocks beyond the boulevard.

Riedwaan waited. In the distance, the foghorn wailed into the night. 'Are those the terms? For us to have a conversation?' he asked.

'Mouton called,' said Clare. 'There's a lot to discuss.'

'You're telling me? I'll be there when I can,' he said. 'On your terms.'

Chapter Thirty-two

CLARE LOOSENED HER hair and leant back on the sofa, drifting with the haunting music that filled the room. The sea, moving with repetitive restlessness beyond the grey rocks, lulled her and she gave up trying to archive the fragmented information she had gleaned. Instead, she gave herself over to the pleasure of being at home, cocooned in the textures and views she had chosen. She picked up a celebrity gossip magazine that Rita must have left behind. Five pages of the antics of footballers' wives and she was asleep, her hair tumbling over one outstretched arm.

The hand under Clare's shirt caressed her bare skin. She arched towards it instinctively, fitting her breast into the familiar palm, a tiny involuntary gasp parting her lips as forefinger and thumb teased her sleepy nipple to a rosy peak. She breathed in the familiar smell: the tang of cigarette smoke, cold night air, biker's leather. The low laugh pulled her awake and she brought her knee up hard, the groan telling her she was satisfyingly on target. Clare opened her eyes to see Riedwaan leaning over her. She pushed herself upright, straightening her clothes and pinning up her hair.

Riedwaan sat down beside her, keeping a wary eye on Fritz, who had leapt to a belated but impressive defence of her mistress.

'That was a nice welcome,' he grinned. 'The first bit.'

'How did you get in?' Clare was wide awake now. She sat on the edge of the couch and decided to ignore the self-satisfied smile playing in the corners of Riedwaan's eyes.

'Spare key.' Riedwaan dropped it on the table.

'You copied one?' Clare's skin was fiery where Riedwaan's hand had been. 'You broke in.'

'You could look at it like that, I suppose.'

'What do you mean, you could look at it like that?' she snapped. But she was pleased to see him and he knew it.

'I've brought you a peace offering.'

'What?'

'Coffee and a message from Shorty de Lange,' said Riedwaan. 'He says he's got some news for you.'

'I accept,' she said, holding out her hand for the steaming espresso.

'On one condition.' Riedwaan held the coffee just out of her reach.

'This is like the Gaza Strip,' said Clare. 'First an invasion, then unilateral conditions.'

'It's felt a bit like Gaza to me recently.' Riedwaan ran his fingers along the inside of her arm. 'But the strip sounds good.'

'What's the condition?' asked Clare, folding her arms.

'You stop being so angry with me,' said Riedwaan.

Clare considered, her head on one side. 'Okay,' she capitulated. 'It's late and I'm tired. Give me the coffee and I'll consider an armed truce.'

Riedwaan put the coffee down and pulled her towards him. 'No haggling?'

'I thought you said ballistics had something for me,' said Clare, disentangling herself. 'That was part of the deal.'

'Shorty wants to meet,' said Riedwaan, letting go reluctantly.

'What? Now?' Clare looked at her watch. It was close to eleven.

'Yup. He's waiting.'

The flag above the khaki-green shipping container that served as Cape Town's Ballistic Unit testing range was at half-mast, indicating that the unit was in use. From inside came the muffled thud of bullets. It had to be De Lange. At eleven o'clock, his was the only car left in the parking lot. Riedwaan lit a cigarette and waited. When there was an interval, he banged on the door.

'You still trying to kill yourself, Faizal?' At six foot six, Shorty de Lange looked like a Viking. He pushed open the door, releasing the smell of cordite into the cold night air.

'Sounded like Baghdad in there,' said Riedwaan, grinding his cigarette under his heel.

'Taxis,' said De Lange, 'are worse when they get going. I tell you, they're cooking now. Three shootouts today. Two commuters dead, a little kid shot walking to school. Two drivers. It's a fucking war.' He tucked the AK-47 he had been testing under his arm so that he could lock up.

Clare got out of the car as Riedwaan and De Lange walked over to the low buildings that housed De Lange's office.

'Hi, Shorty,' she said, joining them.

'Clare,' he said, a delighted smile on his face. 'A sight for sore eyes, as always. What a pleasure to see you. You need an Irish coffee?'

'I'd love one.'

De Lange ducked into his office, then took them through to the bar. One wall was covered with pictures of his rugby-playing days. He looked around. 'No kettle,' he said. 'You'll have to settle for whisky.'

'Suits me,' said Riedwaan.

'You pour then, Faizal. One for me too. Here you go, Clare.' De Lange tossed a folder onto the bar counter. He looked pleased with himself.

Clare flicked open the report, excitement flooding through her. She smoothed out the crisp pages. Nobody would accuse De Lange of being talkative, but his pictures were. There were two images of the striations on a bullet. They would match if you over-laid the one with the other in the same way as a fingerprint would. The concentric patterns were the unique print of the gun from which they had been fired.

'Where did you get this?' she asked.

'There's more.' De Lange unrolled a long sheet of white paper. The image spread out on the table was an explosion of colourful lines, branching off from clusters of dates and place names.

'What is this?' asked Clare. 'A family tree?'

'It is, in a way,' said De Lange. 'Although a tree of death would be a better way of describing it. I told you I've been working on the gang wars. I started mapping them to see if I could link specific firearms to different crime scenes. This one was done during an upsurge of fighting about drug turf and taxi routes. I fed your bullets from Wal-vis Bay into our computer system, and, bang, this is what came up.' He pointed to a small gold star on a branch that ended in a cul-de-sac.

'All on its own?' Clare leaned in to decipher De Lange's writ-ing. 'In McGregor? Who was it?'

'I don't usually ask,' said De Lange. 'If I start with a name, then next thing I've got a wife and kids crying and then objectivity is in its moer.' He pushed the docket towards Clare. 'I pulled this for you, though. Ex-army. A Major Hofmeyr found in a vineyard off the main road into McGregor a few years ago. His car was left at the farm entrance, and two little girls found him at midday. He'd been dead for a few hours already. According to the pathologist he was shot at about seven in the morning.'

Clare paged through the thin report. There wasn't much to go on. Major Hofmeyr was survived by his wife and daughter, but there were very few details for such a gruesome killing. 'No evidence?' Clare looked up at De Lange.

'No tracks, no witnesses. Nothing.'

'Nothing except a bullet embedded in the tree where Hofmeyr's body was found,' Riedwaan pointed out.

'The police speculated a gang killing, maybe an initiation,' said De Lange. 'He was tortured. His skin was carved up, all over. It hung in ribbons, looked like broekie lace.'

Clare turned to the crime-scene photographs. A man's body was slumped against the tree, blood and flies crusting the shattered forehead and lacerated chest. 'Hofmeyr must've welcomed the final shot when it came,' she said, looking at the skin hanging from his fit soldier's body.

'Could've been a hired gun,' Riedwaan said to De Lange. 'What does it cost now, a weekend special on the Flats? Fifty bucks to hire, ammo thrown in?'

'Pretty much,' said De Lange. 'But how did it get to Walvis Bay?'

'A gun like that could easily make its way up the West Coast,' said Riedwaan. 'The border is as porous as a sieve, so it could be in Walvis Bay in a couple of days.'

'I've thought of it,' said De Lange. 'But I've never seen this before or since. It bothered me, this one. That's why I kept a copy of the docket.'

'What bothered you?' asked Clare.

'Same thing that bothered Februarie, the officer who investigated the case. The ammunition,' said De Lange. 'Full metal jacket. That's professional. It's what the security industry uses, the military. Not drug lowlife.'

'We'll check it out tomorrow,' said Clare. 'Talk to his wife. Is she still in McGregor?'

De Lange nodded. It seemed he knew more about surviving relatives than he cared to admit. 'Keep those then,' he said, pouring himself another whisky. 'You go ahead. I've got some things to finish.'

IT WAS NEARLY one o'clock before Clare and Riedwaan were back on the empty highway. 'Does he ever go home?' Clare asked.

'No,' Riedwaan replied. 'He's looking for the gun that killed her.'

The whole force knew that the murder of De Lange's wife had nearly killed him too. She'd been shot in a botched hijacking over a year ago. 'He's convinced that once he gets *that* gun,' said Riedwaan, 'then he's got the tik-head who killed her, and his life will be what it was before. In the meantime, he's trying to keep track of every stray bullet in the Cape.'

'Which works for us,' said Clare, looking out at the cityscape. Compared to the desert sky the few visible stars were faint, eclipsed by the carpet of streetlights and the flashing neon signs.

'We'll see.' Riedwaan parked in front of Clare's apartment.

His hand on the back of her neck stopped her from opening the car door. He turned to look at her, his face faceted by the orange glow of the street lamp. He brushed his thumb across her full bottom lip, silencing her protest.

'I missed you,' he said, moving his hand down her neck, seeking out the hollow at the base of her throat, down further, his hands on her breasts, knowing, peaking her nipples beneath his palms. Clare closed her eyes. Riedwaan's skin was warm against hers as he kissed eyes, ears, mouth, tunnelling desire through her. She put her hands on his chest, felt his breath coming sharper, faster. Gathering what was left of her will, she pushed him away.

'I can't do this.' Clare yanked the door open and got out. She stood on the pavement, her arms folded across her chest. Riedwaan looked straight ahead at the Atlantic hurling itself at the rocks.

'You're coming to McGregor tomorrow?' she asked. She was starting to shiver.

'I'll pick you up at six.' Riedwaan started the car. Still Clare stood on the pavement. 'Go in,' he said. 'I can't leave till you're inside.'

'I ...' Clare started.

'You what?'

'I ... I'll see you later.' She disappeared up the staircase.

When her bedroom light came on, Riedwaan drove home. He let himself in to his empty house and sat down in his only chair. He couldn't decide which maudlin cliché suited him better: Leonard Cohen or Tom Waits. So he sat and smoked until the dawn call to prayer crackled from the mosque down the road.

Chapter Thirty-three

CLARE WAS READY and waiting when Riedwaan fetched her at five-thirty. Dressed in a black poloneck, black trousers, her hair tamed, lipstick in place, she had the carapace of her professional self firmly back in place.

Riedwaan took the N1 through the dilapidated fringes of Cape Town towards the forbidding mountains that were the gateway to the interior. McGregor was eighty kilometres beyond them. The sun was up, stirring the hamlet awake, when they reached it. Smoke wisped from the crowded houses on the eastern edge of town. Higher up the hill, larger houses were spread out around a sturdy white church. A few children in sports uniforms were chattering their way to school along the main road.

'Voortrekker Road.' Riedwaan read the sign in disbelief. 'This is like a movie set. No burglar bars. No armed response. How do they sleep?'

'I'm with you. You'll survive,' said Clare. 'Lie your urban hackles down.'

'I don't like it.' Riedwaan tapped his fingers as he waited for an old lady to coax her moth-eaten terrier across the road. 'It's like the whole place is waiting for something to happen.'

'Something did happen. Why else would we be here?'

'Connecting things will be tricky,' said Riedwaan. 'If there is a connection.'

'It's worth a shot, so to speak,' said Clare. 'Mill Street. Turn here.'

Goedgevonden was the last house. A low, dry-packed wall kept the flinty Karoo scrub out of the lush garden. They hadn't called. Clare and Riedwaan preferred to see people without warning, before the battlements of the self could be checked for a breach.

'That's a welcome mat, not a dog,' said Riedwaan, ringing the bicycle bell on the gate as a German Shepherd ambled over to the gate and whined. A woman straightened up from her rose bed behind the wall.

'Mrs Hofmeyr?' asked Riedwaan.

The woman who approached, secateurs glinting in her hand, was maybe fifty-five, her iron-grey bun severe. She looked at Clare, took Riedwaan in.

'Can I help you?'

The dog was at its mistress's side with a single click of her fingers, its eyes wary. Not such a doormat after all.

'I'm Riedwaan Faizal, SAPS special investigations. This is Dr Clare Hart. It's about your husband Captain Hofmeyr.'

Mrs Hofmeyr squinted into the sun. 'Have you got new evidence?' she asked.

'Not exactly,' Riedwaan replied. 'But we need to speak to you to find out.'

'If you've driven from Cape Town, I'm sure you'll need some coffee. Come into the kitchen. We can talk more privately there.'

They followed her inside and sat down at a scrubbed yellow-wood table. The coffee pot hissed on the stove. *Moerkoffie.* Mrs Hofmeyr slipped a doily off the milk jug. Its little fringe of glass beads clicked in the silence, disturbing the cat coiled asleep on a blue cushion. The animal took one look at Riedwaan and arched its back and hissed.

'What is it with me and cats?' Riedwaan muttered.

'Rasputin isn't used to visitors,' said Mrs Hofmeyr, stroking the cat's gun-metal coat.

'We need to ask you some questions about Captain Hofmeyr's death,' said Clare. Murder was too brutal a word for the ordered domesticity of the room.

'Major Hofmeyr,' corrected his widow. 'Why do you want to stir it up again?'

'I'm very sorry,' said Clare, 'but we suspect that the weapon used to shoot your husband has been used in another crime.'

'How awful,' whispered Mrs Hofmeyr, bringing her hand to her mouth. 'Near here?'

'In Namibia,' said Riedwaan. 'Walvis Bay.'

Mrs Hofmeyr frowned. 'What happened?'

'Four shootings,' said Riedwaan. 'It'd be a great help if you could tell us what happened to your husband.'

'I've already told everything to the police, but all right. He was shot in the head. Close range, single pistol shot. I identified him.' Mrs Hofmeyr trembled, but there were no tears. She had used up her quota long ago. 'He looked so young again when I saw him. All those years gone. A life erased.'

'What time did he leave the house?' asked Clare.

'Early. Before seven, I'd say. I was asleep when he left. When I woke at seven-thirty the tea he had left for me was ice cold.' She twisted her cup in its saucer. 'Who would want to torture him?'

Riedwaan could think of quite a few people who might want to leave a trellis of knife wounds on a man who had commanded a special operations unit during the dirtiest years of South Africa's war in Namibia. Hearts and minds. You could say that Hofmeyr's killer got both. He didn't say that.

'One of the officers here said it was gangsters,' said Mrs Hofmeyr. 'People in the village said some 28s had been here.'

The number gangs. South Africa's apocryphal grim reapers, trailing fear and destruction in their wake. Sliding like a knife through the soft underbelly of a country where all felt their houses to be chalked with crosses, where the vultures of fear circled above the living. The perfect slipstream for another kind of killer, well dressed, without tinted windows, to follow. He would have been smoke against a heat-whitened sky, invisible until the roar of the flames was too close. If he existed.

'They never traced them?' asked Riedwaan.

'No,' said Mrs Hofmeyr, acidly. 'How often do the police find anyone?'

Riedwaan shifted in his chair. He had no answer for that.

'What did he do, Major Hofmeyr, with his time?' Clare changed tack. 'After the army?'

'Rugby-coaching at the school. He'd started teaching science too. He was a physicist. The army was good to ambitious Afrikaners born on the wrong side of the tracks. Teaching science was his way of saying sorry for what happened' – she hesitated – 'for what happened before.'

'He see anyone from his army days?'

'Not really. He was a loner. After Bishop Tutu's thing, the dust settled and we didn't see anyone much. I suppose they didn't need each other any more, didn't need to check up on who was going to say what. Sometimes his old army friends would come through, drink a bit, hunt a bit in season, but other than that the past just went away. We were quiet here. I liked it like that.' She twisted the obsolete wedding ring on her left hand.

'I'm sorry to bring up the past,' said Clare.

Mrs Hofmeyr shook her head. 'Where does it start? That's what I never know about the past. Kobus was a soldier. The army was his life and 1994 was the end of it. Is that the beginning or the end of the past?'

'That's why you came to McGregor?' Clare asked.

'I don't think my husband cared where he went. He just came here to wait until his heart stopped beating.'

'Depression?'

Mrs Hofmeyr batted the word away with a dismissive hand. 'Psychological labels. Human beings aren't bottles of jam. Depressed, obsessive compulsive, paranoid. Giving it a name doesn't make it feel any different.'

'He came out of it?' Clare guessed.

Mrs Hofmeyr looked up at her, surprised. 'He did. Slowly. Despite himself. It helped that our daughter came to visit with her baby from Australia. The first time they had spoken in fifteen years, but not even he could fight with a baby. It was as if some knot inside him loosened, released the man I had married. I don't know. He kept on worrying about the world, about terrorists and bombs, and about what could happen to his *skattebol*.'

'What was he like, your husband?' asked Clare.

Mrs Hofmeyr sighed as she cleared away the coffee cups. 'If you want a sense of my husband, go and look at his den.' She opened the kitchen door and gestured down the passageway. 'I suppose you could say that is what his world shrunk to.'

Apart from the kitchen, the house was dim. The shutters were closed, the curtains drawn. It had the stillness of a museum. Clare opened a door off the passage. A masculine seclusion, free of ornaments. It was irresistible. She stepped inside. The desk was clean, the letter opener and pen standing in quartz holders. A perfect desert rose on an ugly little plinth held down a pile of till slips. Clare checked the dates. All from a few days before Hofmeyr was killed: bottle store, DIY, cigarettes and a paper from the café. Next to the desk was a hollowed-out elephant's foot. A trophy hunt. Caprivi, Kaokoland, Angola. Clare wondered where the helicopters had hovered, machine-gun bullets studding into the fleeing animals below. She pictured the elephant cows herding their panic-stricken young towards the tree line. One sinking to her knees as her calf nudged her with his forehead, then retreated and watched as the men, laughing, hopped down to hack off the cow's foot as the last light in her wise eyes was extinguished. Then again, the murdered man could just as easily have bought it in a junk shop and brought it home for a laugh.

One wall was covered with photographs. Clare went to look at them. A 1960s wedding picture. Later, Mrs Hofmeyr in a halter-neck top, a baby in her arms. Then another baby, the first child now a thoughtful little boy bracketed around his mother's slim legs. Another photo showed a sturdy young woman on a speed-boat, a greying Major Hofmeyr grinned next to her.

'My daughter,' said Mrs Hofmeyr, coming to stand next to Clare. 'She moved to Australia.'

'They seem happy here,' said Clare.

'They were,' Mrs Hofmeyr replied. 'Eventually.'

Clare guessed that politics would have come between them. A father with a decorated career in the defence force of the apartheid years did not go down well in the new South Africa.

Mrs Hofmeyr trailed a finger across a picture of her husband saluting troops on a dusty parade ground. The undulating sweep of sand was unmistakable. Strange, though, to see the vast plain covered with tents. They seemed to stretch from horizon to horizon, a regatta of triangular khaki sails on a sea of sand.

'Walvis Bay?' asked Clare.

'Where else? It looks so different now,' said Mrs Hofmeyr.

'How long were you there for?'

'You want me to give you the hours and seconds? The heartbeats?' Her bitterness flared, a naked flame. 'We were there from 1989 to 1994. Five years, three months and eleven days. Before that at the weapons testing site in Vastrap in the Northern Cape. God knows what we were supposed to do there in the middle of the Kalahari Desert. No people. No trees. Nothing but heat and dust and secrets. Not a place to go if you had a family.'

The large photograph hanging behind the door caught Clare's attention. She stopped, arrested by the photograph of Major Hofmeyr. Lithe and brown, his eyes the blue of the sky above the dune rising in a majestic sweep behind him. Three soldiers, equally confident, were draped over a dusty Bedford. The man next to Hofmeyr, his swagger evident in his muscular, khaki-clad legs, had a hard face. The third one was as thin as a whip, his expression shadowed by his cap.

'That was Kobus's unit.' Mrs Hofmeyr pointed to the date on the bottom. 'It was taken when they were disbanding. This was the last picture of all of them before they returned.'

'They came back then?'

'Kobus and a couple of officers wrapped up the last things, then came back. The troops returned by truck and on the train.'

'You know them? The others?' Riedwaan asked.

Mrs Hofmeyr shook her head. 'Kobus kept us separate, me and his life.' She stood closer to the photograph. 'I can't remember their names.' She pointed to the shadowed figure. 'He came to the house sometimes near the end. He and Kobus would talk. He never said anything to me. This one' – she pointed at the man next to Hofmeyr – 'had such a young wife. She was a dancer before she married.' She frowned at the tug of memory. 'Maylene or Marlene was her name. Something unusual.'

Clare pictured a house on the edge of the dunes. A bracelet of bruises. 'Not Darlene?' she asked.

'That was it: Darlene. Her husband stamped on her ankle at a party. He said she'd been flirting. She never danced again.'

Darlene walking down a dim, polished passage. The awkward gait. A surname jettisoned to mark the end of a marriage. 'She's still there,' said Clare.

'In Walvis Bay?' Mrs Hofmeyr was appalled. 'I suppose it was the only way she could escape her husband.'

'You never went back?' asked Riedwaan.

'Never. Neither did my husband. There was nothing left for him there. Or the others. They all got sent home to garden and become security guards in the new South Africa.' She stood transfixed by the picture as if it were a cobra weaving in front of her. 'He said it was better to leave things in the past, where they belonged. Walvis Bay was the place where all his dreams died. Fool's gold is what he called the past.' Mrs Hofmeyr tapped the photograph of her husband standing in a typical soldier's pose, unfiltered cigarette in his hand. 'A fool,' she said. 'They were all fools.'

'Did your husband keep any kind of record of his time there?' asked Riedwaan.

'Never. He kept everything in his head. Habit from working with classified stuff. He was proud of the fact that he remembered everything even though he wrote nothing down.'

They stood looking at the fading photographs. Deep within the house, a clock chimed ten.

'There's nothing else,' said Mrs Hofmeyr, 'is there?'

'HE NEVER FOUGHT back.' Clare broke the silence of the journey. They had travelled from McGregor to the outskirts of Cape Town without saying a word.

'Hofmeyr?' Riedwaan's thoughts had been elsewhere.

'There were no injuries. No defensive injuries. You think he wanted to die? Just gave up?'

'It's possible he felt certain he was going to die and decided just to go with it, without the ritual of begging and pleading and trying to run away,' Riedwaan suggested. 'Or he knew his killer and he'd reached the end of a road that only the two of them knew about. The war in Namibia was a dirty one, and most of the dirt was brushed under the carpet.'

'That's not much help, is it?' Clare played with the new puzzle pieces Mrs Hofmeyr had given her. 'I guess we should talk to Darlene Ruyters again. Find out about her ex-husband.' There were links, but no perfect fits. 'She's not very forthcoming, though. If she knows something, I doubt she'll talk.'

'Let's go and talk to the investigating officer, if he's sober enough.'

'You know him?'

'Eberard Februarie. Old connection,' said Riedwaan, taking the Stellenbosch turn-off. 'I probably owe him a drink anyway.'

Chapter Thirty-four

THE STELLENBOSCH POLICE station was quiet when Clare and Riedwaan arrived. Clare waited in the car while Riedwaan went inside to extricate the officer who had worked on the Hofmeyr case.

'Where's Captain Februarie?' he asked a bored-looking constable in the tea room. Talking to Eberard Februarie always cheered him up. No one had hit rock bottom at quite the same speed as the former narcotics unit captain.

'Out.' The woman ate another biscuit.

'Out where, Constable?' said Riedwaan, patiently.

'Are you a cop?' She looked him up and down.

'I suppose you think I dress this badly for fun?' said Riedwaan. The constable looked at him blankly. 'Of course I'm a cop. Captain Faizal.'

'Captain Februarie's investigating a case.'

'Which case?'

'He didn't write it on the board.' It was true. Everybody else had a neatly printed note next to their names on the whiteboard. Everybody except Februarie, that is.

'Can I have his cell number?'

'Sure.' The constable flipped through a grimy file. It was the wrong file. She found the right file. Found the right page. Found the number. Found a pencil. Found a piece of paper. Wrote it down. When she looked up to give it to Riedwaan, he was gone. She shrugged and went back to her tea.

Riedwaan and Clare were already three blocks away. The chances of Februarie not being at the Royal Hotel on a Saturday morning were minimal. Riedwaan pushed open the saloon doors, letting Clare precede him. It was dim inside the bar. The smell of last night's drinking hung on the air. There was only one cigarette going: Februarie's. He was sitting in the corner, a Castle lager in front of him.

Riedwaan sat down on the stool next to him. 'Breakfast?' he asked.

'Faizal, you fucker. What are you doing here?'

'Come to see you. You're looking good.' It was not quite true. But Riedwaan had seen him look much worse at this time of day.

'I'm cutting back, man. This is my first.'

'Why don't you just stop?' asked Riedwaan.

'Not good to rush things,' said Februarie. 'You can shock your system. That's not healthy.'

'This is Clare Hart,' said Riedwaan, his hand on Clare's elbow.

'Hello,' said Clare.

Februarie looked her over, taking in her slim figure, the determined set to her jaw. 'The head-case doctor. I've heard about you,' he grunted. 'I didn't know they only let you out under guard these days, Faizal.'

'As charming as ever,' Riedwaan retorted. He ordered a Coke for himself and a soda for Clare and waited for the barman to leave. 'The constable said you were working on a case.'

'Of course I'm working on a case. I'm always working on a case. Someone's bicycle will be stolen any minute, then I'll have another case. You?'

'No, I'm working too.'

'You're lucky they left you in town, man. This exile story is terrible. It'll kill you quicker than cigarettes.'

Riedwaan took the hint and offered him one. Februarie took two.

'You want something, Faizal? Or is this just a social call?'

'We wanted to ask you about a case.'

'So, ask.' Februarie inhaled deeply, then coughed.

'You sound like you're going to die, Februarie.'

'I told you, it's being out here in the countryside. It's unhealthy.'

'Tell us about that shooting in McGregor,' said Clare.

'The army major? Hofmeyr?' Februarie asked. He shifted his eyes from Riedwaan to Clare. Sharp. Calculating. In spite of the drink. 'Why you asking?'

'I'm on a case in Namibia. Looks like a serial killer,' said Clare. 'But the bullet found in the head of one of the boys threw up a match with Hofmeyr.'

'Shorty de Lange tell you that?' Februarie guessed.

'He did,' said Riedwaan.

'All I know is they pulled that case from me quicker than a virgin crosses her legs.' Februarie drained his glass.

'You think it was a gang hit?' Clare asked.

'Nah,' said Februarie. 'Andrew,' he called the barman over. 'Pour me another beer; you're not pretty enough to be useful just standing around.' He turned to Riedwaan again. 'I thought it was something else. They tortured him first. It looked professional to me, not the usual mess a tik-head leaves. Whoever did it wanted something specific.'

'Have you got any idea what?' asked Riedwaan.

Februarie shrugged. 'He was in the army. Old regime. Special ops. He probably knew stuff. They all did, those fuckers. The list of people who want them dead is longer than the list that wants them alive.'

'What did he know?'

'I'm speculating. The case was pulled, I told you. Some desk jockey said they were shifting it higher. Giving it priority.'

'What happened?'

'Don't fuck with me, Faizal. You know what happens when that happens. The case dies.'

Februarie drank his beer. Riedwaan drank his Coke. Clare watched them.

'There was one thing,' Februarie said at last.

'I thought there might be,' said Riedwaan. 'You follow it up?'

'Of course I did.' Februarie was affronted. 'That's when the case was kicked upstairs and I got stolen-bicycle duty.'

'Sorry.' Riedwaan put down enough money to cover the drinks. 'What was it?'

'They were army,' Februarie continued. 'The killers.'

'How do you know?' asked Clare.

'The way he was tortured. They used to do that in Namibia. To insurgents, if they caught them. To civilians, if they were bored.'

Riedwaan was quiet.

'So watch your back in Walvis Bay,' muttered Februarie.

'That's touching,' said Riedwaan. 'You find out anything else?'

'After I got taken off the case?'

'Ja.'

'Sommer for the cause of justice?' said Februarie.

'Something like that.'

'Do I look like I have a death wish? My life might look like a fuck-up, but it's the only one I've got.'

Riedwaan waited. He and Februarie went back a long way and he had learnt to read the man's silences. The barman went to the other end of the counter to serve a new customer.

'I've got an old friend,' said Februarie. 'She did a search for me. Nothing on Hofmeyr. Fuck-all in any army record, old or new.' He looked up at Riedwaan. 'Funny that, for a decorated major, wouldn't you say?'

'Hilarious,' said Riedwaan.

'His unit's there on the record,' said Februarie. 'But no Major Hofmeyr. No fellow officers either, those ones you'll find in the picture in his study. Erased, all of them.'

'So you gave up?'

'Nearly,' said Februarie, finishing his beer.

'Then I found a footnote in one of those truth and reconciliation cases that went nowhere. Some secret weapons-testing site up north.'

'Yes?' said Riedwaan.

'There was a reference to this covert unit in Walvis Bay. There was a Hofmeyr there. A major. He and a couple of friends were implicated. The whole thing folded, so nothing more was heard about Major Hofmeyr.'

'Until he was shot.'

'Exactly,' said Februarie. 'Until he was shot.'

'I owe you,' said Riedwaan.

'You want me to check out his friends?' asked Februarie.

'Depends how many bicycles get stolen.'

'Fuck you too, Faizal.' Februarie counted the money Riedwaan had left on the bar and ordered another beer.

THE GATHERING CLOUDS had thickened when Clare and Riedwaan got outside. It was starting to drizzle.

'I'll be in Walvis Bay in a day or two,' Riedwaan said. 'I'll see what I can find out by then.'

Clare checked her watch. 'I hope I'm going to make it to the airport,' she said.

'You *are* going to make it,' said Riedwaan. There had been an accident on the highway. Rubbernecking drivers had slowed the traffic to a crawl. He pulled in to the emergency lane and speeded past, siren blaring.

'I always wondered why you kept that thing,' said Clare, with a smile.

'You're going to make it,' said Riedwaan, taking the plunge, 'without asking me a single question.'

'I need to think,' said Clare. 'It's not making sense. It could be that the gun used to kill Hofmeyr was sold or stolen. Male victims, there's a match, I suppose, but Hofmeyr was cut up before he was shot.'

'I wasn't thinking about Hofmeyr.'

'I know,' said Clare, 'it's those boys that get me.'

The rain started to come down in earnest, making it difficult to see through the windscreen.

'I was thinking about us,' said Riedwaan.

'Don't start again,' said Clare, holding her hands up. 'This is your thing, your wife here, all that. Why must I take the responsibility for talking about it?'

Riedwaan took the airport turn-off, parking outside the international departure drop-in. He turned to face Clare. 'She never came.'

Clare glanced at her watch again. She had five minutes before check-in closed. 'Why didn't you say anything?'

'I tried to talk to you,' said Riedwaan. 'I've e-mailed you, but you disappear behind work and theories and business.' He stopped, startled at this uncharacteristic burst of articulateness. It was a mistake. Clare opened the car door, slipping her bag over shoulder and the thin Hofmeyr file underarm.

'You know this whole debacle could've been avoided if you'd just said something in the beginning?'

'I know.' Riedwaan's dark eyes flashed with the temper he had been keeping in check. 'And you wouldn't give me an inch. I'm trying to fix things, with Shazia, with my daughter.' Riedwaan got out of the car too. He leant on the roof, his eyes on Clare until she looked away. 'With you too,' he said softly.

'Riedwaan, it's not going to fix, especially not in the five minutes I have before the flight is closed. Just forget it. Let's just get this case done.' Clare was through the automatic doors before Riedwaan could say another word. They closed behind her, leaving him with nothing but his own reflection and a couple of porters shaking their heads in sympathy.

'Women,' said one of them mournfully.

'Women,' agreed Riedwaan.

FIVE O'CLOCK THE next morning and Riedwaan was throwing a couple of pairs of jeans, four clean shirts and underwear into the bike's pannier. He wheeled his bike into the cobbled street. The foghorn wailed as the sea mist stole through the sleeping suburbs fringing the Atlantic. In the distance, the whine of a car or two. Clubbers heading home, Riedwaan's favourite time of day. He fired the bike's engine. Two minutes and he was on the elevated freeway above the harbour, where construction cranes, still as herons at the water's edge, waited for the day's activity to return.

Riedwaan accelerated north where the road ribboned into the clear morning. He had hairpinned up the first mountain pass by the time the sun was up, the roar of the bike lifting his mood.

It was getting hot when he refuelled. Riedwaan checked his map. A hundred or so kilometres to the Namibian border.

An hour later, he was through the border and driving through the emptiness of southern Namibia. Marooned in the desert, a thousand kilometres northwest, was Walvis Bay.

Chapter Thirty-five

In the cool sanctuary of his laboratory, thirty kilometres north of Walvis Bay, Tertius Myburgh picked up a cloth and wiped down his microscope, though his equipment was immaculate. His prepared solutions waited for him, labelled, ordered. His heart beat faster. It always did before he plunged into the secret world of plants. He set to work on the pathetic bundles Clare Hart had brought. The dead boys' shoes were covered in pollen. Invisible hieroglyphs that mapped the journeys they had made.

He prepared his first slide and placed it on the stage, leaning in to the eyepiece and adjusting the lens to bring the grains of pollen into focus. He exhaled. They floated before him, the cellulose grains that carried the fragile male plants to a waiting female, if there was one. More often, they were stranded on unreceptive surfaces. Like a murdered boy's shoes. Myburgh prepared another slide, then another, and another. He matched the pollen grains against what he already had, checking off the species that flowered in response to the desert's waterless spring.

No *Sarcocornia*. The humble, stubby-fingered plant grew in profusion in the shallow, saline water around the lagoon and in the river mouths along the coast. It occurred for about two kilometres inland. If there was none on the boy's shoes, then it meant that their Calvary was further inland.

Plenty of *Tamarix* pollen. Not surprising, as tamarisks grew in profusion in the Kuiseb. They also grew from Cape Town to Jerusalem. He would need more.

There were traces of *Acanthosicyos horridus*, the seasonal !nara plant that crept from the Orange River in the south over the dunes to the Kuiseb. The spiny melons provided food for the Topnaars, the desert people, and their animals, and the inherited stands were as valuable as the secret sources of water in the desert. Myburgh paused to admire their distinctive pollen walls covered with exquisite striations, which, under his microscope, looked as if someone had drawn meditative fingers through sand.

He found *Trianthema hereroensis* pollen, a tough plant that occurred from the Kuiseb River for about a hundred and fifty kilometres to the north. The overlap of the plant distribution was bang on the Kuiseb Delta.

Myburgh was beginning to see the outline of a map for Clare Hart, but he needed more coordinates. One distinctive, triangular pollen pattern eluded him. There were traces of it on all four pairs of shoes. He checked back through Clare's samples.

Nothing.

He picked up Mannheimer and Dreyer's classic *Plants and Pollens of the World* and flicked through, finding the matching pattern that would help him place the pollen. Fear dry-tonguing his neck, Myburgh propped a ladder against the bookcase so that he could reach the top shelf, which held the stained, cloth-bound book that he had hidden months earlier and tried to forget. He opened Virginia Meyer's blue journal. It was still filled with her detailed drawings, her cramped notes on ethno-botany, gleaned from Spyt, the wary old Topnaar man who had shared what he knew about the plants of the Namib, the desert's secret treasure trove. Myburgh paged through it until he came to the last page of entries. Times, abbreviations, Latin names. He ignored those. Instead, he cracked the book open and swabbed the margin. He wiped what he had collected onto a glass slide. A thin yellow smear appeared down the centre of the pane. He placed this on the microscope's stage, the eyepiece cold against his skin once more. His hands shook as he adjusted the lens. They appeared with magical precision, the distinctive triangular pollen grains, perfect equilateral triangles.

Myrtaceae: *Eucalyptus*. The ghost gum.

The scientist lifted his head and stared at the surf. He heard again Virginia Meyer's soft voice, telling him of secrets too dirty, conspiracies too complex, which she had unearthed in the heat-raddled desert. He closed his eyes and pressed his palms against his lids, but he failed to block the memory of a car upturned, its wheels spinning against the blue sky.

In the back, the boy Oscar sits in wordless terror. In the front, his mother's life trickles down her face, into her hair, the same colour as the boy's halo of curls. It runs into her unblinking eyes, over her hands and pools on the floor. Eventually, it seeps into the orange sand at the base of a tall alien tree.

Myburgh shook off the memory with an effort and returned to his desk to type up his findings, the routine of recording method, results and conclusions soothing him. He printed the document and put it into a large envelope with the journal. He thought for a long time about what his discovery might mean for pretty Dr Hart; then he locked his laboratory and slipped away, taking care not to be seen.

Chapter Thirty-six

CLARE PARKED NEXT to Tamar's car when she got to the Walvis Bay police station on Monday morning. She was impatient to be busy after the town's Sunday torpor. The constable at reception greeted her as though she had been gone for weeks. Clare could see a strip of light coming from Tamar Damases's office. She knocked and went inside.

'How was your Cape Town trip?' Tamar asked, after offering Clare a cup of tea.

'Interesting,' said Clare.

'Chinese interesting?' Tamar gave her a sidelong glance.

'Pretty much,' said Clare, with a rueful smile. 'Ballistics tracked that bullet we found in Lazarus Beukes.'

'To the murder in McGregor. Peculiar,' said Tamar. 'I spoke to Captain Faizal.'

'Same gun,' said Clare, 'doesn't make it the same killer. Guns change hands so fast and for so little. How were the interviews about Lazarus?'

'No family, so no one to break the news to,' said Tamar. 'Should have been a relief that, but it made me feel worse. The other kids told me he was in town on Wednesday, doing his usual trick, selling out-of-date newspapers. The little kids who were with him went back to the dump. They don't get a meal if they're late. Lazarus said he'd be along later. He wasn't, but nobody thought much of that. He's older, did his own thing anyway.'

'Did they notice he was missing on Thursday?' asked Clare.

'They did. They were afraid.'

'But nobody said anything?'

'Habits don't change that quickly,' Tamar said. 'They're boys for one, so no telling tales. And second, the police give them a hard time. Particularly some of my own colleagues.' She rose and picked up her jacket. 'I'm going to the school. Mr Erasmus has asked me to talk to the Grade 1s. They all want to know what we did with the body, if we're going to catch the murderer. If they're safe. Would you like to come with me?'

'I'll come,' said Clare, finishing her tea. 'I want to see Darlene Ruyters anyway.'

Tamar picked up her keys and they walked out together. 'You missed Mara Thomson's farewell party, by the way,' she told Clare. 'The school hosted a little ceremony for her.'

'How did it go?'

'Sad, considering the circumstances. I think she felt that everything she'd worked for came to nothing.'

THEY ARRIVED AT the school at the end of first break. Tamar parked under the palm tree as the bell rang. Erasmus came out to welcome them while the older children drifted back to class.

He directed them to the section of the school that overlooked the playground where Kaiser Apollis's body had been found. The corridor that housed the youngest children was crowded with satchels and pungent lunchboxes. Solemn-faced six-year-olds dropping glass, paper and tins into recycling bins stared at them as they walked to Darlene Ruyters's classroom. It had a clear view of the playground, the emptied yellow swings slow-moving in the breeze.

Darlene Ruyters sat at her desk, her right arm around a plump, pig-tailed girl. The child spun around when she saw Clare and Tamar at the door. Darlene patted the little girl on her bottom, despatching her back to her seat.

'Good morning, Captain, Doctor.' Darlene extended her slender right hand. The children shuffled to their feet and greeted the two interlopers in a singsong chorus. A wave from Darlene seated them again.

'Finish your seascapes,' she told the class. Small heads bowed over sheets of colourful paper. After a few furtive glances, they were absorbed once more in scissors and glue and bits of glitter. As Tamar discussed what she'd tell the children with Darlene, Clare drifted to the back of the classroom. A series of poster-sized self-portraits were pinned to the wall. Cheery collages with a smiling child, a few blonde, most dark, at the centre of each one. Pictures of parents, siblings, houses ranging from modest to mansion, ice creams, braaied fish – the small, familiar pleasures that made sense of life for a child.

The lone redhead caught Clare's eye. Oscar. He had given himself wild hair out of orange twine. When she turned to look for the original, his green eyes were riveted to her. She smiled at him. He looked down at once, a startling blush creeping up from under his collar.

Clare looked at his portrait again. The images were skeletal, arresting, executed in the colours and form of the rock paintings found in the desert. Oscar's drawings told a story that the other children, who could speak and shout and laugh, did not need to. Clare looked at his picture of a woman with a mass of hair twisted out of fraying yellow wool. The next picture had the same feeling of bell-jarred silence. A man and boy sat side by side; in a second chair, a woman, taut as a wire, watching television. Another drawing with the woman absent, and Oscar plastered to the man's side, his limbs uncurled as if they had been released from invisible ropes. Ordinary scenes made extraordinary because of the sense of menace that pervaded them.

Clare felt Oscar's presence next to her, as she had on the couple of occasions when he had fallen in step beside her on the boulevard. She looked down, startled to see the contusion on the cheekbone, just below his left eye, and a small, livid tear in the tender skin. Clare put her hand on Oscar's thin shoulder; feeling across his back where there would be more bruises. The child winced.

'What happened?' asked Clare, concerned. Oscar avoided her gaze as he tumbled his hands over each other.

'You fell?' she asked. 'Off your bike?'

He nodded and pointed to the single photograph on the wall. It was fuzzy, printed on cheap paper.

'Mara?' asked Clare, bending closer. The boy nodded.

'You'll miss her now she's gone.' In the photograph Mara Thomson stood exultant on top of a dune, arms and face lifted towards the sun, eyes closed in delight. The shadow of the photographer had splashed against her feet, giving the picture an odd perspective.

Oscar was seated next to her shadowed feet, swathed in a hat and long sleeves.

'You know the desert though, don't you? That's the place you went with your mother, isn't it?'

Oscar nodded, shoulders bowed like an old man.

'Clare?' Tamar and Darlene Ruyters were looking at her. So were the children.

'Sorry,' said Clare. 'I was lost there for a minute.'

Oscar looked down, the thick fringe of auburn eyelashes hiding any expression.

'Mrs Ruyters says the children will want to ask you some questions too,' said Tamar. 'They're always curious about foreigners.'

'Being South African is hardly foreign,' said Clare.

Darlene raised an eyebrow. 'They think Swakopmund is a foreign country and it's only thirty kilometres away.'

'Let them ask, then,' said Clare, smiling.

'Thank you, it'll help them be less ...'

'Afraid?' offered Clare.

'I was going to say fascinated.'

Tamar explained that the dead boy had been taken to the morgue. And that they were safe. The half-moon of children sitting at her feet stared at her with wide, solemn eyes. Only the bravest had questions: where would he be buried? Could they go to his funeral? Tamar fielded them with practised empathy. Soon the children had sidled closer and she got them talking about other things.

'This has been a big help,' Darlene said when she had winkled Tamar away from the children and ushered them out of the classroom. 'Thank you.'

'That little redhead,' Clare said.

'Oscar?' said Darlene.

'Yes,' said Clare. 'His face is bruised.'

'Oh, Tamar can tell you, we have such bad cases ...' Darlene's voice trailed off. She looked at Tamar for support.

'What do you think?' Clare was thinking that somebody's ring held a trace of the child's blood in its setting.

'I don't know what to think,' said Darlene. 'The children come to school with bruises, but you want to see some of the mothers on a Monday. They bear the brunt of it.' She closed the classroom door behind them. The corridor was cold and quiet after the buzz of the children.

'I met an old friend of yours,' said Clare. 'In McGregor.' Her voice was loud in the empty corridor.

'Oh?' Wary.

'Mrs Hofmeyr,' said Clare, watching Darlene closely. 'She told me why you stopped dancing.'

'I've got to get back to my class.' Darlene cut her short.

'It was an army boot on your ankle.'

'So what if it was?' hissed Darlene. 'Since when is it a crime to be beaten?' She put out her hand to open the door. The amethyst bracelet of bruises Clare had seen a few days earlier gleamed citron.

'You've got my number.' Clare placed her index finger on Darlene's wrist.

'I don't need it.' Darlene had her mask-like smile back in place when she stepped back into the classroom. Her voice calling her giggling charges back to order followed Tamar and Clare down the passage.

Chapter Thirty-seven

IT TOOK FOREVER for the lights of Walvis Bay to roll up towards Riedwaan. He had slept over in Solitaire, a half-abandoned hamlet in the southern Namib Desert. The miles are longer on roads where there is nothing to measure distance. The last stretch through the Namib had been bone-shattering. No other vehicles except a donkey cart. Not even telephone poles. He tried phoning Clare, but all he got was an automated voice telling him she was out of range and that he should try later.

'This whole country is out of range.' He said it aloud, just to hear a human voice. Then he dialled Tamar Damases's number.

'Yes?'

'Sorry to call so late,' he said. 'I thought I'd be in before sunset.'

Tamar laughed. 'Did you believe the map? They make things look much closer than they are. You must be finished.'

'I am,' said Riedwaan. 'I need a shower and some sleep before I do anything.'

'You're booked into a guesthouse on the lagoon. It's called Burning Shore Lodge. Don't be deceived by the fancy name, but it's close to the station and to where Clare's staying.'

Riedwaan jotted down the address. The town was quiet, only the pizza place open. He was hungry but too tired to stop. He hoped there would be something for him to eat where he was headed.

The guesthouse was a facebrick nightmare on the lagoon. It seemed to have been designed to avoid the view. Riedwaan rang three times before someone buzzed him in. He pushed his bike into the courtyard.

The only light on was at the bar. Inside, the walls were covered with signed snaps of Hollywood celebrities who had washed up on this barren stretch of coast to make B-grade movies, a couple to give birth to A-list children.

An overweight man took down Riedwaan's details and gave him a key.

'Show him to his room, Rusty,' he said to a morose youth hunched over a beer at the counter.

The boy heaved himself off his stool. He was a replica of his father, down to the tatty white vest and the plain cigarette curling smoke between his fingers.

'This way.' The boy eyed Riedwaan and thought better of offering to take his bags.

The room was clean and, if one ignored the red and black colour scheme, comfortable.

'Thanks.' Riedwaan dumped his bags on the floor. 'Can I get something to eat?'

'Nah,' said the boy. 'We only do breakfast.'

'Jesus, man. I've ridden from Solitaire with nothing to eat. Can't you do me a toasted sandwich or something?'

'Ham?' said Rusty.

'With a name like Faizal? You must be joking,' said Riedwaan. The boy looked blank.

'Get me cheese or something.'

'Come through to the bar. I'll get it for you. But you explain to my dad.'

'I'll be there in ten minutes.'

Riedwaan opened the curtains. The fog had closed in. He couldn't make out if he was looking at a parking lot or the lagoon. He closed them again and went to shower. The hot water dissolved two days of grime and stiff muscles. He pulled on his jeans and a clean shirt and went through to the bar.

His supper was waiting: toasted white bread and cheese, swimming in butter, no sign of salad. Lots of tomato sauce. Just how he liked it.

'You want a drink to go with that?' said the old man.

'Whisky. No ice,' said Riedwaan.

The man poured him a double. 'Name's Boss,' he said. 'What you doing up here? A holiday?'

'Kind of,' said Riedwaan, his mouth full. 'This is a good sandwich.' He washed it down with the whisky. 'Boss. Is that a nickname?'

'Short for Basson. My surname.' He poured himself a shot and shook a cigarette out of the pack lying on the bar. 'You want one?'

Riedwaan took one and leant forward so his host could light it for him.

'So where you headed?' asked Boss.

'I'm going to be here for a bit. Not sure how long.'

'Where you from?'

'Cape Town.' Food, whisky and a cigarette. Riedwaan felt human again.

'Oh,' said Boss. 'The States.'

It was Riedwaan's turn to look blank. 'The States?'

Rusty rolled his eyes back. 'It's what they used to call South Africa pre-94, when there were all those little fake countries. Transkei, Ciskei. All those independent states. You remember, the whole apartheid thing.'

'Oh that,' Riedwaan said dryly. 'I remember.'

'What line of work are you in?' asked Boss.

'Investigations,' said Riedwaan.

'Insurance?'

'No.' Riedwaan pushed his glass forward for another shot.

'You must be in the police,' said Rusty, a rare flash of understanding in his eyes. 'Remember, Pop, Captain Damases made the booking?'

They both eyed Riedwaan. Riedwaan stubbed out his cigarette.

'You working up here then?' asked Boss.

'A bit.' Riedwaan did not care to elaborate.

'Those fishing scams?'

'Not really,' said Riedwaan. 'Thanks for supper. I need to sleep.'

'It's those kids they keep finding in the desert, I bet,' said Rusty. Another light-bulb flash. He was going to wear himself out at this rate. 'I think it's a sailor. One of those Russians. They're all faggots. Drinking vodka, living on those ships for so long. What do you say, Pop?'

Boss ignored his son, turning to rinse the glasses in the sink.

'You must know that lady policeman staying at the cottages down the road,' Rusty said excitedly.

'I think I do,' said Riedwaan, getting up.

'She's hot,' said Rusty. 'I've seen her run past here in the mornings. Nice little tits. I bet I could get her to work up a sweat for me.'

Rusty's fingers were in Riedwaan's muscular hand, bent further back than their original specifications should have allowed.

Riedwaan's voice was low, intimate in Rusty's ear. 'You go near her and you'll be combing the desert for your balls.'

The boy rubbed his hand. He decided it was best to say nothing.

Riedwaan finished his whisky. 'What time is breakfast?'

'Six-thirty on. You want bacon and eggs?'

'No bacon. Just the eggs. Thanks.'

Riedwaan went back to his room and checked his cellphone. A missed call. Yasmin, his daughter. Damn, he'd forgotten his bi-weekly call. He pulled off his boots and lay on the bed, meaning to phone Clare. Instead, he fell at once into that deep, untroubled sleep that is the gift of innocence or physical exhaustion.

Chapter Thirty-eight

FOUR O'CLOCK AND Clare was wide awake, her duvet on the floor, a sheet tangled around her bare legs. Her dreams had been horrible: the dead boys winking at her with their bloody third eyes. The laugh of the hyena echoed through her subconscious, mocking her in a language she could not understand. She got up, opened her stoep doors and stepped onto the balcony. The silence pressed in with the fog. Not a sound, not a car. Roosting seabirds rustled their wings, calling softly, occasionally, as if to reassure themselves that they weren't alone in the vast salt marshes. The cold, and the pulse of an idea, drove Clare back inside; if she couldn't sleep, she might as well work.

She dressed quickly, flattening two cups of coffee in quick succession. The sound of her car starting was so loud she was convinced that she had woken the whole town, but nothing stirred. No lights came on.

A sleepy night sergeant waved her through the police station gates. In the special ops room, dim light filtered in from the street, making Clare's pinned-up victims look like a macabre boy band.

She flooded the room with neon and sat down at her desk. Opening her notebook, she drew up columns, one for each boy. The first victim with nothing on his chest. Then 2, 3. The missing number 4, and 5, the last one. Five columns, four bodies. Clare wrote down what she knew about them, what she knew about their deaths. Then she wrote down what she didn't know.

She made another column for the killer. Nothing to put there, but a bullet matched to a shooting two thousand kilometres away, and a white vehicle glimpsed in the dark. A predator that slipped through the night, unheard. Utmost secrecy and yet the bodies displayed where it would be impossible to miss them. She looked again at the map of the place where Lazarus had been found. One road in. One road out. Beyond it, tracks of sand unmarked by vehicles; the only tracks left were those of animals. Kaiser Apollis, too. Moved unseen and in silence. How? When she reached for the answer glimmering on the horizon of thought, it slipped away like a mirage on a desert road.

Debit and credit. No matter which way she juggled it, she could not get the books to balance. The truth was hidden below the surface, like the rivers that coursed deep underground. Clare put her head on her arms and closed her eyes to think and promptly fell asleep. Fully clothed, under a flickering neon light, Clare did not dream at all.

IT WAS THE smell of fresh coffee that woke her. 'Not like you to sleep on the job.' A voice that should have been in her dreams but wasn't, a gentle hand smoothing the hair from her forehead.

'Riedwaan.' Delight in her voice. She looked a mess; she could feel it. Hair all over the place, her cheek red from where it had rested on her sleeve. 'What are you doing here?'

'I made you coffee. Here.' Riedwaan pushed a steaming cup across the desk. 'And I got you a Florentine from the Venus Bakery. Your favourite.'

The honeyed almonds glistened in their nest of chocolate and dried fruit. Clare picked it up. It was too early in the morning to resist. She bit into the tiny biscuit. It was delicious. Useful too, because she couldn't eat and grin. Which was what she felt like doing, seeing Riedwaan sitting on the edge of her desk.

'Thanks for letting me know you were here,' she said, with her mouth full.

'I did try. Check your phone.'

Clare pulled it out of her pocket. 'Damn. So you did. It's been on silent.'

'What are you doing here?' asked Riedwaan.

'I couldn't sleep,' said Clare.

'You could've fooled me.'

'In bed I couldn't,' she said.

'So you came in here?' asked Riedwaan. 'Odd choice for soothing company.'

'I'm going crazy with them.' Clare gestured to the boys on the wall. 'Just as I feel I have something, it vanishes like water on hot sand. Have you seen Captain Damases?' she asked.

'Not yet. Only Van Wyk, I think it is. He's about as warm as a KGB agent.'

'That's Van Wyk for you,' said Clare. 'I don't think South Africans are at the top of his hit parade. Did you meet Elias Karamata?'

'Looks like a prizefighter? He said I'd find you in here.'

'Oh God, I suppose everyone knows I've been sleeping here.'

'Pretty much.' Riedwaan walked over to the displays, concentrating in turn on each of the four clusters, absorbing what Clare and Tamar had set out.

'I'm impressed,' he said. 'Fritz Woestyn, the one without a number carved on his chest, he was the first one?'

'Yes. We've been thinking of him as Number 1. Head shot, but not as close as the others. No tattooing that the pathologist could see. So definitely more than two, three metres. The others are all close-up.'

'Show me where he was found.'

Clare pointed to a red pin on the aerial map. 'His body was dumped here, but it wasn't where he was shot.' Riedwaan was standing close to her, raising the tiny hairs on her arms.

'Some guys checking a fifty-kilometre stretch just happened to find him?' asked Riedwaan.

Clare nodded. Riedwaan thought of the vast desert he had just passed through.

'You could go missing in this desert and not be found for weeks,' Clare said, reading his mind. 'The chances of the boys' discovery were so slim that whoever shot him probably calculated that he wouldn't be found until he'd been reduced to just another heap of bones. Or they dumped him where they knew he'd be found.'

'The others?' asked Riedwaan. 'Jones, Apollis, Beukes. Run me through them.'

'The killings get more elaborate after that first one. Nicanor Jones with the 2; Kaiser Apollis had a 3 on his chest. Then a skip to Lazarus Beukes with a 5.'

'Where's your Number 4?'

'Alive and well, I hope. No one's been reported missing.' Clare fanned out a series of close-ups: the faces, their mutilated chests, the missing finger joints on the left hands. 'It's the same person killing them,' she said. 'We don't have a bullet from each scene, but it looks like the same calibre gun and the same rope – nylon washing line – on the wrists. Same victim profile, too. Marginal boy, fifteen or so, fey, small, nobody to look for him. Also, there's a time thing. It looks like the murders were done on or around a Friday night, except for Lazarus. At least close to the weekend.'

'And your man?' asked Riedwaan. 'Where does he hang out?'

'This is the only place I can fix him,' said Clare, pointing to the first red pin on the map.

'The takeaway place at the lagoon?' said Riedwaan.

'Lover's Hill. They went there. Well, I know for sure that Kaiser Apollis was there. The cook saw him on the Friday evening he was killed. He ordered some food and then got into a car a few metres down the road.'

'Okay,' said Riedwaan. 'I'm with you. What happens?'

'This guy picks them up somewhere, probably in town where it wouldn't be noticed. Then he drives out, dropping them off to get something to eat. The cook noticed Kaiser because it was quiet, but otherwise the boys would be in and out. Invisible. Then they go outside, walk down the road a bit and get back into the car and they drive out into the desert.'

'There's no sign of recent sexual assault, is there?' said Riedwaan, checking the post-mortem results.

'No. Maybe he's impotent. Maybe he's a romantic. Maybe they laugh at him, threaten him. Maybe he gets his kicks in his own special way.'

'By shooting them?' asked Riedwaan.

'Maybe.'

'So who moves them?'

'Maybe I'm looking at this all wrong ...' Clare's voice trailed off as she stared at the accumulating bank of information. 'Maybe he meets someone out there. They both do something together ...'

'What's he like, this romantic of yours?'

'He'd have to be a loner, maybe a shift worker, so no one notices late comings and goings.' Clare finished her coffee. 'A textbook killer for a textbook case.'

Riedwaan walked over to the window and looked out over the flat, featureless town. 'How do people get around this place?' he asked.

'On foot or bike, if you're poor,' said Clare. 'A 4x4 if you're somebody.' She cocked her head and looked at her display. 'He'd have a car, or access to a car. Enough money to lure these kids and then buy them food. Something to drink. I'd put his age at around thirty-five, forty. Maybe a bit more. He might be someone the kids think they could take advantage of, but they'd go with just about anyone with a bit of cash.'

'Even after a couple of them have been killed?' asked Ried-waan. 'It must seem like someone they can trust, someone they don't expect to be a danger.'

'I agree,' said Clare. 'Someone they wouldn't see as a threat. The car will also look like everyone else's here.'

'White double cab, if what I've seen is anything to go by,' said Riedwaan. 'What would've triggered this spree?'

'Something unravels, the guy ropes of self-control snap,' said Clare. 'Stress does it usually. And there you go: a killer on the loose.' She looked at the pictures of Lazarus's bloodied face. 'Who-ever it is knows how to seduce. There's no sign of a struggle and such an intimate death. Blood would splatter on your hands and face as you fire. Quite a sophisticated rush in a way, the symbolism of it: the union, the consummation. Weird.'

'With you involved it's going to be weird, Clare,' said Riedwaan, looking at the pictures of a dismembered hand. 'You're sure it's someone local?'

'Whoever's doing this knows this place very well. He wouldn't be able to be invisible otherwise.' She paced up and down in front of the pinboard, stopping in front of the photograph of Kaiser Apollis's shrouded figure. 'My profile's still off-kilter,' she said.

'Why do you say that?'

'The display aspect of the murders. Herman Shipanga went on about bodies being exhibited as a kind of warning. It's not just the rush that comes with pulling the trigger. Our killer's trying to communicate something too, through the bodies. Out in the Kuiseb, where Lazarus's body was found, you had to ask how he got to be there exactly, where Chanel would find him. I keep thinking: someone knows this place, knows where people will stop in this vast desert, knows its secrets and can work with them. I wonder—'

The door swung open, interrupting Clare. It was Tamar. 'Did you sleep well, Riedwaan?' she asked. 'Comfortable where we put you?'

'Good bar, good bed, good food. Thanks.'

Clare had hardly noticed Tamar come in. 'What *is* this?' she said, almost to herself. She was rifling through the photographs, pulling out the one Tamar had taken of the alleyway behind the schoolyard where Kaiser Apollis had been found. She spun around. 'Riedwaan?'

'Morning to you too, Clare,' said Tamar.

Riedwaan peered at the photograph. 'Looks like dirt to me,' he said, puzzled, passing it to Tamar.

'It's shit,' said Clare.

'What did you say?' Riedwaan looked at Clare, startled. She saved swearing for emergencies. A grainy crime-scene photo was not an emergency.

Clare strode over to the desk, opened the interview file and flipped through the transcripts. 'Remember, what you asked me, Riedwaan?'

'Which question?' he said. 'There were twenty or more.'

'About how people get around?'

'Yes, by bike, foot, car … it was just a check.'

'Okay then,' said Clare. 'Look at this.' She brandished a carefully typed page. 'Tamar, remember, you said the recyclers use the alley behind the school.'

'They do,' said Tamar.

'And that woman we talked to, the one hanging up her washing, said she heard nothing?'

'I remember.'

Clare walked back to the pinboard. 'When I came back with Helena Kotze after we found Lazarus, I saw a family going home on their donkey cart. I didn't hear them until I was practically upon them. You wouldn't really hear a cart if you were inside and the television was on.' She pointed to a small heap of dung in the photograph. 'Look here,' she said. 'A pile of donkey shit, right by the opening of the fence. They must've passed right here and we never thought to question them.'

Riedwaan was still confused. 'Who uses donkey carts?'

'The Topnaars,' said Clare. 'The desert people. Their settlements are marked on the aerial survey photos. Here.' She gestured to a series of little black crosses. 'If you look closely, you'll see their shanties. Hot as hell they are. I just didn't put recyclers and the

Topnaars together. But of course it would be them, scavenging bits of scrap for the cash even they need to survive.'

'It's so risky,' said Riedwaan.

Clare turned to look at him. 'Not if you've got nothing left to lose.'

'Your invisible man?' Tamar said to Clare. 'A Topnaar?'

'Who else moves with such ease through the Namib?'

'A desert nomad doesn't fit with your profile,' Riedwaan noted. 'They're as poor as the dead kids.'

'No,' said Clare, 'but surely they'd know who's moving in and out of the Kuiseb. They'd see.'

'Wouldn't they tell?' asked Riedwaan.

'Not necessarily,' said Tamar thoughtfully. 'They're a marginal people, pushed further and further out. Persecuted by the army, silenced by this administration that wants them all settled and schooled and controllable. The Topnaars have a couple of hundred years' worth of knowing that the underdog gets the blame. If they found a body, they'd want it as far away from their land as possible.'

'So they wouldn't want to attract attention.' Riedwaan was looking at the map.

'Tertius Myburgh mentioned an old man called Spyt to me. Virginia Meyer used to work with him, because he knew the desert like the back of his hand. Do you know him?' Clare asked Tamar.

'I know of him,' said Tamar. 'He's very secretive, avoids people like the plague. He doesn't speak.'

'Give me a straight-down-the-line gangster any day,' muttered Riedwaan.

'I think we should try to talk to him,' said Clare. 'Stupid of me, not to have gone out there before.'

'We can give it a shot,' said Tamar sceptically. 'We've got to show Riedwaan around anyway, so we'll kill two birds this way. I'll get Van Wyk and Elias. Meet you outside in five minutes?'

Clare nodded.

'Your profile doesn't fit,' Riedwaan said again as Tamar left the room.

'What if there are two people involved?' asked Clare. Her voice was very quiet.

Riedwaan pulled on his jacket, suddenly chilled. 'Two?' he prompted.

'One who kills.' Clare tapped her pen on the window as she stared towards the desert. 'For whatever reason. And another who displays.'

Chapter Thirty-nine

'SPYT'S GOING TO hear us long before we're even close,' said Elias Karamata. 'We won't find him unless he wants to be found.'

Clare, Riedwaan, Tamar and Karamata had left Van Wyk at the station. Claiming that he wanted to see what else the South African experts had missed was his tactful way of putting it. After showing Riedwaan where the bodies had been found, they had gone from one Topnaar settlement in the Kuiseb to the next, each one drier and dustier than the last. An old woman, her weathered skin the same texture as her cloak, had said she knew where Spyt lived. She had led them through a lattice of desiccated tributaries to a desolate refuge.

'It looks as if he lives here alone,' said Clare. Unlike the other settlements, there were no dogs, no goats and no bug-eyed children staring at them from the inside of tin huts.

The camp was well hidden, backed up against a protrusion of black rock. Rusting lumps of metal and old tyres lay around between the little pyramids of bottles and old tins.

'Bully beef,' Tamar said, picking up an old tin. 'Old army issue. This must be twenty years old.'

Nothing moved on the black rocks. High above them a lone vulture drifted in the wash of blue sky. The Namib's eyes and ears, its silent witness. Like Spyt, Clare thought, hidden in a place that even his practised eyes would struggle to find.

'*Eitsma miere*, Spyt,' Tamar Damases called in Nama, the ancient mother tongue that she and Spyt shared. Her voice echoed off the rocks, the only reply.

The old woman led them around the side of the rocky protrusion to a small cave. A ring of stones circled the shelter, demarcating the point at which the desert ended and Spyt's dwelling began. A fireplace marked the epicentre of the domestic circle, the coals half-covered with sand.

'Still hot,' said Riedwaan, putting his hand close. The back of Clare's neck prickled as if she were being watched. She looked about; there was nothing but a lizard sunning itself on a rock.

A shallow oval of bark had been abandoned alongside the cave. Karamata picked it up and moved it back and forth between his hands, winnowing the wild grass seed Spyt must have harvested from a termite heap. He blew away the husks, and the breeze caught them, dust-devilling them across the sand. The chaff landed in the fireplace, the coals flaring briefly. 'You make pap with these,' he explained to Clare and Riedwaan. 'Spyt has to eat food that's as soft as a baby's because of his mouth.'

'His name means regret in Afrikaans,' said Riedwaan. 'What happened to him?'

Tamar asked their wizened guide, who burst into an animated tale in Nama. Clare could not understand a word, but the lilt of the tonal language, punctuated by a complex series of clicks, carried her with the emotional flow of the tale.

Tamar translated: 'She says that when he was a toddler his mother went to work on a farm on the edge of the Namib. Spyt ate caustic soda and it dissolved the inside of his mouth. That's why his mother took him back into the Namib. They lived together, just the two of them until she died. Then he lived alone. It was his mother who taught him how to hunt, how to hide.'

'Must've been why the military were always after him,' said Karamata.

'Were they?' Riedwaan asked.

'Oh yes.' Karamata gestured at the sand sprawling into the horizon. 'They made him work as a tracker for a while. They wanted to know everything about the desert, claim it, then own it and keep everything secret.'

'Let's look around,' said Tamar, 'but I don't think he's going to pitch.'

Clare went into the small cave shelter. It was narrow, dark beyond the splash of light at the entrance. There were few things inside, a sleeping roll, a leather bag, a pair of handmade shoes with pieces of tyre serving as the soles. Strips of cloth hung off a hook. Clare touched the fabric. It had perished from the heat, but the green stripe was still visible. The faint lettering too.

'Looks like old army sheeting,' said Riedwaan, following Clare into the cave. 'SWATF. The letters make the green stripe.'

The smell of years of wood smoke, of stale human sleep was overwhelming. Clare stepped outside, her heart pounding. It was a relief to be in the open air, but it did nothing to clarify her dervishing thoughts.

'A scavenger,' said Riedwaan, ducking out of the cave. 'Looks like he collected all sorts of rubbish lying about the desert, but not your boys. They were kept for a couple of days at the most and then displayed where you couldn't miss them. And they couldn't have been kept in there. It's too hot. Mouton said that the bodies must've been kept somewhere cool.'

'Give me your binoculars,' said Clare. 'I'm climbing up there to have a look.' She scrambled to the top of the cliff face and scanned the desert. The sand roiled in the east, where it had been agitated by the wind. Apart from the slender sentinel of a distant gum tree, there was nothing to see that way. To the south and west was a sea of dunes, some covered with spiny !nara plants, which flowed towards the ocean. Nothing moved. No tracks. No trail of dust to indicate a retreating cart.

'What've you got?' asked Riedwaan.

'Nothing,' said Clare, climbing down again. 'No donkeys, no cart, no Spyt, no tracks. Just sand.'

'You have to learn to see,' said Tamar. 'Not just to look.' She tugged Clare's arm, getting her to crouch alongside her. The light, angled low, transformed the blank slate of the desert sand, revealing the crisscrossings of jackal, oryx, lizards, the circular twist of seed pods eddied by the wind. And wheel tracks, barely visible. Neat crescents, close together, paired.

'Your donkeys.' Tamar stood up.

'That way?' asked Clare, pointing down the gulley that twisted away from them.

Tamar nodded. 'Elias, stay here on the off-chance he comes back.'

Clare and Riedwaan followed Tamar past a midden. Bones and shells, and other waste that had no further human use, were scattered about. They went on further; the ground became increasingly flinty.

Tamar stopped. 'I've lost them,' she said, frustration clear in her voice. Clare looked ahead. The shallow canyon they had entered broke into a labyrinth of tributaries. The sunlight shimmered on the mica, distorting the distances.

'Where to begin?' asked Clare.

'We'll need a helicopter if you want to pursue this,' said Riedwaan, turning back.

Tamar followed him, drinking from her water bottle. Clare waited. The silence the other two left in their wake was profound. She could hear the rush of her own blood, pulsing with frustration.

The sound came when she was halfway back to Spyt's cave. The sharp clink of a stone dislodged. Clare stopped, every sense alert. She looked about. Nothing but sand and rock and the sheer wall of the canyon. An agama eyed her, its reptilian body vibrating with anticipated movement. Clare let out her breath. The lizard bolted, vanishing straight into the rock. Curious, Clare went over to see where he had gone. To her surprise, she found a fissure in the rock, eroded by some prehistoric river that had long since changed its course. She stepped through the entrance into an amphitheatre of rock.

In the shade of an acacia thicket stood two creamy white donkeys. The animals shifted, pulling their tethers tight, as Clare approached them. She made a series of quiet, soothing clicks deep in her throat, and the donkeys were still again, motionless except for the occasional twitch of a velvet ear.

The entrance to the second cave was a dark opening in the cliff, a cool vestibule to the large cavern that opened to the right.

Clare ran back to the entrance. 'Riedwaan,' she yelled, her voice echoing behind her. 'Tamar, come back.'

The other two returned, Riedwaan's look of anxiety disappearing as soon as he saw Clare was unharmed.

'I think this is it,' said Clare, leading them back.

It was cool inside the cave, as dark as a crypt. A bat, disturbed by their presence, swooped low as they entered. Clare shivered at the little rush of air it left in its wake.

Riedwaan flicked on his torch and passed it to Clare. She shone it around the cave, bringing the beam to rest on the cart standing right at the back of the cave. It glinted in the light. The cart had been made from the back of an old bakkie. It had a bench in the front for the driver. Clare went closer and shone her torch over the back. Several empty jerry cans were secured on one side of it. On the other was a narrow space fitted with an old mattress, blotted with dark stains.

Riedwaan let out a long, low whistle. 'You are so lucky, Clare. What were the chances?'

'This'll teach you to be a nature lover,' she teased.

'We're going to need luminal to see if that's blood,' said Tamar, businesslike.

'You've got some here?' Riedwaan asked, impressed.

'I have. And a UV light.'

'Sharp,' said Riedwaan. 'Field forensics.'

'If you've got six months, then send the cart to Windhoek and file an official request to move and test a vehicle,' said Tamar. 'This works. If we need more we take it all in and fill in the forms.'

'Where is the stuff?' asked Riedwaan.

'On the truck. There's a trunk on the back.'

Riedwaan slipped out of the cave entrance. Clare switched off the torch while she and Tamar waited, sheltered from the heat of the desert. Safe and cool and restful. It was not a bad place to be alone.

'You'll need a slow exposure to get the patterning ... if there is any.'

Clare jumped. She hadn't heard Riedwaan come back. He handed Clare the camera and sprayed the luminal over the back of the cart. Tamar held up her handmade ultraviolet light. For a second, there was nothing, then it glowed purple, a small patch on one end of the mattress.

'We'll send that through to the lab,' said Riedwaan. 'But I know what they'll take five pages to tell us: something or somebody was on this, something not that long dead. But they didn't die here.' He pointed to the contained patterning. 'It would've pooled a little when it was moved for transport. Post-mortem.' Riedwaan looked around the cool, clean cave. 'Doesn't look like they were killed here either.'

'No,' said Clare. She shone the torch into the recesses of the cave. On the floor were gossamer heaps. Wings, discarded exo-skeletons. She arced the beam up towards the roof, the light expos-ing the huddled, roosting bats.

Riedwaan ducked instinctively as a dozen or so of the tiny, dis-turbed creatures took off.

'These must be the bats whose droppings got caught in Kaiser Apollis's hair.'

'So what was Spyt doing, bringing dead bodies here and then dropping them off in public again?' Tamar asked the question they were all thinking as they walked back towards Karamata and the vehicle. 'And how are we going to find him if he doesn't want to talk to us?'

'Why would Spyt have done this?' wondered Clare. 'Knowing that eventually someone would come out here and look for him? What was he trying to say to—?'

The roar of a vehicle cresting the dune cut Clare off.

'We've got company,' said Karamata as they joined him.

The doors opened and Van Wyk emerged, followed by Calvin Goagab, incongruous in his city suit.

Goagab reached them first. 'Mayor D'Almeida will be pleased to have a suspect after so much investment in this case,' he said. 'We should get back to the press conference.'

'What are you talking about, Calvin?' Tamar's voice rose with fury.

'Captain Damases,' Van Wyk interrupted. 'I tried to call you, but got no reply. So, I called Mr Goagab.'

'You know there's no cellphone reception out here, Van Wyk.' Tamar's voice vibrated with anger. 'And you were supposed to be checking interviews, not making public announcements.' She watched him as one would watch an unpredictable dog. 'What did Van Wyk tell you, Calvin?'

'That our experts have led us to a suspect,' Goagab replied. 'We're very pleased. It'll allow me to justify the expense.' He nodded towards Clare and Riedwaan. 'And it vindicates my policy to get the desert nomads properly settled.'

'He's not a suspect yet,' Clare observed.

'Oh, we'll have him soon enough and then he will be.' Van Wyk put his hand on Tamar's shoulder. 'The mayor is waiting for you to address the press conference, Captain Damases. We'd better head back if we're to make the news tonight.'

'We'll discuss this, Van Wyk,' said Tamar. 'This insubordination.'

'I did a little check,' he replied, 'and I don't think we'll be discussing anything in the near future. I see our very progressive leave policy stipulates that pregnant officers go on leave from the seventh month. I looked at your medical records and noticed that your due date is next week.'

'How dare you go through my private records?' asked Tamar.

'We care, Captain Damases,' said Goagab, with an oily smile. 'Our administration's concern for gender issues means that we can't allow you to jeopardise your unborn child. We must ask you to return to town immediately.'

Speechless with rage, Tamar looked from Van Wyk to Goagab.

'Let's go, Captain,' Karamata said, his hand on Tamar's elbow. He walked her back to the vehicle.

Van Wyk turned to Riedwaan. 'It's going to look good, Captain Faizal. An almost-arrest the day you arrive,' he said. 'I'm sure you're looking forward to addressing the media. It's all been set up.'

'I wouldn't like to see what Spyt looks like after a night in the cells with him in charge,' Clare said under her breath, watching Van Wyk and Goagab swagger back to their vehicle.

'I'm not sure I want to see what we are going to look like after this press conference,' said Riedwaan.

They joined Tamar and Karamata at the car and were forced to follow Van Wyk and Goagab out of the Kuiseb, tagging behind in the vehicle's dusty wake. Van Wyk angled his rear-view mirror so that he could catch Clare's eye. He grinned. He had won his battle. She'd helped him win. Clare wished she could figure out what the war was.

Chapter Forty

THE YACHT CLUB bar was still crowded at eight-thirty when Clare arrived. The after-work crowd had gone home, but the professional drinkers had settled in for the night. A fug of smoke had settled over the bar.

'Give the lady a drink,' ordered a belligerent drunk. 'She looks like she could do with it.'

'No, thank you.' Clare raised a deflecting hand at the whisky sloshed into a shot glass. She ordered wine and went to sit in one of the booths. Calvin Goagab's press conference had been worse than she imagined, with Goagab and Van Wyk posturing before the cameras, and Clare expressing doubt in spite of all the evidence.

'I said: give the lady a fucking drink.' The drunk's voice rose a threatening notch.

'Tell him, thank you, but no.' Clare fixed her blue eyes on the barman.

'Frigid bitch,' muttered the heavy-set man on the other side of the bar. 'Just a bit of hospitality.'

'She's not interested.' A woman's voice. 'She's not going to get interested either, so why don't you leave her alone?' Clare was surprised to see that her defender was Gretchen von Trotha, seated a few seats away from the drunken men.

'Thanks,' she mouthed, raising her glass in salute.

'You stay out of this, Gretchen,' said the man.

Gretchen did not bother to reply, turning her attention instead to the lean man beside her. Clare recognised him from Der Blaue Engel: the man who had pulled Gretchen from the icy Atlantic. It looked as though he was still cashing in on her debt to him. Gretchen certainly looked adoring.

'Sorry I'm late.' Riedwaan slid into the opposite side of the booth, distracting Clare.

'It's fine,' she said. 'You look cleaner and calmer.'

'You need a drink?' he asked. 'I need a double after that. More like a lynching than a press conference.'

'I'm fine.' She tapped her full wine glass and scanned the bar. Gretchen had vanished, so had the man she'd been with.

Riedwaan came back with his whisky and a new pack of cigarettes. 'I have to eat,' he said, taking the menus from a plump waitress. 'I'm starved. Steak and chips for me,' he said.

'Steak? At the sea? Order the fish.' There was no arguing with that.

'What do you think about Spyt?' Clare asked when the waitress had left with their orders.

Riedwaan buttered some bread and took a bite. 'I don't think it was him. But the local politicians want the Topnaars out of the way. This is all a convenient way of getting this land claim business to disappear. But Nampol have to work that out themselves. Let's just hope they do it before someone else dies.'

'I feel it'll be my fault if anything happens to Spyt. I don't like the thought of Van Wyk and his cronies hunting him like a dog.'

'I don't think they'll catch him that easily.' Riedwaan said. 'What's happened with Tertius Myburgh, by the way?' he asked, shaking a cigarette from his pack.

'I'm still waiting for his pollen analysis,' said Clare. 'I'd love one of those. I need it after this afternoon.'

'Have one.' Riedwaan lit one for her and placed it between her lips.

'Smoking's like sex,' said Clare, inhaling deeply. 'It seems such a good idea at night. Not so brilliant when you wake up in the morning.'

'You can give that back to me then,' said Riedwaan.

'No, let me smoke it,' she said. 'Just so that I can remember what a stupid idea it is.'

'The smoking or the sex?' said Riedwaan.

'I haven't decided yet,' said Clare, tension coiled in her belly. 'I feel so stupid, that I set myself up. Van Wyk and Goagab had me checkmated at that press conference. All that bullshit about Cain and Abel, nomads being vagrants. Just an excuse to persecute people whose land you want.' Clare took a deep drag of the cigarette. 'Yes, it was my idea. Yes, I went out there. Yes, there was evidence that the bodies were in Spyt's cave at some stage. And me like an idiot, saying he didn't kill them.' Clare put out her half-smoked cigarette when the waitress brought their food. 'While Goagab and his goons are flattening the desert in their 4x4s, there's a killer sitting eating dinner and planning Number 6.'

'There's nothing more we can do tonight,' Riedwaan pointed out.

'What're we going to be able to do tomorrow?' snapped Clare. 'Van Wyk has pushed Tamar into a bureaucratic corner and me and you are supposed to be off the case.'

'Not quite,' said Riedwaan. 'But let's leave that for tomorrow.' He put his hand on hers. 'Right now the moon is nearly full. I'm here, you're here, so why don't we talk about something else?'

'Okay,' said Clare. She took her hand away and fussed with her table mat. 'Suggest something.'

'Smoking maybe,' said Riedwaan.

Clare didn't laugh.

'Me? You?'

'Me and you?' Clare toyed with the idea of asking him about Yasmin, or of telling him she was sorry that she hadn't listened to him earlier, but she couldn't find a way to start. She gave up and pushed her food around her plate. She looked at Riedwaan, looked away.

'Talking about something other than work take away your appetite?'

'No,' she said. 'It's just that my stomach's in a knot.'

'Does your having dinner with me mean I'm forgiven?'

'Don't rush me.' Clare picked up her wine glass. 'I'm deciding.'

'I'm useless on parole,' Riedwaan warned. 'It brings out the worst in me.'

'You're not—'

Clare's phone rang. She looked at the screen. 'I've got to take this,' she said. 'It's Constance.'

Riedwaan shook his head at her, irritated, but Clare had already taken the call. He waited for a second, but all her attention was focused on the identical twin murmuring into her ear, drawing her away from him and into a place he could never follow.

He picked up his cigarettes and went to the bar.

The barman poured him a sympathetic double whisky.

Chapter Forty-one

THE DARK WAS thinning when Clare awoke, smiling, expecting to find herself circled in Riedwaan's arm. Then she remembered that she had gone to bed alone. She got up and opened the curtains. A sodden west wind was blowing. She pulled on her tracksuit and a waterproof jacket, zipping her phone into her pocket as she left her room. She headed north towards the harbour. Once she was past the Burning Shore Lodge, she found her stride, finally eliminating all thoughts of Riedwaan.

Sweat bloomed under Clare's shirt. She slowed as the path narrowed, snaking between the lagoon shore and a new hotel. Discarded building materials and other debris littered the track. She waved at the little red-haired boy sitting huddled on a bench.

'Hello, Oscar,' she called as she went past. 'You're up early.'

He raised one hand in reply, his face solemn.

She whipped her phone out of her pocket when it rang.

'Riedwaan?' He had said he'd call first thing.

There was nothing but a hollow echo.

'Hello?'

No answer. The chill played over Clare's skin. She ducked behind a wall when her phone rang again.

'Hello?'

'Is that Dr Hart?' An unfamiliar voice. Faraway. Foreign.

'It is.'

'I'm sorry to disturb you. I know it's early.'

'Who is this?' asked Clare.

'She didn't arrive,' a woman said.

'Who didn't arrive?'

'Mara.' There was a break in the woman's voice. 'This is Lily Thomson. Mara's mother.'

'How did you get my number?' Clare asked.

'I phoned the police station. The man I spoke to, Van Wyk' – she struggled with the unfamiliar name – 'said it was too soon to do anything. He gave me your number when I asked for you.'

'Where are you?'

'I'm at home again, aren't I?' Lily Thomson replied. Clare envisaged the bleak courtyard of the housing estate that Mara had escaped. 'I went to Heathrow.'

'Yes?' prompted Clare, unease prickling the nape of her neck.

'She didn't come. She was meant to be on that flight. That's all I know and all I can find out, because she's not answering her phone.'

'Might she have changed her mind?'

Lily Thomson clutched at Clare's straw. 'That's what I said to myself: she's changed her mind. I tried her mobile.' Her voice broke. 'But she's not picking up.'

Clare pictured Lily Thomson in her spring-cleaned flat. The supermarket flowers on the kitchen table. Mara's single bed made up in crisp white sheets, a chocolate under the pillow, teddies perked.

'Mara told me about you coming there from South Africa,' Lily Thomson continued. 'About the investigation. She was so upset about those boys. That's just how she is, our Mara: always responsible, trying to make the world right, especially after that trip that went all wrong.'

'What trip?' asked Clare. Anxiety tightened her spine. Mara and her soccer team. She had known the murdered boys better than anyone else had.

'She took them camping or something,' said Mrs Thomson. 'She felt so guilty about leaving them out there in the desert like that. But I told her it was fine, if it was the only time she could see her boyfriend, that Juan Carlos, then why not? She was so head-over-heels and she knew she didn't have long with him.'

Clare thought of the last time she had seen Mara, entwined with Juan Carlos, sharing fish and chips, glowing with whatever he had been doing to her to make her so hungry.

'Did you report her missing?'

'I tried. They said they have this all the time with travellers, with volunteers. They meet a new person, go somewhere else. To Botswana. Maybe Cape Town. That the mothers panic because it's Africa. Van Wyk said to wait twenty-four hours.' She stifled a sob. 'But when do I start counting, Dr Hart? When she didn't come I thought the worst. I thought ...'

Panic hit Lily Thomson, doubling her over. It was impossible for her to say what she had thought, as if saying the words would conjure up what she feared most.

'Please find her for me, Dr Hart. I'm so far from there. You speak English. You can understand me. You knew her.'

Lily Thomson caught it. Clare did too, that slip into the past tense.

CLARE SET OFF at a run for George Meyer's gloomy house where Mara had rented a room. She clung to the hope that she would find her and Juan Carlos asleep in a tangle of sheets and salty limbs. When she got there, the only signs of life were in the kitchen. Clare knocked over Oscar's fishing rod standing at the back door. She righted it, disentangling it from the roll of washing line as Gretchen, wrapped in her sky-blue robe, opened the door.

'Yes?' Gretchen jabbed her cigarette into her mouth, still stained with last night's lipstick. Smoke curled up to the ceiling.

George Meyer and Oscar were sitting opposite each other at the kitchen table, Oscar staring down at the rheumy eye of a fried egg. He looked up at Clare, his face lighting up. George Meyer paled.

'Dr Hart, please come in,' he said. 'How can we help?'

'I'm looking for Mara,' Clare said as she walked inside.

'She left.' Gretchen tossed her cigarette into the remains of her coffee.

'When?'

'Yesterday, must've been,' said Meyer. 'The Lufthansa flight.'

'You didn't see her?'

'No.' He shook his head. 'I saw her on Sunday evening. She had supper with me and Oscar and then she went out with her Spanish friend.'

'How was she going to go to the airport?'

'I offered her a lift, but she said she was sorted,' said Gretchen. 'Go and look; her room's empty. She took all her stuff.'

'What time did she leave?' Clare asked.

'I don't know.' Gretchen's mouth twisted, thin as wire, around a fresh cigarette. 'I work late. I must've been asleep.'

Oscar coughed, his delicate ribcage heaving under his shirt. 'Do you want to show me Mara's room?' Clare asked. 'Do you mind?' She turned to George Meyer.

He shook his head.

Oscar slipped his hand into hers and led her down the passage to Mara's room.

Stripped bare of Mara's belongings, the room was smaller than Clare remembered. The overhead light had been left burning, the bulb feeble in the daylight. A pile of soiled bed linen was bundled on the floor. On the bedside table were a couple of abandoned paperbacks and an old *People* magazine. Clare sat down on the bed. The little boy sat next to her. The mattress sagged, leaning the child's warm body against her.

'Where is she, Oscar?'

Oscar's hand in hers was clammy, as he tugged her off the bed and led her to the other side of the room. There he lifted up a loose square of carpet to reveal a shallow depression in the concrete.

'What is this?'

Oscar lifted out a cheerful yellow and red Kodak envelope, taking out some folded drawings, childish representations of Walvis Bay, the desert, and trees against orange sand.

'Did you do these?'

Oscar nodded again, pointing to where he had written his name. An O bisected with an M inside a heart.

'They're good.'

Clare took out the photographs. They were mostly of Mara. With her mother in London, looking triumphant and nervous at Heathrow. Standing against a Tropic of Capricorn road sign, her arms spread, bisecting the featureless plain behind her. Surrounded by grinning children at a school. Camping in the Namib.

Her soccer team holding a cup, looking like the cats that had the cream.

Oscar was growing agitated, tugging at Clare's arm. 'What is it?' she asked.

He pointed at the pictures again.

'Are you upset that she left the drawing you gave her?'

Oscar inclined his head. His expression was unreadable.

'Was she in a hurry to—?'

Oscar was shaking his head before she was halfway through her sentence.

'You don't think she would've left a present behind?'

Oscar nodded, this time certain. He turned to face the window that overlooked the concrete yard of the house and lifted his index finger, seeming to point to the sky. Clare frowned, struggling to see through the grime and dew misting up the glass. Oscar touched the pane. He wasn't pointing; he was drawing, tracing a familiar shape in the condensation on the window: the scored-through heart on Clare's bedroom window which had so startled her.

'That was you,' she said, 'watching me.'

Oscar's nod was almost imperceptible.

'You were checking on me. Did you watch Mara, too?'

The child nodded, tears welling in his eyes. Clare's heart went out to the fragile boy. The little Clare knew of Mara convinced her that she would not have rejected the child's shy gesture of love.

'And Mara wouldn't leave a present behind, because she loved you,' she guessed.

Oscar nodded again.

'What happened to her, Oscar?'

He shook his head violently and then stopped, his eyes fixed behind Clare's shoulder. She turned to see Gretchen leaning against the door frame. Clare wondered how long she'd been there.

'Silly boy,' Gretchen laughed, low in her throat. 'Why would she keep your stupid pictures?'

'When did you see her last?' Clare asked Gretchen.

'Sunday night,' said Gretchen, giving it some thought. 'She was at the bar of Der Blaue Engel. I was working.'

'Who was she with?'

'Juan Carlos.' Gretchen was quick to answer. 'Her boyfriend. She loved him, Oscar, not you.'

'Do you know what time she left?' asked Clare. She felt Oscar shake.

'I did my show,' said Gretchen. 'I left straight after. Maybe two?'

When I got home, everything was dark. I watched TV for a while, then I went to bed. She would've left while I was still asleep. Her flight was nine-thirty. So check-in time seven-thirty for international.'

'You didn't hear a taxi come? A car?' Clare put her hand on Oscar's shoulder.

'No,' Gretchen said blandly. 'I sleep deeply. Is there anything else we can help you with, Dr Hart?'

'No,' said Clare. 'Not now.'

Gretchen lingered in the doorway until Clare stood up to leave, then she turned and ascended the stairs, her blue gown sweeping over the steps. Oscar tucked the envelope into Clare's jacket pocket as they walked back to the kitchen. He fiddled with his fishing bag, humming to himself to fill the space around him, and then he took his rod from behind the kitchen door, averting his eyes from Mara's empty room. The sound of running water came from the bathroom upstairs.

'You'll excuse us, Dr Hart?' said Meyer. 'I have to get to work.'

George Meyer picked up his keys and walked Clare to the front gate. 'Be a good boy, Oscar,' he said, as the boy wheeled his bike around to the front.

'Call me if you hear anything about Mara.' Clare said it to George, but her hand was resting on Oscar's cheek. She felt him nod.

Chapter Forty-two

CLARE CUT BACK alongside the rubbish-snagged razor wire that sequestered the harbour from the town. She called Tamar, but her phone went straight to voicemail, so she left a message with the news about Mara. She turned in at the police station. At seven in the morning, the parking lot was empty except for Van Wyk's white 4x4.

She pushed open the office door, her running shoe protesting against the linoleum floor. Van Wyk was engrossed in whatever was on his computer screen, his hand on the mouse. One click and the image shut down. So did his expression.

'I'm surprised to see you here, Dr Hart.' The hurried crackle told Clare that he had hit sleep mode. 'After yesterday. But if you're looking for Captain Damases, you're a bit early.'

'I'm always early,' said Clare, wondering what had piqued Van Wyk's interest in office work. 'But this morning I also had a call. So I thought I'd come and see you about it.'

'The media?' Van Wyk said 'For another interview with our ... expert from South Africa? I'd say your case is dead in the water.

It's just a matter of time before we find that old desert beggar.' He leant back in his chair, arms behind his head, legs splayed, the denim tight across his thighs. The door clicked shut behind Clare, making her jump.

'It was Mara's mother,' she said. 'Mrs Thomson.'

A pause, a heartbeat long. 'What must I say to the mother? That her daughter got an itch for a sailor?'

'Has it crossed your mind that something might have happened to her?' said Clare.

Van Wyk spread out his hands and examined his fingernails. 'If she's dead, her body'll pitch up sometime, and we'll send her home in a box. If she's alive, she'll run out of money and go home anyway. All the same in the end.'

'To you maybe. Not to the desperate woman I had on the phone.'

Van Wyk uncoiled himself from his chair, his pupils pinpricks. 'Mara was nothing but trouble. She lodged a complaint against me after we picked up one of those street kids of hers stealing in the harbour. She got me shunted into this pointless fucking unit. And now it's my job to look after a stupid little foreign slut who can't keep her knees together?'

'She's missing, Sergeant,' said Clare.

Van Wyk was close to her now. Clare kept her eyes on his.

'You don't belong here, Dr Hart.' His fingers closed around her wrists. The bones shifted when he twisted. 'Just like Mara didn't, so you stay away from things that don't belong to you.'

'Don't you ever threaten me,' said Clare, bringing her right knee up, fast and accurate.

Van Wyk let her go, his eyes glazing with pain as the office door flung open.

'Morning, Clare.' It was Karamata, cheerful and crisply dressed for the new day. 'Morning, Van Wyk. You're here—' He looked from Clare to Van Wyk. 'Is something wrong?'

'Everything's fine,' Van Wyk managed to say. 'I was working most of the night. Dr Hart and I were just talking about solving cases, weren't we?' He didn't give Clare a chance to reply and walked down the passage, his tall, thin body cutting through a sudden flood of early-morning arrivals.

Clare flexed her wrists. She made herself breathe deeply, slowing her heart rate and ordering her jumbled thoughts. 'He's like a hand grenade without a pin,' she said.

'Oh, you mustn't worry about him too much,' said Karamata. 'He's always touchy first thing in the morning.'

'I won't,' said Clare, with feeling. 'I was worrying about Mara Thomson. Her mother called to say she never arrived home.'

Karamata stirred sugar into his tea and shook his head. 'If we followed up every report like this, we'd never do anything else. She'll call her mother when her money runs out.' His cellphone rang. He nodded at Clare and went into the corridor, firing a rapid volley of Herero into the receiver.

Clare sat down at Van Wyk's desk to get Mara's number from the case dockets on the shared server. She found it quickly and dialled. Mara wasn't answering. Unease, long since upgraded to anxiety, turned into fear.

Clare massaged her wrists, working out what to do, watching the screensaver on Van Wyk's computer. Her curiosity was piqued at his unprecedented diligence. She didn't imagine he'd been working on an expense report on the hunt for Spyt. She reached for the mouse. There were a couple of cases in the documents folder, but when Clare opened them, they were empty. She called up the mail programme minimised on the bar at the bottom of the screen. Viagra spam, a couple of e-mail memos from police headquarters in Windhoek. Routine stuff from Tamar. The sent box was sparse too. Nothing in the delete box either. She checked the file history. Nothing there. Clare sat back in the chair for a second. There was one last thing for her to try. She went to the recent items in the menu. Google. She clicked on the search history. One website only. Van Wyk had spent some time on it.

The site was dark, almost black. Explicit content warnings competed with the pop-ups of beckoning girls inviting viewers to 'cum see my first time'. So this is what he does in his spare time, Clare thought. Her mouth dry, she clicked on the entrance portal. The names and images of twenty half-naked women appeared. Amateur shots in suburban homes, classrooms, offices. Clare scrolled down the web page. The photos had been posted from all over the world, but they had two things in common: the youthfulness of the girls and the subtle brutality of their submission. In offices, classrooms and toy shops, around family dinner tables and in everyday places, were images of girls doing everyday things. One click transformed the image, and the girl was stripped, splayed and penetrated.

Clare scrolled through the images, but there was nothing to identify the anonymous postings. She was about to log out when the name of a video link caught her eye: Namib Nature Girls. Clare opened the first video. It was grainy, downloaded from a handheld camera, but it made her stomach turn. It was Van Wyk all right. He was standing in his uniform, his cap jaunty, his belt unbuckled, poised behind a naked, spread-eagled body. It was impossible to identify the recipient of Van Wyk's attentions. Then the film cut to a wide shot.

Clare froze. The ghost-smell of a putrefying cat caught at her throat. The altar, the ring of stones, the amphitheatre, the encircling trees. She looked closer at the body on the altar. It was a girl, her eyes glazed, limbs limp, a blank smile on her face. Her clothes in a pile on the floor. She looked drugged. LaToyah or Minki. The names scrawled on the cave. And Chesney, the other name. It must have been him holding the camera. There were other videos too. She flicked through the site, looking for Mara, but there was no sign of her. There were no boys either. The videos were strictly heterosexual. There were a couple of Angolan girls who Clare had noticed hanging around the entrance of the docks, so young that the breasts had barely budded on their skinny chests. She wondered how much these girls, paying in kind in the revolting little films, paid him in cash as well. Fury surged through her as she e-mailed the link to Tamar and hurried out of the office.

RIEDWAAN WAS PACING in front of the cottage when Clare got back. 'Where were you?' He flicked his cigarette away and followed her in. 'What took you so long?'

'What's the matter with you?' Clare asked.

'Unfamiliar territory.' Riedwaan's desire for an argument had ebbed as soon as he had Clare safe in front of him again. 'It puts me on edge.'

'I went past the station,' said Clare, making coffee.

'So early?'

'I got a call from Mara Thomson's mother,' Clare said. 'From London. Mara was meant to arrive there yesterday, but she never got off the plane.' Riedwaan looked blank. 'Mara volunteered at the school, teaching the homeless kids soccer,' she explained.

'So what's bothering you?' he asked.

'She knew those boys better than most people in this town,' said Clare, the kernel of anxiety unfurling from the pit of her stomach. She pushed the coffee away. The caffeine would only make her feel worse. 'She looked like them, too.'

'Did you go past her place?'

'Yes, and all her stuff's gone.'

'Boyfriend?' Riedwaan knew more about missing girls than he cared to.

'Yes,' said Clare. 'A sailor. Nice looking. I've met him.'

'If she's young and she has a boyfriend, that can mean two things,' said Riedwaan. 'She's safe and fucking him silly and her mother will be furious. Or she's dead. Either way, the boyfriend's your first port of call.'

'I'm going to see if she missed her flight first,' said Clare.

'Fine. I'll catch you later.' Riedwaan stopped in the doorway, silhouetted by the sun. 'Clare,' he said.

'What?' She turned from the sink where she had been rinsing her cup.

'You'll call me if you need me?'

'Of course, I'll call you.'

Clare locked the door behind Riedwaan, walked to the bathroom and turned on the shower tap. Her wrists hurt. They would look like Darlene's by tomorrow. It was only when was in the shower, hot water needling down her back, that she realised that she hadn't told Riedwaan about Van Wyk. She pulled on her clothes, wishing that she had.

Chapter Forty-three

RIEDWAAN'S CELLPHONE BEEPED as he parked his bike outside the police station. *Call me*, read the text. He dialled, smiling.

'Februarie, you cheap bastard.' Riedwaan could hear maudlin country music playing in the background.

'You still interested in that murder in McGregor?' Februarie grunted.

'You had an outbreak of altruism or what?' Riedwaan closed the door to the office. Neither Karamata nor Van Wyk was in. Tamar's door was closed.

'You wouldn't know altruism if it gave you a blow job,' said Februarie.

'What then?' said Riedwaan. 'You think I'm phoning you back because I like the sound of your voice? Just like I came to see you because of your pretty face.'

'As charming as ever, Faizal. No wonder you're such a one-hit wonder with women.'

'What have you got?'

'Some more background on your Major Hofmeyr. Seems he started in Pretoria with some obscure unit doing research. He was from the wrong side of the tracks with no links in the Afrikaner establishment. But he was a bright boy and he did well. Soon he had a beautiful wife from one of the oldest Cape families, nice house, fancy car, and trips overseas. Then he was transferred to another unit and sent to some hellhole in the Kalahari where–'

'Vastrap,' Riedwaan interrupted. 'His wife's already told us. She was less clear about what he did there.'

'That's the odd thing,' said Februarie. 'It looks like it was a promotion. More trips overseas. More money. He didn't do the party circuit like some of the others, but he had what he wanted in terms of research and travel. I can't find much, but it looks like it was weapons development and testing.'

'What kind of weapons?'

'Possibly nuclear. It looks like it was part of Operation Total Onslaught, PW Botha's baby. Born in 1972, baptised with the Soweto riots in 1976. The best minds; the best facilities; unlimited funding. It makes sense that it would be nuclear.'

'And then?'

'He was sent to Namibia in the eighties, where you could do what you liked, pretty much. Play God, and no one would ever know. And if they found out, what would they do about it?'

'Why was he shunted sideways?'

'Can't say if he was really. It was all classified. And shredded in the early nineties before Mandela could say *amandla*. De Klerk sold them down the river by decommissioning unilaterally in 1990.'

'What else have you got?'

'Well, I had another look at that TRC stuff. Like I said, Hofmeyr's name came up in a few of the hearings. The usual things: torture, a few extra-judicial killings, assaults. Him and two others, all from the same unit in Namibia, but it didn't look like he was going to apply for amnesty. And because nobody said anything, it just went away.' Februarie paused. 'Never happened for me,' he added.

'You fucked up in the wrong direction, Februarie. You went after the guys with money to buy enough politicians to make their own parliament.'

'That's my problem with altruism,' said Februarie.

'It's terminal,' said Riedwaan. 'You're born with it. This therapy session is costing me five bucks a minute. I'm sure you can get it cheaper down there. Tell me what happened.'

'Extra-judicial killings,' Februarie mused. 'A good concept that – always makes me wonder what a judicial killing is.'

'No philosophy either, Februarie. What else? How is this connected to Hofmeyr's murder?' Riedwaan tried not to sound impatient; withholding information was Februarie's favourite game.

'Ja, well, Hofmeyr had a change of heart. He approached someone to make a full disclosure about what they'd been doing up there in Walvis Bay. Him and his friends.'

'He must've stood out like a parade ground corporal in a ballet tutu,' said Riedwaan.

'Funny, you mention Tutu. The only person who looked like he might be happy about it was the Arch. Hofmeyr wanted forgiveness, I suppose. The major was dying of cancer, so I guess he was afraid of that final court date. His offer was shoved from one desk to another, and then he was murdered. So it all went away overnight.'

'Until you started looking,' said Riedwaan.

'I was shafted,' said Februarie. 'Apparently my paperwork was bad.'

'Was it?'

'Of course it was. My paperwork's fucking terrible. But it always was before I got into any of this.'

'Why then?' asked Riedwaan.

'I found out that he had visitors before he died,' said Februarie, after a pause.

'Who told you?'

'The maid. Who else?'

'She see them?'

'No. Hofmeyr told her not to come for a couple of days. But the woman who worked next door told her anyway. Two men. They argued on the second night. Then they left, and two days later, he was dead. Too many coincidences. The visitors while the wife was away. The convenient gangsters.'

'You think it was the wife?'

'You know what I think of wives,' said Februarie. Riedwaan knew. The whole force knew. Februarie's wife left him for her boss. Februarie had refused to take the fact that the boss was solvent, always sober and never violent as mitigating circumstances.

'But no. Not her. It's the visitors. I've been looking for them since I last saw you.'

'And did you find them?' Riedwaan felt his fingertips tingle in anticipation.

'No. But I did get the names of the two friends Hofmeyr was going to implicate in his disclosure.'

'Where did you get this from?'

'It might be hard for you to swallow, Faizal, but I still have a few chips to call in.'

'Who are they?' Riedwaan asked. 'Hofmeyr's friends?'

'Malan.'

'Malan?'

'Malan.' Februarie was enjoying Riedwaan's discomfort.

'Now there's a helpful name. There must be thousands of them.'

'This one runs a security consulting business out of Goodwood in Cape Town.'

Riedwaan knew the area well, poor and working class, clinging to respectability despite the backyards filled with cars on bricks. 'You got a number for him?'

'Jesus, Faizal. You ever heard of a phone book? Phoenix Engineering. Look it up.'

'Give it to me, Februarie. I know you've got it.'

'Okay, I'm standing in front of the place right now,' Februarie laughed.

'I thought you were at the Royal,' said Riedwaan. 'That shit music I heard in the background.'

'Don't insult the Man in Black,' said Februarie. 'That was Johnny Cash on my new tape deck.'

'Sorry, sorry,' said Riedwaan. 'Tell me what you see.'

Februarie was parked at the end of a littered cul-de-sac. 'Spanish burglar bars on the front,' he said. 'A pile of mail at the front door. Nothing inside. Empty. Everyone gone.'

'When would you say?' asked Riedwaan.

'The neighbours round here aren't that chatty, but one old lady told me no one's been here for a month.'

'She know the people?'

'No. Keeps her curtains shut. This isn't the type of neighbourhood where you pay too much attention to what your neighbours do. All she would say was that a man came here, used it for storage. Then he left and … nothing. I've done a company search. Not much, except some import/export permits to Pakistan.'

'And the other one?' asked Riedwaan.

'The other who?'

'Hofmeyr's other friend?'

'Oh him … Janus Renko.'

'Russian. That must've caused him trouble in the army.'

'From what I heard, he didn't take any shit. Parents were immigrants.'

'Do you know where he is?'

'No sign of him for ten years. No parents, no siblings. No ex-wives like Malan. No children like Hofmeyr. Could be he changed his name. Maybe he bought another passport, moved elsewhere,' said Februarie. 'Could be dead, in which case you'll be hunting a ghost.'

'Where did your witness in McGregor see them?' asked Riedwaan, lighting a cigarette and going over to look at Clare's display.

'She didn't. All she saw was two extra sets of dirty sheets a couple of days before the major was shot. Made me wonder who Hofmeyr had had to stay.'

'Thanks, Februarie. I'll buy you a case of beer when I'm back.'

Riedwaan put down the phone and looked again at the places the boys had been found. A triangulation between Rooibank, the Kuiseb Delta and the ugly cinder-brick town. Pretty much the area where South Africa had camped thousands of miserable, sand-blasted conscripts in their decades-long war in Namibia. Why would any of these men come back? Walvis Bay had been about the worst army posting anyone could get.

Riedwaan looked closely at the pictures of Kaiser Apollis, Fritz Woestyn, Nicanor Jones and Lazarus Beukes. Why would anyone bother to shoot them? Scrawny little rejects, unlikely to live past their teens anyway.

He sat down at Clare's desk and opened her neat folders, looking for her interview transcripts. Details. The devil gave himself away in the detail. Riedwaan opened the first interview and started to read again.

Chapter Forty-four

THE PLUMP BLONDE put down her coffee when Clare pushed open the door of the only travel agency in Walvis Bay.

'Can I help you?' she asked, almost cracking her heavy make-up with the first smile of the day.

'Morning, Sabina,' Clare said as she sat down opposite her.

'Have you been here before?' The girl looked disconcerted.

Clare pointed to the girl's name tag.

'Of course,' said Sabina. 'How can I help you?' She pecked at her keyboard with crimson-tipped nails, bringing the computer to life.

'I was wondering if you knew Mara Thomson.'

'Yes.' The girl's pretty mouth closed on the single syllable. 'I booked her ticket home for her. So if you're looking for her, she's gone. She would've left yesterday.'

'Will you check her booking for me?' Clare asked.

'Sure,' said Sabina. The printer muttered and whirred. 'Here you go. Yesterday. Lufthansa. Nine-thirty a.m.'

'Did you issue the ticket?'

'Oh yes. A week ago.'

'How did she pay?'

'Credit card,' said Sabina. 'But it wasn't hers. Someone from England paid. Look here. Mrs Lily Thomson, it says. Battersea. Where's that?'

'It's in London,' said Clare. 'Can I keep this?'

'Sure. Is there something wrong?'

'She never arrived. Her mother phoned this morning, frantic.'

'Shame!' Sabina's hand went straight to her mouth, though her eyes glittered at the prospect of gossip. 'Poor lady. I told Mara she was leaving it late.'

'Leaving what late?'

'Telling Juan Carlos she was going home. It's hard for them when they stay long, these foreigners. I warned her that Juan Carlos would be angry if she didn't give him enough warning. Her boyfriend. He's Spanish and a sailor. You know how they like to be the ones who leave, not the other way round.'

Clare did not know that, but she let it slide.

'You ask my boyfriend.' Sabina wrote down an address on a slip of paper and handed it to Clare. 'They had a terrible fight, Mara and Juan Carlos, outside the club where Nicolai works.'

'Which club is that?' Clare asked.

'Der Blaue Engel. You must've been there. Everyone goes.' Sabina paused. 'Check at the airport first, but if she didn't leave, go around and wake Nicolai up. He'll know what's what.'

As Clare left, she heard the girl sharing the news with a friend over the telephone. Mara's disappearance and Clare's interest would not stay secret for long.

THE MORNING PLANE to Walvis Bay had landed, loaded and taken off again by the time Clare had parked her car and entered the bleak airport terminal.

'Flight's left,' the check-in clerk told Clare as she approached the counter. He settled his shades on his nose and zipped up his bag.

'I'm not flying,' said Clare. 'I wanted to see if somebody flew yesterday.'

'Can't help you. The flight lists are confidential.'

'It's important. I'm investigating a missing person.' Official idiocy provoked in Clare an overwhelming desire to inflict grievous bodily harm. 'A girl who was meant to arrive in London and didn't.'

'Then you must get a warrant and come back.'

The man stood up, slipped on his jacket and went through the door behind his chair, closing it in Clare's face.

Clare suppressed an urge to swear. A customs official drinking tea at the café table gestured to her.

'Dr Hart,' the official said. 'Did you miss your flight?' It was the large woman who had stamped Clare's passport when she arrived.

'I'm not leaving,' Clare explained. 'I was trying to find out if somebody left on the Lufthansa flight yesterday.'

'That plane,' said the customs official, 'it was two hours late. It left at eleven-thirty eventually. Everyone was crazy here. Who were you looking for?'

'An English girl. I can't find her here, and she never arrived in London. The check-in clerk refused to help.'

'I can help you.' The official looked around. There was nobody in the terminal. 'Follow me.'

The woman led Clare through the restricted area to a heavy metal door. She twisted the combination lock, and the safe swung open, revealing an untidy Aladdin's cave of boxes, full of small square emigration forms.

'There must be thousands of them here,' said Clare.

'Ja, there are,' beamed the customs official. 'If your lady's here, we'll find her.' She picked up a box and cut open the seal. Lying on top was a muddle of forms from the previous day. She gave half of them to Clare. 'What's her name?' she asked.

'Mara Thomson,' said Clare. 'Thin, brown skin, lots of wild hair.'

'I didn't see her,' said the woman, ferreting through the forms. 'But she could've been processed by one of my colleagues.'

They sat down on the floor and rifled through the forms, deciphering the cramped handwriting of yesterday's passengers. Most of them had ticked 'holiday' under 'reason for visit', a few 'business'.

Clare read through the last form for the second time, fear returning, as cold as ice, in the pit of her stomach. 'It's not here,' she said. 'Could she have got on without handing in a form?'

'Not at all,' the woman bristled. 'We're very professional. Maybe she just changed her plans, didn't tell anyone. Young people are like that.'

Clare thanked the woman and went back to her car. She stood without getting in for some time, looking at the horizon. A fiery haze was erasing the thin line separating the sand and sky. A gust of east wind blew sand into her eyes. For the first time since she had arrived in Walvis Bay, she felt the implacable heat of the desert.

Chapter Forty-five

'WHAT?' A MAN's bleary eye appeared through a crack in the door. The heavy chain did not let the door three inches from the steel frame.

'Police,' chanced Clare. 'I have a question for you.'

A sharp-featured man unchained the lock. Nicolai, with a dirty sarong wrapped around him, was as unattractive a sight as his dingy flat above Der Blaue Engel.

'Come into the kitchen. I need some coffee.' Clare followed him into a gloomy room. A week's worth of dishes stood in the sink.

'I know you,' he said, sitting down at the table. 'You came in the bar the other night. Gretchen was dancing.' He smiled, revealing uneven and slightly yellow teeth.

'That's me,' said Clare, sitting down.

'So, Miss …'

'Dr Hart,' said Clare.

'So, Doctor,' Nicolai drawled, 'to what do I owe the honour of your presence?'

'I'm looking for Mara Thomson.'

'Why are you asking me?' The man's voice rose defensively.

'I wanted to speak to her. I heard she was at Der Blaue Engel the night before last.'

The sound of running water came from the direction where Clare guessed the bathroom was. It stopped, thickening the silence in the rancid kitchen. 'Where is she?' she asked.

'How the fuck would I know?'

'Did you see her last night?' Clare persisted.

'No.'

'The night before?'

'Yes. What's the deal? She's a big girl.'

'Who was she there with?'

'Juan Carlos, her boyfriend. Works on the *Alhantra*. Spanish. Pretty boy. I thought he went the other way, but then he arrived there with Mara. Not my type, English virgins,' said Nicolai, 'so you won't find her anywhere here.'

Nicolai leant back, his eyes sliding away from Clare to the doorway. 'This is more my type,' he added.

A Rubenesque woman strolled into the kitchen. She looked Clare over dismissively, poured herself a cup of coffee and strolled out again. Clare wondered if the woman had met Sabina.

'The maid,' said Nicolai, with a smirk. 'We were doing the bed.'

'When did Mara leave Der Blaue Engel?'

'Sometime after Gretchen's show.' Nicolai sipped his coffee. 'Must've been about two. She and Juan Carlos had a fight. Why don't you ask *him* where she is?'

Clare ignored his question. 'What did they argue about?'

'How should I know?' Nicolai said glibly. 'I went outside and saw them in the parking lot. They'd both been drinking. She was crying. He looked angry. Same old, same old.'

'Did they come back inside?'

'Juan Carlos came back later. I didn't see her again. He was upset and said that she'd walked home. Later he left with Ragnar Johansson. You know him, I think?' Clare nodded. 'Ask him. But the last time I checked there wasn't a law that the barman has to know what his customers do in their spare time.'

'There isn't,' said Clare, standing up. 'But there'll be consequences if you're withholding information.'

Nicolai stood too. 'If what I've heard is correct, Dr Hart, you've been paid by me and my fellow taxpayers to catch the motherfucker who's been cleaning up Walvis Bay.' Again, the suggestive smirk. It made his ratty features even less attractive. 'She looked very like those boys of hers, Mara did. Let's hope for her sake there hasn't been a mix-up.' Nicolai moved even closer to Clare. The implication of what he said, his breath rank in her face, made her shiver. 'Now, if you'll excuse me, I have some housework to finish.'

Clare needed no further encouragement. She breathed a sigh of relief as she went down the stairs from Nicolai's apartment. When she got to her car, she pulled out her phone and dialled Tamar's number; she was going to need help getting to Juan Carlos.

'Tamar.' Clare was very happy to hear her voice. 'Mara never arrived home.'

'I got your message,' said Tamar, concerned.

'I've checked at the airport. She didn't take her flight, but all her stuff's gone from George Meyer's house.'

'You need to go out to the *Alhantra* to talk to Juan Carlos?' Tamar guessed.

'As soon as possible,' said Clare.

'I'll organise you a motorboat. Give me a few minutes.'

'Thanks. Any news about Spyt?'

'I'm not holding my breath,' said Tamar. 'Spyt knows this desert too well. If he is found it'll be because he wants to be caught. Van Wyk disappeared out that way early. The evidence that the boys could've been there is all Goagab needs to get his lynch mob going. At least it gives me a bit of breathing space.'

'Did you look at that website I sent you?' Clare had almost forgotten to ask.

'I did. I'm working out what to do. I'm not sure if he's done anything illegal. The site claims all the girls are over eighteen. If they are, my hands are tied.' There was a beat of silence. 'I'm also putting out fires here,' Tamar added.

'What?' asked Clare. 'Riedwaan?'

'He and Goagab haven't exactly hit it off,' said Tamar. 'I had Goagab in my office, raging that the reason we invited you here was to look for a killer, not for young Englishwomen who stir up trouble.'

'I need to know if she was more than just their soccer coach,' said Clare. 'We need to find her.'

THE SKIPPER AND speedboat were ready, the engine idling, when Clare got to the harbour. Five minutes later, the nose of the boat was chopping through the swell, to where the *Alhantra* and other ships were anchored, beyond the bay, where they could avoid harbour fees.

Clare plunged her hands into the front pocket of her jacket, her fingers wrapping around the envelope of Mara's photographs. More precious than a passport, which could be replaced by enduring the supercilious smile of a British embassy official. She opened the envelope, sheltering it from the wind with her body, to look at Mara's well-thumbed photos, the dainty drawings Oscar had done for her. The surreal whimsy of the drawing of a tree, ghostly against the endless dunes, hinted at the child's strange inner world. It was a haunting image. Why had Mara left them?

There was the picture of Mara and Oscar together. Mara searching for a place to belong; the mute boy, yearning for affection. The image caught their fragility and isolation. Mara and Oscar. They had understood each other. The little boy knew that Mara would never leave her pictures, her memories.

That is what he had been trying to make Clare understand.

Clare put herself in the place of the silent, unnoticed boy. She pictured him opening the door off the kitchen. She saw him glide down the passage, a silent red-haired ghost, into Mara's room. Oscar would have found her room emptied but for the photographs hidden in their secret place. He had given them to Clare, so that she would do something.

Clare looked at them again. The last picture, the date in the corner six weeks earlier, was the photograph of Mara and her team. She had the triumphant smile of someone who has beaten the self-timer. She stood in the middle of the group, wiry-haired, boyish, wearing skinny jeans, with her arms around two boys who had turned up dead. The thought that the predator she was hunting had seen the same androgynous likeness in Mara goosefleshed Clare's arms. She put the envelope back in her pocket.

The water unfurled a fringe behind the boat until it came to a bobby halt next to the *Alhantra*. The ship was high in the water, its hold emptied of fish. A ladder lolled like a tongue down the side. At the top of it stood Ragnar Johansson. Clare swallowed the fear that had balled tight and cold in her stomach. She put her hands on the ladder and began to climb, thinking of Mara at the rubbish dump, playing soccer in the dust and broken glass.

So needy of love, of acceptance. She thought of her twined around Juan Carlos and wondered if Mara had given everything of herself over to him, if he had made her pay the ultimate price to assuage his loneliness.

Ragnar helped Clare aboard, his delight in seeing her obvious; his disappointment, when Clare told him the real purpose of her visit, equally apparent. He had half-hoped she had come to find him.

'Wait here,' said Ragnar, escorting Clare to the bridge. 'I'll fetch him for you.'

Ragnar took the steps into the dim interior of the vessel. The metal door screeched when he pushed it open. 'Juan Carlos,' he called into the gloomy cabin. The Spaniard lay on the top bunk. He grunted, without looking down to see who it was. 'You have a visitor.'

Juan Carlos turned onto his back and punched the metal ceiling above him. He licked the blood welling red on his knuckles, then he swung his legs off the side of his bunk and dropped, agile as a cat, to the floor and followed Ragnar to the bridge. He stopped when he saw Clare Hart, pulling his rosary beads from his pocket and passing them through his fingers until the crucifix halted them. Mara had given them to him. If he held the wood to his nose, it whispered of the hot interior.

'You know Dr Hart?' asked Ragnar.

Juan Carlos nodded.

'Where is Mara Thomson?' Clare dispensed with the formalities.

'In London,' said Juan Carlos, the vein at the base of his throat pulsing. He looked from Clare to Ragnar and back again. 'She left yesterday.'

'She never arrived,' said Clare. The creak of the ship was loud in the silence that Clare let stretch between them.

'Maybe she didn't go to her mother's house,' Juan Carlos tried. 'Her mother drive her crazy. So lonely.'

'She didn't check in at the airport.' Clare stepped closer to him. 'Where is she?'

'I don't know.'

'You were with her the night before she left.' Clare kept her voice low, intimately aggressive. 'You went home with her, made love to her, I imagine.'

Juan Carlos shook his head. 'No, no, I said goodbye and then I come back on board.' He looked at Ragnar. 'I had a pass. Twenty-four hours.'

Clare took Juan Carlos's hand in hers, tracing his bloodied knuckles, the scratch along his sinewy wrist, his signet ring, a silver skull and crossbones.

'You didn't take her to the airport?'

'She didn't want me to go with her,' he said. 'What's happened to her? Why are you here?' He snatched his hand back.

'Why did you hit her?' asked Clare.

'I love her.' Juan Carlos said the words with no trace of irony.

Clare pictured the darkened parking lot. The hand raised. Mara's smooth cheek. The ring tearing open her taut skin. The contusion that would be developing.

'I was angry because she was leaving,' Juan Carlos went on. 'I was … I don't know the word.'

'Upset?' said Clare.

'Yes, yes, upset. I was very upset. She was too. She was sad to go from Namibia; she loved it here, her work. She was sad for saying goodbye to me too. So we fight. And then she go away.' He looked Clare in the eye, shifting the balance of power away from her. 'You never fight with someone before you go away?'

'That is the last you saw of her?' Clare shifted the control back. 'In the parking lot? Where you hit her?'

'Yes,' he said, leaning against the metal railing. 'No.'

'You were away from the bar a while.' Clare listened to Juan Carlos's beads clicking persistently in the quiet. 'Nicolai says an hour. That's a long time to spend in a parking lot.'

'Okay, okay,' said Juan Carlos, lighting a cigarette. 'She left. I was very angry to start with, but then I think, is she home? I want to tell her I am sorry, so I follow her. Nothing. She was walking fast when she left, so I go to her house. Her light is on and I knock on her window. She doesn't answer. I call her phone. She doesn't answer. I think she's in the bath maybe. But she doesn't want to speak to me. I leave her a message to call me, that I'm sorry. It's cold and I don't want to wake up the other people in the house. She's angry. She's still a woman, even if she looks like a boy. And I think, what more can I do? So I come back to the bar.' He looked at Ragnar, who nodded.

'What time was that?' Clare asked.

'About three, three-thirty, I suppose,' Ragnar answered. 'Just before I left.'

'Then I get her text message to say sorry the next morning from the airport. Here, look.' Juan Carlos pulled his phone out of his pocket, found the text message and shoved the screen in front of Clare. 'I was already on board ship,' he said. 'I couldn't see her again. I sent her a text, but nothing. It's too late. She was on the plane already.'

'You hit her because you were upset, and she forgave you that easily?' asked Clare. 'You're lying, Juan Carlos.'

'You see that?' Juan Carlos flung his arm towards the desert. The wind whipped tongues of flame-coloured sand into the sky.

The sandstorm was preparing to strike the bunkered town. 'That is what we fought about,' he spat.

'I'm not following you,' said Clare. 'Explain.'

'The east wind … it is on its way,' Juan Carlos continued. His tone was resigned. 'It was the same weather the weekend that we fight.'

'What happened that weekend?'

'She went out to the desert, and the east wind, it was blowing. She take her soccer boys – Kaiser Apollis, Lazarus Beukes, I can't remember the other names – to camp in the Kuiseb River. It was a reward because they did well in some five-a-side tournament. We came in to port for the weekend and I phone her. She didn't want to come back, because she always put them first. She say that's what they needed to see: someone putting them first. But I tell her to leave them and come and see me. I say she should fetch them in the morning. I told her they were used to looking after themselves. That they would be fine. It was true.'

Juan Carlos watched a gull turn on a column of air, mesmerised by its flight. 'They *were* fine that weekend, except the one who got sick. That is what we fight about. She felt bad that she left them out there. She blames herself. We went back to fetch them the next day and they were not there. She found them later at the dump. They say they had walked back; that is why the young one, he got sick.'

'And that's why you hit her?' asked Clare.

'I didn't want her to tell you.' Juan Carlos looked down at his feet. 'She wanted to come to you or the other lady cop and tell you that she had been with them all and that now they were all dead. She was crazy about it. I tell her it was just coincidence. I was saying, no, if she tells, then the police will want to question her and me. And the ship is sailing tomorrow. If the police want to ask questions, then I can't go too and I won't get my fishing bonus.'

'How many boys did you say there were there?' asked Clare.

'Five. It was the five-a-side tournament.'

Two. Three. Five. One with no marking. One unaccounted for. Clare calculated how long it would take to get to the dump when she was finished. Half an hour, she reckoned.

'You'll have to stay on board,' said Clare. 'Captain Johansson will keep you under guard.'

'Why?' Juan Carlos pleaded. 'What have I done?'

'You were the last person seen with her,' said Clare. 'If you'd prefer you can come ashore and go to the cells.'

Juan Carlos paled.

'I'll need your cellphone.' Clare held out her hand.

'For what?' asked Juan Carlos. 'I tell you already, she text me.'

'I want to track all the calls on your phone,' said Clare. 'Calls in and out. You can choose: I take your phone and check, or you can come in with me and I put you in the cells for refusing to cooperate.'

Clare was bluffing, but he was a foreigner, wanting to get home. It worked. Juan Carlos handed her the phone, the fight gone out of him.

'Ragnar,' she said, 'can you keep him under guard?'

'No problem,' said Ragnar. 'We're out of here soon. If you want him longer, and you've got grounds, I'll have to hand him over to the Namibian police.'

Ragnar walked with Clare to the top of the ladder. 'You think he did something to that girl?' he asked.

'The odds are against him.'

'You're not a gambler, Clare.'

'No, I'm not. But I won't take any more chances either. If Mara knew something about what happened to those boys, then Juan Carlos might too. I'd watch him. It might be for his own sake.' Clare stepped onto the ladder to climb down to the speedboat waiting for her. 'Where are you headed?' she asked.

'Luanda tomorrow, after the shareholders' inspection,' said Ragnar. 'Then Spain. You can imagine that I need this like a hole in the head.'

Chapter Forty-six

IT WAS QUIET at the rubbish dump. The first flurry of trucks had come and gone and the incinerator was pluming smoke into the sky. The boys who had been so eager to greet Clare the first time she had visited slunk away. She went to the lean-to where Kaiser Apollis and Fritz Woestyn had shared a mattress. The bed was untouched, as was their meagre assortment of garments. One of the braver boys hovered in the doorway, a younger child sheltering behind him.

Clare called him over and showed him Mara's team photograph. 'Where is this boy?' she asked.

The boy's expression closed down like a mask. 'Ronaldo's gone,' he said, his voice low.

'Where?'

The boy shrugged. 'Miss Mara took him.'

'Mara took him? Where? Where did she take him?' Clare's voice wavered.

'To the desert.' Emotion flickered in the boy's eyes, but Clare could not read it. 'He never came back again.'

'Okay, where did she take him?' Clare softened her tone.

'Ask Mr Meyer,' the boy said. 'He knows where they go.'

The younger boy cupped his hands and looked at Clare, eyes wide, pleading. 'You got some change for bread, madam?' Clare fished in her bag for money.

George Meyer was alone in his office, his hands folded on the empty desk. His tie, knotted too tight below the Adam's apple, bulged a fold of skin onto his collar.

'What do you want this time, Dr Hart?' he asked when Clare appeared in the doorway.

'These boys. Four are dead. Now Mara's missing.' Clare propped the photograph against his hands. 'Where is this one?'

Meyer picked up the photograph and looked at the frail boy. The child's bony ribs tented the skin on his chest. 'Ronaldo. I haven't seen him for a while. He was sick.' He handed the photograph back to Clare.

'Where will I find him?' said Clare. 'If he isn't dead yet.' Clare leant close to Meyer. She kept the impatience from her voice.

'The only place that would take him would be the Sisters of Mercy.'

Clare remembered Lazarus's fear of the nuns. 'Where are they, these Sisters of Mercy?'

'Out in the Kuiseb, past the delta. The road to Rooibank. You'll see the turn-off there.'

'A convent?' asked Clare.

'It's a hospice now. The sisters take people who no one else wants.'

'And it was Mara who took him there?'

'Yes. Those boys on the dump are like a pack; they look after their own. But this child was the runt of the litter. Mara was attached to him. She has a thing for underdogs. Why do you think she liked Oscar?' Meyer's voice snagged in his throat. 'Or me for that matter?'

CLARE TURNED OFF the tar road, leaving the row of pylons and phone lines that trudged on to the airport. There was nothing to see but the mesmerising expanse of gravel rolling up to meet the car, then fanning dust behind her. The outcrop of black rock reared above the red sand like the exposed skeleton of some ancient animal. Clare bumped down the track towards it, surprised by the alluring green cleft in the heat-cracked surface. The convent had been built into the cool overhangs and caves that formed the oasis.

Clare parked and walked down the swept path that led into a perfect amphitheatre. A woman came towards her, her welcoming smile a startling splash of white against her dark skin. A loose wimple covered her head, her gnarled feet secured in sturdy sandals. A Sister of Mercy.

'Welcome.' The woman took Clare's hand between her cool palms. 'Come out of the sun.' She led Clare to a shaded veranda. 'Wait here. I'll fetch the Mother Superior.'

Clare sat on a bench and closed her eyes, the cloistered tranquillity of the oasis working its seductive magic on her.

'My child.' A gentle voice broke the spell.

Clare opened her eyes. A tall woman stood before her. Her habit fell from broad shoulders which looked as if they carried the weight of the Lord with ease. The hand she offered Clare was muscular, calloused. Her face had been weathered down to its essence: a beaked nose, arched iron-grey eyebrows, a tapestry of lines and crevices on the tanned skin.

'I'm Sister Rosa. You're welcome here.' Her accented English gave an old-fashioned lilt to her words.

'Good morning, Sister. I'm Clare Hart.'

'You have no bags with you. I presume that you want something specific from us?'

'I wanted to ask you some questions about a child who was brought here,' Clare explained.

'Follow me.' Sister Rosa's habit swished wide, drawing Clare into its wake. Clare followed her into a cool study. On a low table was a pile of dog-eared pamphlets about prayer and meditation, healing and love, HIV/Aids and dying with dignity.

'What is it that you are looking for?' Sister Rosa asked, sitting down.

'A boy,' said Clare. 'I'm hoping he is here with you, alive.'

'His name?' asked Sister Rosa.

'Ronaldo. That's all I know. He doesn't seem to have a surname.'

Sister Rosa opened a leather-bound ledger. She flicked through it until she found the page dedicated to him. 'Here you are.' She pushed it over to Clare. 'All I have about him.'

The notes were brief: the boy's name. His age: barely fourteen. Parents: unknown. Previous address: none. Date of arrival: four weeks earlier, just before Fritz Woestyn was found dead by the pipeline.

'A young English girl, Mara Thomson, brought him here,' said Clare.

'Poor child,' said Sister Rosa. 'She lost her heart to this place.'

'You knew her well?'

Sister Rosa nodded. 'She came out here a few times.'

'Four of the boy's friends are dead. And now Mara has disappeared,' said Clare.

'Where is she?' Sister Rosa's voice was full of concern.

'I'm trying to find that out,' said Clare. 'When last did you see her?'

'About a week ago. She came to see this boy you seek.'

'I'd like to see him. Maybe he can help.'

'Come this way then,' said the nun after a moment's hesitation. 'He has some lucid moments.'

Clare followed Sister Rosa down a path shaded by tamarisks. At the end of it was a sparse row of old stone-crossed graves. Alongside these was an abundance of new mounds, lozenge-shaped heaps with wooden crosses. The newest graves had posies of veld flowers on them. The rest were bare. Sister Rosa passed the graveyard and walked towards a stone building shaded by vivid green trees.

The interior of the building was dim and cool. An old nun, her face wrinkled as a walnut, rose as they entered. 'The sick boy?' Sister Rosa asked the nun. The woman pointed to an open door and they went inside.

'There he is, your Ronaldo.'

A child, impossibly thin, lay on a narrow bed with a drip attached to his arm. His breathing was laboured; the lips were cracked and dry; his skin was a dull grey. There was a photograph on the bedside table. The same boy propped against plumped pillows, a toothy grin on his gaunt face.

'Mara took that the last time she was here,' said Sister Rosa. 'He was so pleased with it.' She moistened a cloth under the tap and wiped the boy's face. Ronaldo's eyes flickered open, then closed again.

'Mara knew how ill he is?' Clare asked.

'She phoned a couple of days ago and I had to tell her he was much worse,' said Sister Rosa. 'It happens like that, with his condition, but she was distraught. Kept on saying it was her fault.'

'Has Mara brought other boys to you?'

'No,' said Sister Rosa. 'Only him, although she used to raise money for us. Ronaldo played in her soccer team and she said something about him being pushed too hard. It must've broken his immune system, because he collapsed after a camping trip that Mara had organised for the team. She brought him here afterwards, asking us to keep quiet. Ronaldo was afraid other people would find out. There's a terrible stigma about this illness.'

'What's killing him?' asked Clare.

'Technically, a single-digit CD4 count. He has no immune system and a host of secondary infections. That's what will stop his heart from beating in the end.' Sister Rosa stroked the boy's forehead. 'But his heart was broken a long time before.'

'Abuse?' asked Clare.

'Abuse, poverty, Aids. It's not hard for a child to support himself in a place like Walvis Bay, but the way he had to make a living is a death sentence. It was too late for treatment when we got him, so I suppose you could say he came here to die.' Sister Rosa turned to Clare. 'What was it that you wanted to ask him?'

'I wanted to ask him about that camping trip in the desert.' Clare looked down at the boy, the sheets barely raised over his emaciated body. 'About where they went and what happened. Seems to me it was the start of something that played out to a very bloody finish.'

'At least these have healed,' said Sister Rosa, picking up the child's right hand and smoothing open the palm.

'What was there?'

'Blisters, deep ones. It's only the scars now. They were infected and then healed so slowly. Poor child, he was in agony.' She drew Ronaldo's thin sheet up to his chin and smoothed his pillows.

'Do you know what they were from?' asked Clare, her pulse quickening.

'I asked him; he said it was from the digging they did, but I couldn't work out where. Somewhere in the desert. Maybe they had casual work on the water pipeline. He had some money when Mara brought him.' The nun opened the Bible lying next to the boy's bed. There was forty Namibian dollars in notes tucked into Revelations. Clare thought about Kaiser Apollis and the diary with one hundred dollars in it. She tried to remember the boy's hands, but all she could picture was the tipless Apollo finger.

'He was terrified of the desert,' Sister Rosa continued. 'It must've been torture for him to camp there with Mara. I sat up with him one night. The moon was full, and he couldn't sleep with the curtains open. He kept saying they would see him.'

'Who?'

'Who knows?' said Sister Rosa. 'Whoever it is that you see when your temperature hits forty.'

There was no point in asking the boy any questions. Each shallow breath marked a loosening of Ronaldo's tenuous hold on life. Clare stood up and followed Sister Rosa to the entrance lobby. The old nun they had passed on the way in nodded politely to her.

'Did anybody come to see the boy apart from Mara?' Clare asked on impulse.

'Nobody,' said Sister Rosa. 'Except you.'

'You,' the old nun interrupted, 'and one of the missionaries.'

'Who are they?' Clare swung around to face the woman.

'The Christian Ladies' Mission. A group of worthy wives. Protestants,' Sister Rosa said with a wry smile. 'They work with prostitutes. They rarely come out here. I suppose they've given up on us Catholics.'

'When was that, Sister?' Clare asked the old nun.

'Three days ago,' she replied. 'Just before Ronaldo started slipping away from us.'

'What was she doing here?' Sister Rosa asked. 'Why was I not informed?'

'I'm sorry, Sister,' said the older nun. 'I forgot my sewing in the convent and when I came back the woman was here. The child was very upset, but I got her to leave and he settled down again.'

'Did you know her?' Clare asked.

'She was young. Fair. I don't know her name. She said she wanted to save him, but I think that even she could see that it was too late.' The nun hesitated. 'They can be ... agitating, reformed sinners. Zealous.'

'You'll find them easily, Dr Hart,' Sister Rosa said. 'They have their haven, as they call it, down near the docks.' The woman's hand on Clare's elbow propelled Clare back into the heat.

CLARE'S CAR WAS a furnace when she got back to it. She opened the window, letting the hot air escape before she got in. The heat swam on the surface of rocks, the road and the car as she drove back to Walvis Bay, mirroring her thoughts. What did Mara know? Why had she hidden the boy Ronaldo out here? And why had she not said anything? Why had Lazarus said nothing? This circuit of questions was interrupted only when Clare found the Christian Ladies' Mission. It was situated opposite Der Blaue Engel, where the ladies could keep an eye on their husbands while saving the town from moral turpitude. Housed on the ground floor of an ugly facebrick building, the entrance to the Mission was decorated with watercolour landscapes and crocheted doilies, no doubt donated by its members.

The woman who got up to greet Clare was slender, her hair set in even, rigid waves. 'Dr Hart?'

Clare was getting used to strangers knowing her name. She nodded.

'How can I help you?'

'I need to know about one of your members who visited a boy out at the Catholic hospice in the desert.'

'Why, may I ask, should I give you this information?' The woman's mouth was a red-lipsticked slot in her face.

'I'm working on the investigation into the recent murders of—'

'The boys?' the woman interrupted.

'Them,' said Clare.

'Well,' said the woman, pursing her lips, 'we've tried to reach out to street children before, especially the Aids orphans. But it's difficult to get children who have strayed from the authority of adults to conform.'

'Which of your members would've visited him there?' asked Clare.

'I'll check in the record book. But I can't imagine anybody did. When was it?'

Clare gave her the date, and the woman opened the book and paged through to the relevant entry. 'Nothing then.' She shook her head. 'Not to the convent at any rate.'

'The woman who visited him was blonde apparently. Young,' Clare said.

The woman frowned. 'I can't think of anybody who fits that particular description.' She pushed the ledger over to Clare. 'And see for yourself. Nobody went out that day. Everything's logged, because our volunteers can claim for petrol.'

'Would one of your members have gone without filling in the forms?' asked Clare.

The woman drew herself up, offended. 'All our volunteers are working here towards salvation and rehabilitation. Part of that process means that they must follow procedures in all situations. The leadership, and I include myself in that, are unwavering about such details.'

'Who could it have been, then?'

'Dr Hart, I'm a lay preacher, not a detective.'

Chapter Forty-seven

RIEDWAAN WAS IN the special ops room, a takeaway coffee in hand and Clare's notes and several official-looking printouts spread out in front of him. The sheets spiralled on a gust of wind when she opened the door.

'Where've you been?' Riedwaan got up to retrieve the pages.

'Out in the desert,' said Clare. 'At sea.'

'That's how I feel, going through all of this.' He gestured to Clare's notes.

'Did I miss anything?'

'Nothing that I can see.' Riedwaan sat down again and picked up a heap of papers. 'I was just checking through these car rentals. See who's been passing through.'

'Any patterns?' Clare asked.

'Not yet. German tourists mainly. A few businessmen coming up for meetings. I'm working through them. You haven't come across the name Phoenix Engineering while you've been here?'

'Doesn't ring a bell,' said Clare. 'Why? Are they on your list?'

'Februarie mentioned the name to me,' he said. 'He phoned earlier about Hofmeyr's murder. It's the name of a company that one of Hofmeyr's connections set up after he left the army. A guy called Malan.'

'Haven't heard of him either,' said Clare. She picked up the car hire lists, scanning the names. 'No Phoenixes here,' she said. 'Although there're a couple of other Greek names sprinkled in. Here's one: Siren Swimwear. That sounds promising. How about this one: Centaur Consulting?'

'The advantages of a classical education revealed,' said Riedwaan.

'Funny ha-ha,' said Clare. She scanned the list again. 'There's also Arizona Iced Tea and New York Trading and Washington Pan-African Ministries. What're you looking for?'

'I'm just casting about for an easy answer, I guess. A psycho ex-soldier running amok would be easy to explain. It'd certainly make the Namibians happy.'

'You've had Goagab on your back then?' Clare sat down on the edge of the desk.

'I had the pleasure. He was in here demanding a resolution before his tourism press junket or whatever it is that makes him sweat in his Hugo Boss shirts.' Riedwaan crumpled his coffee cup and pitched it into the bin on the other side of the room. 'Tell me about Mara's sailor boy. You think he did something to her?'

'I don't know what he's hiding, but he implied that she was.'

'You could hide an army out here and no one would find it,' said Riedwaan, pointing to the waves of sand on the map.

A movement at the door caught their eye, and they both looked up to find Tamar standing in the doorway. 'You see nothing,' she said, her voice soft. 'Everything's hidden by the heat and the distance, then these dunes pick up their skirts and move and everything's exposed. What did you find out about Mara?' she asked Clare.

Clare gave her the rundown: that Mara and Juan Carlos had fought about a camping trip; that Mara had wanted to tell the police that she'd left the boys alone in the desert while she was servicing Juan Carlos's needs for the night; that the boys were being targeted now; and that Juan Carlos had shut her up.

'They fought about it again the night before Mara was supposed to leave,' Clare said. 'Mara went home and he says he went back to the club. Says he never saw her again, though she apparently sent him a text message from the airport.'

'What do you think?' Tamar asked Clare.

'About him?'

'About her, her and the boys?'

'Hard to say. If someone is targeting homeless pretty boys, then it could be a coincidence, I suppose. She was working with them, spending more time with them than anyone else does, so a "wrong place, wrong time" is possible.'

'Funny things, coincidences,' said Riedwaan.

'Never happens in movies, because no one will ever believe them,' said Tamar. 'In real life they happen all the time. Wrong place, wrong time. There's you: dead.'

'She left all her photographs behind.' Clare put the envelope of snapshots on the table.

'Memories go sour sometimes.' Riedwaan flicked through them. 'You move on, leave the past behind. Could be that.'

Clare was sceptical, but said nothing. 'Tamar, do you know the Sisters of Mercy?' she asked. 'Out in the desert, in an old castle?'

'Yes, towards Rooibank. There's an oasis there. Some German count built a castle for the love of his life and she never came. So he donated it to the Catholic Church, specifying that it be run as a convent. Now it's a hospice.'

'There's a lesson in that,' said Riedwaan. 'I'm not quite sure what.'

'Why do you ask?' said Tamar.

Clare picked up the photograph of Mara and the five-a-side team and pointed to Ronaldo. 'A boy who played in Mara's team was out there. George Meyer told me about him. I went to talk to him.'

'What did he say?' asked Tamar.

'Nothing. He's on his way out,' said Clare. 'Full-blown Aids. Too far gone for treatment.'

'He's the last boy alive,' Riedwaan said. 'Her whole team, red-carded.'

'There's something else,' said Clare. 'The Mother Superior told me a woman had visited him. She thought it was one of the Christian Mission ladies, but I went past there and they have no record of anyone visiting.'

A sudden gust of the east wind sprayed sand against the office window. Clare jumped, then continued: 'His hands were infected when he came in, blisters all over the palms. His illness was triggered by exhausting himself doing some kind of digging.'

'Digging where?' asked Tamar. 'None of those kids would be picked up to work. First, nobody would trust them, and, second, if anyone did hire them, they'd be bust under the child labour law – one of the many unintended consequences of a progressive constitution.'

'Catch 22,' said Clare.

'I wonder what they were digging for,' Riedwaan said. He opened the files of autopsy photographs and sorted out the close-ups. 'Look at this.' Kaiser Apollis and Lazarus Beukes both had thin, livid marks across their palms.

'Could be blisters,' said Clare, looking at the photographs. 'Easy to pass over in a homeless child whose hands and feet would be rough and cracked.'

'You get anything else from your interview with Juan Carlos?' asked Tamar.

'His phone.' Clare held it up. 'I want to check out his story about the night Mara went missing. I've asked Ragnar Johansson to keep him on board until you've decided if you want to keep him here. In the meantime, I want to check some phone records.'

'There's a place out in the industrial area that'll figure it out for you in no time.' Tamar wrote down the address. 'Cell City. They'll help you out.'

'Did you talk to Van Wyk?' Clare asked Tamar, folding the piece of paper.

Tamar shook her head. 'He's still out of cellphone range. He's scouring the desert with Goagab, but I did find Chesney, the name we saw painted on the cave. Turns out he's Van Wyk's nephew.'

The mention of Chesney's name made Clare shiver: Chesney, Minki, LaToyah, the heat and the stench of the dead cat. 'What did he say?' she asked.

'Not much at first,' said Tamar. 'But Elias can be persuasive when he needs to be. He convinced Chesney that it'd be simpler if he just showed him a couple of files, his web cam, and some other incriminating evidence. The girl you saw, LaToyah, is fifteen, so as far as Van Wyk goes, it'll be a fairly straightforward case of statutory rape.'

'All we need to do is find him then,' said Clare.

'What's this?' Riedwaan asked. 'Van Wyk been cradle-snatching?'

'A cop getting freebies off the girls he protects. Oldest trick in the policeman's book,' said Tamar. 'How about you find this killer now.' She was standing in the doorway, keys in hand. 'My water broke half an hour ago and I'm off to have this baby in peace.'

Riedwaan went pale. 'We'll take the bike.' He tossed Clare the spare helmet.

Outside, the sun sparkled off the razor wire, the snagged plastic flapping, its colour bleaching in the heat. Even the black slagheap across the road managed to give off an ebony gleam.

Clare slipped her arms around Riedwaan and her hands under his jacket.

'It is better with you here,' she said as they drove through town.

'I was waiting for you to say that,' said Riedwaan.

'Only because I like having a driver,' she teased him. 'There it is. Cell City.'

THE TWO CHINLESS wonders who ran the cellphone shop looked as if they could hack into the Pentagon. Darren was blond, his hair hanging in greasy rats' tails over the faded picture on his T-shirt – some heavy metal group doomed to permanent obscurity, Clare hoped. She explained that they wanted to know where Mara's last SMS had come from.

'No problem,' he said.

'You want a list of all the numbers called? Texts?' asked Carl. He had dark hair, and was as soft and blubbery as his friend was bony. 'I can download the pictures too.'

'That'd be great,' said Clare, writing down Mara's number. 'How long will it take?'

'I can do that for you straight away,' he said. 'Darren'll take a bit of time, but this is a small town, so there's just a couple of thousand cell users. Do you want to come back?'

'We'll wait.'

Darren beamed up at them from behind his laptop. 'Go get some coffee there.' He pointed to a Portuguese café across the road. 'A watched hacker never cracks.'

Carl found this hilarious. He emitted a series of stricken hoots that passed for a laugh.

'Come on,' Riedwaan said to Clare. 'We'll get some coffee.'

The café served unexpectedly good coffee. They took their cups and some rolls to the only table outside.

'So, tell me about Van Wyk,' said Riedwaan.

Clare smiled grimly as she told him of Van Wyk's sidelines in extortion and amateur porn. Nothing pleased her more than ridding the world of another corrupt bully.

They had just finished eating when Carl undulated across the road. He grabbed a Coke and a Peppermint Crisp on his way to their table.

'Darren,' he said admiringly. 'He's a fucking wizard.' He placed a single sheet of paper on the greasy tablecloth. A list of numbers in one column, coordinates in the other. Carl bit off half of his chocolate bar before pointing to the last number. 'There you go. The SMS you were looking for. That's it.'

'Where was it sent from?' asked Riedwaan.

'The airport tower is where it's first logged.'

'So she was there?'

'Who was there?' Carl shovelled the second half of the bar into his mouth and washed it down with Coke.

'Mara Thomson. The girl who sent the message.'

'This one?' Carl scrolled through the photos in Juan Carlos's cellphone, stopping when he got to one of Mara, naked on a sand dune, smiling at the phone camera.

'That's the one.'

'So pretty,' said Carl wistfully. 'What's she done that you're looking for her?'

'It's what she hasn't done that's worrying me,' said Clare. 'She left Walvis Bay, but never arrived in London. Her boyfriend claims that the last he heard from her was this SMS from the airport.'

'Well, from the tower closest to the airport. But that covers quite a range out there. It could be anywhere from the Kuiseb Delta to Rooibank.'

'These other numbers?' Clare asked.

'Recent calls. A couple to Spain. The others are all local numbers. Looks like whoever's phone this is had this girl's number on speed dial.'

'I tried to call her earlier,' said Clare. 'It just says the number is unavailable and to try again later.'

'That means she's out of range or her phone is off,' Carl explained. 'Or her battery's dead.'

'If Mara was in the vicinity of the airport,' said Clare, 'then why did she never go in?'

'Oh no,' said Carl, excited at the prospect of playing detective, 'she got on the plane all right. Check this out.' He pointed to a column on the next page, listing all the SMS messages. 'This is what she said.'

Riedwaan looked at the screen: *On the plane. Sorry. I love U. X Mara.*

'I saw that,' said Clare. 'But it seemed pretty standard to me. Anybody could have sent that text.'

'Amateurish as a cover,' said Riedwaan. 'Someone was going to phone when she didn't get to London.'

'But if you go missing in the desert, it can be a long time before anyone finds you,' said Clare, deciphering the columns of digital information that Darren had teased from the phone.

'Unless you're a homeless boy. Then after two days you're stuck up like a billboard advertising the fact that someone really didn't like you.'

'Have a look at this.' Clare pointed to the time the message was received: nine-twenty.

Riedwaan and Carl looked at her blankly.

'Her plane was two hours late. Nobody was even on the plane until eleven.'

Riedwaan parked his bike outside the station. Clare was heading for the door before he even had a chance to switch off the engine.

'That schoolteacher you mentioned in McGregor,' Riedwaan called after her. 'Did she marry again?'

'Darlene?' Clare turned around, remembering that she had meant to talk to her again.

Riedwaan nodded.

'No, she'd had enough of men after her first husband. She just shed her married name. Why do you—?'

The shrill sound of Clare's phone interjected. She took it out of her pocket and looked at the flashing screen. 'Tertius Myburgh,' she said to Riedwaan. 'My pollen expert. I thought he'd vanished.

Let me take this.' She held the receiver to her ear and nodded a greeting at the receptionist as she entered the station.

Riedwaan followed her down the passage in a daze, his manner unusually calm.

Clare sat down at her desk and disconnected. 'He's got my results,' she said, reaching for a mapbook. 'I'm going to meet him at Dolphin Beach. It's halfway between Walvis Bay and Swakopmund.'

'Can you handle this on your own?' asked Riedwaan. 'There's something I must do.'

'I'll call you when I'm back,' said Clare, grabbing her keys. 'Where are you going?'

'To see your ballet-dancing divorcée,' Riedwaan smiled. 'Darlene Ruyters. To find out what she can tell me about centaurs and phoenixes.'

Chapter Forty-eight

ONE KICK WOULD have ripped the newly installed chain out of the door, but Riedwaan rang the doorbell.

'Yes?' Darlene Ruyters opened the door a crack.

'Captain Faizal. Police.' Riedwaan always felt stupid holding up his badge like an American movie cop, but he did it anyway. People watched so much television these days they expected it. Darlene put out a hand for the badge before sliding back the chain and letting him in. Riedwaan stepped into the gloomy hallway. The smell of a thousand houses he had visited: the combination of yesterday's cooking and fear.

'Where is he, Darlene?'

Darlene's eyes widened. 'There's nobody here.' She crossed her arms. She wasn't wearing a bra.

Pushing past her, Riedwaan went down the passage. He opened the first door, Darlene's bedroom. Peach nylon lace and pale-green walls. A worn, shaggy carpet and a pile of teddy bears on the bed. He opened the next door: a bed, a table, a chair, a lamp. Not a thing out of place, but the windows closed, and the smell of a man in the stale air.

'Where's he gone?' Riedwaan demanded.

Darlene was right behind him, her dark hair framing her pale, once-beautiful face. 'You can see. There's no one,' she said, turning away, but Riedwaan caught her arm and swung her around again, light as a bird against his arm. The bruises on her wrists had faded to shadows. Riedwaan nudged her collar away from her neck. There was a livid contusion on her clavicle. He felt the back of her head. She winced. The skin there was broken.

'Tell me where he is,' said Riedwaan. 'Your house guest, who left such a charming thank-you gift.'

'I don't know what you're talking about,' Darlene whispered. Riedwaan let her go. She swayed on her bare feet.

'The guy who hired the car. Centaur Consulting,' said Riedwaan. He pulled the car-hire forms out of his pocket and showed them to her. 'Fifty-three 2nd Avenue. Your address. He hasn't returned the car yet. Your ex-husband.'

'Malan.' The name twisted Darlene's mouth as if it were poison. She slid down the wall until she was folded, small as a child, on the floor.

Riedwaan was unmoved. 'When did he leave?'

Darlene stopped resisting, a drowning woman too tired to fight any more. 'The day before yesterday,' she whispered.

'Where did he go?' Riedwaan knelt down in front of her. He lifted her chin so that she had to look at him.

'To cash in his pension.' Darlene laughed, her bitterness corrosive.

'What're you talking about?' said Riedwaan. 'I'm out of time.'

'What are you going to do? Hit me too?' She looked him up and down. 'I'm an expert in that area and *you*,' she spat, 'haven't got it in you.'

'Why did Malan come here to you?' asked Riedwaan.

'I don't know. He didn't explain. He wanted somewhere to stay. Somewhere where he wouldn't be seen. I don't know.' Darlene got up slowly, the pain of movement making her wince.

'You didn't refuse?'

'This is what I got *without* arguing.' Darlene unbuttoned her blouse. Her delicate body was black and blue to the waist. 'I thought, it can't last forever. And it didn't. He left.'

Riedwaan put out his hands and gently buttoned up her blouse again. 'Where will I find him?' he asked.

'If he's not out in the desert then I hope to God he's gone.'

'The desert?'

'The sand on his boots. He made me clean them for old times' sake. They were full of the golden dust you find further in. Fool's gold.'

'Why would he be back? Think, Darlene.'

She shook her head. 'I don't know. But if I know them at all, I can guess.'

'Them?' Riedwaan took her by the shoulders. She winced again.

'Malan. Hofmeyr.' She waved her hand dismissively. 'Except he's dead now.'

'Janus Renko?' Riedwaan tested.

A shadow passed over Darlene's face. 'I haven't heard *that* name in a long time.'

'You haven't seen him?' asked Riedwaan.

'Not since the South African army left, and please, God, I won't see him again. He made my husband and Hofmeyr look like Sunday school teachers.'

Darlene took a packet out of her back pocket and fingered out a cigarette. Riedwaan held out his lighter for her.

'What was this pension?' he asked.

Darlene shook her head again.

'Guess then, Darlene. Guess.' Riedwaan kept the urgency out of his voice. It was like coaxing a wild bird to take food from his hand.

'I'd say it's something to do with the weapons they worked on during the war.'

'What?'

'You saw all that stuff, guerrilla fighters drugged and dropped from planes. People bleeding to death after being detained. Drugs that made your heart stop. Where do you think they practised?'

'Where did they do this?' asked Riedwaan.

'First at Vastrap, then they had a place out in the Namib, in the Kuiseb Delta somewhere. I never went there.'

'Would they have taken anyone else out there?' asked Riedwaan. 'Boys, maybe?'

She considered the possibility. 'Not likely,' she said, holding out her bruised hands. 'It's women he likes to see grovel and beg. He's very old South Africa, so if he had boys out there it's because there was hard labour to be done.'

'Where would they go,' said Riedwaan, 'if they've come back? Tell me, Darlene. If they've come back for some of their old toys and you say nothing, you'll have way more than a couple of homeless kids on your conscience.'

Darlene's resistance crumbled. 'There's one place. I'll show you.' Riedwaan followed her as she walked down the passage. 'Here.' She pointed to an old survey map taped to the wall. 'It's a map of the Kuiseb before the big flood a few years ago. This was an old army site, before the river changed course after the flood.' She pointed to a marking next to the old Kuiseb River. 'It's this area around the old railway line that caused all the trouble between the Topnaars and the army; it was full of !nara plants. Now it's giving Goagab headaches. Maybe that's where they tried to go. Some kind of sick reunion.'

'Can I take this?' Riedwaan asked.

Darlene nodded and Riedwaan rolled up the map.

He closed the front door behind him and heard the chain rattle as Darlene locked herself in. She must have slid down the wall and crouched there, because he did not hear her footsteps recede.

RIEDWAAN'S BIKE SURGED to life. He made the short trip back to the station in record time. He closed the special ops room door and called Phiri, pleading with his acid-sounding secretary that she get him out of his weekly planning meeting. While he waited for Phiri to call back, he looked at Clare's map of where the dead boys had been found. Two, three, five, the first one with nothing. He plotted possible trajectories, trying to figure out where they had been killed from where they had been dumped. Two of them in the east; two in the west. No-man's-land in the middle.

'Faizal?' Phiri called back in five minutes.

'Sir, I'm glad you—'

'I had a call from someone called Van Wyk,' Phiri cut him short. 'He tells me that Captain Damases is off the case and that he's in command and, thanks, but no thanks for the assistance. I then had a call from Town Councillor Goagab saying that, apart from apprehending the suspected serial killer, who seems to be some kind of desert bogeyman, the show's over. What've you done this time?'

'I've done my job,' said Riedwaan.

'That's what I was afraid of,' said Phiri.

'Goagab and Van Wyk would like to see it as solved,' said Riedwaan.

'You and Clare don't?'

'No,' said Riedwaan.

'Despite the fact that the luminal showed positive for blood on the cart?' Phiri asked.

'The Topnaar could've moved the bodies when the boys were already dead,' Riedwaan explained. 'But I don't think he killed them. You dump a body out here, and no one will find it. Vultures, predators, heat. All you'll have is bleached bones in a couple of weeks. I'd put money on that Topnaar moving these boys to draw attention to their murders.'

'What for?' asked Phiri, puzzled.

'There's a weapons test site that a special ops unit used to use,' said Riedwaan. 'Bang in the middle of the Topnaar land. I want to check it out.'

'That's it?' said Phiri.

'That, and the fact that a couple of old soldiers who used to be involved in covert stuff seem to have been around.'

'That lot are finished, Faizal. They are all practising their golf swings in Wilderness.'

'If your intelligence is correct, this little game is not about ideology,' said Riedwaan. 'This is about money.'

There was a long pause. Riedwaan waited it out. 'What sort of weapons?' asked Phiri. 'What sort of money?'

'The records are all gone,' said Riedwaan, 'but I'd say bio-chemical.'

'I have one card left to keep you there,' Phiri said reluctantly. 'And that's a bluff. You've got twenty-four hours.'

'Thank you, sir,' said Riedwaan, breathing a silent sigh.

'This had better be good,' warned Phiri. 'If it's not, there's a post in Pofadder that needs filling.'

'I'm sorry, sir,' Riedwaan cut in, 'but I have a call waiting.' He saw with relief that it was Clare.

'What've you got?' he asked as he switched calls.

'Nothing yet,' said Clare. 'Myburgh hasn't pitched.'

'Wait for him,' said Riedwaan. 'I'm going to check out an old military site. If Karamata's around, I'll get him to take me.'

'Good plan,' said Clare. 'Elias knows the area well. What did Darlene tell you?'

'That her ex-husband's been back.'

'Surprise, surprise,' said Clare. 'With those bruises, who else? You think he's been killing these boys?'

'Why come all the way to Walvis Bay to kill street children?' said Riedwaan. 'There are enough in Cape Town.'

'Another coincidence?' Clare asked.

'That's what's bugging me. We'll discuss it over dinner.'

Chapter Forty-nine

CLARE WAS WATCHING the fishermen, their rods sticking up like insects' feelers above the shoreline, when the battered red bakkie drew up next to her. She got out, the sand blowing off the desert stinging her calves. Tertius Myburgh unlocked the door and she slid in next to him, holding the door against the wind.

'Here,' said Myburgh, pushing an envelope across the cracked seat. He was tense; his hands were shaking.

Dr Clare Harriet Hart. Her full name in black ink: like an accusation. Clare opened it. Five pages of Myburgh's dense, looped cursive. Clare spread out the pollen report on her lap.

'There's the list,' said Myburgh. '*Tamarix. Trianthema hereroensis, Acanthosicyos horridus.*'

'What does that tell me?' asked Clare.

'The *Tamarix* and the *Hereroensis* grow in the Kuiseb River. This is where you'll find them.' He pulled out a map and sketched out two intersecting arcs. 'This section is where they overlap.'

'That's a huge area,' said Clare. The flicker of hope disappeared into the empty wastes that Myburgh's long, tapering fingers indicated.

'Well,' said Myburgh, 'you can cut out this bit. If they'd been near the mouth, you'd have found *Sarcocornia*, a stubby little succulent. You'll have seen fields of it beyond the lagoon. Nothing on them. They didn't even walk through it.'

'So they could've been anywhere in this area, except for this two-kilometre sliver near the shore?'

'No.' Myburgh looked around the parking lot before continuing: 'There's the *Acanthosicyos horridus*, the !nara plants that the Topnaar harvest. These grow in restricted areas along the vegetative dunes. It looks like a melon. Sweet, nutritious, full of fluid. Just what you need in a desert, but they only grow a few kilometres inland.'

'So that restricts us to this area, more or less?' asked Clare, pointing to the area of the Kuiseb Delta and just beyond.

Myburgh nodded.

'That's still a huge area.' Clare turned to look at the ocean of sand, rolling far beyond the horizon.

'Your needle in a haystack,' said Myburgh. 'I've got it for you.'

'What do you mean?'

'*Myrtaceae: Eucalyptus.*' Myburgh's dark eyes gleamed as he held out the branch to her: dark, pungent foliage, pale bark. 'The ghost gum,' he said. 'An Australian, alien. It would've had to have been planted near a water source.'

'How sure are you that you're right?' asked Clare.

'There'll only be a couple of spots in the Namib with this combination of plants.'

'So where do I start?' said Clare.

'With the gum, anywhere where there was human habitation,' said Myburgh, unfolding an aerial photograph. 'I looked and the only places I could find gum trees were these: two tourist camps and this old military area.'

Clare thought of Riedwaan's proposed destination. 'That's in the middle of nowhere,' she said, the puzzle pieces in her hand; the composite they made as shifting as the mirage dancing on the desert.

'It's the best I can do, I'm afraid,' Myburgh said, 'but there's more.' He handed Clare a slim journal, dark blue with embossed initials on it: VM.

Clare opened it. 'Whose is this?'

'Virginia Meyer's,' said Myburgh. 'It's all that was left of her work.'

Clare flipped through the book, glancing at the pages filled with spidery notes, the whimsical drawings of plants, birds and dunescapes so like her mute son's. Outside, the rising wind moaned around the car.

'I don't understand.' Clare looked up at Myburgh.

'I tested her diary for pollen,' he said, 'and it was a match. They were in the same place, Virginia and those boys.'

Clare's face remained expressionless.

'She was on her way to see me when the accident happened,' Myburgh explained. 'She'd been dead twelve hours when Spyt found them. Oscar couldn't loosen his seatbelt, so he was trapped, covered in her blood and flies. Spyt managed to resuscitate the child and get him help. And he brought me this.' Myburgh gestured to the journal. 'It had been hidden under Oscar's seat.'

'Why?' said Clare.

'Virginia wasn't where she should have been.' Myburgh must have crossed his Rubicon of doubt. When he spoke, his voice was quiet. 'It was the only bit of her work recovered after the accident. Everything else was gone. No one would've found them if Spyt hadn't come across them. She was on a side road out of the Kuiseb.'

'What was she doing there?'

'Virginia loved the Namib,' said Myburgh, 'and was enraged with the South African army and what they'd done to it. I always thought she was paranoid, seeing conspiracies everywhere. She was obsessed, Dr Hart, convinced that her beloved desert had been contaminated by the army. She kept on trying to expose what had happened, what she was convinced was happening again. She would've done anything to stop it.'

'Contaminated with what?' asked Clare. 'The South Africans left more than ten years ago.'

'They took their hardware,' said Myburgh, 'but they left some damaged people behind, as scarred and littered as the desert.'

'What had they been testing?' asked Clare.

'Overtly, the usual heavy weapons,' said Myburgh. 'Virginia was convinced there had been covert bio-chemical testing. Diseases, viruses, poisons that had leached into the underground water, and driven the Topnaars from their own land. Just before the accident, she phoned me to say there was something else, something much worse. She was afraid to tell me over the phone.' Myburgh looked away before continuing: 'She said the water table would be contaminated because of what they'd done.' He rubbed his eyes. 'Virginia was so paranoid, Dr Hart. It seemed easier at the time just to leave it.'

Clare thought of Fritz Woestyn, his lifeless body propped on the water pipeline, the artery pumping water into Walvis Bay, the lifeblood of the marooned town. 'Contaminated with what?' she asked.

'It didn't make sense to me then, still doesn't, because she said it in Afrikaans, but it stuck because she never spoke Afrikaans. She said it was the language of oppression.' Myburgh paused. 'She told me she was *vasgetrap*. Trapped fast. At least that is what I thought she said.'

'*Vasgetrap, vasgetrap*,' Clare repeated the syllables to herself. The word conjured up the quiet house in McGregor, the den with the elephant's foot. Mrs Hofmeyr with her iron-grey hair talking about her dead husband, her years as an army wife. 'She didn't say Vastrap, did she?' Clare asked.

'Vastrap, yes, that was it.' Myburgh looked at her. 'What is it?'

'It was a military base in South Africa, a secret weapons-testing site in the middle of the Kalahari Desert.'

A horrible image was forming in Clare's mind. She turned back to the last page of Virginia Meyer's diary. The digits 2, 3 and 5 were ringed in red. Clare looked at Myburgh's beaked profile.

'Tertius,' she asked, 'what do the numbers 2, 3 and 5 mean?'

'Nothing,' he said.

'Stop lying to me,' said Clare.

'Well, 235 is nothing on its own,' said Myburgh, his voice a monotone, his eyes trained on the heaving sea. 'Except with uranium. U-235 is an isotope. Highly enriched uranium. It's what you use for a nuclear weapon.'

Myburgh looked Clare in the eye for the first time, his knuckles were white on the steering wheel.

'That's what she meant about the desert being contaminated, Dr Hart. Those boys and Virginia Meyer, they were in the same place and now they're all dead.'

Chapter Fifty

THE SOUND OF the off-road bike was a flinty staccato across the plain. Riedwaan stopped to get his bearings. He had gone to find Karamata, but there had been no sign of him at his desk, and Riedwaan hadn't looked for him for long. He preferred being alone. The sun bellied orange over the sea as he passed the place where Lazarus Beukes had been found, but the shallow valley was a dead end, blocked by a wall of sand. So he left the relative sanctuary of the dry Kuiseb River behind him, trusting that his cheap Chinese GPS would see him through the expanse of desert.

The disused railway track, a spine from which the desert fell away, soft as a woman's flesh, came from the north, running aground in an ocean of red sand. Riedwaan checked the coordinates against the GPS. They told him the same thing as his old survey map: he needed to be on the other side of this waterless strait. Out here, the temperature would strip a body of its cloak of skin, hair and flesh. In weeks, he'd be nothing but white bones and a skull staring up at the blue vault of the sky. Riedwaan calculated the descent of the first dune and the elevation of the second and pitched over the edge, opening the throttle to the full, praying that the momentum would carry him to the top. It did, but all he had in front of him was another dune, then another.

Again Riedwaan took his bearings, trying not to picture his own demise. He made himself go on, following, more or less, the tracks of a vehicle that had preceded him. Three more dunes, and the railway reappeared, its ironwood sleepers scattered like matchsticks in the sand. A kilometre ahead was his destination. He could just make it out: some scrubby bushes and a gnarled eucalyptus tree next to two weathered huts. Riedwaan rode alongside the railway line, stopping under the tree, a ghostly sentinel in the dunes. Apart from the rattle of seeds feathered across the sand by the east wind, the place was silent.

The ground fell away from the huts towards two concrete-capped mounds. They could have been a century old, or a single decade. The tracks he had followed were neither, thought Riedwaan, bending down to get a closer look at the compacted earth. A heavy vehicle, a Land Rover perhaps, had passed through recently. An empty bottle of brandy lay discarded against the pale tree trunk. Scattered near it were a few cigarette butts. Riedwaan bent down to look. Two different brands.

It was cooler in the shade, but that did not account for the chill that played over Riedwaan's skin. A grimy white T-shirt was snagged against the bole of the tree, sweat stains indelible under the arms. The Pesca-Marina logo was only half-hidden by the shovel lying on top of it. Riedwaan stood where the men must have stood, the image forming as crisp as a nightmare in his mind. The back door of a vehicle would have opened, releasing the men's hurriedly collected human cargo – five boys, hired to harvest a deadly crop planted in another lifetime. Riedwaan lit a cigarette, imagining how their presence would have absorbed the vestiges of warmth from the night air.

The brandy, neat, burning down the throat of one man, then the other. Impossible to say how many, but Riedwaan would put his money on two. The men watching the activity below them would have been accustomed to the backs of others bending rhythmically to their wills.

For the boys, coming out here must have seemed safer than standing against a wall, legs astride, for a paunchy truck driver or a sailor with a knife. They wouldn't question a hundred for the night. Sickness or fear might have tightened the chest of one boy, hot from digging. The youngest boy slipping off his shirt, the moon sculpting his slender torso, as he stopped to rest. But when he caught the man's eye on him, as cold as a switchblade, he would have bent down again. And dug.

Riedwaan's mouth was dry from the heat. He fetched his water from the bike and tried to phone Clare. No reception under the tree, so he walked towards the shelters. One bar, he noted. The door to the first hut was ajar. Two bars. He dialled, ducking inside to avoid the sun.

The blow came without warning. For a brief moment before silence blossomed from agony, Riedwaan heard it: the quiet crack of his own skull.

Chapter Fifty-one

THERE WAS NO one at the station when Clare got back from her meeting with Tertius Myburgh. She closed the door to the special ops room and sat down at her desk. She dialled Riedwaan's number. Nothing. A flash on her screen told her she had a call waiting.

'Dr Hart?' It was Karamata.

'Yes?'

'George Meyer's son is missing.'

'Where from?' Clare felt faint at the inevitability of it, her own failure to protect the child.

'Kuisebmond beach.' Clare knew the beach. It was a crescent of grey, littered sand near the harbour.

'I'll come over.' Clare cut the connection, but not the image of cold water creeping over the face of a lonely, wide-eyed boy.

She drove fast along the beach road, which glistened like a strip of kelp stranded by a receding tide on the high-water mark. Karamata was there with a couple of uniformed officers. George Meyer stood with his hands thrust into his pockets, his shoulders hunched. The vehicles blocked off the area of beach where the boy had been. The wind was too strong for tape.

'He must've been here,' said Karamata, beckoning Clare over.

The yellow rod was wedged into the ground. Next to it was Oscar's khaki bag. The bottle of water was still full. A half-eaten sandwich was wedged in next to his bait. Peanut butter and Marmite.

'You didn't see him again, did you?' Meyer asked Clare. The question was framed around the hopes to which the parents of missing children cling. But with George Meyer, it was a formality. Hope was absent.

'I didn't see him,' said Clare, her chest tight with sadness.

'He was upset this morning after you were there. He was upset that Mara had left. I thought maybe he'd tried to find you.' Meyer moved out of the way of a wave that reached up the beach. It retreated, leaving a fringe of foam. 'He liked you, Dr Hart. He thought you'd be able to find Mara and bring her back.'

Clare saw Oscar's face before her, eyes accusing at her inability to understand his mute explanations. 'When did he disappear?'

'When I got home at lunch time, he was gone. His rod was gone too, so I came looking for him at the beach. I found the bike and the rod. No Oscar.'

'He wouldn't have gone off somewhere?'

'Not without his bike,' Meyer said.

'That taxi driver saw him here earlier.' Karamata gestured towards a man leaning against a battered red Toyota, talking to a couple of uniformed officers.

'The sea's been rough today,' said Meyer. 'He couldn't swim.'

Rough and cold, Clare thought. The Atlantic was not a place for a little boy alone.

'They're going to put a radio alert out,' Meyer said.

'And we'll search the harbour,' Karamata added. 'Why don't you go home, Mr Meyer? Maybe he's been somewhere and he'll turn up.'

'Maybe.' Meyer looked at the keys in his hand as if he had never seen them before.

'I'll take you back.' Karamata pointed to the police car. Meyer walked towards it, obedient as a child.

'Where was he?' Clare asked Karamata.

'At work all the time. I checked. They were doing an audit, so he was with the accountant. There will be a search, so there won't be anyone at the station for a while.'

'Did you speak to Captain Faizal?' Clare asked. 'I thought he'd arranged with you to take him to the Kuiseb Delta.'

'He's said nothing to me.'

'I can't get hold of him,' said Clare.

'I hope he doesn't go out there alone,' said Karamata. 'It looks so easy on the map, but once you're in the desert a map's useless, especially with this east wind.'

'Don't count on it, Elias,' said Clare. She knew Riedwaan too well to assume he'd do the sensible thing. She tried his number again. 'Caller out of range,' said the electronic voice. 'Try again later.'

'I have a sea search,' said Karamata. 'All I need is a desert search during a sandstorm.'

With an effort of will, Clare put her anxiety about Riedwaan on hold. 'You've spoken to Gretchen, I presume?' she asked.

'I did,' said Karamata. 'On the phone. She said she was in the bath when Oscar left the house.'

'That polite?' Clare raised an eyebrow.

'Not actually,' said Karamata, with a rueful smile. 'She told me to fuck off, that he wasn't anything to do with her and that she was busy.'

'Charming.' Clare looked out at the choppy sea. 'He was a little boy to be out fishing alone.'

'Nobody's child,' said Karamata. 'There are so many of them here, not all of them poor.'

'Who uses this beach, Elias?'

'The Chinese come and fish here. Couples with nowhere else to go. Kids come to fish. No one else really.' Karamata's phone was ringing. 'I must go and speak to the divers. They're here.'

Clare picked her way to the last rocks on the small headland that protected the harbour and looked back at the beach where Oscar had left his rod and his frugal picnic. Litter circled the small bay, nudging against the man-made promontory where she stood. The first diver splashed off the bobbing rescue vessel. If the boy had drowned, then his body would have been sucked down and flung up here, against these rocks. She worked her way back, her heart beating fast when she spotted a red smudge, but it was an old piece of T-shirt.

A wave ran high up the beach, obliterating all trace of Oscar and those who had been looking for him. Half an hour later and nobody would have known where he had stood and cast his line. Clare looked up the beach towards the road. The sand behind where Oscar's things had been had not yet been smoothed by the water. She walked towards his last-known location. Several mussel shells lay crushed in the disturbed sand. It looked as though a vehicle had stopped right behind where Oscar had been standing. It had stopped and then reversed and gone back onto the road.

Clare picked up a fragment of shell.

Oscar wouldn't have gone swimming and he hadn't fallen in. They weren't going to find Oscar's body here. She felt it with chilling certainty. Someone had picked him up and taken him elsewhere. Someone he had had to obey. Clare thought of the portraits hanging in her gallery. Each had slipped from life without a ripple.

Fritz Woestyn.

Nicanor Jones.

Kaiser Apollis.

Lazarus Beukes.

Mara Thomson. A girl, but so similar. The slenderness of the limbs, the brown skin, the faces planed and angled.

Now Oscar.

The coda to this symphony of pain. Small, russet-haired, pale ... he struck the wrong note.

Clare dropped her head into her hands and imagined herself sliding under the translucent skin of the child, the silhouette of evil taking shape in her mind. She pictured him watching Mara pack, holding the break in his heart in, locking away this new loss with the loss of his mother. And then before the allotted, dreaded time of the taxi, before the final flurry of packing and goodbye, a gun in her back. The middle of the night. The shadow-man removing his last witness. Mara's room brutally emptied of everything except the secret pictures that she and Oscar shared.

Mara hurtling towards the desert, her life receding with the grey fishing village sinking behind the horizon. Oscar shrinking back, unheard, unseen, except for the crack in the upstairs curtain. And now he was gone, the witness. Like the others. Killed not for the way they looked, but for what they knew.

Clare looked out to sea. A fishing ship, laden and low in the water, made her way between the buoys towards the quay where the *Alhantra* had docked to be loaded. One last shot, thought Clare, at finding where they had all connected.

She parked outside the Pesca-Marina factory as the shift-change siren went, the silver fish in the logo catching the light. She slipped in unnoticed through the stream of workers on their way out. On the wharf, front-end loaders scurried back and forth, heavy with stacked boxes. She went past the men concentrating on offloading the catch and slipped on board. There was no sign of Ragnar Johansson on the bridge, so she went below in search of Juan Carlos.

The second-last cabin door was closed. There was no answer when she knocked, but, to her surprise, when she tried the handle it opened. She went in and sat down to wait. It didn't take long for the door handle to turn again. Juan Carlos closed the door behind him, the expression on his handsome face unreadable.

'Dr Hart,' he said. 'Again.' The hum of the engines preparing to sail seemed to have restored his confidence.

'You're free to move about?' Clare asked.

'Change of command.'

'I need to know where Mara went camping,' said Clare.

'You didn't get a warrant?' Clare's beat of hesitation was enough for him. 'What do you have to trade?'

'You're free to go,' Clare bluffed. 'No word to the police in Spain, so no trouble when you dock.'

'I'm innocent?'

'Not the word I'd have chosen,' said Clare. She took out her map. The coordinates Myburgh had given her needed to be narrowed, and fast.

She spread it out in front of Juan Carlos. 'Show me.' The tone of her voice brooked no argument.

'Here. This is where Mara went.' Juan Carlos took the pen from her hand and marked a place with a sure, black X alongside a railway line. An arc of dunes had moved across it, severing the dry tributary from the rest of the delta.

Clare thought of Lazarus Beukes, the no-entry signs shining in the dark. She had been there, or near there, before. The hairs on her arms stood on end. 'What happened there with Mara?' she asked.

'Nothing. I've told you. She went with those street boys of hers. She loved them.' He smiled a slow, smug smile. 'But she loved me more. Once I show her how.'

'What do you mean?' Clare did not like him so close to her. He made her skin crawl.

'I told you, I got a pass, so I call her and tell her to meet me. She left them out there. Her boys. It was late. We met. We made love. She go back to fetch them, but they were gone. She found them at the dump again. They say they walked.'

'All of them? Were they all there?'

Juan Carlos looked down and said nothing. Clare waited.

'Okay, okay, all except for one,' he said at last. 'He only turn up later … dead.'

'Why didn't you tell me earlier? Why didn't Mara say anything?'

'She was too ashamed. She was afraid. She say she should have stayed with them. Take your pick.'

'Which one's your choice?' asked Clare.

'It was me or them.' His eyes glinted with the subtle charge of sexual power.

'What did you do, Juan Carlos?' asked Clare. 'Four boys are dead and a girl who loved you is missing.'

'The ship is full. I've made my money. I don't want delays,' Juan Carlos shrugged. 'Why would I do something?'

'Where is Captain Johansson?' asked Clare.

'Go and check on the bridge.' Juan Carlos turned his back on her. 'I say nothing more.'

The passage was a relief after the closeness of the cabin. Clare went up to the bridge before the boxes were stowed. A half-smoked pack of Marlboros was wedged on the barometer. It was Ragnar Johansson's brand, but there was no other sign of him. Clare looked below. The centre of the ship was open as the winch lowered packed fish into the refrigerated hold. She guessed that Ragnar would be directing things from below.

There was a metal staircase near the bridge. Clare closed the door behind her and swung down. The metal banister was slick and cold and her feet tingled as she spiralled down into the dark hold.

Ragnar wasn't on the first level. She asked one of the packers if he had seen him, but he shook his head. Clare went lower into the ship's belly. It was eerie, just the roar of the engines and the thud of the winch as it lowered its precious load. Something gleamed on the floor next to the packed and padlocked cold room. A Zippo. Clare picked the lighter up and rubbed away the dark fluid staining the engraving of a mermaid. Not Ragnar's, but familiar. She slipped it into her pocket.

'Are you looking for something?' Clare swung around. She didn't recognise the voice. Light and chill, as dry as ice.

The man was blocking the light in the narrow corridor. He had his cellphone up, directed at Clare, and he snapped her as she turned.

'Hey, what are you doing?' she asked, furious. 'Who the hell are you?' But she remembered the leanness. She had seen him at Der Blaue Engel. It was the man who had pulled Gretchen out of the sea.

'I like a record of the people who come onto my ship without permission.' The man was blade-thin, his face sculpted, handsome. He pressed a button on his phone, a smile creasing his tanned cheeks. Then he slipped his phone into his pocket and looked directly at Clare for the first time. 'Janus Renko. The new owner.'

'I've seen you,' said Clare. 'With Gretchen von Trotha.'

He raised an eyebrow.

'I'm looking for the captain,' said Clare. 'Where is he?'

Renko lit a cigarette. 'Ragnar Johansson?' He flicked the name away with the match. When he took off his dark glasses, he exposed pale, blank eyes. 'Ragnar went kite-boarding.'

'When will he be back?' Clare asked. Renko had not moved from the doorway. Clare glanced towards the light behind him, the smell of diesel oil, cold and fish heavy in the air. Renko smiled at her discomfort.

'He was made an offer he couldn't refuse,' he said.

The churn of the engines crescendoed. The ship was ready to sail.

'We're on our way, Dr Hart.' He rolled her name in his mouth, the intimacy of it was chilling. 'If I speak to him, I'll tell him you were here.'

Then Renko's hand was on her elbow, his grip a vice, propelling her back down the icy corridor, walking her faster than was comfortable. Clare's heart hammered against her ribs when she saw the refrigerated room ahead of her, the door into its icy maw now ajar.

She tried to pull free, but Renko had her arm twisted up her back. He was very close, his arm, sinewy and hard, was round her throat, cutting her breath. He laughed when she kicked backwards at him.

'This can be slow, Clare.' His voice sibilant, his breath intimate on her neck. 'Or it can be qui—'

'Janus!' A voice from above. 'Goagab's here with your authorisation. He wants us out of here.'

Renko's grip loosened an involuntary fraction, enough for Clare to twist herself free of him. In three strides, she was clear of him and past the startled harbour master holding out a sheaf of papers. Back on the deck, she dashed towards the gangplank; the shouts of the men she pushed out of her way were snatched away by the wind. Clare sprinted past the packers, through the ice shed and out of the factory gates.

Chapter Fifty-two

CLARE YANKED HER car into gear and cut in front of a hooting taxi, her heart thudding against her chest. She drove towards the lagoon, the tears coming without her noticing.

There was no truck and no dog at Ragnar's flat. She looked across at the harbour to see that the *Alhantra* was halfway down the narrow shipping channel, heading for the open sea. She drove back along the lagoon, but there was no sign of Ragnar there either. One place left to look. In five minutes, Clare was bumping along the track that led into the salt marshes where the Kuiseb Delta blurred into the sea. A dangerous place to kite-board, but one that Ragnar loved.

The first thing she saw as she approached the beach was the Labrador circling the vehicle, yelping in distress. The kite-board was still tied to the roof racks, ready. Clare did not like the feeling in her chest. It felt like something hard and cold was expanding, squashing the air from her lungs. She drove towards Ragnar's truck.

'Come boy,' Clare called to the dog.

The dog whined, but refused to move away from the vehicle. Clare approached slowly, expecting the worst, but Ragnar was sitting inside, staring straight ahead at the sea. Clare opened the door and to her horror he toppled towards her. She caught him in her arms. He beamed up at her, his eyes ice blue, the wound in his forehead blooming. He was warm against her breast, his blood on her shirt a cheerful red. Clare bit back a scream. She manoeuvred him back into the seat and placed a finger against his neck. A pulse.

'I'm getting you help,' she said.

Ragnar started to slide towards her again. She propped her hip against his weight and pulled out her phone. Her hands were shaking, but she managed to key in Tamar's number. It was ten rings before anyone answered. Clare counted every one of them. It felt like a lifetime.

'Hello.'

'Tamar?' asked Clare. The voice didn't sound right.

'She's asleep right now.'

'Helena?' said Clare.

'Yes,' said Dr Kotze. 'I'm sorry—'

'It's Clare Hart. Send an ambulance.' Clare could not get the words out fast enough. 'The road past the saltworks, towards Pelican Point. Ragnar Johansson. Head shot. He's still alive but only just.' She disconnected without waiting for an answer.

Ragnar slipped further. Clare dropped her phone and turned to the stricken man. She pulled his seatbelt across his chest to hold him upright.

'Keep still,' said Clare, her heart thudding. 'The ambulance is coming.'

'Angel.' Ragnar's breath was feather-soft against her ear. The blue eyes flared. The wound in his forehead oozed, and his eyelids started to flutter.

'Don't pass out, Ragnar. Look at me. Talk to me.'

Ragnar obeyed and looked up at Clare, struggling to focus, his breathing coming in sharp jerks. There was nothing to do but wait. Clare looked out at the deserted beach; it was hard to believe that on other days, it would be dotted with kites and dogs, and families enjoying a weekend outing.

Ragnar groaned and his eyes rolled.

'Come on, Ragnar.' Clare touched his face. 'Stay with me.' She settled him against the door and went around to the back of the truck in search of water. When she came back, the blood from his forehead had trickled over his lips. She sprinkled the water over his mouth.

'Talk to me, Ragnar. Tell me who did this to you.'

'Angel,' he slurred.

'Not yet,' said Clare. 'No angels for you.' She cradled his blood-ied head, counting the minutes.

A chopper at last, she could hear it. Ragnar inched his hand across the seat, as if he were looking for something. There was nothing there.

'Here's help for you now. Hang on.'

The helicopter hovered, buffeted by the rising wind blowing off the desert. An enormous flock of flamingos took off, turning the sky deep pink as they circled before heading for safety. Two paramedics jumped out, neat as paratroopers.

'What happened?' the first one asked as soon as he was within earshot.

The sound of the chopper drowned out Clare's attempts to explain. She stepped aside so the paramedic could see Ragnar.

The colour drained from the man's ruddy face.

'Shit,' he said as he bent over him. 'Pulse is here. Just.' He signalled the other paramedic over. 'Let's get him out of here.' There was an efficient flurry of drips and needles.

'Where are you taking him?' Clare asked.

'To Windhoek,' the man said. 'There's no ICU at the coast.'

Clare restrained the frantic dog. 'Will he make it?' She was starting to shake.

'If he made it this long, he has a chance. Sometimes the bullet lodges between the brain lobes. If nothing's damaged, he might make it,' said the paramedic.

Clare stood back, watching as the paramedics worked to stabilise Ragnar before lifting him into the chopper. They pulled the door closed and were gone, lifting up and over the dunes. Clare closed her eyes, but it did not drive away the image of Ragnar's punctured forehead.

She walked around to the other side of Ragnar's truck and opened it. A file of official-looking papers fell out. She picked them up, wondering if it was what Ragnar had been looking for. The Walvis Bay Port Authority letterhead. Records of load, of taxes paid, of inspections done, of a route filed. Spain via Luanda.

Clare thought of the *Alhantra* rocking next to the stone quay. Its sudden turn of fortune. Two. Three. Five. It was adding up. Ragnar was a sore loser and she knew he'd bent the law before: illegal crayfish, some dope, a bit of recreational coke. But transporting the ingredients for a dirty bomb was not his thing. He must have found out about his ship's secret cargo and threatened to talk. The helicopter had vanished, leaving only the wind and the calls of seabirds in its wake.

Clare snapped the file closed as a car door slammed behind her. It was Van Wyk and a sergeant she did not recognise.

'Captain Damases is off this case,' said Van Wyk. 'And I'm on it.' He held out a hand and Clare reluctantly handed over Ragnar's file. 'It's an offence to remove evidence from a crime scene,' he added, tossing the file into his vehicle. 'I'm running this case now, Dr Hart. So I suggest you run along.'

Clare let a violent fantasy that involved her, Van Wyk and a machine gun run its course before getting back into her car, his smile a knife in her back. She calmed herself with the knowledge that Tamar's inquiry would put him behind bars and wipe that arrogant smile off his face for a long time.

The maternity ward was surprisingly quiet. It was not visiting time, but Clare had slipped in without anyone noticing. Tamar's room was at the end of the passage. A single bunch of flowers – hand-picked by Tupac and Angela, Clare guessed – stood by her bedside. The aftermath of labour had smoothed the guarded toughness from her face. She looked fifteen, lying on her heap of starched white pillows. The baby curled in her arms was slack with sleep, a drop of milk pearled in the corner of its small, pink mouth.

'Tamar,' Clare whispered. 'Tamar.' It felt like sacrilege to wake her.

Tamar opened her eyes, and the illusion of the Madonna vanished. 'Hi.' She drew her child closer to her before she smiled. 'What is it?'

'I'm sorry, I know you're off the case, but I really need your help.'

'Any time,' said Tamar. 'What is it?'

Clare closed the door and told Tamar. The horror of it seeped through Tamar's exhausted postpartum tranquillity like a poison. The baby's face crumpled in distress, feeling its mother slipping away from it.

'Pass me my phone. It's in my bag.' Tamar rocked the child and it settled again, lulled. Clare handed her the phone.

'We'll do a swap,' said Tamar. 'You take her.'

'Who is she?' asked Clare, taking the infant. 'This new little person.'

The child was unbelievably light in her arms.

'Rachel.' Tamar ran a gentle finger over her baby's plump cheek. 'Rachel Damases.'

Clare looked at the child. 'She's beautiful.'

Clare watched Tamar's features sharpen and her eyes focus as she made the calls Clare needed.

'It's done,' Tamar said, snapping the phone closed. 'Now you do what you have to.'

She held out her arms for her baby and Clare handed Rachel over.

'Look in that drawer,' said Tamar.

Clare walked to the bedside table and pulled open the drawer. It contained a tube of cream and a pistol.

'You can leave me the hand cream,' said Tamar.

Chapter Fifty-three

OUT IN THE desert, Riedwaan's stomach had hollowed beneath his jeans, but the belt buckle stood clear of his skin. He could feel the place where the sun had bored heat through the metal to brand the tender skin. He tried to calculate how long he had been out, measuring the air in even packages of breath. In. Then out. Pacing himself.

He remembered the road, winding through the tamarisk trees. He had passed the no-entry sign where Lazarus Beukes had been found. He had gone on, his bike churning the virgin sand in the riverbed. He had found the place Darlene had told him about, the tree a dark-green sentinel, a couple of kilometres east of Spyt's makeshift hideout. He could see the old railway tracks sinking into the heaped sand. The ruined roof of the huts, the rafters protruding like the ribs of a carcass picked clean by scavengers. The stationmaster's house, the red sand curved through the windows, heaped like treasure in the front rooms. The track. The end of the track, the riverbed again, the ghost gum tree towering above him, the entrance to the hut. Then nothing. Except this blinding pain.

Riedwaan opened his eyes. The sun was dipping west. He closed his eyes against the searing light, the sand whirling in the wind. He made his mind work. Remember.

There had been tracks everywhere. He had gone into the building. A pick, shovels too, standing against the wall. New ones. A boy's peaked cap, tossed in a corner. The pit, recently dug. A single drum standing against the wall, the hazard sign visible beneath the crusted sand. The others had been dug up and were no doubt now on the *Alhantra*, moving towards their targets like deadly wraiths. The pain. That's when it had come, from behind him when he stood inside the room.

'You're awake.' A woman's voice. Riedwaan could just make out her figure stacking a pile of wood into an ashy hearth. Her fire would be going in minutes. His eyes fluttered closed.

He opened them again and looked at the woman standing above him now, her hair gleaming in the angled light. Riedwaan tried to move his arms. They were tied tight around the trunk of a tree, the slender nylon rope cutting into his wrists. The ground was hard. Riedwaan's cellphone was in his back pocket. It bit into his back. He shifted his weight and hoped it was on silent. His gun was gone.

'Who are you?' Riedwaan's own voice sounded unfamiliar. It hurt his cracked lips when he spoke. The woman dropped to her knees beside him, fanning her cool fingertips over his hot skin. He concentrated on her face, trying to get his vision to stabilise.

'Your guardian angel.' Her voice was husky. 'You're going to need one. The Namib Desert's not safe.' She held out her hand. 'Oh, you can't shake. Sorry.' She returned to the fire and turned the metal fence dropper she had placed in it. The tip glowed an ominous red.

'Water,' Riedwaan begged.

The woman turned to look at him, not a glimmer of compassion in her pale-blue eyes. 'You must learn to ask nicely.' A shadow passed over her face. Pure menace.

She pressed the dropper into the smooth skin on Riedwaan's chest. The acrid smell of charred skin hit him before the pain convulsed his body. He bit down on his bottom lip, the taste of his own blood sharp on his tongue.

'A perfect circle,' the woman said, admiring the mark she had made. She lifted the rod to do it again.

'Give me some water,' croaked Riedwaan, watching her face, trying to judge how far she would go, how much he could take. 'Please.'

'You can do better than that,' she laughed, the soft red dunes echoing the curves of her body, but she put the rod down.

Riedwaan felt like he was walking a tightrope in the dark. If he was sure-footed, he might rekindle some empathy in her. If he got it wrong, he would fall, triggering a release of cruelty.

He thought of Clare, the gentleness in her face when she thought no one was watching her. Yasmin, his daughter. She would be calling tomorrow at their usual time.

Riedwaan knew if he drifted, he was going to pass out. And if the woman drifted any further, the slender thread of empathy would snap and he would die. He fought off the siren call of unconsciousness.

Shift things.

That's what he had learnt when he had trained as a hostage negotiator. Shift things and get them to talk, to trust you. Then the hostages have a chance of survival. It seemed like a rather fragile straw to cling to now that he was the hostage. Unlike Clare, he was a betting man, but he didn't like to think of his odds.

'Talk to me,' said Riedwaan, watching the woman, ignoring the stabbing pain in his bound arms, his seared chest. She was so at home, preparing things. The fire, the rope, the gun. Riedwaan had not picked a winner in this charnel-house hostess. He had to bring her back to him.

'Give me some water.' He said the words with an authority he did not feel. His tongue was swelling in his throat.

The woman glided towards him and held the flask to his mouth, the liquid pouring in, hot and choking at the back of his throat. She was so close Riedwaan could feel the warmth of her body, smell the unsettling, feral mix of perfume and adrenaline. Her hair swung over her shoulder and brushed his skin. It was bleached and porous, the colour and texture of dried grass left from last year's rain. The desert wind made it crackle with static.

'Just swallow,' she said, holding his chin expertly. Riedwaan choked, his lungs burned, but the alcohol gave him a kickstart. 'It's only the first time that's really bad,' she added.

Riedwaan looked at her face. Her cheekbones, the sweep of her eyebrows were sculpted, beautiful, but the eyes were blank. All he could see in them was his own reflection, twice in miniature.

'Who taught you that?' he asked. He could imagine. She had such a perfect mouth, full and red. Made for a certain kind of love.

The woman sat down opposite him, intrigued by his question.

'A boyfriend?' guessed Riedwaan. 'A teacher?'

She clasped her slim arms around her knees, as if folding her forgotten vulnerability away from his prying gaze.

'Your mother's boyfriend?'

The woman said nothing, but she shivered. Riedwaan was on target. He had to keep her talking.

'Your mother?' The wind had dropped and Riedwaan's words reverberated in the sudden lull. The pain in his arms was unbearable. He was glad of it. It distracted him from the charred skin on his chest. He inched himself higher up the tree.

'Not my real mother,' the woman spoke at last, though she did not look at Riedwaan. 'The woman who took me after my mother died.'

'Tell me what she made you do,' Riedwaan coaxed.

The woman got up and walked away as if she had not heard Riedwaan. She walked into the hut, leaving him alone. Riedwaan moved his body a little higher up the tree. The trunk narrowed a little, a dry cycle must have stunted its growth.

When the woman returned, she was holding a box of menthol cigarettes and a lighter. Riedwaan, though desperate for nicotine, feared what she might do. 'Can you—?'

'He was old,' the woman interrupted. 'In the army, but he always smelt dirty. He used to come to see her.'

Riedwaan nodded. 'And he decided he liked the look of you?'

Again, she seemed not to hear him. 'I choked and he hit me, but she made me finish.' The memory of it danced like a blue flame as she raised her expressionless eyes to stare at Riedwaan. 'Once you get used to it,' she said, 'it's such an easy way to pay the rent.'

Riedwaan kept moving his body upwards. He could flex his wrists a little now. 'How old were you?' he asked.

The woman picked up a stick and jabbed it into the sand. 'I was eleven.'

Riedwaan pictured the hand, nails lacquered red, holding the child's small, round chin to wipe her face clean.

'Tell me about those boys you shot,' said Riedwaan.

'What about them?' she asked.

'So close,' he said. 'You did it so close. I'm impressed.'

Her eyes glittered. An arc of light again. He had to keep her facing him.

'Tell me about it, what it felt like.'

She hesitated.

'Come,' he said. 'You don't want to rush this, do you? When I'm gone, then your fun is over.' It was true; he could see it in her face. Clare would be impressed with him, he thought. His new conversational ways with women. 'How did you feel?' he pressed.

'How do you think?'

'Like no one could argue with you. Powerful.'

'More than that.' She came closer.

'Tell me,' he said. 'Tell me where it all began.'

'I can tell you where it's going to end.'

'With me?'

The woman smiled at him and lit a cigarette. 'Why not? Any requests?'

'A cigarette,' he said.

She held the cigarette to his lips.

'But we aren't at the ending yet, are we? So why don't you start with the first one, Fritz Woestyn?'

'Oh, was that his name?' she asked. 'I didn't do him.'

'Who killed him, then?'

The woman hesitated. 'Don't be clever with me. You think I'd betray him, my guardian angel. I told you, you need one.'

'Nicanor Jones?'

'He was sweet,' said the woman. 'My dry run.'

'The others?'

'Those were all mine. You'll see later,' she said. 'I've learnt to be a good shot.'

'I can't wait,' muttered Riedwaan.

The woman stirred the fire with the fence dropper. He didn't think he could endure another session. 'Why?' he asked. It was a weak question, he knew, but he had to do something.

'Why what?' the woman shrugged.

'Why did you do it? Love?'

'I suppose you could call it that.' She considered the notion.

'Who are we waiting for, out here in the middle of nowhere?' Riedwaan asked.

'This time' – she leaned close to him – 'it'll be just the two of us. Tête-à-tête.'

'So why did you do it?'

'It made me feel. He made me feel, standing close to me. Here.' She put her hands on her hips. 'Close.'

Riedwaan could feel it with her. The man behind her, close, his hands under her elbows, adjusting them, helping her aim, sliding back the smooth upper arms, under the breasts. Stepping back as she fired to watch the dénouement. There didn't seem any reason why it shouldn't be pleasurable.

'Why did the Topnaar move them?' Riedwaan asked.

'I don't know,' she said, agitated. 'I don't know who moved them. Nobody's business, but ours.'

'And why didn't you stop?'

'We had to finish what we started.' She looked at him, surprised that this logic had eluded him. 'That is what he taught me; to finish what you start.' She stirred the fire, mesmerised by its flames. 'And I always pay what I owe.'

'So now you get the clean-up?'

Rage flared in the woman's eyes. 'He's not like that.'

Her phone purred on cue. She fished it out of her jeans and looked at the screen. Riedwaan watched the pulse at the base of her slender throat. He inched his arms up the tree, closer to where it narrowed. Blood oozed where his skin tore on the rough bark.

'Who?' he managed to say. 'Who's not like that?'

The woman laughed, the sound low, malignant. 'You think you're so clever, making me talk to you, distracting me. You think I haven't seen it before?' she sneered. 'You'll stop being so full of yourself when you meet him. He'll fix you as soon as he's finished.'

'Finished with what?'

'Your little doctor friend.'

Riedwaan was quiet. The stakes had just notched higher, and the woman knew it.

'You want to see?' She held up her cellphone, so Riedwaan could see the screen: Clare, half-turned, startled, in a narrow passageway.

Horror made him lucid. Riedwaan played his last card. 'You believe he's coming back for you?' he asked.

'He's coming,' said the woman, petulantly.

'He's finished with you. He didn't even bother to kill you, did he?' The air pulsed. The wind was rising again, fast, and visibility was dropping.

For a moment, the ghost of the broken child the woman had been softened the carapace of her adult face. But only for a moment. It was gone when she started to strip. She unbuttoned her shirt. Off it came and her bra, her jeans, the shoes, the watch, even her rings.

Riedwaan watched her, riveted. A quick shower and any traces of his blood on her skin would be gone. This perfect woman, naked except for the wings tattooed on her back and the pistol in her right hand. She flicked off the safety catch. She was so close, he could feel the warmth of her. It chilled him. She touched the gun against his forehead – cold, like a dog's snout, and stepped back.

Knees soft, elbows locked.

She breathed in slowly.

Then out.

She knew what she was doing.

Chapter Fifty-four

VISIBILITY WAS GETTING worse. Clare could see a few metres ahead. That was it. The wind was a keening banshee. It hurled the sand in stinging waves off the tops of the dune, driving them down like vengeful furies that flayed the skin and tore at the eyes and ears. Her mouth was soon filled with choking red dust. Clare stopped to orientate herself. The stand of trees was thick, the black bark coated with mica. She fought her way towards the outflung arm of dune in the lee of the wind. Here, the wind was less constricting and she could make out the outlines of trees. She was close. She had to get to the top of the dune. She looked for the signs of human habitation that would be there. Eucalyptus. Here in the desert it would have been planted and nurtured for some time so that its delving roots could tap into the subterranean lake where the Namib hoarded its water. She closed her eyes and pictured the aerial map. If she pulled it out here, it would be whipped out of her hands.

She had seen the eucalyptus earlier, exactly as Oscar had drawn it, with its dark spire squared against the undulating horizontality of the desert. She had seen it and then it had disappeared, so it must be behind the ruff of dunes that had formed in the last flood. She would have to go up and over the dune she was sheltering against. Due east. At least the wind would help her orientate herself: she had to face down the valkyries of sand that screamed past her towards the sea. It was horrible going forward: two steps forward was one backwards. Her throat was dry and cracked, and her muscles screamed at her to stop. There was a momentary lull. An absolute and deafening silence fell. The dust hung in abeyance, waiting for the next onslaught.

Janus Renko. The unfamiliar name. The hard face familiar. And not just from Der Blaue Engel. The chord it had struck echoed through the chaos of sandy wind. The quiet kitchen. Clare saw it with startling clarity: the woman with her gun-metal hair, pointing out her husband in the desert. In the photo, one arm draped over a friend, the unknown man standing aloof, shadowed. The same face, distilled down to its cruel essence. The half-empty ship. The numbers: 2, 3 and 5. Coded for her, inscribed upon the dead boys' chests by Spyt, the desert's silent witness. The drums loaded, not with the obscuring load of fish, but with the deadly treasure dug up by five boys, watched, found and delivered by Spyt.

Two, three, five. Unleashed in air or water, a stealthy death no one could fight. Enriched uranium: more than a pension that. A fortune for anyone willing to sell mass murder to the jostling numbers eager and able to make a dirty bomb. She couldn't think of that now. Not here. She was concentrating on one life. One death.

She was on the summit. Below, a vortex of red dust writhed beneath the yoke of the wind. Her heart thudded at the thought that she had lost her way, but the storm was so wild, the only thing to do was to struggle towards the tree she had glimpsed earlier. It offered the only sanctuary. She plunged over the edge of a dune, into the comparative silence in the well of sand. She rested, recovering from the assault of the wind.

Ahead of her was a mound where the desert had heaped against something. Shelter. She made her way to it. The shape, the outline, a flash of colour. The familiarity of it caught like a cry in the throat. She crawled forward and collapsed against the mound.

Mara.

Clare repressed the hot flare of panic. Face to face with her, the girl's expression rigid, the eye sockets already emptied. The final bullet a rose on her forehead. Beautiful, for a split second. Mara had been dead a good twenty-four hours, by the looks of her. The wind howled over the top of her discarded body, her outstretched hands covered in sand. Clare brushed the insects away from the girl's face, curling her hand into hers. Mara's paisley jacket was open, hanging loose from her body, revealing her white shirt. A few strands of hair stuck in the bloodstain drying on her sleeve.

Clare touched the stain. It was still moist. She picked up one of the blood-sticky hairs. It was a deep auburn where it wasn't stained. The colour of the dunes where Mara lay.

It could only be Oscar's hair. There was a faint impression on the sand where the boy had curled, nestling into the stiffening curve of the dead girl's body. He had crawled here, inching his way across the dune, as she had, to find shelter. Clare shivered, looking out into the wind-blurred sand. There was no sign of the boy.

She wound her scarf tighter around her face. The series of regular impressions leading away from Mara's body was nearly obscured. The lure of them, the possibility that they were footprints, that Oscar was alive, was overwhelming. Clare stood up and looked north, the direction into which the tracks vanished. There was a gulley on the other side of the dunes, and then nothing but an ocean of dancing sand. If she followed these ephemeral marks she would be lost in minutes. Oscar had survived the desert before. She had to hope that he could do it again.

She struggled up the incline, leaving Mara's lifeless body to be buried in the desert. Below, she could make out the broken spine of the railway line and the eucalyptus standing in solitary splendour, marking where someone had tried to make a home, or coax a crop out of the sand. Clare made her way down, zigzagging along the contour, dreading what she was going to find. The wind had sculpted the sand over the low scrubby bushes, rocks and any detritus that lay on this dry tributary. It moulded sand over everything, making the shifting landscape surreal, blurred by the whirl of fool's gold.

Clare crouched as her eye registered a movement at the tree. A woman with her knees parted and bent just a fraction. The arms locked, clasped in front of her body. The man bound and watching the woman's face as one would watch a weaving mamba.

Riedwaan.

Clare slipped the dust-sticky safety off Tamar's gun. Before her mind had a chance to even register, she fired.

RIEDWAAN FELT THE blood spurt from his right wrist as he wrenched it free. He grabbed the metal rod beside him and brought it across the woman's knees as she fired, felling her like a hamstrung animal. She lay across his lap, completely motionless. He worked his left arm free and slipped his arms around her. They were both slick with her blood. There had to have been two shots; Riedwaan was sure of it. That was the only thing that explained the sound. He turned Gretchen around to reveal a gunshot wound on her shoulder.

'Well caught.' The catch in Clare's voice undid her attempt at a joke.

Riedwaan looked up. 'About time,' he said. The blood was rushing back into his arms. It was excruciating, but the sight of Clare was like a shot of morphine. 'Who is this?' he asked. 'If you don't mind me asking.'

Clare knelt beside the bleeding woman and turned her head towards her. The woman moaned.

'The Blue Angel,' said Clare. 'I thought it might be.'

'A friend of yours?' said Riedwaan. He pulled off his shirt and wrapped it around Gretchen's naked form.

'In a manner of speaking. You could say we have a couple of mutual acquaintances.'

'She's not going to last long,' said Riedwaan. He pulled out his phone and gave it to Clare. 'You dial. My hands aren't working that well at the moment.'

Clare took the phone and dialled Tamar's number, ducking into the hut to get reception.

Riedwaan found his cigarettes. He put one between his lips and felt around for his lighter. It was gone.

'You don't have a light, I suppose?' he said to Clare as she came out of the hut.

'I do actually,' she said, offering him the Zippo with the mermaid on it. 'I picked it up outside the freezer just before Gretchen's friend tried to push me inside.'

Riedwaan turned the lighter over in his hand so that he could read the inscription: Magnus Malan. He lit his cigarette. 'On the *Alhantra*?' he asked.

Clare nodded.

'No sign of its owner?'

'Just a trace of blood.'

Riedwaan took a deep drag. 'How much will you bet that Darlene's husband is freezing in the hold with his uranium cakes?'

Clare sat down next to him and watched him smoke. 'I'm not much for betting,' she said. 'But if I were, the odds would be so low it wouldn't be worthwhile.'

She thought about kissing him, but the sound of the helicopter approaching drowned out the wind and by then it was too late.

Chapter Fifty-five

THE BUNDLE OF dollars Janus Renko handed over to the port
captain in Luanda meant that the *Alhantra* had no trouble docking
at the Angolan port. He leant against the rail, waiting for his man.
He had not met him before, but they all looked the same: shirt
pressed and crisp despite the humidity, linen suit, shades mirrored,
black hair precisely cut. He scanned the girls displaying their wares
on the other side of the razor wire. There. Newly budded breasts.
The girl held his eye, deliberately hooked a nipple on a barb. One
crimson bead of blood spread across her tight white shirt.

'Delivery complete?'

Renko turned towards the soft voice.

'Of course.' He took the case the man had placed at his feet and
opened it. The diamonds, nestled on green velvet, winked at him,
complicit, true.

'You want to look below?' Renko asked, putting his eyepiece
away.

The man shrugged, his expression hidden behind his dark
glasses. 'It's there. We checked.'

Renko handed over the ship's papers. The keys. Docking papers. Orange roughy, such a delicacy. Especially the way this lot was going to be prepared. Renko disembarked, avoiding the filth on the wharf. The girl peeled away from the others. She fell into step beside Renko once he was clear of the docks.

'You lonely?'

Renko checked his watch. He had a couple of hours.

'A little,' he smiled.

When his plane flew low over the Luanda Hilton, the sun was dropping westward, the roofs of the town shining in its light. In the east, darkness.

Hours later, the stars hung low. On the horizon, Scorpio setting as the plane touched down. Janus Renko's shirt was white against the smooth, dark skin of his neck, despite the long flight to Johannesburg. He was tired. It took a second before he noticed the man in the black suit peel away from the shelter of the wall.

That fraction of time was all Phiri needed. The Browning was hard in Renko's kidneys; his arms high up his back, the sharp intake of breath indicating just how far.

'Funny,' said Phiri, his mouth close to the man's ear. 'A perfect fit.'

Renko knew better than to fight. 'Goagab?' he asked.

'Singing like a bird,' said Phiri.

In the time it had taken Renko to get to Johannesburg, Goagab's fear of prison had him confessing to every crime he'd ever even considered committing. The *Alhantra*, he told Karamata, had been ferrying six cakes of uranium 235. The highly enriched uranium had been siphoned off from Vastrap and buried in the Namib by Hofmeyr and Malan when they were in charge of destroying the nuclear programme in 1990. The cakes had been buried there for over ten years, waiting for Janus Renko to broker a deal with some Pakistani businessmen. When he did, Goagab had signed off the safe passage to Spain for a cut.

'One city, one cake,' Phiri said. 'Enough highly enriched uranium to make dirty bombs for six European cities. Which were they? Paris? Berlin? Antwerp?'

'You'll be sorry for this,' said Renko calmly, 'when my lawyer gets hold of you.'

'I hear the Americans are clearing a cell for you in Guantanamo,' Phiri continued, unperturbed. 'But I think that might have to wait a bit. That little mermaid you pulled out of the water in Walvis Bay, the one you got to shoot those boys who did your dirty work, she's decided that her debt to you was cashed up when you left without her.'

'A whore,' said Renko. 'Any lawyer would shred her in court.'

'Hell hath no fury ...' Phiri let the phrase linger. 'After Clare Hart put a bullet through her shoulder, and then kept her alive long enough to get her to ICU, it seems she switched allegiance,' he went on. 'Never underestimate a woman scorned. Dr Hart got the lot. You. Gretchen. The boys. Johansson, who incidentally looks like he'll be testifying, too. Malan.'

'Malan.' The name erupted from Renko. 'Too fucking lazy to do his own labour.'

'We found him,' said Phiri. 'Not a pleasant sight. What did you use? A filleting knife?'

Renko was silent again, contained fury vibrating through his body.

'Now, if you'll excuse me ...' Phiri pulled out his cellphone and dialled the number. 'Faizal,' he said when Riedwaan picked up. 'Tell Dr Hart we've got her man.'

RIEDWAAN PUT HIS finger on Clare's lips, stopping her question. She waited impatiently, recognising Phiri's voice on the other end of the line but unable to make out what he was saying amidst the noise of the restaurant.

'They got him,' Riedwaan said, snapping his phone shut. 'And his cargo.'

'I've had enough to eat,' said Clare, relief washing over her. 'Shall we go?'

Riedwaan signalled for the bill. He winced. The skin on his chest was healing and his shoulder had been expertly bandaged by Helena Kotze, but even after three days in hospital, movement was not easy.

Outside the restaurant, it was clear, the sky heavy with stars. A curlew on the lagoon called, the sound piercing the cold night. Riedwaan put his arm around Clare's waist.

'Sexy dress this. I was wondering who you were going to wear it for.'

Clare unlocked her cottage door. Somehow, they had walked past Burning Shore Lodge.

'You want some coffee?' she asked, running a tentative finger down his neck.

'Maybe a whisky.'

Clare poured two and took them through to the sitting room.

'You didn't miss these?' Riedwaan put his hand into his jacket pocket and pulled out a scrap of silk.

'Whose are those?' Clare grabbed the black knickers.

'Yours, I hope,' he laughed. 'I took them before you left Cape Town. A memento.'

Clare reached under her skirt and pulled off the pair she was wearing. 'You want me to check?'

'Not really.' He caught both her hands in one of his. The other one he slid up her bare thigh. 'I'd just have to take them off again.'

'True,' said Clare, pulling him with her onto the couch. 'And that would be a waste of time.'

Scorpio Setting ...

Oscar.

You hear it, your name formed as a series of soft clicks in the back of a throat. A drop, then two, of water on your lips, your eyelids. You open your eyes. The familiar weathered face: Spyt.

You try to say his name. Nothing comes but a croak. The man sweeps the flies sipping from your forehead, split by a rock. He disentangles you from the dead woman, Mara, lifting you into his arms, cradling you against his chest. He carries you to the cool shelter of his cave, out of the wind. The silence in the wake of the storm is overwhelming. Spyt lays you down, gentling his donkeys, restless at the intrusion, before he sets to work on you ...

Three days later, the moon is full, obliterating all but the brightest stars. Spyt puts out a hand for you. Together you listen, ears catching the distant purr of an engine, which is nothing but a texture in the silence. You retreat deeper into the shadows when the lights break over the dune, sweeping across the moonlit sand. When the engine cuts, the restored silence is deafening.

Their voices are low murmurs as the couple unpacks, lights a fire. The pungent smoke purls into the sky. It is getting colder. The man twists the long rope of the woman's hair in his hands. She sinks into him. The soft undulation of their bodies mimics the desert, radiating away from them. When they subside into sleep, the old man walks with you down to the dying fire. In sleep, the woman has turned her back on the man, but his hand rests on her hip. She is familiar, this woman, the woman who reads your mind. It is Clare. You have watched her sleep before, standing by her window, tracing a heart in the mist your breath made.

Spyt crouches, holding your hand close to her mouth. Her breath is warm on your palm.

When the moon arcs up and over, sinking into the ocean to the west, the cold desert wind knifes down the gully, rattling dry grasses. She turns towards the sleeping man; you imagine her breasts soft on his chest. Spyt takes your hand, and the two of you leave. The man and woman will head south to Cape Town, and you, here, will melt into the sheltering desert.

A jackal cries, unfurling the rosy dawn. Scorpio defers to the new light and sinks below the horizon.

Acknowledgements

THANKS TO WILLIE Visser and Sharon Roberts, for patiently explaining ballistics to me and for teaching me to shoot straight; to Johan Kok, for detailed information on blood splatter patterns and forensics in out-of-the-way places; to Leanne Dreyer, for introducing me to the microscopic wonderland of pollens and forensic palynology; to Colleen Mannheimer, who told me which plants grow where in the Namib Desert; to Bruno Nebe, for rescuing me at the last minute with information about the bats that live in the Kuiseb River; to Johann Dempers, for giving me so many rivetingly gory pathology lessons; and to Andrew Brown, for letting me borrow his wonderful Coldsleep Lullaby cop, Eberard Februarie. Special thanks to Martha Evans for being such a creative and patient editor, and to my literary agent, Isobel Dixon, my heartfelt thanks. Also, to Michelle Matthews, for having faith again.

Any mistakes and all fabrications are mine.

About the Author

MARGIE ORFORD is an award-winning journalist and an internationally acclaimed writer. Her thriller series, starring investigative journalist and profiler Dr Clare Hart, has been translated into more than eight languages. She was born in London, grew up in Namibia and was educated in South Africa. She lives with her family in Cape Town.

www.margieorford.com

Visit www.AuthorTracker.com for exclusive information on your favorite HarperCollins authors.

RESILIENT HEART

RESILIENT HEART

A Story of Crossing Cultures,
Building Bridges and
Embracing Uncertainty

LEAH KADWELL

ISBN9798645120139

Cover Design by Jacquelyn Cork
Cover Photo from Free Adobe Stock Images
Author Photo by Tammy Brice

CONTENTS

INTRODUCTION

I have been writing "books" for as long as I can remember. It began of course with reading as many books as I could get my little hands on as a kid. My mom filled our house with books and my memories are filled with her reading books (mostly Stephen King, of course) and making reading the most natural thing to do. We would go to the big library in Southfield, Michigan, and I would check out as many books as they would let me. I loved the stories the books contained and they fueled my imagination for my play.

I wanted to take my reading a step further, though. I wanted to be the writer of those stories. I wanted to create the things that people would read. I can remember very clearly taking pages and pages of notebook paper, writing out my rambling stories, then piecing them together and calling them my books. I wrote stories and plays and knew that they were excellent pieces of literary craftsmanship. I didn't know who was going to read them or who would ever perform the plays that I wrote, but it didn't matter. They were my creations and I was proud of them. Someday, I thought, I'll be a real author. I had a voice, I had something to say,

and I knew that the world was going to hear me speak loud and clear.

Then, of course, life got in the way. And by "in the way", I don't think I'm really talking about being too busy to write. I think what I mean is that life discouraged me from writing. It felt like I lost my voice. I lost the confidence that my voice mattered. I began to believe that everything that I wanted to say had already been said by someone else. That everything I wanted to say could be said better by someone else. That no one would want to read what I had to say. I lost all confidence in my writing. Sure, I would write a few stories here and there to communicate our cultural learnings from India to our friends and family back home. But when it came to truly exposing my heart? No, I was no longer allowed to do that. The world had removed my right to do that. Or at least that's what I thought.

But then, so many years later, the stories that had been building up inside me began to force their way out. There was no possibility of containing them any more. From time to time during our tenure in India, a book title would pop out of my brain. But now it was more intense. Whole outlines for books would emerge onto the page without any effort. The words flew out of my fingers onto the keyboard seemingly without going through my conscious thought system. I would stand back, read what I had written and wonder where it had come from. The words had to come out. The emotions tied to my experiences had to be expressed. They could no longer be held back. My mental and emotional health depended on this.

My therapist agreed. He encouraged my almost obsessive journaling. I had started carrying with me a variety of journals. One for "serious" journaling. One for "emergency" journaling.

One for journaling related to "work". I no longer felt safe if I didn't have access to paper and pen. If I couldn't let the words out onto paper, it was as if the emotions would eat me alive. So I wrote. And wrote. And wrote. And finally one day, I knew it was time. It was time to start with the exercise that would capture the years of my life that were most dear to me, the most meaningful, the most impactful. It was time to write about India. The nation that I love so much and to which I have dedicated my life. It would be my first book, a memoir. This is the book you hold in your hands right now.

Instead of a chronological history of every event that happened, or, heaven forbid, a tell-all gossip rag of my intimate and private opinions of everyone I met and worked with over the years, I wanted this memoir to be a collection of the most important things that I learned while we lived in India. I wanted to be able to look back at our time in India and see how God had worked in our lives while he was at the same time working in the lives of the billion people around us. I knew there would be themes that emerged and was so glad that the themes came to me so quickly and clearly. In this book, you'll read about those themes of learning and I give them to you not only for my own reflection and benefit, but because I feel like all of us, to some degree, need to learn these things. We all encounter cultures different from our own. We all struggle with relationships. We all fear uncertainty. I hope that my experiences and the things that I've learned will help you as you face these issues in your life and seek to move forward with confidence in all that God has created you to do.

In the review process of this memoir, so many people asked me to include more stories. More stories, they shouted! So I have included three distinct chapters entitled "Heart Stories... " where

I do just that. I've included stories both silly and serious, both joyful and heartbreaking. The stories reflect our lives, but also the work that we did while we were there. I hope the stories will not only be interesting, but also inspiring and a source of learning for all those who read. Our lives are made up of stories and we feel so privileged to have been a part of these moments and know our lives have been formed by the things God allowed us to experience during this precious time overseas.

Oh, one more thing. Unless otherwise noted, I changed all the names of the people I refer to in this book. Many of you reading may know the people I've mentioned, so it might be fun for you to guess who they are. Every story I've written comes from a place of love for people who mean so much to me.

Leah Kadwell
Shoreview, Minnesota
September, 2020

P.S. Don't Skip the Epilogue!!

PROLOGUE

The tears were running down my cheeks and pooling on the slightly scratched screen of my phone, which I clutched, white-knuckled in my lap. It was 3:00am and all around me was noise and action and distraction as already exhausted passengers boarded the plane. They were trying to shove their overstuffed carry-on suitcases into the always-too-small overhead compartments. They were wrangling uncooperative children into seats so that those same children, zombie-like due to the late night departure, could immediately begin kicking the seat in front of them. This mass of humanity that was crammed into a vessel that looks huge from the outside, but in reality is tiny on the inside, was sitting, then standing, then sitting again in what seemed to be a badly choreographed dance, somehow unable to find the spot which would be their home for the next 16 hours. The air was already beginning to get stale and it was clear that not everyone had bathed and used deodorant before boarding the flight. Announcements from a frustrated, yet overly polite flight attendant were blaring overhead, while her desperate colleagues battled their way up and down the aisles pleading with people to take their seats and fasten their seatbelts. They were largely unsuccessful in their diligent efforts. Their faces reflected their desperate state and betrayed their thoughts which questioned how they could have possibly chosen this particular profession. "You'll get to travel," people said. "It'll be fun."

Although I can recall all the details now, I didn't notice any of these clearly obvious things in the moment. I was still shaking from what had happened only moments earlier. My heart was pounding and my hands were sweating. My mind was racing through the events of the evening. Even though some part of me

had been expecting this day to come for 20 years, the shock of it all was still too much to take.

I wiped the pool of tears from my phone's screen and began texting one, then another, and still another of my faithful buddies who were certainly wondering where I was. Yesterday had been a normal workday where I'd seen my friends and colleagues in the office and we made plans for meetings and projects. We'd laughed and drank coffee from my contraband Keurig machine that everyone thought was a marvel. How does it make coffee so fast? We'd eaten lunch together and talked about politics and sports and laughed playfully at the antics of the boss's grandson. We'd worried together about how we were going to raise the needed funding for our schools and healthcare projects. The work we were doing was making such a transformative difference in the lives of so many people, we were driven to power it with resources. I had driven my little red Volkswagen home from the office and cooked dinner (chicken, again...) and gone to bed as usual. Nothing out of the ordinary, nothing new to report. Yes, it had been a "normal" day.

But then today? Everything changed. Things were no longer "normal". I'd gone radio silent for almost 24 hours, which was highly unusual for me, a tech-addicted 40-something Gen-X-er. My 20-something-aged friends who were chronically attached to their phones had been reaching out asking me how I was doing, what I was doing, where I was. Their messages to me became more urgent throughout the day, confused as to why I was not communicating with them as usual. "Please," they said. "Are you ok?" Every time my phone sounded off its characteristic "ding", my stomach churned and my brain, fully clouded now, searched for a way to let them know what was going on. All day it pained

me that I couldn't tell them or give them any details on my whereabouts. But now that I was safely in my window seat on the plane, I was moderately relieved that I could reply. Although "relieved" is probably not the most accurate description of what I was feeling since I felt like vomiting every time I hit send.

My messages to them were cryptic at best: "I'm going on a trip and I don't know when I'll be back." "I'm sorry I wasn't there to say goodbye this time." "Please pray for me; I'm not doing well." They must've wondered what in the world was going on. Worried, even. Trying to piece together the scraps of non-detail that I had offered up. I had traveled many times alone. On my own I had traveled to North America, Europe, Asia, and really never thought about the fact that no one was with me. It was my job. It was what I was required to do. However, on this particular night, I felt alone. I felt isolated. I felt targeted. And in the midst of these lonely feelings, I couldn't gain solace from those who loved me. I couldn't tell them what was happening. I had to just send off a few words, imbibed with as much love as possible, then put my phone on airplane mode, lean my head against the window and hope that someday I'd be able to explain it all. The tears flowed even more freely now.

Soon enough my seatmate arrived. She was an elderly Indian woman wearing a multi-colored sari along with a burgundy sweater, grey wooly socks and dark blue sneakers. She was following what appeared to be her son and daughter-in-law and their children who had arranged for her to sit in the front "bulkhead" seat (whatever that means), even though they were seated further back in the aircraft. This lovely woman struggled even to carry her small suitcase, let alone lift it above her head into the bin. Thankfully, her son helped her with this burden and she

5

was free. She sat down next to me grasping her black leather purse against her chest and a white embroidered handkerchief in her hand. She sat down carefully, gracefully. Her golden bangles clinked together as she inserted the metal tip into the buckle of her seatbelt. She had a quiet spirit about her and I was thankful on my night of trauma to have this grey-haired matriarch's presence so near to me. I looked over at her with my tear-stained face and smiled. She seemed to notice my damp cheeks and smeared mascara and, bridging the language gap with the international and all-pervasive symbol of love and affection, she smiled back. In that moment, I felt cared for by a one-in-a-billion stranger and my bruised and aching heart felt just a little less alone.

The airplane lurched backward, somehow signaling to my brain that I was now safe, despite the events that had happened earlier that evening. I was unexpectedly leaving the beautiful, diverse, sometimes confusing land that I loved, but at least I would soon be in the arms of my family once again. I had to keep that reunion in my mind throughout the ordeal I had endured.

Even as this feeling of safety and a mild wave of relief washed over me as we roared down the runway and took off into the night sky headed west, my mind raced back a few hours to the moment I stood in the long line to clear the exit immigration process in India's capital city of New Delhi. People from what seemed like every nation of the world surrounded me. New Delhi is such a cosmopolitan city with visitors and residents coming and going from a wide range of countries for a wide range of reasons. All those people were now packed into the immigration hall standing in a line that curled round and round like we were all at Disney World waiting to ride Space Mountain. However, the end

of this line held something much different for me on this particular trip.

As I stood in the "queue" as they call it in India, I watched as passenger after passenger quickly went through the required steps of schlepping themselves and all their luggage up to the counter and presenting their passports and boarding passes to the immigration officials as they prepared to leave the country. The passports were scanned and stamped, and people were sent on their way, generally without incident. I had gone through this ritual at least a hundred times before in India alone, not to mention all the other nations I'd traveled to over the years. I knew the drill. I knew what to expect. I knew what would happen. Or, should I say, what was supposed to happen. Tonight, for me, was different.

Even though I knew what to expect, I sensed in my heart that perhaps things were not going to go as smoothly as I had hoped. I was leaving India quickly and unexpectedly due to some incidents that had spiraled well out of my control. I didn't want to leave, but I had to. I expected that I would leave for a couple months and then come back and resume life as before. But as I was walking up to the immigration counter, I felt more nervous than usual. The butterflies in my stomach were flapping their wings furiously and my chest was tightening with anxiety. Still, I presented a calm face, hoping that my outwardly peaceful demeanor would not betray what was going on inside. "Please, Lord," I prayed with a little more urgency than usual. "Let me get through this without a problem." I'm sure God heard my desperate prayer in that moment. But as we all know, sometimes God has other plans.

I gave my passport to the immigration official and he took it as usual. He opened it to the picture page and scanned it into his

computer. Within moments, I could tell that all was not as it should be. Although his face was characteristically stoic, he stared at the monitor in an unusual way as if seeing something he was not expecting to see. Without removing his gaze from the screen, he grasped for a small scrap of white paper and his black pen and began copying down line after line. I didn't know what he was writing, even though I tried my best to casually glance over the barrier to catch a glimpse. I didn't dare ask because I knew the situation was grim. I had heard too many horror stories of people facing challenges at immigration.

When we are guests of other nations, we place ourselves at the mercy of their laws and regulations. In some nations, those laws and regulations are so much different than our own that they are difficult to interpret and understand. In other countries, the rules change quickly and without notice. Most times those in violation of these immigration requirements may not even know they are in violation. They have in good faith entered the country to visit, to do business, or in some way to help better the nation through humanitarian work or simply by building relationships with its citizens. Nevertheless, we as foreign nationals visiting must obey the local laws. If at any time it is determined that we have not complied with the laws of the land, we are asked to leave. Usually permanently. I feared this was what was happening to me now.

I stood silently, watching this man continue to write things on his scrap of paper. Minutes passed. People behind me in line must've wondered what in the world was going on and what I had done to garner so much attention from this official. I could feel their eyes staring at me. I could hear sleepy children getting restless and starting to cry as they waited their turn. Even the

temperature in the immigration hall seemed to rise as the hands on the clock kept on moving. My emotions were raging. I wanted to cry. I wanted to scream. I wanted to just grab my passport and run through security and get on the plane. I was longing to know exactly what was happening. The uncertainty was killing me. What was he writing down? Is there any way this was going to turn out positively? What were they going to stamp in my passport? Were they going to let me leave the country? Would I end up spending the night in jail? I tried to be calm, but expecting the worst is a nerve-wracking pastime. It was all becoming too much.

After about half an hour of writing, the man pushed back his squeaky chair and stood to his feet. "Come," he said sternly, without looking me in the eye. Even he knew this was going to be difficult for me. I followed him, not knowing where we were going. Even though he was not physically touching me, I felt as if I was being escorted roughly to some kind of holding cell to await my fate. In reality, he was taking me to another desk where another official sat, this one with more power and more authority. My guy presented the papers he had written along with my passport. They spoke to each other quietly in Hindi. My poor hearing and even poorer Hindi-language skills prevented me from hearing them, even though I strained to catch any bit of information. The new man looked at me with disdain, sat down, scanned my passport and confirmed all that the first official had told him.

More minutes passed, but soon enough the man rose from his chair and said, "Come." This time he took me behind the desks, handed me my passport and said, "Go." Wait. What just happened? No explanation? No documents telling me I'd been kicked out of the country? No holding cell? No rebuke for

supposedly breaking the laws of the land? The uncertainty was too much to take, so I bravely asked, "Sir, can you tell me what is going on?" He looked at me with his stone-set eyes and simply replied, "No," and walked away. I was left holding my passport and boarding pass in one hand, my carry on bag in the other with a bewildered look on my face. I knew that yes, I had just been "blacklisted" from ever entering India again (or at least for a long time), but surely there had to be more pomp and circumstance to go with it. Hmm. Apparently not.

I turned and went through security and eventually got on the plane. All of these fresh and painful memories swirled in my head as the plane had now leveled off at its cruising altitude. I had left India. I would not return. I would not see those dear friends on the other end of my text messages again. I would not get to see the results of 20 years of blood, sweat and tears laboring in both the good times and the bad times of the trenches. I would become an outsider. I pictured the faces of those I loved and became consumed once again with grief. The tears flowed down my already damp cheeks and although I tried to turn my head, the dear Indian grandmother seated next to me sensed my sorrow and gave my knee a gentle pat. Once again, despite India's multitude of languages, most of which I did not know, the barrier of communication had been breached with one small gesture.

I looked out into the night sky and to the Arabian Sea below wondering what life would be like now. For most of my adult life I had lived in a culture that was not my own. I had given my life to a cause that had brought betterment and transformation to millions. Millions. It was no small thing. What a privilege. What a blessing. But now perhaps it was all gone. For the second time

that night I cried out to God, "Please Lord! Let me get through this…." Would I survive?

PART ONE:
CROSSING CULTURES

CHAPTER ONE

Whenever I think of that night on the plane leaving India and the hours I spent crying over what I believed I had lost, I am reminded of the only other time I had cried on an airplane: The day so many years before that we left America to move to India.

We were young. We were newlyweds. We owned nothing. We had packed all our worldly belongings into four suitcases and decided to move to the other side of the world. We had fallen in love with India on a three-week trip we had taken a year earlier. The people of India, her culture, and the pace of life all captured our hearts and we had longed to return. But for us it wasn't just somewhere we wanted to visit occasionally on vacation. We knew we wouldn't be satisfied returning for a week or two every year. We felt called. We felt compelled to make a permanent change. We had heard the voice of God speak clearly to us and we were ready and willing to respond. As we had spent time with people on that first trip in 1997 and listened to their stories and learned about their lives, we saw such great potential for full-life transformation. We wanted to play a significant part in bringing that transformation. We had some ideas of what we could do and what our roles might look like, but most of all, our hearts had been opened and we were ready to move forward with this new thing we believed God had prepared specifically for us.

We had returned from that short initial trip with a vision for our future and a renewed sense of purpose. Sure, we had struggled during our time there. It was a time in India's history before globalization had truly touched the nation. There were infrastructure challenges we had never before imagined. We didn't have running (or hot!) water for showers or laundry. There was no electricity. The food was challenging to eat and we had to wait hours for our water to be purified. The smells were overwhelmingly noxious and the traffic was the heaviest and most snarled we'd ever experienced. Despite all that, however, the decision was an easy one. We were aware and ready to overcome any obstacle that was presented to us in a life in India. We never felt fear or uncertainty. We never had to make a pros and cons list. Sure, there were cons, but nothing could break our newfound focus or divert us from this passionately chosen path. We were moving to India and it was a good thing.

In some ways, though, despite our absolute certainty, the decision to relocate our lives and commit ourselves to this new reality came as a surprise. Prior to going to India the first time, we had never eaten Indian food. We didn't watch Bollywood movies or listen to Hindi music. We did not have a collection of Indian handicrafts in our small one-bedroom apartment, and we certainly had no interest in indigenous Indian art. We had never cultivated an interest in the East Indian community in our own neighborhood. In fact, at the time, I think we only knew maybe one person of Indian heritage. (Ashamedly, I went to high school with two sisters of Indian heritage, spent time in their home, and learned how to pronounce their very Indian last name. But it never occurred to me that they were Indian. In fact, I never even

viewed them as "foreign" or different from me in any way. I guess I had a very low cross-cultural awareness quotient in those days!)

India had never been on our radar. To be truly honest, India wasn't really on anyone's radar at the time. Lots of people were moving overseas to serve in Africa, China or the Middle East, but not India. In fact, one time when we told someone we were moving to India, she replied, "Indiana?" We laughed, but it reminded us how unfamiliar our little world was with this nation we had chosen. Despite all these things, upon spending just a couple days in India, the love for India and its dear people was sown immediately and deeply into our hearts. It was as if this affection and calling had always been there. Our lives were forever and profoundly changed.

When we began telling other people we were moving to India, almost every single person said, "Of course you are!" That's exactly what it felt like. It was natural. It was the obvious next step in life for both Kevin and me. We had both grown up in families where the Church and serving the community were valued above most other things. I can remember being a young girl of probably four or five when my grandfather took me into the inner city of Detroit, Michigan, to its Rescue Mission. This was definitely no place for little girls. We entered through the back door which was heavily gated and locked with black, iron bars. Our tour of the place included introduction to drug paraphernalia and the temporary sleeping quarters where both drug addicts and prostitutes could take confidential refuge for a few nights, especially during the brutal Midwestern winters. I sang songs, I served soup, and I greeted each resident with an enthusiastic smile accompanied by a bashful "hello". My grandpa brought me to this place not for the shock value, but instead to show me first-hand

that we are called to love everyone, especially those who are different than us and those who are struggling in life. In a sense, by entering this place and embracing those we found within, I was, at a young age, already crossing cultures as Grandpa took me from the comforts of suburbia into the desperation and poverty of the inner city.

Grandpa wasn't the only one with a ministry. My grandmother volunteered with the Billy Graham Evangelistic Association. My other grandmother was a deaconess. My mother supported and prayed for a variety of missionaries, faithfully sang in the choir, and mentored younger women. My father was a gifted musician and spent every Sunday behind the console of a pipe organ. My aunt and uncle were missionaries in France. My cousin, the first in our family to go to a four-year university, studied Bible and became a pastor. My parents and grandparents modeled what I later learned to identify as missional living and altruistic service. They served because they loved God and they loved people. They did not serve to get recognition. They never had an ulterior motive, nor did they expect anything in return. They loved God and this was their sole motivation.

When we were old enough, both Kevin and I began to get actively involved in all kinds of ministries. By the time we were young adults, you name it, we had done it: Children's Sunday School, Youth Group, College Ministry, Choir, Bible Study, Summer Camps, Service Projects, Fund Raising, Overseas Trips. We quickly gained a reputation as reliable volunteers. If someone in the church needed something done, they called us. We often were called upon to start a new ministry or to fill a last-minute need. People knew that if they asked us to do something, it would get done. We were well-versed in how to build relationships, run

ministry programs, and help people apply the Bible to their lives. Therefore, when the day came that we announced that we were moving to India, it seemed to make sense to us and to everyone we knew that we would take our skills, our zeal and our steadfast commitment to God and His Church to the "next level", so to speak, and do what we knew to do in a land far, far away.

When we announced to our parents that we were moving to India, they were supportive. (Yes, we simply "announced" this big, life-altering news to them. In our 20s we weren't ones to ask for feedback. We just announced our intentions and hoped those closest to us would accept our decisions. Geesh.) Our parents knew our passion for ministry and, along with others, felt like this was the next natural step in our service experience. While my parents had seen the natural progression of me moving further and further from home throughout the years to pursue whatever I wanted to achieve, Kevin's parents took a little more time to come to terms with the idea. They definitely recognized Kevin's love for people and passion for ministry, and so the idea of us serving God in this radical way was not unusual to them. However, they initially thought this would be a two-year experience that we would perhaps "get out of our systems" and then return to life as normal. However, as they began to see our love for India and drive to bring transformation to the nation, they, too, realized this was our life calling and they threw their wholehearted support behind all that we were seeking to do. We were so thankful that our family members were charter members of our home team and were faithful prayer warriors for us, standing in the gap for us, even in these early days of the unknown.

But it wasn't just our ministry skills that convinced us, our parents and others that moving to India was the right choice for

us. There was a sense that moving overseas to live in a developing nation was going to take a special quality, a unique capacity, and a depth of character beyond just the ability to travel and make new friends. It was going to take resilience. It was going to require us to be capable of facing problems and challenges head on, unafraid of the unknown, and willing to conquer even the most seemingly insurmountable obstacles. Resilience is not something you can learn from a book. Resilience is only gained through experience, through heartbreak, through trial, and through tenacity. I didn't know it at the time, but resilience would become the #1 major theme of my life. It would be the common thread that took me from childhood, through the turbulent teen years and into adulthood living in another culture. Resilience is what saw me through and helped me to thrive in the midst of unimaginable troubles and unspeakable joys. Being resilient never meant that my problems went away or became easier. But with time and experience, I was better able to weather the storms that came my way. We, of course, knew only a little of the resilience it would require to live in India when we signed on the dotted line and made the commitment to spend our lives living cross-culturally. At the beginning, we generally viewed India through rose-colored glasses, even though we were somewhat aware of some of the realities we would face. But more than anything else, we would be called to be resilient. And this was something for which God had been preparing us our entire lives.

Growing up in middle class families in the Midwest in the 1970s and 1980s, life was good. I grew up playing outside 'til dark, safely riding my blue Schwinn bike miles from home, and hanging out with my childhood buddies, then teenage friends. My grandparents lived next door, so there was always an abundance

of family nearby. I still remember getting home from school and making toasted cheese sandwiches with Pepperidge Farms pumpernickel bread and Kraft American cheese, then making a batch of boxed brownies and licking both the wooden spoon and the mixing bowl clean of any of that sweet and gooey brownie batter. (It's a wonder any brownies actually made it to the baking pan.) It was a relatively carefree life surrounded by adults who cared for me, protected me, and gave me boundaries in which I should operate, but by-and-large let me make my own decisions about school, relationships, church, and ministry. I remember feeling like I was in control of my own destiny.

Living in Detroit, Michigan, my life revolved around sports. Whether it was going to Detroit Tigers baseball games or cheering for the University of Michigan Wolverines in their latest bowl game, we were super fans. We had the jerseys and the hats. We had the baseball cards and knew all the stats. We followed the schedules and the standings religiously in the newspaper. The nights we spent at Grandma's house while waiting for my mom to finish her afternoon shift at the hospital were spent listening to Ernie Harwell call baseball games on the radio. We were on a first-name basis with all the players on all the teams and, despite the fact that we'd never met any of them personally, they were a part of our home life and our emotions were often based on their performance. The night the Detroit Tigers won the 1984 World Series was one of the happiest nights of my life. The Detroit Lions football team, however, was a constant source of disappointment. Sports was our life.

When I was old enough to start playing on an organized softball team, I was on the field. I had been "practicing" in my backyard for years, hitting a whiffle ball as far as it would go,

perfecting my "pitching" to my younger brother who somehow always played with me despite the fact that I always won. We broke our share of windows and climbed our share of fences chasing after balls that went astray. Participating in sports became an important part of my life. I won awards and eventually sports paid for my college education. I loved being part of a team. I loved practicing. I loved performing. I learned very quickly the thrill of victory and the disappointment of defeat. The disappointment never lasted long, though. There was always another chance to play, another chance to hit that ball long and far, out of the reach of our opponent.

By the time I reached junior high, I was playing basketball, volleyball and running track, in addition to keeping up with summer softball. My mom supported me and came to every game faithfully. It was her support and the support of my coaches that encouraged me to continue working hard, even when I knew my skills weren't up to the mark. I felt compelled and driven to improve. There were so many days that I arrived early to practice or stayed late to shoot just a few more free throws, hit just a few more balls off the pitching machine, or serve just a few more balls over the net. Truth be told, I wanted to be the best. I knew to be the best, I had to work harder than everyone else, stay later, do more reps. In some sports I was the best. In others, not so much. But no matter what I wanted to do, I felt the support of my mom. After every game, win or lose, we went to Baskin Robbins to celebrate (or commiserate) with a double-dip cone of mint chocolate chip. I knew I was loved. I knew that win or lose life would go on. I knew that even in all those horrible basketball games when I didn't even get to play, that I was still a good and valued person. I didn't realize it at the time, but through the glory

of sports, I was learning resilience at an early age. I was learning to bounce back. I was learning to thrive.

Money always seemed tight in my childhood home. The love overflowed, but the money not so much. I grew up in a single-parent home in which my mother worked hard as a high-ranking, expertly skilled nurse in a leading area hospital. Because she was the boss, she was often the one "on call" overnight. My younger brother and I were used to hearing the phone ring in the middle of the night, followed by a short trip to finish sleeping the night at my grandmother's house next door. We had everything we needed in life and most of the things we wanted. Both my parents did everything they could to provide for us. But as students at an upper class college-prep private school, the evil of comparison often raised its ugly head. Our house was smaller than all my friends' houses. My clothes weren't as fashionable. My haircut was too simple, my shoes weren't the latest trend, I didn't know how to apply makeup to my acne-prone face, and I never carried a cute purse from class to class.

Nevertheless, I have only happy memories from my childhood home. Even though I knew our house was small, it never felt too small. It felt sufficient. It had everything we needed. I don't remember ever actually longing for a larger home. Surely, if I had a bigger bedroom it would've only been that much harder to clean! I was satisfied with what we had even though I didn't know it in the moment. The house was warm, we had more than enough food, and the love and acceptance of family was always there. Learning this attitude of contentment and sufficiency would serve me well in later years when electricity and running water were not always guaranteed, when there were no options in the

supermarket and choices were made for us on such "simple" things as paint colors, number of bedrooms, and furniture.

I was also a child of divorce during a time in history when divorce was still uncommon and shameful. The early years after my parents' divorce were often filled with prying eyes gazing at us as we sat in our usual pew in church. Was it disdain? Was it pity? Was it judgment? Probably all of the above. Christians can do a lot of good in this world in the name of Jesus, but sometimes they're not so good at loving people who are struggling. I was eight years old when my parents got divorced and I didn't need people's pity or judgment. I needed their love. I didn't have any other friends whose parents were divorced at that time, so I didn't have any other behavior to model my own upon. We went to a bit of counseling to sort through our emotions and the divorced life became our new normal. It was fine. I didn't know any different.

What I didn't know at the time, however, was that the shame of living in a home affected by divorce would shape me. I always felt that there was something not good enough with me, despite the love that both my mom and my dad poured out on me, despite the success of my sports and ministry experiences. Compared to others who came from "normal" homes, I was tainted, scarred, and wounded in a way that was never going to heal. Shame defined me and my relationships, both with people and with my God. I could not accept God's grace for my life because I was ashamed of the ways I constantly failed him. I remember as I child begging God to forgive me of my sins every night before I went to sleep. I lived in fear that if I didn't do my morning devotions, God would condemn me to a bad day without His protection and without His favor. At its worst, as a young girl, I even feared losing my salvation and repeatedly asked Jesus into

my heart over and over again. Those were some challenging nights in my childhood bed, wondering if God would still be willing to accept me.

Further to my relationship with God, I couldn't believe that people would ever love me because I would never measure up to their expectations. These were all deep-seated interior battles I faced and most of the time didn't understand until much later. What was astounding to me, though, was that even in experiencing this sometimes-debilitating shame, I was being prepared for my time in India. India is a Shame and Honor culture as most Asian countries are. My internal struggles with shame during my younger years gave me a head start in beginning to understand what shame could mean to an entire culture that operated out of a fear of the implications of being shamed.

Despite the psychological scars I suffered because of the divorce, my parents did an amazing job in expressing to both me and my younger brother that they loved us, would never leave us, and that we were an absolutely important part of both of their lives, even though life would look different in the future after they split up. We lived with my mother, but my father never moved far away and we saw him twice a week. I knew I had two parents who loved me, who worked hard to provide for me, and supported me in whatever I wanted to do. Once again, I was learning to be resilient. I was confronted with challenges that not many children at that time had to face and I weathered them. Life had thrown young eight-year-old me a curve ball and I had to learn to cope. And I did. It was not easy. There were tears and frustrations and so many nights filled with the unknown. But through it all, I developed strength and stamina that would serve me well later in

life when I needed to face uncertainty and all the hard things that life would throw my way.

Life has such a funny, yet miraculous way of preparing us for what we will encounter. God has designed our lives in such a way that we will be ready to conquer what He has planned for us. His plans are so good and so detailed. I firmly believe that everything in our lives is simply a training ground for us as we seek out and fulfill His ultimate purpose. Yes, we have free will and the freedom to choose our own destiny. But God knows even that. My life as a child growing up in the Midwest playing softball, learning to recover from losses, dealing with life in a middle class home, and being a child of divorce all taught me such valuable lessons and life skills that I had no way of knowing would benefit me as I got on that airplane in 1998 and flew off to live on the other side of the world. As a child, I think I knew that God wanted to use me for some plan that was greater than my own. I didn't know what that was and I didn't know I would end up in India. But I was willing to go wherever He led me and do whatever He asked me to do. I didn't know it at the time, but He was equipping me so that when the time came, I would be ready. I would have the skills, attitudes and resilience needed to thrive in a culture that was not my own. In fact, it was a culture so opposite from my own that, even as I sat crying in that airplane seat next to my new husband, having just said goodbye to our friends and family and ready to fly off to the other side of the world, God had more than adequately prepared me for the grand adventure I could never have imagined was waiting for me when my tears had long-dried and the airplane landed in Hyderabad, India, 24 hours later.

CHAPTER TWO

We had been to India twice before, so we thought we knew what to expect. India is a vibrant, unexpected, colorful, amazing culture. Its rich history and vast population combine to create an astounding variety of sights, smells, sounds, attitudes and traditions. We would come to realize quickly that there is something new to learn every day in India. We would never completely understand everything about this massive nation, but this would only be part of its remarkable charm. India is not for the faint of heart. Its extremes assault the senses and leave us exhausted emotionally as we try to process all that our minds are attempting to absorb. Sure, we thought we knew what to expect when we stepped off of that jet bridge and into our new life abroad. However, we began almost immediately to expect the unexpected. And it was that sense of the unexpected that drew us even more powerfully to this endearing nation that had captured our hearts.

We stepped out of the airport terminal in the city of Hyderabad, our new home, and were immediately hit with the humidity of a southern Florida beach town, despite the relatively manageable middle-of-the-night temperatures. Sure, the daytime temps would reach in to the 90s, but right now, at 2:00am, it wasn't that warm. It was appropriate that our first encounter with India on this, our inaugural night in the country was the weather. The weather in India is an integral part of cultural awareness. It is

a topic of daily conversation despite the much more subtle changes experienced in this tropical climate. Whether it is the extreme, debilitating heat of an Indian summer or the overwhelming downpour of a monsoon rain, people's lives revolve around the weather and its impact on society. Not enough rain? Farmers' crops refuse to grow and they face bankruptcy and certain economic failure. Too much rain? Farmers' crops are drowned and they face the same financial fate. Homeless people are confronted with experiencing hypothermia and death in the winter, even though temperatures never dip below 40 degrees Fahrenheit. Underdeveloped infrastructure results in putting India's people in peril and at the mercy of Mother Nature.

Pushing our airport luggage carts with all our worldly possessions contained in four suitcases in front of us, it was now time to find our ride. Someone was arranged to be there to pick us up. Who? We didn't know. But someone. Our pace slowed and people started backing up behind us, eager for us to move forward. Our eyes darted around feverishly trying to locate any indication of familiarity, anyone who looked remotely like they were there to receive us. There were about 200 Indian men who, ashamedly, all looked the same to us, holding signs made of white 8 ½ x 11 paper with black ink on them. Where was our name? How would we find him? All of the names on all of the signs appeared to be Indian names. We were, after all, the only "white" people we'd seen in the airport. Surely that would reveal our obvious identity to the person awaiting our arrival.

Finally, after what seemed like an eternity, a man with a bright smile and friendly eyes emerged from the crowd and dashed toward us. Here he was! Ready to receive us. "Mr. Kevin?" he said, greeting us both hesitantly yet enthusiastically. That is, by the way,

how we would forever be known in this land. "Mr. and Mrs. Kevin". It is traditional in many parts of India for people to use only their first name as their main source of identity. They pass their first name on to their wife and then their children. I would be greeted as "Mrs. Kevin" by drivers, hotel owners, tour guides, pizza delivery guys, and school staff members. Sometimes I even forgot that "Kadwell" was actually my last name. (In other parts of India, the surname is used. I learned that the naming practice varied by state and by region, but I never finally determined the exact formula or protocol to predict who would use what name. The safest bet was simply to ask someone what they preferred. Even birth certificates were sometimes not the name people eventually used. In most cases, the "official" name became whatever they used on their school registration papers. Those became their permanent records and were rarely changed after that, even if they somehow contained a spelling error or other discrepancy.)

"Kevin", of course, is not a common Indian name, and so over the years new acquaintances would innocently butcher it. We heard everything from Kelvin and Calvin to Kewin, We learned to answer to just about anything that sounded close. My own name, "Leah" was rarely used. That was okay. I quickly learned that my identity as a woman was firmly rooted in my identity as Kevin's wife. I began to realize how good it was that I was married. If I was a single woman, my worth would have been significantly diminished. Marriage gave me value. When I got pregnant? Whoa. Then I had really fulfilled my destiny. Things were certainly different here.

As he reached out to shake Kevin's hand, our new friend and driver told us his name, but I didn't understand what he said. My

"India ears" as I came to call them later, had not yet developed. Even though he was speaking English to us and, I would learn later that his name was not that difficult to pronounce, I still didn't understand. I could blame it on jet lag, but in reality, I just hadn't yet learned to hear my friend's accent correctly. I felt embarrassed that I wouldn't be able to thank him by name later or remember his name when he drove us again. When I look back at my journals recording our first impressions of our arrival in India, I chuckle at what I thought his name was. Clearly, I was not hearing correctly, nor did I have a good grasp on what traditional Indian names were yet. I would learn. It would take time, but I would learn. Years later, when those coveted "India ears" were fully developed, I would act as a "translator" for other newly arrived foreigners. I translated English to English, of course, but the new arrivals were so thankful for my services.

Regardless of my ability to understand his name at that time, he took my luggage cart joyfully. I would discover rapidly that as a foreign woman in India, I would rarely carry my own luggage, packages, bags or any kind of burden which required any form of moving from here to there. There was no use arguing. It was a cultural honor for someone else to assist me. Even though it was uncomfortable and tremendously humbling for me at first, I allowed this lovely man to push my luggage cart as we headed out into the overcrowded parking lot. He led us toward the big, blue 15-passenger van in which he would take us to our temporary home. We didn't know where we were going or how long we would be there. We just decided to trust.

We piled ourselves into the road-worn and slightly dented van and off we went. The plexi-glass windows were wide open and some refreshingly cool night air was flowing freely through

the vehicle, whipping my already unbrushed hair into a frenzy. That cool night air was also infused with the smells of the city. Garbage was burning on street corners. The smell of sewage surfaced as we traveled by storm drains and slum settlements. The pungent odor of diesel exhaust materialized with every passing truck that was rushing through the city to make an early morning delivery. These were all new smells to us that would soon become part of our India experience. With every return trip to India, no matter how long we'd been gone, the permanently imprinted memory of these smells would transport us in our minds to our beloved Indian home long before we reached our front door. Although the smells themselves were not pleasant, the memories associated with them became dear to us and a part of our story that nothing else could ever replace.

On this particular night, in the early morning hours, the traffic we had experienced in earlier trips to India was not there. It was, after all, the middle of the night, so apparently all the cars and their drivers were at home sleeping. We zoomed through the streets and eventually arrived at the 11-acre campus that would be the hub of all our activities for the next 20 years. It was, however, completely unfamiliar on that night. A security guard dressed in a black uniform with red tassels on his shoulders who looked to be at least 70 years old, looked through the windows of our vehicle, deemed us not to be a threat to the property and opened the clunky black front gate which squealed and resisted as he pushed it on its rusty tracks. Driving inside, we craned our necks to peer up at the brightly lit coconut trees lining the driveway. It looked beautiful. Tropical. Like paradise. We ambled over the rocky roads until we arrived at some humble guest accommodations near the rear of the property.

Our new driver friend helped us unload our belongings into one of the apartments which was painted with whitewash, was lit with fluorescent tube lights, had mosquitos flying freely, and smelled like mothballs and cleaning solvent. As we stepped into the bedroom for the first time and glanced at the beds, the sheets looked sufficiently clean. Clean enough, at least, for our exhausted bodies to collapse upon and get some much needed rest after the emotional and physical toll of the travel we had just endured. There was a noisy and dusty window air conditioner unit that we turned on as soon as we entered the room. It did a marginal job of projecting some cooler air into the room. It was good enough. There were no blankets on the bed, but we wouldn't need them. We fell into the bed and immediately went to sleep. We were exhausted, but we were thrilled. We were home.

The next day would come to represent a lot of what we would experience during our time in India. We awoke to the sounds of roosters crowing. This surprised us because we were not on a farm and we hadn't seen any chickens roaming around the property when we arrived the night before. Nonetheless there were roosters somewhere eager to announce the coming of the new day, even before the sun rose over the horizon. It was as if these humble roosters were the nation of India's thoughtfully-provided natural alarm clock, the first sign of one of the country's most characteristic qualities: India is a land of extreme hospitality.

Before moving to India, I believed hospitality was some combination of hosting people for a Martha Stewart-style dinner party or creating the perfectly decorated guest room for them to stay for the weekend. But Indians take hospitality to the next level. Their ability to host their guests is so superior to that of other

nations that it has become cliché. Walk into any hotel in North America and the likelihood that the general manager is of Indian descent is unusually high. Hospitality is in the Indian DNA. I suppose there could be some debate about whether this hospitality is truly genuine or not. Is their service of others truly selfless? Or is it in expectation of a blessing from their gods? An insurance policy against bad future karma? Who knows. There can be no argument, however, that they go the extra mile for their guests and sacrifice their own personal comfort for the sake of those who are visiting. We experienced that hospitality over and over again during our entire tenure living abroad. Our first week in India was a fantastic example of this exceptional hospitality.

Before we had arrived in India, our new friends and colleagues had rented a simple two-bedroom duplex for us. We had given them the authorization to simply find us a place to live. We were interested in living in a home that was similar to everyone else's home, there were only two of us, and we had only a small budget to pay the rent, so something simple would certainly be sufficient. It wasn't until much later that we discovered that it was unusual for foreigners to occupy a home sight unseen. Usually people spent up to a month touring the city searching for exactly the right place. That thought had never occurred to us. We simply let someone else choose. The home was good enough for us and we loved the place they chose. As I reflect on our love for our first Indian home, and realize how simple it was, I can only credit our satisfaction with it to growing up in an equally simple childhood home and learning from an early age what sufficiency meant. I am thankful that I had that upbringing which made it easier to thrive in simple surroundings once we arrived overseas. Upon arriving in that humble two-

bedroom rented duplex, what didn't occur to us immediately was that our new colleagues had taken the time to scour the city for an appropriate rental property for us. We would learn later that it took a lot of time and negotiation and wasn't an easy process. Their graciousness and hospitality began even before we arrived.

The home was not furnished, however, so we had to buy furniture and appliances to fill up the place. We had a meager budget, so, again, our choices were limited. We were okay with that. We toured a couple of our new friends' homes to see what kind of furniture they had and then decided to buy items that were similar. So, two days after we arrived in the country, we piled back into the big blue 15-passenger van that we were now more familiar with, and we headed out into the city, our big bundle of recently exchanged Indian Rupees stuffed into our fashionable fanny packs. Our shopping expedition began with us meeting more Indian colleagues, another newlywed couple like us, who would become fast friends. They had given up a week of their lives to take us shopping. He had lots of work to do, she had the house to keep. Nonetheless, they dropped it all and joyfully clamored into the big blue van with us as if it was the best way they could spend their week. Indian Hospitality! Remarkable.

He had a sense of humor that wouldn't quit and she was surely the city's top shopping negotiator. She knew how to treat shopkeepers with respect, and yet drive a hard bargain at the same time. She knew what items were worth and when prices were being unnecessarily inflated. Many times, after we had selected an appliance or some dishes or our bed linens, she would kick us out of the store (lovingly) while she went to work on the actual purchasing process. She knew that our white skin would add an extra "tax" that she couldn't bear to pay. This kind of hard-core

negotiating was a skill I never acquired. One time I went to the market and tried to negotiate the price on a kilogram of carrots. I believe I ultimately paid more than the original asking price. I am good at many things and have many skills. Negotiating is not one of them. So after a while I simply gave up and just began paying whatever anyone asked me to pay. If I knew the product wasn't worth what the seller was asking, I simply didn't buy it.

Indians are, of course, fantastic at negotiating. They've grown up learning to bargain with the best of them. But foreigners visiting India? Foreigners LOVE the concept of negotiating prices when they come to India. It's as if they think the ability to command a discount on goods and services is their magical right and that paying full price is equated to, forgive me, being cheated. No matter how low the price, it seems everyone who visits India wants to get a discount. Perhaps my empathy for shop owners ran too deep, but I was always concerned with what the items were worth. If a dress looked to be worth 500 Rupees, I was glad to pay 500 Rupees. But surely, some (good-hearted?) tourist would come along and offer only 200 Rupees. That would hurt my heart. After all, the man had to make a living. There were likely many mouths to feed. In addition to my irritation over possibly inappropriate bargaining, I developed a rather specific (and eccentric?) pet peeve during my time in India when it came to the topic of negotiating.

My pet peeve developed concerning the terminology about the act of negotiation. Time and time again, foreigners would arrive in India and announce that they were so excited to go shopping so they could "barter". I knew what they meant (they weren't bartering, they were bargaining!!), but it usually took every ounce of self-control not to correct them and instruct them on the correct usage of the word "barter" and inform them of what they

actually wanted to do. As a point of reference for all of those dear guests to Incredible India, I hereby offer this shopping terminology tutorial:

> *To Purchase: To acquire something by paying for it; to buy*
> *To Negotiate: To reach an agreement or compromise (on price) by discussion with others*
> *To Barter: To exchange goods or services for other goods or services without using money*
> *To Bargain: To negotiate the terms and conditions of a transaction*

You're welcome.

Our dear colleagues knew all the best places to go to find exactly what we needed for our new home. We hit the town as soon as the stores opened and didn't return home 'til well after dark. We were amazed at how far our Rupees were going. We had arrived in India at a time when the US Dollar was worth only 35 Rupees per 1 US Dollar. The big infrastructure boom seen at the turn of the century still hadn't hit Hyderabad and prices remained remarkably low and more than reasonable. We eventually outfitted our entire home including furniture, appliances, linens, dishes and electronics for only US$2,000. That figure would rise rapidly over the next few years, and so we felt as if we had gotten in on the ground floor. We had entered India while it still existed in innocence and we considered that a divine privilege. The roads had not yet become crowded with cars and SUVs. The cities had not yet built all the overpasses and elevated highways. The number of skyscrapers was still few. People still shopped at

vegetable markets instead of supermarkets, and one-stop shopping at multi-level department stores was unheard of.

We had two years of this glorious cultural wonderland and we were so thankful. India and its culture is a marvel that is only glimpsed in the films and photos, but fully experienced personally by seeing the sights, smelling the smells, tasting the foods, and interacting with her beautiful people.

CHAPTER THREE

As the days, weeks and months went by and we journeyed through the normal stages of culture shock and began to dip our toes into the water of the lengthy and complicated process of cultural adjustment to this fascinating nation, the love in our hearts for India and her people only grew. We quickly came to the realization that we enjoyed learning about the culture more than we had expected. Seemingly simple trips to buy clothes and household goods turned into powerful lessons about how society operated, what they believed, and their value system. To be honest, it was exhausting at times, even though it was equally exhilarating. We would arrive home after a day roaming about town and we would fall into bed, certain that our brains could not possibly take in and process one more thing. We learned that an inevitable part of culture shock is "culture fatigue". We would become weary of being confronted with so many new bits of information day after day, minute after minute. Living overseas is filled with innumerable pressures and expectations that cause physical, mental and emotional lethargy. But somehow, after a good night's sleep, we would awake refreshed and ready to take on a new day.

The first few times I went shopping for clothes in India were times of unexpected learning for me. Sure, I knew we would be shopping for Indian dresses which were so much different than the American clothes I had worn all my life. Sure, we would be

shopping in the city markets which were a complete departure from the American shopping malls I had frequented almost weekly since I was a teenager. But beyond that, my expectations fell enormously short of what I was about to experience.

Our colleagues took us into the market where we passed by five or six perfectly good-looking clothing stores before carefully selecting one and going inside. They greeted the shop workers cordially and an older man who looked like he was clearly in charge came to personally welcome us, the foreigners, to his shop with pride, a beaming smile and a warm handshake. We were immediately greeted with the smell of burning incense and saw that near the entrance of the shop there was a small Hindu idol that had been garlanded with small yellow and white flowers, painted with turmeric, and had a slice of coconut and half a lemon sitting near it, both dotted with chili powder. We had seen similar idols in other shops all around the city. Some were obvious Hindu deities, but in other places they looked more Buddhist, and a few even had crosses with pictures of Jesus.

As we looked around the shop, we saw that there were fabrics everywhere. I didn't know which were saris and which were salwar kameez dresses. In every direction the colors were bright, vibrant, and shouting at me to look closer. I initially tried just to look at the shelves containing the goods. But instead, we were insistently led to the back of the store and told to sit down on some plastic stools adjacent to a white-sheet-clad padded platform where a male shop worker was sitting cross-legged, waiting for our impending arrival. Without any instruction from us, other workers from all corners of the shop began pulling dresses off the shelves, and throwing them through the air to the man sitting in front of us. He tore them out of their clear plastic packages and opened

them wide for me to see. Bright orange and vibrant yellow, lime green and fluorescent pink. Teal blue and pastel purple, black and red. The brilliance of the hues nearly assaulted my visual senses. Colors of clothing like I'd never seen before were now displayed with grandeur before me and I was expected to choose one. (Well, actually, I was expected to choose five or six, but I only had the mental bandwidth to choose one at that point.) I began gently touching the fabric, unsure of what to do. None of the colors were what I would normally choose. I was on sensory overload. Culture shock, indeed!

"Do you have any dark green?" I asked sheepishly.

The man looked at me with disdain. Nonetheless he ordered up "green". He handed me lime green, kelly green, blues, yellows, and a few reds thrown in for good measure. None were the forest green I was picturing in my head. This was definitely not Macy's. I was not in America anymore. I was going to have to change my expectations of what my wardrobe would include going forward. I bravely chose orange and pink and some pastel blue. Somehow I also managed to find some maroon, which I thought was miraculous. There were no sizes on the dresses. I was heavier than any Indian woman I had ever seen, so the shopkeeper suggested I get "Free Size" which I assumed meant "Extra Large". I just hoped that, after all this mental effort to endure this colorful assault, that everything would fit. (They did.) All during the process, they kept opening dress after dress after dress and just laying one on top of the other until the pile of unselected dresses was massive. I pleaded with him to stop opening the dresses and let me view them while they were still folded neatly and in the packaging. He refused. Instead, another younger store employee began folding the dresses again and re-shelving them. I felt

uncomfortable and guilty for all this extra work I was creating. No one in the shop, however, seemed to mind. It was all part of the job, apparently.

Not long into our dress shopping experience, another younger store employee brought a carefully balanced tray with glasses of water and some small cookies for us. Kevin and I glanced at each other, wondering if it would be safe to drink this water from which we did not know where it came. Believing it would be rude to refuse, we each took a glass and sipped carefully, hoping our stomachs would inexplicably be protected from whatever harmful bacteria might be contained therein. We gobbled down the cookies (called "Digestive Biscuits") with glee. Shopping was helping us work up quite an appetite.

When I had selected my dresses, it was time to pay. The shop owner was sitting at a rickety wooden desk on top of which was a time-worn cash register. He wrote out a small paper bill for my goods and handed it to another shop worker who handed it to Kevin. We gave the shop worker the cash and he handed it back to the shop owner who deposited it in the cash register. He pulled out a rubber stamp and stamped our receipt and gave it to us along with a hearty thank you and another smiling handshake. Little did we know that this would be the beginning of a years-long relationship with this particular dress shop. We would bring many visitors to India to this shop and the shop owner would become our casual friend. Even when his store location changed twice, we followed him. He introduced us to his sons who eventually took over the family business. We were thrilled to have had this cultural experience.

As we began processing our dress shopping experience, however, there were so many things we realized we didn't understand.

- Why were there separate employees for every task in the shop?
- Why were all the colors of the dresses so bright and intense?
- Why did our Indian friends drink their glass of water all in one go while we sipped ours delicately?
- Why did we have to remove our shoes before entering the shop?
- Why did they insist on opening every dress and showing it to us fully and creating so much work for themselves rather than just leaving it in the package?
- Why were there no female workers?
- Why did he stamp our receipt with a rubber stamp?
- Why were there slices of lemon and a coconut near their idol?

...and really, so many more questions. We didn't have any answers. Nothing we'd read up until that point gave us any of this in-depth information. No one sat us down and gave us a clear, intentional explanation of what was happening or what we experienced.

We came to realize quickly that "culture" was going to be more than just noticing material things about a culture. It was going to mean so much more than just being able to identify foods and clothing and traffic patterns. In our few months of

preparation before moving to India, we were thrilled to take a course designed by missiologist Donald K. Smith called "Creating Understanding". His book of the same title described culture as an onion, noting that there are different layers of culture that must be peeled back and revealed in order to fully understand the people and their nation. Our arrival in India and our pre-arrival study had only allowed us to see the first layer of the Indian cultural onion: behaviors and artifacts. We had tasted the food. We had bought the clothing. We had listened to the music. We had heard some of the languages. We saw water buffalos and goats in the streets. We shopped for vegetables in an open-air market. When we wrote home, we had such fun describing all of these base-layer experiences and our friends and families were astounded that we were able to survive a culture that was so much different than our own.

But we felt compelled to go deeper. Our love for India and her people urged us to learn more, to create understanding in our own minds so that we could build deeper relationships and find true acceptance in this beautiful community into which we had transplanted ourselves. It was time for a deep dive and this deep dive meant peeling back the layers of the culture onion.

Traditionally and at its most basic levels, there are two deeper layers to the culture onion model as described by Smith: Norms and Values, and then Basic Assumptions and Worldview. This would be the world and the mentality we would live in for 20 years. Everyday experiences became rich with meaning and significance when viewed through our cultural interpretation filter. We learned to ask questions, the right questions, and never rest until we got the answers. We wanted to move past the surface

observations and into the hidden cultural strata that was there if we would only go looking.

One of the biggest areas of Indian culture learning into which we were dragged kicking and screaming was Indian orientation to and attitude toward time. American culture is obsessively time-oriented. We schedule our lives and our events down to the second and become irritated with people who are late. We condition our children from an early age in school to be on time to class, to turn in their assignments on time, and to use their time wisely. If children do not measure up to the expectations with regard to time, they face negative consequences: detention, bad grades, or a stern talking-to. India, however, from the first day we arrived, seemed very different in this regard.

During our first week of shopping for all our household goods, we were told to be ready to leave by 9:00am. Our new friends and shopping guides, as wonderful and gracious as they were, never showed up 'til closer to 10:00am. We sat (mostly) patiently on the front steps of the offices waiting for them to arrive, wondering if we got the time wrong or if they had been in an accident. When they did arrive, an hour late, there were no apologies. There was no acknowledgement that we had been waiting for them. We bottled our feelings that first day, thinking surely it was an anomaly. The next day, however, the same thing happened. And the day after that. Our frustration began growing and then our cynicism.

We went to a house-warming celebration which was slated to start at 6:30pm. We arrived there at 6:25pm, were the first ones there, and the hosts weren't even dressed yet. The decorations were still being put up and the food hadn't even started cooking. The festivities didn't get underway until almost 8:00pm. "How can

people operate like this?" we questioned exasperatedly. Children's birthday parties were the same, as were weddings, funerals and anniversary gatherings. We were always the first ones to arrive at any event and it was always so uncomfortable. We tried to go a little late, but nevertheless, we'd still be "early". In later years, I adopted a "social timing" policy that drove Kevin crazy. If we were going to a social engagement, I wouldn't allow us to even leave the house until the "start time" of the event. Still, we were generally the first ones to arrive.

In later years, we became part of the leadership of a growing church congregation and we were having trouble getting people to come to church on time. The service was supposed to start at 9:00am. However, more than half the congregation didn't come until 9:45am or even 10:00am. It was a long service, so they still arrived for (most of) the sermon, but it was concerning to us that they were missing the worship time (and the offering!). So we changed the service time to 10:00am thinking it would be easier for people to come on time. But no! People still came 45-60 minutes late. It was simply how they operated. No matter what time we made the service, they would arrive late.

So naturally, we had to question, in Indian culture, is arriving after the appointed start time considered "late"? We began to realize that no, it was not late. There was absolutely no negative connotation for arriving after that appointed start time. In fact, we were told that it was a sign of social status to arrive later than the start time. The more important you were, the later you came. You wanted people to wait for you. You wanted people to know you were there. You wanted them to be honored by your presence. It had nothing to do with time at all. It had everything to do with status and class and position in society.

Initially, these extreme differences from our own culture caused us to call into question the legitimacy of this cultural norm with regard to time. As we focused only on the outer layer of the culture and observed only the surface-level behaviors that we could see and experience initially, our emotions and propensity to judge started getting in the way of our learning. We felt there **should** be negative connotation to being late. Maybe this was something we could teach our Indian friends. We could work to change this aspect of the culture. And the idea that someone would choose to arrive late to show others how important they thought they were? That was, in our opinion, the height of hubris. This was certainly another cultural "flaw" that required fixing. Moreover, the mere fact that there was such a strong class/status system in Indian society was something that surely needed to be overthrown. We were there to take care of all of these things, at least within our sphere of influence.

Thankfully, however, we took some time to think about these things before we set off on our quest to personally change the centuries-old culture of India and be the saviors of more than one billion diverse and deeply respected people. We remembered back to our Creating Understanding class and recalled that there were likely more facets to the culture that we had yet to uncover.

The reality is, we all cross multiple cultural barriers every day. Those barriers don't have to be national boundaries. They can be age barriers, social barriers, society barriers, gender barriers, sexual barriers or professional barriers. Culture is such a crucial part of the fabric of our lives and is one of the ways God has created each of us in a unique and wonderful way. Despite God's beautiful design, however, crossing cultures is never easy. It is always difficult and full of challenges, whether it is crossing into a new

country, or whether it's just entering into the home of someone who was brought up differently than we were.

We learn from an early age how to talk to people of a different culture than our own. At its most basic level, girls and boys learn that there are differences between them and even toddlers learn how to navigate those cultural differences between the genders. As we get older, we realize there are great cultural gaps between the "haves" and the "have-nots" in our high schools. Those who "have not" learn how to navigate the foreign culture of those who have more than they do and how to protect themselves from the shame and social embarrassment so many teenagers face.

Later in life, we attend universities which expose us as young adults to people who are greatly different from us. We have to learn how to get along with them, sit side by side with them in class, and learn with them through books and lectures and all that college life has to offer. As we enter the work force, we are forced to bridge the cultural gaps between white-collar and blue-collar workers. As we travel for work and vacation with our families and make our way around this beautiful country that is America, we learn that there are different "languages" that people from different parts of the country speak. Sure, we might all be speaking English, but the accents and the vocabulary can diverge significantly with what we may have been taught as a child. We learn that the way people from different backgrounds dress can vary and can therefore reveal a lot about their upbringing and their socio-economic status. Interacting within all of these immense cultural disparities teaches all of us a lot about life and about people and about how we will respond emotionally to the vast array of situations in which we find ourselves.

But(!) despite all of the trials that we can face while trying to traverse through the landscape of the cultural mosaic, taking the time to experience and learn from cultures different than our own makes our lives better. We must make sincere efforts and challenge ourselves to absorb as much from the cultures that surround us. Even though culture shock and cultural adaptation are exhausting and pressure filled, we cannot withdraw our determination to understand those around us. Learning from other people's lives broadens our own experiences and gains us entry into a world of beauty and richness that we can in no other way know. In fact, I believe that learning from other cultures can also help to deepen our own empathy for others. Our heart for people is expanded when we understand their life situation more fully. We know what they've been through and how they might be thinking. We can have more love and compassion for them as they deal with life's challenges in the way they've been taught since childhood. We can pray more effectively and minister to them in ways that will be more meaningful and on point. Ultimately, we are more able to love people unconditionally when we understand better their culture and see them through the eyes of love, acceptance and cultural sensitivity. Really, we see them as Jesus does.

I am certain that my life is at least one hundred times better not simply because we lived in India. Physical proximity does not guarantee acquisition of knowledge and understanding. We could have lived there for our full 20-year tenure and never truly have experienced the culture. I am sad to say that I witnessed others live their lives in India in a way that remained only on the surface, missing out on the abundant opportunities to delve into the abundance of all that was around them. That always made me so

sad. What was so remarkable for us and what changed our lives forever was the fact that we intentionally chose to peel back layer after layer of the culture onion and reveal the profound, meaningful aspects of Indian life that were hidden beneath the surface, not easily accessed without the effort of study, examination and deep inquiry. It was these efforts to understand that went a long way toward helping us to be resilient in later years when times got really hard. When we were hit with problems that were so complex that we felt like we were at the end of ourselves, we were able to rebound because of our knowledge of the culture and how it required us to respond. You don't have to travel the world to encounter new cultures. Just look around you and get to know the people God has put divinely in your path. There are cultures just waiting to be explored and understood. Take a risk and get to know them. Your life will be so much better as a result.

CHAPTER FOUR

Prior to arriving in India, we had prepared ourselves well enough to know to ask questions and listen to the answers. We knew that asking one question and getting one answer would never be enough. We knew to probe deeper. We knew about the culture onion and this was the time to start applying that knowledge. It was time to learn about the culture by examining its values and worldview. We also knew something that was challenging to come to terms with: sometimes the answers we discovered wouldn't be what we expected at all.

We liked to ask questions and seek answers to all that we encountered every day during our life in India. There was never a day in our entire 20 years that we didn't learn something new or experience something that was fresh and unfamiliar. We grew to love that part of our life there! But sometimes the answers we got to our never-ending questions didn't make sense. Or sometimes the answers we got seemed contradictory to other things we had learned in months past. Or sometimes, the answers we got stood in opposition to what we considered long-held beliefs. And of course, sometimes we didn't get answers at all.

The contradictions and the times of opposition were initially the hardest to process. We were not alone in that. Time and time again, friends and visitors would come to India and would be confronted with a cultural norm that was confusing, unclear or otherwise complicated and they would be left without the clarity

they desired, without the answers that would bring them the certainty American culture values. "How can this be?" they would ask. "Surely something is wrong with that." I must admit, there were lots of times in the early days that Kevin and I would sit at our dinner table in the evenings discussing the day and wondering what we had gotten ourselves into by loving this culture so much.

One of the first jobs that Kevin and I had when we moved to India was teaching English to young people in their 20s who came from small, remote, rural villages with absolutely no exposure to the English language. It was an attempt to teach English as a foreign language to people who knew many Indian languages, but to whom English was a near impossible feat. Most of these young people also had not excelled academically and did not have the study skills required to organize themselves in such a way to achieve success in schooling of any kind. Nevertheless, we prepared a curriculum and began teaching. Why did they choose us to teach English? We did not have any teaching experience nor any English language college degrees. We were chosen simply because we spoke English and, therefore, certainly, we could teach it. Well, let's just say they were probably wrong.

We had all the best and highest hopes for our students! We taught enthusiastically, prepared worksheets and games and role plays. We did everything we could to transfer all the simplest, most basic knowledge about the English language into the brains of these young and eager Christian workers. They were so friendly and wanted to please us so badly. They loved to talk to us in their broken English and wanted so desperately to learn. They smiled with their brightest, toothy grins, and always shook our hands with fantastic enthusiasm before and after class. They listened and

took notes and showed all the promise of students who were grasping all the material.

Oh my. How wrong we were.

When we administered the first of several tests, we were shocked to see the pathetic results. More than half the class failed. They clearly were not grasping what we were teaching. They likely were not even understanding most of the words we were saying as we were trying our level best to teach them. So we tried harder! It never occurred to us to get a translator or employ any help from nationals. (We were still so new.) So we soldiered on, desperate to see an improvement in their performance.

We administered the second test and, remarkably, their grades improved dramatically! Those who had previously failed were now getting As. Wow! What a miraculous turnaround! What great teachers we were! But then we began to look at the papers more closely. We examined the answers and compared the papers one to another. It became clear all too quickly that in actuality, the students had cheated. There were one or two students who already knew English before they came to our class and they had "graciously" allowed others to copy their answers. How they accomplished this under our watchful eye is still a mystery. But they did it.

We were devastated. How could these supposedly godly students who were establishing churches and sharing the love of Christ, for heaven's sake, commit this egregious sin of stealing other people's answers?! This was truly unforgivable and we had to put a stop to it immediately. We brought the offending students in for confrontation. We demanded apologies and the promise to change their ways. We reported them to the school's principal and

threatened a failing grade if this behavior continued. We were assured it would not happen again.

But then it happened again.

And again.

And again.

We were bewildered. What in the world was happening? How could these students who claimed to love Jesus so much continue in their woeful ways? They knew the Ten Commandments. They supposedly knew what they were doing was not right. And yet they persisted. Nothing we did, nothing we said, nothing we threatened would get them to stop copying one another's papers. We felt like failures as teachers and, frankly, as Christians. We were somehow unable to disciple these young people in the ways of the Lord.

What we didn't see at that time, however, was that we weren't going up against a moral issue. We were facing a cultural issue. "Right" and "wrong" and "sin" weren't even in the minds of these students at all. They were deep in the recesses of their cultural upbringing and we simply were not understanding it. We couldn't see it. We were frustrated and would only learn years later what was actually going on.

You see, we had grown up in a culture, whether it was all of American culture, or whether it was simply our strict religious upbringing, that was very black and white. There was right and there was wrong. There was cheating or there was being honest. There was no in between. In all of life, we were called upon to decide between things. We couldn't have both. That perspective that I learned from birth, through childhood, and into my teen years stayed with me long into adulthood. And, ultimately, I carried it to India with me.

54

Upon arrival into India, however, I was immediately confronted with an enormous amount of "grey" in between all the black and white. In this nation of vibrant color and intense flavors and smells, there was always a vast variety of "in between" and lack of clarity and "grey areas" that never seemed to bother anyone. It was a part of the culture. It was simply how everyone thought and acted and processed all of life. It was, evidently, part of the Indian worldview. India is a land of great paradox that tricks you into believing that everything in the Indian culture is indeed black and white. But, no. Things in Indian culture are rarely as they seem. AND THAT'S OK. The Indian sense of right and wrong aligns itself with their cultural values. Those values are different than our American values. Actually, "different" may not be a strong enough word to describe how seemingly completely opposite our American values and Indian values can be sometimes. I initially couldn't understand this concept of values. I didn't know how to talk about it. Many times, I didn't know how to ask questions about it. I wasn't prepared for this paradigm-shifting test of my own internal beliefs. I had assumed that worldviews would be more easily grasped and understood. But I was in for a complete revision of the way I thought and observed and came to conclusions.

What I would learn later in life, was that I had grown up having developed a dualistic mindset. New Mexico's Center for Contemplation and Action is run by Fr. Richard Rohr who has written widely on the topic of dualism. He says, "The dualistic mind is essentially binary, either/or thinking. It knows by comparison, opposition, and differentiation. It uses descriptive words like good/evil, pretty/ugly, smart/stupid, not realizing there may be a hundred degrees between the two ends of each

spectrum. Dualistic thinking works well for the sake of simplification and conversation, but not for the sake of truth or the immense subtlety of actual personal experience. Most of us settle for quick and easy answers..." (Adapted from Richard Rohr, *A Spring Within Us: A Book of Daily Meditations* (CAC Publishing: 2016), 98-99; *Yes, And . . . : Daily Meditations* (Franciscan Media: 2013), 406; and *The Naked Now: Learning to See as the Mystics See* (The Crossroad Publishing Company: 2009), 34-35).

This is exactly how I had grown up. My life and programming up until age 24 or 25 had been one of "comparison, opposition and differentiation". I learned to compete from a very early age. I competed in sports. I competed academically. I competed to be the best Christian. I competed to be the best friend. I had compared myself endlessly to anyone and everyone around me. I was in constant opposition to anyone who did not hold the exact same Christian fundamentalist views that I held. Little did I know that these attitudes and outlooks that were so much a part of me and that I had long fostered were destroying my ability to see the beauty and nuance of my own life and culture. And as I entered India, my dualistic thinking was now putting at risk my ability to comprehend all that was going on around me. Something within me sensed this was happening and wanted to stop it. I wanted to grow. I wanted to go beyond what my life had held thus far. In some ways, through thought, prayer, journaling and processing our new India experiences, God gave me a vision of what life could be like if I could only let go of everything that I knew to be familiar and comfortable and allow him to expand my mind to something only He could show me.

So, after a couple of years of frustration and lack of understanding, I decided to trust the vision God had for me and to go for it. I decided India would be my new training ground. Being resilient enough to survive and ultimately thrive in this place and with these people that I claimed to love so much was going to require that I make a drastic shift in my thinking and ability to process what was happening around me. I decided to be open to changing everything I knew to be true and seek after what God was waiting to reveal to me. I learned about dualism (although I didn't know the term at the time) and how to conquer it in India because of the richness and complexity of the culture. I embarked on a journey that would revitalize my intellectual and spiritual consciousness in a way that I could never have expected. Things were no longer "good" or "bad", they were just different. And I would come to learn that "different" was best.

This promotion of the idea that India was just "different" was something that would become almost cliché for me as I worked with countless international groups that visited India over the years. They constantly wanted answers. They constantly wanted to know what was right and what was wrong. They wanted some kind of authority or expert to instruct them on how to live in India. They wanted their experience to be well-defined and easy to understand. However, this in itself was a return to dualistic thinking. William Perry says that, "In dualistic thinking, students rely on authority figures for direction on what is right or wrong. They prefer to memorize and repeat as opposed to analyze and examine, and they are uncomfortable with active and cooperative learning. Facts and figures are comfortable at this level of development; abstract concepts are not."

(https://www.reference.com/world-view/definition-dualistic-thinking-b2e3413148fc213c).

It was interesting the journey God took us on as he led us out of our dualistic thinking. For us and for all of our international friends, there were no experts or gurus or industry icons to lead the way. Really, there were no concrete facts and figures. You would have thought that we would have sat in a classroom and heard remarkable lectures on the topic. Or it would have been natural that we would have read thick academic books about how to modify our thinking. But no. There were stories. There were observations. There were interactions. There were times of processing. Basically, our learning of what was accepted as "right" and acceptable in Indian culture came from our everyday experiences. These experiences often caused us great confusion at times, but upon reflection garnered us great wisdom. Our learning came from things like going to the chicken shop. Our learning came, among other ways, from one of our favorite topics: food.

I was at home in our tiny little kitchen which had been outfitted with a tiny little refrigerator, a tiny little stove, and a few cooking vessels which would certainly suffice for our first months in our newly rented duplex. I was planning on making chicken curry for our dinner. A few days before, a sweet older woman had come over and taught me how to make it. Now I was on my own and I was excited to make my first-ever Indian meal. Kevin got home and came into the kitchen holding a small black plastic shopping bag which was knotted at the top. He handed it to me and as I grasped it in my hands, I immediately knew something was different.

"It's warm," I observed.

"Yes," he said. "They just killed the chicken 5 minutes ago, so it's still fresh."

I immediately dropped the bag on the kitchen counter as if it were going to burn my skin. Ugh, I thought. How was I going to do this? I made Kevin un-package the chicken, rinse the blood and a few remaining feathers off and put it into the pan. As I peered into the pan, I noticed there were still bones in the pieces of chicken, and they weren't cut into any familiar-looking shapes. No drumstick, no wing, no breast, no thigh. Just chunks of chopped up chicken. Again, how was I going to do this? Exasperation seemed to be my new favorite emotion during the first few months in India.

We came to learn that everyone went to the chicken shop when they could afford to add "Non-Veg" to their weekly meal. They would go to the shop where a dozen or more live chickens were crammed into too-small, rusted-out cages. The "chicken-walla" would choose a chicken for you of the approximate weight that you wanted and take it "in back" where he would slit its throat, bleed it out, then pluck its feathers, and cut off its head and feet. Then he'd bring the carcass out to the chopping block and perform what we affectionately termed the "chop-chop" method of butchering. Just take their giant butcher's knife and CHOP CHOP it up into pieces and throw it in a bag.

There were so many things wrong with this picture.

What about hygiene? What about salmonella? Did he actually weigh the chicken pieces to give us our money's worth? How old were the chickens in that cage? Where were they born and grown? What were they fed? How often did he clean the killing area in back? Did he disinfect the killing area or his knife or the chopping block? So. Many. Questions.

In our minds, this whole process was wrong. But in the Indian mind, this was absolutely the right way to handle chicken. They knew, without a shadow of a doubt that their chicken was fresh. They believed they knew where it came from. They had control over cleaning and cooking their own chicken once it came into their hands. They could buy exactly the amount they wanted. They could develop a relationship with their own personal "chicken-walla" who would certainly take care of them month after month, year after year. Sure, there were no government regulations or health department regulations. But that was not a value for our friends. Knowing the seller and guaranteeing freshness were the values. And they were getting what they wanted. What we initially saw as wrong, we learned to see as right when we looked at it through the correct lens and filter.

We had other friends who bought enough rice for a year (100 kilograms!) and then stored it for that year, taking only enough to cook each day. There were no vacuum-sealing or fully air-tight containers. Just a steel bin and some oil. It worked perfectly fine for them. There were no bugs or diseases or bacteria or germs. How they accomplished this, I still don't know to this day. But it worked for them. We saw it as wrong, but our new paradigm taught us that it was the perfect way for a culture that values rice at every meal.

There were other Indian values concerning healthcare and the foods you must eat or not eat to maintain good health. There would be no ice cubes or cold water. No ice cream in the winter or while sick. There were a list of "hot" foods and "cold" foods that were to be eaten only in proper season and in proper temperaments. There was a vast variety of old wives' tales surrounding what foods could make you sick if consumed at

different times. There was no medical basis for any of these beliefs, but our Indian friends held to them so strictly that we ourselves began to believe as well. At first, I tried to "help them change their ways". That was both futile and foolish. These traditions were so deeply held as part of the Indian worldview that no matter how politely they listened to me, they would never be convinced to change their ways.

When I was pregnant with my first child, my very experienced, qualified and specialty maternity doctor insisted that I get a tetanus shot before the birth because "all pregnant women need a tetanus shot." I had just had a tetanus shot 4 years earlier and was desperately afraid of shots, so I told her I didn't think I needed one. She insisted. I insisted back. In fact, I begged her to show me the medical proof that I needed a tetanus shot. She was intrigued by my insistence and agreed to research it. Through this interaction, I learned that most Indian women who came to that maternity hospital to give birth had never had a tetanus shot. They were not required for school or employment. So, yes, they needed to have one in case of accident during the birth. However, I had been the regular recipient of tetanus shots and therefore, was not required to get one. In Indian culture, therefore, it was not "wrong" that all pregnant women should get tetanus shots. They should! They hadn't had one before! Had I not taken the time to investigate the culture a little more, I would have been left simply with a negative impression of Indian medical practices and a lack of confidence for their services. But knowing more about their culture helped me to see that they have good and clear reasons for doing things differently which make sense and are helpful and beneficial to all of society. Ultimately, the Indian worldview was different and it modeled itself in ways that were extremely

different than my own American culture because it is based on a different value system. I was learning how to navigate it and was learning so much in the process.

You see, as Brian Thompson says, "We assume the world is exactly as we've been taught and that our personal memory speaks the truth. These are both conscious assumptions that we knowingly make, but what about the countless assumptions the mind makes on our behalf, that we are unconscious of? What are we missing?" (http://www.zenthinking.net/blog/non-dual-awareness-seeing-through-your-assumptions). Had I held on to my dualistic thinking and not been open to all that God and India had to show me, my assumptions would have limited the truth about India that I could have seen. As I learned to be at peace with the things I didn't understand, and as I opened my mind to accepting values that were not my own, my appreciation for Indian culture grew, and my ability to be resilient in the face of uncertainty was also enhanced. My adventure with challenging dualistic thinking did not end when I left India. In fact, I credit my India experience and all I learned there with my ability to develop my faith further today. Today I carry that non-dual thinking with me even into my new life in America and into my own spiritual life as I deconstruct my faith in Christ and reconstruct it in a way that is more loving to others and ultimately more glorifying to God. I credit India for that change and I am so thankful.

CHAPTER FIVE

very time I tell someone I lived and worked overseas
in another culture for nearly half my adult life, they
are astounded. "Wow," they say. "That's amazing!"
They praise me and glamorize my life in India, assuming it
certainly must have been an experience marked with adventure
and romance and victory and all the best things. Truth be told: It
was.

But the accompanying reality? IT WAS SO HARD.

Sure, there were amazing times that we will never forget. We
experienced the highest of highs as we traveled the world, met
incredible people, ate the finest of international cuisine, and
immersed ourselves in a rich and beautiful culture that in some
ways really became our own. But most days we focused simply on
trying to survive. Most days were actually quite mundane. We did
laundry and washed the dishes. We picked up our children's
scattered toys and wondered when they'd learn to make their own
beds. We went to work and wished we could take more vacations.
We got frustrated with our co-workers and sometimes felt like we
were not needed. Our days were often filled with unmet
expectations, disappointment, confusion, and exhaustion. Yes,
living in another culture and engaging ourselves fully in it was
worth it! But it was never easy.

We made it, though. In fact, we learned not only to survive,
but to thrive. In order to achieve thriving, however, we had to be

incredibly intentional in how we lived our lives, did our work, and interacted with everyone around us. In addition to diving deep into the hidden layers of culture and being willing to approach the culture non-dualistically, there was yet one more essential thing that helped us to thrive during our years in India. This was an attitude we cultivated from the first day we stepped off the plane into our new surroundings. From Day One, we chose to be learners. We asked questions. We listened. We struggled through things that didn't make sense. We fought through the difficulty of trying to understand when all that we thought we believed was challenged.

We would soon find out that being a learner would open doors that were not there previously and expand our base of knowledge as we sought holistic transformation for all those around us. Being a learner helped us make lasting connections that ultimately built the Kingdom of God and set our team up for greater effectiveness.

We would also learn that being a learner meant making an important clarification. We learned that there was a difference between being a learner and being teachable. To make the most of our experience in India, and to make the most of any cross-cultural encounter, we must be **more** than teachable. Our valuable Christian upbringing had taught us that being teachable was one of the three main keys to ministry and discipleship success: Faithful, Available and Teachable. Being teachable is a wonderful and needed thing. If a person is not teachable, they are then obstinate, stubborn and inflexible. They may be completely unwilling to try new things, unable to take feedback, uninterested in personal growth, and participating in things for all the wrong reasons. A teachable person, however, wants to be "fed". They

want to grow. They want to follow and have someone instruct them. They want to serve and take feedback well from others. We need teachable people around us. It is a basic requirement for effective life and ministry.

Being teachable, however, takes a person only so far, especially in a cross-cultural scenario. Being teachable tends to be a passive trait. Teachable people have good intentions, but because their focus is on being "fed", they require someone who will take the initiative to teach and feed them. They rely on someone else to guide and direct them. Even though being teachable could be considered "cleaner", risking fewer mistakes, this lack of risk may ultimately limit their accomplishments and create a lower threshold for their personal development. While those who are teachable take feedback well when others give it, they don't necessarily seek out feedback proactively.

We saw many good, teachable people come through India over the years. They did well. They learned many things. However, they didn't get to the deeper levels of cultural adaptation that would have helped them truly thrive. We ourselves were the same during our first couple of years overseas. We thought being teachable would be enough. For some people, maybe it is enough. But we wanted more. We wanted not just to see and hear and smell and speak. We wanted to understand and absorb all of India and make it our own. This would mean we would have to find and adopt an attitude that was more complex. Ultimately, we would choose to be learners.

However, being learners was not something we'd ever been instructed about from any book or in any class. A few of our life mentors along the way had modeled it for us, but we were basically on our own. We were flying blind. We had to figure

things out without assistance and take the initiative if we wanted to make the kind of progress we so deeply desired. It would be hard work. It would be a challenge. A marathon, not a sprint. But we were ready to go.

One of the first things we quickly realized on our journey to be learners is that we didn't know it all. The American culture from which we came bred us to be confident and certain. It placed high value on being an expert and knowing everything there is to know. Before we came to India we studied books, attended classes, watched films and interviewed nationals. What more could there be to learn? During our first two years we observed everything we could observe. We studied the lives of our newfound friends. We ate all the new foods. We wore all the Indian clothes. Surely by now we were the experts. But we were not. There was a never-ending amount of things to learn. As we sought to build community and play our role in the lives of others, we quickly learned that we had to embrace an attitude of humility and openness with regard to Indian culture. This would be the only way to learn meaningful things and realize the abundance that God wanted to pour out on us as we served Him in that great land.

One of the things that drew us to India was the seeming lack of any kind of focused ministry for young people. Both Kevin and I had spent a good amount of our lives working with junior high and high school students in America and we felt sure of the fact that God was calling us to develop and implement youth ministry curriculum in India and then train Indian youth leaders to take vibrant, indigenous youth ministries forward. When we arrived in India, along with all of the cultural learning that we were doing, we kept our eyes wide open for young people with whom we could interact. We wanted to spend time with teenagers. We

wanted to mentor and disciple them at this crucial formative age. We basically wanted to take everything we had learned in the US and transfer it directly into our new Indian experience. We thought we knew just about everything there was to know about youth ministry. We had years of experience under our belts. We had been successful youth leaders in the US. What could go wrong?

Well, a lot.

The very first thing we had to learn about "young people" in India, was that teenagers weren't considered "youth". They were considered "children". In fact, as the months and years went by, and as we discovered more information about the culture and its norms, we unveiled the fact that in many cases, people are considered "children" until they get married. This means, a 19- or 20-year-old still attends Children's Sunday School, lives in his parents' home, doesn't work a job, and has little independence. Yes, things changed some during our two decades abroad, especially in the cities, but the general cultural traditions remained. We were not going to do youth ministry with teenagers. It simply was not a viable option. Kevin began to do "youth" ministry with 25-year-old men who worked as volunteers with our organization. He could see in them the same adolescent mentality that we had witnessed in 15-year-olds back home. They had the same enthusiasm for life, the same fearless attitude, the same lack of respect for authority, and the same sense of overall freedom of young people without a care in the world. Our paradigm for youth ministry had to change. We had to learn what it meant to do youth ministry in India. We didn't know it all. The faster we accepted that inevitable fact, the more we could be learners who would truly gain cultural understanding.

As the years passed, as we met more and more people, and as our experiences became fuller and more significant because of our position as learners, we eventually concluded that all cross-cultural situations benefit from those who seek to be learners. We became enthusiastic proponents of the concept of Becoming a Learner. As we assumed leadership positions, we made sure that all our orientation materials included some training on this new attitude we challenged everyone to adopt. But it wasn't just for India. No matter who we are or what stage of life we might find ourselves in, we can benefit from adopting the posture of a learner. Sure, we can have a wealth of ministry experience, academic pedigree or extensive professional acumen, but the simple truth is we have so much to learn from the others who are around us. This attitude of humility and eagerness to learn more will bridge the relationship gap and endear us to those with whom we are living and working.

To be a learner, we must open ourselves and our minds to the possibility that there are still things out there others can teach us. We must spend time with our leaders and colleagues, asking meaningful questions, listening to the answers, learning about their experiences, and allowing them to educate us. This intentional effort to learn will surprise us with new insight and a greater awareness that ultimately will deepen our bond to others and build a camaraderie that will show itself in how we are able to live in harmony and serve sacrificially.

As we discover new things on our quest to be a learner, we must be ready to suspend judgment of the ways things are said, done or implemented. We might be outraged or confused by the way things are done before we fully understand why they are done. "They don't do things the way we would do them!" we might say in irritation and disbelief. But in reality, our willingness to consider

new and different methods and ideas can be the key to finding understanding and an attitude of acceptance. When we can realize that we truly have many things to learn and that we do not know everything, we can take the first steps forward in building relationships and serving God in exciting ways.

Once we finally humbled ourselves and realized we had so much to learn, we began seeing all the ways God had placed specific people in our lives to teach us. Most times, they were the people we least expected to teach us things. We embraced the remarkable truth that God had immersed us in the community in Hyderabad, India, among delightful (and sometimes initially frustrating) people intentionally and in His divine plan. Although it took some time, we eventually realized that the best people from which to learn were those right there around us.

The Indian women were a marvel to me. Lucy was one of my colleagues who taught me so much about what it meant to be a wife, a mother and a woman of God. Lucy was a leader in the ministry for many years before she got married. She had always longed to have a husband, but God was choosing not to provide in her timing. She prayed and she waited, confident that God held her in the palm of His hand and had her best interests in His plan. Eventually, God provided. By Indian standards, she was basically an "old maid", waiting until her early 30s to get married. She had thought all hope was lost until God sent her Charles. After marriage, the two were so deeply in love that people joked about how they openly held hands and took loving photos together. Lucy was a strong woman. Charles, was a humble, sensitive man. It would have been very easy for Lucy to dominate her husband, but Indian culture would never allow such a thing. She therefore

humbled herself to serve her husband and be his helpmate. It was a beautiful sacrifice of love.

It wasn't long until their daughter was born and their family was complete. Together, they poured themselves into the life of their growing daughter. Lucy helped her study and cooked all her favorite foods. She was the light of their life. She had the prettiest dresses and the best of everything they could afford on their meager ministry salary. Lucy quit her leadership-level job with the ministry to stay home and raise her daughter. Many thought she would be resentful of her new position as housewife and mother, but Lucy reveled in the roles. She became known for her perfectly clean house, her delicious, hot meals, and her daughter's excellent grades at school.

Church and their Christian faith was a major part of Lucy's life. She not only attended church every week (as was expected!), but she was also a major leader of the women's fellowship that met monthly, and she led prayer meetings and Bible studies whenever the needs arose. She studied her Bible every morning, reading the scriptures from cover to cover once a year. She claimed the promises of God in her own life and in the life of her family members. She prayed fervently for those who were sick and often visited them. All of these things she did consistently and faithfully, even when she was tired from keeping the house, even when she had stayed up very late helping her daughter study for an exam. People could count on Lucy and she served them with a joyful heart.

Whenever I interacted with Lucy, that authentic joy and enthusiasm for life, her family and her faith always came through loud and clear. It helped me to examine my own life and taught me the kind of wife, mother and Christ-follower I wanted to be.

Observing her life and learning from it often times convicted me of ways in which I was falling short, not in my actions, but in my attitudes. Why couldn't I clean my house with a joyful heart? Why couldn't I be less resentful of the time I had to spend with my children? Why couldn't I pray and then wait on God patiently when He chose to take time to answer? Lucy was an inspiration to me and as I chose to be a learner, she taught me oh so much, even though she never knew she did.

Learning from those God has placed in our lives isn't just for those living overseas. Yes, it is helpful to have a culture mentor when posted abroad. However, there is so much we can learn in our own home cultures from our family members, colleagues, church friends, acquaintances, or even strangers we meet on the street. Sure, we can learn professionally and academically, but we can also learn holistically as well. Even if the people around seem less educated, less accomplished, or seem to have fewer specialized skills than we do, we can learn abundantly from them: spiritually, physically, intellectually and socially. We can learn new things about God from these dear people alongside us that we would never have learned on our own. We can learn about marriage and parenting and how to do church. We can glean fresh ideas on health and schooling and hospitality. We can learn what Jesus means to them and how He might be present in the same way for us. The actual learning isn't the only or ultimate advantage to being a learner in these situations. Humbly garnering whatever you can from people hand-picked by God to minister to us goes a long way toward deeper fellowship, relational strength, and increased effectiveness of the community.

Relationships with others are ultimately the bottom line and end goal to any learning situation. And one of our biggest points

of learning during our time in India was something with which people in all cultures all over the world struggle, probably on a daily basis. It's a topic of controversy in American marriages. It is the subject of both gender and racial equality debates. And so when I learned that this topic would help me build better relationships and adapt more effectively to the beloved culture of India, I wasn't sure what I thought, let alone what other people would think when I tried to explain it to them. Another key to becoming a learner? Choosing to submit.

Submission. Oh boy. In this world so focused on equality and equal rights, the word "submission" is oft maligned and discarded. But, my friends, God calls us to submit to one another in love. It's one of His commands. He expects it of us. I can still remember the day, the year before we moved to India, when I was asked to submit to the leadership of someone younger than me, someone with less ministry experience, and someone whose personality was so much different than mine. I could have rallied the troops against him, but inwardly I knew that was not the right thing to do. In fact, I was the next logical choice to lead the ministry. But it didn't happen that way. God had called this young man to be my leader. I had to make an intentional choice to submit to his leadership. In the end, it worked out well and the ministry grew under his leadership. With time, I saw God's plan at work. It didn't come naturally, though. I had to make a choice to submit. I didn't know it at the time, but I was being a learner.

An intentional decision to submit to the leadership God has placed over you can build relationship bridges and develop synergy faster and with more success. This takes a deliberate effort on our part to yield any real or perceived authority we believe we may have to those who are actually in leadership over us. It takes

humility and a desire to follow those leaders, even when we may not fully understand what that leadership is doing or why they make certain decisions. Being a learner means abandoning our own need for authority. It means giving up our right to be in charge. It means being patient enough to wait for God's plan and His ways to be made clear. We must learn from our leaders. To do that, we must enthusiastically submit. This is especially important in cross-cultural situations in order to achieve any acceptable level of cultural adaptation. Submission shows our new national friends we are serious about building trust and relationships with them.

Submitting to national leadership was probably one of the most challenging and controversial things that we encountered with foreigners coming to live and serve in India during our many years there. The organization we were working with had an early history of foreign leaders, but those foreign leaders eventually gave way to Indian national leaders who were well-trained and well-equipped to lead their own national and indigenous work. Even though it was obvious that the Indians were more than capable to lead the work, the incredibly talented and high-powered foreign recruits that joined us to serve in India found submitting to the Indians extraordinarily challenging. After all, they were industry experts. They were leaders in their field. They were coming not only to serve, but to guide and consult and give of their valuable time and efforts. The Indians should follow and be grateful. However, this is not the way of the learner. And this is not the way to gain cultural knowledge, adapt and find true acceptance.

We were the first foreign nationals to come to the organization to serve fully under Indian leadership. We came in as junior workers who held no leadership roles. We tried to fulfill

those roles as faithfully as we could. Both Kevin and I were used to following strong leaders. But we had to quickly learn how Indian leaders, most specifically **our** Indian leaders, led. This required us to put all our cultural knowledge to use. We had to observe their behavior and listen to their words, but then also peel back the layers of that now illustrious culture onion and actually figure out how to operate under their leadership when the direction they gave to us was different from the direction we had been given in our own home culture. For a couple years we struggled to figure out how to manage our day-to-day work activities. We never really knew if we were doing well or if we were falling short of expectations. However, over time, and through a lot of careful and intentional exploration and analysis on our part (and a LOT of mistakes!), we figured out how to follow well. It became easy to submit. Our stance as learners had paid big dividends.

As we thought about the topic of submission as learners, however, we realized that God calls us to more than submission to our leaders. We are also created to submit in love to one another. This submission creates an atmosphere where learning can take place. Others can challenge us. Others can generate space in which we can think and consider and deliberate. That won't happen, though, if we don't recognize their authority over us in Christ. Submission is not easy. It comes with a lot of mess. But mutual submission to one another brings with it a beauty that grows relationships and draws people to the love of Jesus. Cultivating a culture of learning requires it. A culture of learning propels us to achieve greater things together than we ever could achieve on our own. Being a learner gives us the resilience to bounce back when times get tough. Although choosing to become

a learner of cultures of all kinds may not come naturally, it is ultimately worth the effort as we seek to live a Kingdom Life and bring the love of the Father God to all those around us. We were so thankful that we had the grand blessing of experiencing and living in the Indian culture with all its wild complexity and diverse beauty. We are thankful that we made all the efforts over two decades to learn deeply about it and that we were rewarded with a level of cultural adaptation, acceptance and trust by our Indian friends and colleagues that few ever find.

HEART STORIES...
PART ONE

We were so excited. Everyone told us that this would be one of the highlights of our time in India. A cultural goldmine. There would be colors and sounds and smells and crowds of people and music. We felt so lucky: It was only the first month that we'd been in India and we were already going to an Indian wedding. We were certain that we would learn so much. Sunil and Sunitha told us about the event that was coming up the next day. We personally hadn't received an invitation, but they told us the bride and groom would love it if we were in attendance. I began planning what I would wear: a sari, of course (if I could tie it properly). I only had two to choose from at that point, a purple one that I had carefully chosen, or an orange one that I had been given as a gift. I loved them both. I thought about my hair and makeup, excited to get dressed up, despite the heat that caused me to be a sweaty mess and prevented me from truly looking my best. I believe I put my hair up and didn't wear makeup. The fresh-faced look was all I could manage in the heat that I would soon learn was the "cool season".

The day of the wedding arrived and we wondered what time we would leave. Our friends would drive us in their car so we wouldn't have to arrive at the event on our motor scooter while wearing our Sunday best. The wedding started at 6:00pm and we thought maybe we'd arrive there at 5:45pm to be sure to get a good seat. We knew that the groom was one of the most popular and beloved people at the church and the place would be packed out. (What we would learn later was that weddings do not start on time in India. Most things do not start "on time" in India... at least by American standards. If the invitation card says 6:00pm, you can count on the fact that the ceremony won't start until

7:00pm or later. We would have been sitting there by ourselves for an awfully long time.)

We called up Sunil and Sunitha to find out our departure time and they informed us, rather nonchalantly, that we wouldn't actually be going to the wedding ceremony itself. It'll be boring, they said. We're just going for the food! After all, wedding crashers should only go for the reception. Wow, what disappointment filled our hearts! We hung up the phone and our shoulders slumped. We would be missing out! Our expectations about our first Indian wedding were quickly going unmet. We desperately wanted to see how an Indian wedding ceremony differed from an American wedding ceremony. Surely there would be rituals and traditions that were so unusual that would be interesting and fascinating and from which we could learn more about this land we were quickly coming to love. But no. We'd only go for the reception. By "boring", of course, what they meant was that we were going to a Christian wedding, which would be remarkably similar to weddings we had been to in America. In fact, the bride would wear a white wedding gown instead of a sari. They would process down the aisle, the ceremony would be in English, there would be Christian hymns sung, and the spoken vows came from the customary Western wedding tradition. It wouldn't really teach us anything about Indian culture and would, in fact, confuse us as to why these people were seemingly denying their own culture in favor of something so "vanilla" and plain compared to the vibrancy of India's color and cultural vitality.

Trying to ignore our disappointment, we then learned that we would also be going late for the reception. There was a program that started the reception and the food would be served only at the end. Once again we were warned that the reception program

would be "boring" and that the only thing we truly would be interested in was the food. We were informed that we would time our arrival strategically to be the first ones in the buffet line, get our food, eat it, then join the receiving line to wish the newly married couple all the best. We were stunned at this arrangement, but it seemed so normal to our friends. Apparently they did this all the time. We were learning from this wedding, but not at all the things we expected we would learn.

We went to the wedding reception. It was indeed very crowded. We were the first ones in line for food. They served from huge vats filled with steaming hot, spicy and fragrant lamb biryani, with eggplant curry and cool, creamy yogurt on the side. The four of us stood huddled together, holding the recycled paper plates filled up with food in our left hand, and eating the best we could with our right hand, trying not to spill and trying not to make a mess of ourselves. (We were still new to eating with our hand in the traditional Indian manner.) The food was hot and spicy, but oh so delicious. Our eyes and noses watered as we gobbled up this tasty and traditional wedding cuisine. We finished the food, washed our hand in the small "hand wash" which was really just a water dispenser over a big plastic bin, and then headed over to greet the newlyweds.

By the time we reached the happy couple, the receiving line was quite short. The bride and groom looked exhausted, but still exhilarated from their special day. They were sweating, but their sweat glistened with a special glow that showed their glee at being united as man and wife. As we approached, they perked up with recognition because they knew our friends Sunil and Sunitha. Of course, they had no idea who we were. Still, they smiled broadly at us, shook our hands, and thanked us for coming. Little did they

know we only came to eat and run. Which is exactly what we did. After making our way through the receiving line, we quickly got back in our friends' car and hurried home. It was actually quite late at night now since the reception and the meal hadn't started until after 9:00pm. We were exhausted from the anticipation and the waiting and the disappointment and the whirlwind of emotion that surrounded the evening.

During our time in India, we would go to other weddings, disappointingly never a Hindu wedding, but many more Christian weddings. Each had its own flavor and unique family traditions. For most of them, though, from that point onward, we attended both the ceremony and the reception and didn't simply crash for the buffet of delicious wedding food. We learned things that night, though. Not what we expected to learn, but we did learn. Perhaps that was the biggest point of our learning that night: to check our expectations at the door and get ready for a remarkably wild ride. India would have lots of surprises in store for us and we had to be ready to receive them. This was just the first of many more to come and we committed ourselves anew to whatever India, in her divine wisdom, had planned for us.

❄❄❄❄

Our time in India was really all about people. It was India's people that compelled us to uproot ourselves at a young age and relocate to the other side of the world when all our friends were buying houses and cars and furniture to start their families. It was the people. Their hearts, their pain, their courage, their needs. We wanted to connect with them. We wanted to pour into their lives. We wanted to know them.

As we got to know people on a more intimate level, time after time we met people who wanted hope. They were desperate for it. They weren't used to having hope like we in the Western Global North are. We in America have an incredible amount of hope. It's part of our worldview. It's built into our DNA. We go through life thinking that we can have whatever we want if we just work hard enough and try. The people we met in India, however, were devoid of this hope. They craved it. But they didn't know how to achieve it. They had been conditioned to believe that there is nothing they can do to change their fate. Their life and its events are set in stone. So why even try to achieve more? Why try to improve their state? There is no hope. But they still crave it. They would do anything within their power to have hope for a better tomorrow.

Prema is one of these people that we met who craved hope.

As a 24-year-old, single Indian woman, she had endured hardship far beyond her years. Her father died unexpectedly when she was only six years old. This is the plight of many young children in a land where disease runs rampant and the health systems are insufficient for rich and poor alike. Her mother was then left to care for the family, but could not provide for young Prema, despite all her best efforts. Making enough money for food, shelter and clothing, the necessities of life, was simply too big a task for this grief-stricken woman who had lost her husband. With great regret, but knowing it was the best choice she could make, Prema's desperate mother sent Prema to live with a family friend who lived in a neighboring village. Prema's mother imagined a better life for Prema, or at least a life with two to three meals every day and maybe schooling.

Sadly, however, the "friend" treated Prema as a servant rather than as a member of the family. She was forced to scrub floors and toilets, and had to sleep on the floor she had just scrubbed without a mat or a blanket. She was fed the leftovers rather than eating with the family. Schooling was out of the question as it would be too much of a financial burden on this family. The worst result of all, though, was that young and innocent Prema was subjected to beatings and rape for more than a decade. Her life had definitely taken a turn for the worse and this was not the life that her mother had imagined for her. It seemed as though the fates were against Prema.

Unfortunately, things went from bad to worse. As a result of the abuse she endured, Prema got pregnant at a young age and her guardians forced her to get married. They could not risk tarnishing their "good name" and reputation in their community. They married young Prema off to a much older man, an alcoholic, who continued with the abuse she faced in her foster home. She tried to endure the torture, and employed every coping mechanism she could think of to survive, but eventually it became too much. She tried to end her life on a number of occasions, but never succeeded.

She had no hope. There was no way that positive talk was going to get her out of this situation. It was nothing a sunny disposition was going to fix. Her future was worse than bleak. It seemed as if the gods had plotted against her and there was no way out of the tortuous existence in which she was living. Even suicide was not saving her. How could she make the pain and agony stop? What was she going to do?

Then, however, unexpectedly, came the day that she attended a women's empowerment program hosted by our organization.

We realized that there were thousands (millions?) of women just like Prema all across India. Women who were suffering at the hand of abusive men, abusive families, trapped in the hell of their dark reality. These women needed a way out, an escape, a way to lift themselves out of the mire of their lives and find the hope that they were longing for so desperately. Prema was one of these women.

She sat quietly in the back of the room filled with dozens of other suffering women and she learned about women's advocacy issues. She learned about health and hygiene. And, perhaps most importantly, she learned about the Eternal Hope others had found in the Living God. Tears rolled down her cheeks as she realized that this was the hope for which she had been yearning. This was the hope that would help her in her most desperate of situations. Suicide was no longer the answer. There was a way forward. There was a way out.

Prema received training in tailoring and eventually was granted her own sewing machine. She was able to escape from her home every day for 6 hours to work in the village center sewing clothes at a tailoring shop and was able to earn enough money to ease the financial burden in her home which had caused so many tensions and problems. As the financial burden was lifted, some of the emotional challenges were alleviated as well. Her husband eventually stopped abusing her and, miraculously one day gave his life to Jesus. Their lives completely turned around and, despite their checkered past, they were set up for a future that was productive and encouraging. Prema finally had long lasting hope which compelled her forward into each new day.

✿ ✿ ✿ ✿

Growing up, family holidays were a special event for me. The Fressel family would gather at my grandmother's house (which was next door to my house) and we would eat until we couldn't eat any more, and laugh and drink chocolate milk out of the special antique green glasses. The days mostly revolved around food, but we would also exchange gag gifts and marvel at cousin Becky's famous, beautifully decorated sugar cookies and wonder what pranks Uncle Bill would play on us kids that year. Holidays were good days filled with good memories. Memories that I hoped to carry into my adult life and into the lives of my children one day.

When we moved to India, I wasn't sure what to expect from holidays. I expected that Indians celebrated holidays differently than we did. I expected that we would learn new holiday traditions. I expected that we would even learn of new holidays to celebrate. What I didn't expect, however, and this was my cultural naiveté showing through, was that there would be American holidays that weren't even known in India. I was very typically American in that way. I figured everyone around the world knew of and appreciated everything that we did. But no. That was not at all true. American Thanksgiving was one of those holidays. No one in India really even knew what that day was. In fact, we always had to say both words: American Thanksgiving. Otherwise it wouldn't make sense to them. But really, why would it? The holiday had nothing to do with their nation. It was purely an American holiday.

Nonetheless, I still wanted to "celebrate" it, even though we had only been in India for less than a month by the time Thanksgiving rolled around for the first time. We had a few

challenges, though. First, we hadn't had enough time to make any friends. We didn't know anyone really well enough to invite them over to our house for a celebration. I was never very good at taking the initiative to build relationships, so this did not come as a surprise to me. So we wouldn't have any guests. There would be no party. Our celebration would just be the two of us. That would be different, but I think I was ok with that.

Second, we didn't know if it was possible to get any of the ingredients we would need to cook a traditional Thanksgiving meal. We assumed we couldn't find a turkey, but what about stuffing and corn and cranberry sauce? At that time, we still shopped at local markets because no supermarkets had opened yet and none of the markets we knew of carried any of those items. In 1998 when we were there, the great infrastructure expansion of the early 2000s had not yet happened in Hyderabad and there was a lack of imported goods. One day in the future I would be able to create a truly authentic American Thanksgiving meal if I was willing to spend the money. But not in 1998. If we wanted to recreate a Thanksgiving meal, I would have to do so with local ingredients and make it completely from scratch. It really wouldn't be the same. That reality began to set in.

Third, being truly realistic, even if we could scour the markets around town to find most of the ingredients to make everything from scratch, I hadn't learned how to cook most things yet. I was still a new homemaker and chef. Our first meal in India was grilled cheese sandwiches and I felt as if that was a triumph. I had a cookbook made for people living overseas, but it had yet to truly provide me the guidance I needed to cook the variety of foods we wanted to eat. I was fearful in the kitchen and lacked any of the confidence I would later have to make homemade bread, roast a

whole chicken, or bake a pumpkin pie. Just thinking about how much progress I made in the kitchen over the years reminds me of what is possible if you're desperate and hungry.

The night before Thanksgiving on that first year in India, I remember feeling sad. I remember feeling a twinge of hopelessness and homesickness. I was happy to be in India and knew that missing out on holidays was part of the adjustment process, but I still longed for the comforts of home. The people, the traditions, the food. As I sat there in our duplex at our small 4-seat dining table wondering what we would eat for our first Thanksgiving abroad, I decided we should somehow focus on being thankful. And for some reason, I correlated being thankful with bean soup. In my mind, the more beans we ate, the more blessings we could thank God for. So we went to the market, bought a wide variety of colored, dried beans and brought them home. The next morning, Thanksgiving morning, I put them in a pot with water and some salt and set them to cooking. It took forever, naturally, since I hadn't soaked them and didn't know how to use my pressure cooker yet. But I tended my "Thankfulness Beans" well and by evening they were tender and warm and ready to eat.

We sat down on Thanksgiving evening to our small, steel bowls filled with steaming hot bean soup and did our best to be thankful. The soup was relatively flavorless and not at all a good substitute for turkey with all the trimmings. However, the simplicity of the dish reminded us of our new simple lifestyle, the people we had come to India to serve, the creativity we would learn to exercise in a vast multitude of situations in the future, and the fact that we were so thankful for so many things in our life.

We were living out our dream, living in a land that we loved, and actively serving God professionally.

Over the years our Thanksgiving celebrations would become much more elaborate. We would go from a two-person celebration in 1998 to a 75-person celebration in 2015. What a difference a couple of decades makes. We became known for our large group gatherings with traditional American meals. Our friends, who became more like family to us, knew well what American Thanksgiving was and looked forward to celebrating with us every year. It became one of our most beloved traditions. However, despite the pomp and circumstance of the years that would follow, I still remember that simple bean soup on our first Thanksgiving in India and its reminder to us all to be thankful in all circumstances.

※ ※ ※ ※

We were newlyweds when we moved to India. When we announced that we were going to India for the first time for a short trip two months after our wedding, people asked us if it was going to be our honeymoon. Definitely not, we replied. When we packed up our suitcases and moved permanently to Hyderabad, we had been married less than two years and really knew nothing about marriage or, to be honest, about each other. We were still getting to know one another since our courtship and engagement were so short. That, combined with preparation to move to the other side of the world did not give us much time to settle in to married life and really establish ourselves as a new family. In India, everything was new, including how we related to one another as husband and wife.

Reflecting upon our lives so many years later, we realized that we learned how to be a married couple in India. We learned through Indian eyes, not American eyes. We didn't go to couples retreats or marriage seminars. We worked on our marriage in the hard work of everyday life living cross culturally. It was not easy. No, it was really hard. We really had no help and many times didn't know what we were doing wrong or what we were doing right. We were just two flawed individuals trying to bring ourselves together as one, building a family in a foreign land.

We often took our cues on marriage from the marriages we viewed around us. These, obviously, were Indian marriages. Those were much different than any American marriages we had ever known. The dynamics between husband and wife were so much different. The husband was definitely the head of every household, with no exceptions. Women did all the cooking, all the household work, and all the childrearing. Men worked far from home for extended periods of time and often were not present for the birth of their children. Abuse of women was, tragically, prevalent in most homes. There were good things in Indian marriages, but there were also some extremely challenging things as well. We certainly had a lot of things to think about and process when it came to the topic of marriage.

And then came the day when we met twenty-five year old Anitha. We met her when we were traveling in North India to attend a series of Christian living meetings where we would get the chance to share from our lives and encourage those who were in attendance. Anitha came to talk to me after one of the conference sessions and had tears overflowing from her eyes. She explained that she had two pre-school age children and her tears were because she had recently faced a family crisis. Slowly, through a

translator, and in her despair, she explained that her husband had abandoned her and the children. One day he was there; the next day he was gone. They had their share of marital problems in these, the early years of their relationship, but Anitha never believed he would leave. Then he did.

Distraught and having no idea how she would survive, she explained that she turned to her family for advice. "Let him go," her father said. "We will take care of you."

"Don't waste your life, dear," her mother cried, "We might be able to convince someone else to marry you." It seemed her parents had even less hope than Anitha did that the two could be reconciled. Anitha was even more confused and discouraged than before. She did not know what she wanted to do.

After some time had passed, and despite the hollow reassurances of her parents, Anitha decided that she did not want to give up. Something deep within her told her to keep trying. So, she had been searching secretly for her husband. She hoped, perhaps unrealistically, one day he would return to her. She wanted to remain faithful to her marriage commitment, something that even in India is losing its value as the cultural norms evolve with the times. Her family and friends thought she was crazy and would end up disappointed.

During her long and possibly disillusioned search, Anitha met one of our colleagues who was a pastor at a local Good Shepherd Church. She told him about her desperate plight. He prayed for her and together they cried out to Jesus for help. In her desperation and longing for hope, Anitha began going to church where she was wrapped in the love of the church members and she also took comfort from God's promises that she found for the first time in the Bible.

I remember listening as she narrated her tragic story and wanting to help in some way. I wanted to give her a plan to find her husband and achieve reconciliation. I wanted to solve her problem for her. Of course, I could not. The cultural implications were too strong. I could not possibly understand what she was going through or how to fix it. But what I could do was pray for her. So I prayed with her that day and then continued to pray for her whenever God brought her to my mind. I was thrilled that she had found Jesus, but a part of me was not satisfied with that alone. I wanted her to be reunited with her husband.

Two months later, after more than a year of longing for his return, I got word from my friends in North India that Anitha's estranged husband phoned her. He pleaded with her for forgiveness and asked if he could return home. Joyfully, Anitha said, "Yes!"

In the months and years that followed, their marriage grew to be stronger than ever and they both became believers who have committed their lives to the Living God. They are maturing in their Christian faith. What a joy it was for us to meet people like Anitha, to see them in the depths of their sorrow, but then to see them be rescued from that sorrow, only to have it replaced with the unspeakable joy that is only available in Christ. What a privilege it was, indeed.

PART TWO:
BUILDING BRIDGES

CHAPTER SIX

Cassie was my first childhood friend. She was a cute, little, blond-haired neighbor girl who lived one block over. I can't remember how we met considering I was six and she was four when we had our picture taken one Easter morning on her front lawn in our adorable little pastel blue Easter dresses with white lace collars. Surely some neighbor had introduced us thinking the two young girls would become fast friends. Well, that neighbor was right. Cassie and I played so happily together for years. We spent endless hours together at each other's homes, spending the night, naming our dolls, playing games, riding our bikes, and eating lots and lots of macaroni and cheese. Her parents still remember me asking, "What are you having?" when Cassie would ask if I wanted to stay for dinner. If it was liver and onions, I suddenly had other plans. Cassie was my best friend and I was thrilled to have her in my life. I have only happy memories of Cassie and what a lovely girl she was. Only happy memories, that is, until I realized that I was not Cassie's best friend.

Her best friend was Lisa. They had known each other longer, went to school together, and their parents spent time together as well. The fact that I believed Cassie probably liked Lisa more than she liked me was heartbreaking to me. At such a young age, I began developing an insecurity surrounding relationships that would remain with me long into adulthood. Actually, it's still with me, even as I write these words today. I have many talents and many good qualities. I have had a variety of successes in life and have won many accolades over the years. I have been put in positions of leadership and given great responsibility for projects and teams and initiatives. I've summited Mt. Kilimanjaro and made it to Everest Base Camp, for goodness' sake! But relationships? This, I'm afraid, has been, in my opinion, my greatest downfall in life. A challenge which has plagued me from childhood until today.

I would go through many more friendships where I felt as if I was not the "chosen one". Sure, I had enough friends. There was always someone to sit by in class, play with at recess, hang out with after school, or go with to the shopping mall. But I craved a deeper relationship with all of my friends that they were either not willing or not able to give to me. This craving for depth of relationship often resulted in me being too clingy, too needy, or too overbearing for my young friends to tolerate. They didn't want that depth of friendship. They wanted fun and frivolity. I wanted seriousness and intensity. For many, it was simply too much. All of my friends had a best friend and it was not me. I was the ultimate "third wheel". It made me feel left out, less than, and unwanted.

I also struggled with what I would later learn was my deeply-held dualistic thinking in relationships. I felt that people could be

my friend or they could be friends with others. They couldn't have it both ways. My jealousy flared voraciously, making my interactions with my "friends" supercharged with emotion and filled with threatening ultimatums. I didn't know what I was doing in the moment, especially as a young girl or teenager. I just knew I felt insecure with regard to relationships. I felt unwanted and as if no one truly liked me. I didn't know what it took to build relationships that lasted. I didn't know how to be friends with multiple people at once. I had plenty of friendly relationships, but none that held my heart safe in theirs. I longed for connection. I longed for the hole I felt so acutely in my heart to be filled. The fact is it never would be filled and I would struggle with loneliness for years to come.

How truly ironic it was, then, that God would call me to live in a nation that is built on relationships. Relationships are the heartbeat of Indian culture. India is a place where relationships are valued over time, over money, over education, over leisure and over all other things. The pace of life is slower because India's people have to create margin in their lives to include unexpected moments of connection with others. Indians would rather be late to an important event than pass up the opportunity to talk to someone they haven't seen in a while. They would rather host an unexpected guest in their house than keep a business appointment in the city. Indians never have strangers in their lives. They can always find someone to talk to, someone whose family heritage is similar to their own, or someone who is willing to listen to the troubles that are plaguing them in the moment.

There seems to be no better example of the sense of community with which the Indian culture is saturated than on the Indian trains. Perhaps the greatest legacy of British colonization,

India's trains are a marvel. Riding the train in India is a culture all its own. Most Indians choose to take the train whenever they have to travel in between cities. It is a massive and complex network of trains that crosses through the landscape without discrimination. Through the cities and villages with an egalitarian composure that spans class boundaries and unites the nation. The trains weave their way, meandering through the plains and up into the hill stations, through the arid deserts and into the lush jungles. The train stations are filled with hawkers selling hot, creamy chai and delicious, salty snacks, spicy curry-based meals and refreshing bottled water, "pan" chewing tobacco and sweet digestive biscuits. Homeless people crowd the platform, taking shelter for the night under the roof of the station, finding safety from the elements and hoping passersby will spare some change with which they can have at least one meal that day. Rats, cockroaches and stray dogs scurry over the tracks in search of food scraps and hoping to avoid the powerful "whack" of a platform guard's stick. Pigeons lurk overhead, longing for stray pieces of left-behind bread and targeting the heads of weary travelers with their droppings.

Once passengers are on the trains, a tightly-knit community emerges. In the "sleeper class", the least expensive and most accessible way to travel, the train compartments are packed out with those who have paid for a seat, and, many times, those who have simply hopped into the cars hoping for a free ride. Passengers sit cheek-to-cheek, their sweaty bodies next to one another in a deodorant-free zone. No one seems to mind the sweat or the smell. It is a part of their humanity, a part of their authentic existence. From the moment they arrive, the conversations begin. They start out with the basics: "Where are you from?" "What do you do?" "How many children do you

have?" Eventually they move on to topics common to society: politics, sports, the economy. No topic is off limits. Some people talk of religion and money. They enter into debate, they argue, perhaps even raise their voices. But then the on-board chai, tomato soup and meals come and any animosity is forgotten. They are one community, enjoying a meal together and ready for a night of rest as the train continues its journey through the Indian countryside.

I always marveled at the way Indians could become friends with absolutely anyone they encountered. I spent a lot of time observing Indian women, especially, talk to one another as if they had been lifelong friends when, in actuality, they had met each other only moments before. Something had drawn them together into an open and free dialogue that bonded them together in ways I had never seen. I would see groups of women sitting cross-legged on the ground, huddled closely around an open fire, rolling wheat-flour chapathi flatbreads to be cooked for their evening meals. Their motions were so well rehearsed and automatic that they didn't at all need to concentrate on what their hands were doing. The small wooden rolling pins in their calloused hands flew over the lumps of brown dough quickly and efficiently, forming the chapathi into a perfectly round circle which was then thrown onto the hot "tava" frying pan where someone else would bake it to perfection. During this entire process, a running dialogue was going among the women. They talked of their children, their husbands, their extended family, their houses, their hopes and dreams for the future, the neighborhood gossip, the economy, and even politics. They knew all the minute details of each other's lives and seemed to truly care about one another. If any of the women had a need, it would be met by someone immediately and without

hesitation. Would I ever be able to reach such pinnacles of relationship prowess?

Well, the answer is no. I never did. I still don't. I spent many years sitting awkwardly in silence with people of all nations, desperate for any topic of conversation to come to my mind. Come on! I would urge myself. Think of an open-ended, meaningful question to ask. But nothing would come. I listened and listened to people talk for hours, unable to contribute anything meaningful to the dialogue. How could people talk to each other so freely, for so long, without letting the conversation lull? It was a mystery to me that I would never solve.

Because of my frustration with my inability to talk freely and build relationships, I fell into the dangerous pit of comparison. I would compare myself to other women, Indian or not, and wish I could be as good at relationships as they were. I would see only the good in them and only the bad in me. I would judge myself harshly. This comparison then turned into competition. If they were better at relationships, then they had basically "won" at life and I had "lost". It was a dark and desperate rabbit hole that I spiraled into with every interaction I encountered. I was bad. They were good. There was basically no hope for me. Why even try? I longed to improve at my relationships, but I found that it took so much effort and, to be honest, it was an amount of effort I was not willing to give. I enjoyed my rest too much, my alone time too much, my own solitude-based interests too much. I was unwilling to give myself to others and sacrifice my own energy and comfort for the sake of relationship.

While preparing to move to India, those who had lived overseas counseled us that a unique part of many cultures was the propensity of nationals to show up at your house at all hours of

the day and night without calling first to announce their arrival. As Americans who value privacy and planning, this would take some time to get used to, but we were looking forward to it and looking forward to building the relationships that would come from people wanting to spend time with us. We would be ready to receive them at a moment's notice. I learned how to make Indian chai (badly at first, then more passably), and always had a supply of Indian cookies in my pantry so I could be a good hostess and offer my guests some refreshment when they came. At first, a few people did indeed come over unannounced. They were curious about the newcomers and were excited to get to know us. They wanted to see how we would choose to live, what our house would look like, what we would eat and what stories we had to tell. It was uncomfortable for us when they came if our house was not perfectly clean or if we were not dressed properly for their visit, but we welcomed them with open arms. I am blessed to have a husband who can talk to anyone about anything for any amount of time. (Perhaps this is why I never achieved that skill!) However, soon, the visitors became few and far between. What was wrong with us? Why was no one coming to see us?

We learned that people thought we didn't want them to visit. They believed we valued our privacy. Why was this? It was because we never visited them. Somehow, despite all our best efforts, we could not overcome the cultural barriers that had been so deeply ingrained in us since birth. Visiting someone unannounced was simply not possible for us. We would call to arrange a visit, but they would claim to be busy and refuse our visit. We would say, "Let's get together," but it never happened. This was discouraging for us and we wished it could be different. But when push came to shove, we didn't go visiting our friends

and colleagues in the same way they wanted to be visited and we paid a relational price because of it. We didn't try hard enough to adapt culturally. We had great relationships at the office, were able to talk freely about ministry and work topics. But when it came to delving deeply into the intimate details of personal life, we were lacking. It seemed as if the relational hurdle of us being "foreigners" and strangers in this land was too much to surpass. But still, surely we could have done better.

What always discouraged me was that we saw foreigners who came later who excelled in building personal relationships with the Indians. They were able to converse freely, visit homes, and create bonds that would last long into the future, long after they had left India and returned home. I remember being filled with jealousy when hearing reports of other Americans being invited for dinners or other social engagements at Indian colleagues' homes. We rarely got invitations. They would post photos of their Indian friends visiting their homes on social media, showing off their great times together. Why did the Indians visit their homes and not ours? These other internationals had somehow found the secret to making connections that we never were able to find. They were beloved because of the time and effort they had taken to invest in the lives of others. They took time to move beyond the office talk and dive headlong into the personal during the late hours of the evening and night that crafted deep rapport that would somehow stand the test of time. I was envious of these connections. Once again my tendency to compare and compete emerged. The eight-year-old little girl in me who felt she had no close friends once again took over the emotional control of my psyche. They had won and I had lost. My dualistic thinking rose to the surface. They were good and I was bad. They were relational

and I was not. They had good qualities and I had none. It was all or nothing for me.

While it's true that some people from Western nations are extremely capable of building relationships with others, in general, Americans do not place huge value on creating these deep and lasting bonds with others. I berate myself still to this day because of my self-perceived inability to create lasting and meaningful relationships. However, as I spend more time observing people, perhaps I need to give myself more grace. Most people likely struggle with relationships because, the truth is, relationships are a challenge! We as Americans are a society of individuals who are inwardly focused and who place a greater value on time and efficiency than we do on the needs of others. Relationships take time which we are not willing to sacrifice. Relationships take effort which we are not willing to exert. Relationships take intentionality which we are not willing to create. Relationships generally do not happen by accident and rarely happen naturally. We need to make them happen and we as a culture simply don't do it. We prefer to isolate ourselves in our single-family homes, reserving our relationship efforts for our nuclear family units and generally no one else. We don't want to bother others. We don't want to intrude on their privacy. Our whole value system is based on individualism, privacy, seclusion, discretion, and confidentiality. So when we are thrown into a culture whose core values include community, relationships, openness, sharing and joint living, it is a shock to the system that breeds discomfort, confusion and emotional instability.

The simple truth is that good relationships take **pursuit**. All of us, no matter what kind of culture we were born into, long for authentic relationships with others. God has created us for

relationship. We long to connect with people on an intimate level and to be seen, heard, and understood. We want someone to notice us, to long to be in our presence, to pursue us. It is this longing to be pursued that can be the key to fostering relationships. When someone feels pursued, they will respond. I can remember when Kevin was pursuing a dating relationship with me when we were in our early 20s. He did what it took to let me know that he wanted a relationship with me. He called. He took me to dinner. He bought me gifts. He left me notes. He gave me flowers. He arranged special outings. He listened to me when I talked and remembered what I said. He pursued me because he wanted a relationship with me. And it worked.

Pursuing someone takes effort, though. It doesn't happen naturally or without trying. What does pursuing someone mean? Pursuing someone means getting to know someone on **their** terms and learning what is important to them. Pursuing someone means being interested in what interests them and loving what they love. Pursuing someone means joining them in their journey wherever they're at, at their pace, on their level. It means extending grace to them and accepting them for who they are. It means not trying to change them, confront them or fix them. Pursuing someone means loving them as God would love them. In essence, pursuing someone means understanding people, how they are wired, how people are different from others, how God has created them uniquely, and how they respond to the challenges of life.

Once someone feels pursued, they will respond relationally. They will return your texts. They will reach out to you. They will ask you questions and respond at length to your questions. They will want to hear from you and will, in turn, pursue you. You will

have built a relationship that will last and that will grow. My fatal flaw in building relationships in India was that I didn't pursue people. I figured they would pursue me. In fact, I mourned over the fact that they didn't pursue me. I should have taken the initiative to create the relationships I longed to have. Yes, I regret that. However, my time in India was a time of maturing and learning for me. I give myself grace when I look back at my time there, especially in this area of relationships. I didn't know then what I know now. Today I pursue people. In fact, I'm known for pursuing people. Others are drawn to me and feel safe with me because I pursue them so strongly. It is a glorious feeling to know that people respond to my relationship-building efforts. I wish I had known these things when I was in India. But I'm glad I know them now and can live the rest of my life implementing this knowledge in the every day.

My struggle with relationships was not only with my Indian colleagues, however. It extended into my relationships with my international colleagues as well and caused me great heartache. I had many more lessons to learn, most of them painful. I would eventually realize that relationships promote resilience, a quality with which I was familiar. I had somehow been able to be resilient in most other areas of my life. But relationships? They were an enigma to me. I needed them. Relationships give us the support we need when times get tough, when our circumstances spiral out of our control. God gave us people in order to give us companionship and camaraderie in the best and worst of times. Without one another, we live in isolation, unable to thrive and without the resources that only come from collaboration with others. Bottom line? We need one another. Without one another we may not survive, let alone thrive. The need for relationships is

only magnified in cross-cultural settings. My inability to foster relationships prohibited me from reaching a level of resilience that I would need to carry me through some of the most difficult years of my life. These years would bring heartbreak and confusion and desperation. I needed people who understood me, who could advocate for me, who could sit with me in times of trouble and listen, comfort and console. Unfortunately, I felt as if I had no one. When I needed it most, a tight-knit community of trusted and caring individuals was nowhere to be found.

CHAPTER SEVEN

I was driving through the crowded Indian streets as I had done many times before. It was heavy, stop-and-go traffic, nearly gridlock. All around me were cars, trucks, motorcycles, mopeds, bicycles, water buffalo, goats, street dogs and pedestrians, all fighting their way to the front of the line of traffic, hoping to get through the intersection first. Men with carts peddling bananas and sunglasses made their way through the small gaps between the vehicles hoping to make a few final sales before heading home for the night. The smell of exhaust fumes was heavy and thick and was permeating through my windows even though they were sealed tight. I cranked the air conditioning in my golden Tata Safari vehicle and kept my foot on the brake and the clutch, hoping the traffic would ease. It was dark outside as people made their way home late in the evening from a long day's work at the office. The neon lights of the shops and the billboards blazed overhead, beckoning our patronage. For me, though, it was all a blur. Sure, I'd seen it all before. I'd been traveling this same road for ten years, years filled mostly with joy and adventure. Tonight's adventure, however, was not filled with joy. It was filled with sorrow and the tears running down my cheeks were only a small indication of both the physical and emotional pain I was in.

The journey, which usually took 40 minutes, took 90 minutes. I was in a hurry, but so was everyone else. As I finally reached my destination, I let out a huge sigh mixed with an exasperated sob

realizing that I would have to find somewhere to park, a near impossible task in this crowded side street which was more like an alleyway already crammed with parked cars of all shapes and sizes. Parking was always something I dreaded, even avoiding shopping centers that did not have parking structures or valet services. Tonight's destination had neither, and so I was left to fend for myself. How would I do this? The road itself was so narrow that if there were cars parked on both sides of the road, there was no space to drive down the middle. The road was also filled with garbage and some of the remaining parking spaces were blocked by large white cows who were having their evening meal out of the neighborhood dumpster. If only I could just nudge these beasts out of the way, I could park! Other spots were occupied by street hawkers selling trinkets which to me seemed completely unnecessary in my present state of mind. Eventually, after making a 3-point turn that took exactly 7 tries, with a great deal of frustration I left my vehicle parked half-crooked in the best place I could find. Let them tow it, I thought. I dragged my aching body out of the car and hobbled toward the entrance of the maternity hospital.

I was familiar with this place. I had given birth to two beautiful and healthy babies in this hospital. I had visited for multiple appointments and ultrasounds and follow up checks. I was a bit of an anomaly here as the hospital's first foreign patient. When I gave birth to Clark and Claire, there was a never-ending stream of nurses and orderlies who came to check on me in my room, simply so they could catch a glimpse of the white lady and her cute little white babies. It could have felt intrusive, but honestly I found it endearing. Apparently I was something special and unique. Why not lean into it. The staff had always treated me

with kindness and respect. I was a huge proponent of this facility for mothers and their babies. I had brought other foreigners to this birthing center when it was time for them to have their babies. Their experiences weren't as good as mine, but their babies were born healthy nonetheless. In general, this was a place of comfort for me. It was founded by Catholics, which meant there were crosses and pictures of Jesus hung indiscriminately all around. More comfort. More peace. However, on this particular night I was feeling anything but comfortable and peaceful.

"I need help," I cried out to the two men sitting at the in-patient registration desk. They looked at me with a bit of fear and confusion. I was a foreigner, I was alone, looked like I was in pain, and my tear-stained face betrayed the emotions that most Indian women hold inside when in public. They seemed to understand the situation was dire and rushed out from behind the desk to escort me to a treatment room. I think they did this as much to help me as they did to get me out of public view so I didn't frighten anyone. The treatment room was simple and empty. It had a metal desk and a wooden chair, as well as a medical examination table on which there was a mostly clean white sheet. There was a white curtain hanging from the ceiling that could be pulled for privacy. There was a single fluorescent tube light on the wall behind the desk which illuminated most of the small room. I don't remember much else about the room because after I sat down in the wooden chair and the receptionist left me alone in the room, I laid my head down on the desk and passed out.

What I assume was a few minutes later, but could have been an hour, a kind lady doctor entered the room and laid her hand on my back, willing me back to life.

"What happened?" she said with compassion.

"I think I'm having a miscarriage," I said.

Sure enough, I was.

Just days before, we had received the surprise news that five years after Claire was born, I was pregnant again with what was most likely twins. We were thrilled and scared at the same time. We had gotten used to the idea of having only two children, even though when we got married we had decided on having four. Was this God's way of fulfilling the original vision He gave to us so many years ago? We decided not to tell anyone of the pregnancy until it was "safe" to do so. Many people wait until 2 months and we were going to do the same. Although my reasons for not wanting to tell anyone were slightly different. Most people don't want to tell anyone for fear of miscarriage or other problems with the baby. I wasn't afraid of losing the babies. I didn't want to tell people because I wanted my privacy. I didn't want anyone else to know what was going on in my life. I didn't want to share my most intimate information with anyone else. I felt as if my life was so much on display as a leader within my work and as a foreigner in a strange land. I wanted to keep this information for myself and not let anyone else in.

You see, this had been my pattern. I never wanted to let anyone in. Whether it was too much effort or because I didn't want them to see me as vulnerable or weak, I didn't want to do what it took to build relationships with people. The other foreigners would gather to have meals together, but I would claim I was too busy. The ladies would gather for shopping expeditions, but I would claim I had to take care of my kids. The other moms would want to bring the kids together to play, but I would claim I had to work. Whether or not I was truly too busy was not the issue. I just couldn't bring myself to create community around me.

It was too much work and it felt too invasive. I didn't make friends. I didn't build relationships. I didn't draw others in. And it cost me dearly.

I believe some of my fear and inability to craft lasting rapport with others stems from the fact that I really didn't know myself very well for most of the years I was in India. I had moved to India during my mid-20s, a time when most people in their own home culture are doing the hard work it takes to figure out who they are, who God has created them to be. People spend those young adult years gaining their independence from their parents and discovering the unique individual they are. While I did some of that while I was in India, most of my 20s were spent doing cultural adaptation. My self-exploration was replaced by learning about India and who I had to be in India, not who Leah Kadwell was as a person distinctively created by God. As a result, I didn't know how to fit me as a person in to community at large. Other people may not have adapted to the Indian culture (and I arrogantly disparaged them for this), but they knew who they were. They knew their place in society. They knew how to interact and how to manufacture bonds that would bring benefit to all. Somehow I missed that class. It was something I couldn't do. I simply wasn't capable of it. It wouldn't be until my mid-40s when I was once again living in America that I would begin to learn more about myself, about who I was and who I was created to be. It wasn't until my mid-40s that building relationships and establishing community would make more sense to me. Somehow I had missed 20 years of emotional and mental maturing with regard to relationships. And because of this, my ability to be resilient in this area was stunted. I suffered because of this in more ways than one.

As I lay there in that hospital bed on the horrible night I miscarried two tiny babies, I reflected on the fact that I had no friends there to be with me. There was no community to rally around me in my time of need. The situation was so bad I even had to drive myself to the hospital while miscarrying. When I tell that bit of the story to people today, so many years later, their faces contort with pity. "I would have helped you!" they often say. But what they don't realize is that all those years ago I was quite a different person and we likely wouldn't have had a relationship at that point in my life. There was absolutely no one to come watch our children in the night so that Kevin and I could go to the hospital together. I had alienated everyone, including my husband. I couldn't share my feelings of hurt, pain and desperation with him and had no one else to whom I could turn. So there I lay in the hospital bed, bleeding, sobbing, wondering what was going to happen. The doctors wondered why I was alone. "Isn't there anyone who can come to be with you?" Oh, if they only knew the awful truth. I was alone and it was my own fault. My lack of investment had cost me so much.

Someone to help me in the hospital at my most vulnerable time was not the only way my inability to connect with others brought me distress. As a leader of approximately 25 foreigners in India at any given time, my lack of transparency with them and dearth of relational ability bred a lack of trust by those under my leadership. They didn't know me, so how could they trust me? They would have conversations amongst themselves when they had challenges, but would never come to me. They didn't allow me to help them because I never allowed them to help me. I was so frustrated when they didn't want my help. But what I didn't see at the time was that I had such a skewed view of community.

These lovely people didn't want to expose their weaknesses to me because I never let my guard down with them. I had read so many books on leadership and even taken multiple Masters level courses on the topic, but nothing could break through the emotional and relational barriers I had carefully built up over time. The betrayals I had experienced with friends in my past had carried over an enormous amount of baggage that prevented me from excelling as a leader. I was a fantastic follower because, as a follower, the requirements for transparency and trust are fewer. But put me in a position of leadership and everything got messed up. In an effort to be strong and valiant, I would shut everyone out. This caused all kinds of problems and prohibited any forward progress for our team.

Despite my inability to build relationships, I was not naïve enough to miss that there was conflict developing between me and my team members. In fact, there were also some problems emerging between me and a few of my Indian colleagues as well. Because of my challenges with connecting with people, in the final three years that I was in India, my communication with most people had broken down. I had completely given up on talking to people, getting to know them, or really even truly listening to them. When I did "listen" to them, I opened the door for them to criticize me and tell me all of the things with which they were struggling. Because I was in leadership, many of my subordinates would, rightly or wrongly, choose me as the target of their complaints. I knew this was happening and I knew that they were simply frustrated and weren't really upset with me. However, after this happened dozens of times, I began to internalize these discouraging interactions. I did not create healthy boundaries and had not created trust-filled relationships to protect myself. Thus,

my emotions began to take a nose-dive. I began to react defensively and emotionally during relatively normal conversations whenever even the smallest amount of conflict or disagreement emerged. I took everything personally and I began to legitimately believe with all my heart that people hated me. I couldn't see any other reality. I believed that people were out to get me, that they wanted my removal not only from leadership, but from India. I believed people wanted me to struggle and to suffer because of all of the things I had supposedly done to them. I was no longer seeing things clearly. I remember on at least four occasions where I left a meeting in tears after having raised my voice in frustration with one of my Indian colleagues. They were certainly the least of my problems. I knew the Indians loved me. They had embraced me over the years and had expressed their affection for me on multiple occasions. But my mental state had deteriorated to such a point that I viewed even them as against me. The truth? I was descending into serious mental illness and there was no stopping this freight train of depression from overwhelming me and destroying my life and ministry.

Eventually, after I'd been 19 years faithfully, and what some would call sacrificially, serving in India, leading to what I had determined was the best of my ability, some of the foreigners on the team under my leadership gathered together behind closed doors on a conference call with my US-based supervisor and aired all their concerns about me. They shared about my emotional immaturity, their lack of trust in me, my perceived propensity toward favoritism, and my overall unfit character as a leader. Most people never find out about these conversations. However, the discussion in its entirety came to my notice and I was devastated. Any trust or relationship that existed, even in a small amount, was

forever dismantled and destroyed. I couldn't face any of them again. I refused to go to the office for fear of seeing any of my international colleagues in passing. I remained at home, alone, secluded in my mental sickness, with no hope of recovery. The closest women I had to calling sisters, Dr. Bethany and Dr. Abigail, saw what was happening to me and suggested I go to a psychiatrist. I went willingly and he medicated me, claiming I was too psychologically far-gone to undergo counseling. I was shocked and skeptical at first, but after a month, the cloud of medication took effect and I no longer cared about all those who seemed to hate me.

At the same time as I began treatment for my mental illness and went through this recovery with the help of the doctors and one dear friend, we as a family were thrust into the biggest trial of our lives. I'll reveal more details later, but here's the gist of it: my husband had been banned from India and I had also been asked to leave the country immediately. This trauma combined with my mental illness was the last straw. I no longer cared about being a good leader. I no longer cared about cultivating relationships. It was over. Life would have to begin anew. I didn't know what the future would hold, but I knew I had hit rock bottom and things could only go up from there. But it wouldn't be with these people. I would have to start a new life, with new friends, in a new home.

Bottom line? I accomplished a lot of good ministry in India. I worked myself out of a job at least four times during my time there. I achieved the ultimate ministry objectives. The ministry grew exponentially during my tenure. What a monumental blessing to have played a part in growing a Macedonian church movement and seeing literally millions of people's lives transformed as a result. However, most of the time I felt as if I

missed out on relationships during my time in India. I never had the opportunity to discover who I was as an individual and this usually precluded me from connecting with others. It caused chaos and hurt. I descended into mental illness as a result. I had the idea that leaders couldn't have relationships. But nothing could be further from the truth. Although many leaders are introverts, they still need relationships. They still need points of genuine, authentic connection to help them grow and develop and build trust.

My struggles in the area of relationships helped me to cultivate a profound personal value for building relationships going forward. Frankly, that's all I want to do now. When others don't respond to my pursuit of them, I'm disappointed and disheartened. They've not been on the journey I've been on, so I understand. But I long for that intense connection with people that can only come from time and shared experiences and laughter and tears and struggle and love. I am thankful for the lessons I learned through fire in India because today I'm able to love others with a love I couldn't find during my tenure overseas. That love is worth all the effort and the reward is eternal.

CHAPTER EIGHT

I have spent many a rainy Saturday afternoon curled up in a chair, journal and pen in hand, pondering all of my catastrophes with relationships. These are not pleasant times and are often accompanied by tears and a feeling of dread that settles ominously and unrelentingly upon my chest. When I reflect on the myriad of missed opportunities, remember the hurt I caused, and recall the wasted hours spent selfishly neglecting others, I am at times overwhelmed with regret. It is easy for me to forget about any good that was accomplished during those decades of honest and pure-hearted work in India. It's also easy to slip into an attitude of self-pity as I berate myself about things I can no longer change or control.

The regret, though, is eased at times with the valuable life lessons I learned and the more developed woman I am today despite the mistakes I made. I learned to value community. I learned to pursue people. I learned to be intentional. I learned to let others in, let them serve me, share with them, be vulnerable, and not to be afraid to loosen my boundaries for the sake of love. Overall and most simply, I learned just to love others. That was the most valuable lesson of all: to love others unconditionally, no matter their so-called faults or the ways in which they would disappoint me. Love them because of their shortcomings and in all the ways they truly needed to be loved. I am so thankful that I learned those lessons, finally, after two decades of really making a

mess of things. But really, isn't that how we all learn things? We have to falter. We have to fall. We have to be willing to pick ourselves up out of the pit and have the courage to move onward and upward. That is what I'm doing now and relying on the grace of others to teach me, even in my middle age, what it means to build relationships that matter, relationships that last, relationships that build others up and bring us all closer to God in the end.

What brings me joy in the midst of my despair and regret over past relationship failure is remembering with thanksgiving the handful of dear people who loved me, taught me and inspired me during those sometimes tumultuous years spent in India. Some for just a year or two, others for my entire India journey, and a couple who continue on even until today. God chose to place remarkable individuals in my life at a time when I didn't know who I was. They didn't care about that, however. They didn't care that I was unbalanced and at times unstable. They didn't care that I didn't always reciprocate the efforts they poured into my life. They didn't care that I was at times over-emotional and defensive. They simply wanted to be a part of my life and give to me whatever it was they had to give. I believe it was relationships with these few people that bolstered my resilience even in the midst of my general relational failure. I couldn't be resilient on my own, so they carried me through. For that I will be forever grateful.

I often said that I wished all my family and friends could come to India to meet the people I cared for in my life there. Many did, indeed, come for a visit. When they came, they fell in love with these people just as I had. They were shining stars in a place of confusion and uncertainty. They were like a drink of refreshment in an otherwise emotionally and relationally dry existence. These people are some that I wish everyone could meet.

But of course, that's not possible. So I want to share their stories here in an effort to encourage anyone who reads about them.

Sunil and Sunitha:
Joy and Mercy

You could always hear his laugh ringing out through the halls of the office. He always had a nickname for everyone. He had funny sayings and hilarious unknown idioms for all situations. His dear wife generally rolled her eyes or laughed along in solidarity. Loved by absolutely everyone, Sunil and Sunitha were some of the first people we met when we moved to India and were the first people we genuinely could call our friends. It was easy to be friends with them. They had a passion for life and loved to laugh. Kevin and Sunil would trade off telling jokes, even if none of us really understood what we were laughing at. We enjoyed getting food together in the city and talking with all the shopkeepers we encountered during long evenings of shopping for household goods. They introduced us to Paradise Biryani, Nanking Lemon Chicken, and Kamat Hotel's Thali Meals. Those foods would bring us an enormous amount of joy over the years and would be some of the things we missed the most when we returned to America. Of course it wasn't just the foods we missed, but it was the joy of sharing those foods with Sunil and Sunitha. They made every meal a banquet of frivolity. What great fun we had.

Occasionally, Kevin and I would start feeling frustrated about life, homesick for America, or uncertain about how we were going to adapt to this new culture. Whenever this happened, Sunil would always know exactly the right thing to say. He was able to encourage us when we needed it and find the positive points in

the most negative of situations. The joy that so obviously overflowed from his warm heart into his kind words lifted our spirits and helped the joy return to our hearts as well. Where did this joy come from? Sunil and Sunitha's story was not one of a life of ease. They had an arranged marriage during which they hadn't even seen one another until the wedding day. And yet their relationship was one of the most loving relationships we had ever seen. They had confidence that the Lord had brought them together and they were so obviously choosing joy. What a difference that made.

They also were desperate for a child, but month after month they were met with disappointment. However, that joy that overflowed from their hearts helped to get them through and helped them to be the best uncle and auntie to all the other children in their life. No matter the challenging situation, they chose joy and it was a genuine reflection of their faith in a joyful, unchanging God who saw them through and provided for them emotionally in a world that could be so cruel and unkind. I had always been a relatively joyful person. But I had never really experienced hardship. It was easy for me to be joyful during all my good times. But here I was learning through this relationship how to embrace joy and be resilient during the hard times as well. It was amazing to see them in operation. Amazing and inspiring all at once.

It was their experience of sorrow that helped push their joyful existence into one of tender mercy for absolutely everyone. They built relationships with people so they could help them. We could rely on them for anything. Whatever we needed, Sunil could source it for us. "Just give me two minutes," he would always say, and then he would pick up the phone, make a call, and

miraculously we would have what we needed. In our first week in Hyderabad, we spent hours and hours with this dynamic young couple, us with all of our intensity of needs and them helping us. It wasn't long before we noticed that they were like this with everyone. They longed to help others and expected nothing in return. In fact, they were loathe to receive help from others. As we got to know them more deeply, it was clear that their desire to help others was more than just an attitude. It was a gift. It was something sewn deep within their hearts. It was a supernatural gift of mercy that they both exhibited with the core of their beings. They couldn't help but love others, notice the pain others were experiencing, and work intentionally to ease that pain. They were filled with so much empathy for others that you could see the pain on their faces when they were interacting with someone else who was in pain.

At the time, I didn't know how to have empathy for others. I didn't understand how other people suffered. I was too young at the time. I hadn't lived. I hadn't suffered. I only had my small amount of life experience to rely on and it didn't allow me to conceive of how others might be feeling. But watching Sunil and Sunitha in action showed me that it was possible to care for others and have mercy for them in their depths of despair. It showed me that relationships are created for bearing others' burdens and journeying with them in both the good and the bad times. Until that point I thought I had to labor through trials on my own. I figured others had to as well. But Sunil and Sunitha's merciful hearts taught me that we should struggle together in community. We were created to battle life's trials together.

Pavel:
Compassion and Pastoral Care

Sitting in my office in Hyderabad, the one without a desk, painted in trendy colors, and furnished with couches, a fridge, a microwave and two coffee makers, I often had visitors looking to take a break from the workday. They would peer in through the small square window in my door to see if I was in and then enter hoping for shelter from whatever storm they were facing that day. There were lots of tears shed in my office by friends and colleagues confronted with frustrations and the unknown. However, there was an equal amount of laughter that could be heard in surrounding offices, creating jealousy in my co-workers who weren't invited to whatever party must certainly be going on. One of my favorite daily visitors was Bishop Pavel. His jolly, grey-haired, 5-foot frame would bounce inside, sit on the couch where he would ask tentatively at first (then more openly) for a cup of my American coffee which he would douse with a heavy hand of buffalo milk, but no sugar. (He was always trying to "cut back".) "Anything special today?" he would ask as he sauntered through the door. I had a habit of baking delicious American cakes and cookies and bringing them to share with folks in the office. Pavel was one of my best customers. We would sit together, drink our coffee, sometimes eat some cookies, and always talk about All. The. Things. He treated me as a confidential friend, someone with whom he could talk about organizational issues, knowing I would keep them private and offer my best, sometimes unsolicited, advice.

Pavel was also a person I knew I could turn to when I believed, rightly or wrongly, that things were unfair. In my dark

days when I saw only through the lens of mental illness, there were many days when I would sit in his office and talk to him about people I felt were treating me badly. He always listened to me patiently and with an extra dose of compassion. He never scolded me for thinking poorly of others, but could see that I was struggling. He was my pastor. He was someone who could listen well and take action if needed. But most times, no action was needed. I just needed a friendly face and a kindhearted person to hear me out, despite my tendency to distort reality during a time when I wrestled with what was real and what was in my imagination. Pavel was also sensitive and perceptive. When I was having a bad day, his pastoral heart knew without me saying anything that I needed some tender loving care. He would come for coffee more often during those times. He would come tell me jokes, ask for my advice more freely, or just come sit near to me during an event, a faithful friend who knew what I needed even if I didn't know.

I would love to be a pastor. Truly, my heart is for caring for people and seeing them grow in the Lord and in their lives. My actions and attitudes didn't always reflect those strong desires which would get distorted at times when I tried to take control over those I sought to serve. But my heart really is for other people's good. I can see potential in others that no one else can see. My strong longing is for people to live up to that potential and achieve great things for God in this world. Sometimes my longing for their greatness outshines their own personal desire! But my intentions are good at their root. I believe I may have learned some of this from Bishop Pavel. He was a pastor at heart and gave people a chance when others weren't willing. He would place people into positions of leadership perhaps before they were

ready, being willing to let their dormant gifts shine while on the job. Sometimes this went very well. Sometimes it backfired. But he was never afraid to let people have the chance to excel. I loved that about him and wanted to implement that in my own leadership and in my own relationships with people. I wanted to adjust my own controlling nature and just let the pure desire for goodness come through. I saw that in Pavel and I wanted it for myself.

Having a pastoral heart can be wearying at times, though. Just as I struggled at times from emotional exhaustion, Pavel did, too. His leaders had to tell him to take a break, take some rest. And when they told him to rest, he did. He retreated to his hometown village in Northeast India and took time off. Because his burden of work and ministry was so heavy, he had to retreat more often than others. He always returned refreshed and ready to take on whatever life was going to throw his way. In this regard, he was the opposite of what I'd learned in Indian culture thus far. I became friends with Pavel after I'd already been in India for probably 12-15 years. Until that time, the values of Sabbath, Vacation and Holiday, were mocked by some of my Indian friends and colleagues as "American" and unnecessary. I guessed, inaccurately, that all Indians must feel that way. Not Pavel. He took rest and encouraged others around him to take rest as well. When he saw me struggling mentally and emotionally, he encouraged me to get away for a week to escape the pressures of work. I didn't listen to him, but I should have. He had a pastoral wisdom that I valued, but apparently didn't value enough to follow. That was certainly my mistake.

Nonetheless, Pavel's compassionate care for me continued and I learned a lot about caring for others as I watched and

learned from him. In my interaction with those under my leadership, I took more time to see their mental and emotional needs. As I saw their holistic health as more important, I spent less time judging them and less time competing with them. I spent more time praying for them and giving them the benefit of the doubt. Perhaps this change in attitude came too late for me, but nonetheless it arrived. I carry that compassion and pastor's heart with me now into the relationships I'm blessed to have in America. Those qualities have developed within me a level of empathy that I've never before experienced. In fact, sometimes, I feel so deeply what others are feeling that it causes me physical pain. I never thought I would be that kind of person. To see the change that God has brought in my heart is remarkable. I believe it is because of Bishop Pavel and his ability to relate to me that the seeds of emotional responsiveness were planted in my heart. I am so thankful.

Annie White:
Graciousness and Unconditional Acceptance

When I grow up, I want to be like Annie White. No, scratch that. I want to be like Annie White *now*. A sweet, generous and radically grounded woman from the Northwestern United States, I knew Annie only marginally before I moved to India. She attended the same church that we attended before we made our big move to the other side of the world. She had known Kevin since he was a teenager when her husband was the youth pastor. She had watched him grow and mature, through the victorious times and also through the challenging and messy times of teenage angst. She has daughters my age, so when Kevin married me and I

was therefore adopted into the greater church family, she got me. She understood me. She knew how to relate to me immediately. I was thrilled, therefore, when she and her husband decided to come spend some extended time with us in India. Her husband had been instrumental in developing some curriculum for our pastors, and she was actively involved in training our healthcare workers. They had come on several short-term trips and had fallen in love with the country almost as much as we had. They were newly retired, but didn't want to spend all their time playing golf and vacationing. They wanted their lives to matter. So they came to India.

My friendship with Annie really began to bloom during our weekly Saturday morning trips to Q-Mart, my beloved grocery store that was an hour from our house, but was worth the drive because it carried all our favorite groceries both from India and abroad. I would pick Annie up at 8:30am on Saturday morning and we would glide across town, missing the morning business traffic, and arrive at Q-Mart just as it was opening. The hour-long drive was a perfect time for us to catch up, to chat about all that had happened during the week. We would share our joys and our struggles with life, culture, marriage, kids. You name it, we shared it. It was an amazing time for me, someone who was learning to crave depth of relationship. Annie was willing to meet me where I needed her and I was so thankful.

What I noticed during our times of discussion, though, was that Annie would never talk ill of anyone else. Never. Not even in a "constructive" way. Not even in a "we need to help this person in their area of weakness" way. She had so much life experience that I thought surely she would have an opinion on how others could improve their lives, their attitudes, their actions or their

skills. But, no. She spoke only positively and with great perspective about everyone we knew. I absolutely marveled at her ability to do this. If I had something even marginally negative to say about someone, she always replied in the positive. It was astounding. You see, I had a problem. Part of my difficulty and challenge with building relationships was my inability to resist judging people. I knew I was right about things and never shied away from believing the worst about others. My spirit of competition fostered this attitude in a big way because I wanted to be better than others. What better way to be the best than to cut other people down. Now, be assured, I didn't voice any of my thoughts in this regard! But they were there in my mind and I had hoped to find a friend that would share in my judgmental ways. That friend would not be Annie White. And her spirit of graciousness and unconditional acceptance challenged me.

If someone we knew was being angry or hostile, she would see them as having a bad day and being in need of encouragement. If someone was not fulfilling their job obligations or was not living up to their potential, she would see them as struggling with self-esteem and in need of being built up. If someone was unable to follow the leadership they were under, she would see them as in need of a gentle touch and more conversation. She was always willing to give everyone the benefit of the doubt. At first, this drove me crazy! I felt that people should be held accountable for their actions. There should be consequences for their indiscretions. How can this mature woman not see all the flaws of these immature, irrational people! But the more time I spent with Annie, the more my perspective changed. The more I began to see through eyes of love. Wow, what a remarkable change. Now, I actually began wanting to extend grace to people as well. I tried to

love people unconditionally and give them what they needed. I hoped to listen more and hear people's hearts. I avoided trying to fix their lives. I didn't want to punish them. My desire to compete with them started to fade. And wouldn't you know it, my relationships began to improve ever-so-slightly, the more I kept Annie in the back of my brain acting as my gentle counselor in my interactions with others. Instead of WWJD (What Would Jesus Do?), my mantra was WWAWD: What Would Annie White Do?

People all around us are struggling and need our support. They certainly don't need our judgment or our condemnation. God doesn't condemn us, so why are we so quick to condemn others? Yes, we are insecure and we need to make ourselves feel better. But the reality is, the more we build each other up, the more we support each other, the more we genuinely love others and seek their good, the more tightly knit our community will be and, ultimately, the better people will feel about themselves. People who feel loved and embraced will perform to the best of their ability. People who feel accepted will follow their leaders and will be a contributing part of any team. I want to be the kind of person who is known for being gracious. I want to be the kind of person who is known for accepting others no matter what they've done, what they've said, or who they claim to be. And I want to be these things because of my relationship with Annie White. I still talk about her even today with my American friends. I'm so thankful for our trips to Q-Mart and so thankful that despite all my flaws, she accepted me and was my friend. I'm able to be more resilient in life and in relationships because of her. I'm a changed woman today because of her. Thank you, Annie White, I really owe you so much.

Vikram:
Creativity and Loyalty

For most of my life, I have claimed (rightly so?) that I am not a creative person. I am firmly a left-brain person. I like words and order and organization. I remember my school-age artist friend Brooke who could draw and paint and sculpt with such ease. I remember feeling so jealous of her artistic abilities as I frowned at my art class creations. I just couldn't do it. The ability wasn't there. And that was how I lived my life. I enjoyed music, but I played music or sang music. I didn't create it. I didn't improvise. I liked words, but I didn't write poetry. Frankly, I didn't even like or understand poetry. That was how I lived my life. I was not creative. That was fact. There was no changing it.

And then I met Vikram. He was a young, charismatic musician who worked with us. He was full of life, had a young spirit, a wide smile and everyone who met him liked him almost immediately. He knew how to talk to people and make them feel good about themselves. His main talent was music. He sang and played every instrument. How he had learned all these things, I'll never know. He just had a God-given talent, I guess. Or maybe it was by necessity. You see, Vikram was one of those people that others called upon to do things when no one else could do them. Perhaps this is why we became friends. Need someone to create a Powerpoint presentation for the pastor to use during his sermon? Ask Vikram. Need someone to take the young people Christmas caroling? Ask Vikram. Need someone to go across town to fetch new camera equipment for our head of photography? Ask Vikram. He always did whatever anyone asked of him without arguing. He knew his place in the organization and played it well. So when we

needed someone to start leading the worship in our church services, they asked Vikram. And he accepted. He recruited a group of young people with varying degrees of musical ability and formed a small band. They practiced when they could and did the best they could leading the congregation in praise and worship week after week. They took well-known songs and crafted their own versions. They sometimes even wrote their own lyrics and encouraged one another to write their own full songs. They might not have been Top-40 hits, but they were trying. They were expressing themselves. They were using the gifts they had to glorify Jesus and they were doing it together as friends, as a team.

I was drawn into that team during my last year in India. Despite the fact that I was 20 years older than most of those young people in the band and could have been their mother, they accepted me as one of their own. And as one of their own, I was simply expected to express my creativity. "But I'm not creative!" I would protest. Vikram and the gang would not accept that answer. Creativity, they demonstrated, could flourish in community, and now it was my turn. They challenged me to sing as I'd never sung before. They challenged me to play the keyboard. They challenged me to worship and dance and pray in creative and seemingly outrageous ways that I could never have done on my own. Vikram and his community rallied around me and how could I do anything else but get joyfully caught up in the flow of their love. For the first time in my life, and in the privacy of my own home, I began writing song lyrics. These lyrics never saw the light of day, but I wrote them. That in itself was a major accomplishment for me. I exercised the "right brain" that God had so obviously given me and created songs. This would never have happened if I had not released myself to become friends with Vikram and his band

of merry followers. The one year I had Vikram in my life was probably the most creative I'd ever been and I'm so thankful.

It was not only my creativity that he encouraged. He connected with young people in the church on such a deep level. It wasn't his charisma or creativity or musical ability that drew them. Vikram was one of the most loving, faithful and loyal people these young people had ever encountered. He himself had not been the recipient of grace during his vital formative teenage years and wanted to offer something greater and more grace-filled for the young people God had put in his life. So, in an effort to love them better, no matter what they did, Vikram defended these young people and remained loyal to them, even amid all their missteps and foibles of teenage life. "Don't worry," he would say. "They'll learn." He had such confidence in them. He was so patient. These qualities were so inspiring. My relationships were always fraught with disdain and conflict because I never had the patient confidence that people would ever learn the things they needed to learn without my intentional intervention. I always felt like I had to speak up, to tell them they were wrong, to set them on the right path. But Vikram knew better. He showed me that waiting for young people (and people of all ages) to learn lessons on their own was the much more powerful way for them to make positive progress in their lives. His willingness to take a long view of their lives and walk alongside them as they journeyed built an incredible amount of trust. His loyalty to them reflected loyalty right back. Those young people would do anything for Vikram. They loved him fiercely and considered him not only their older brother in the Lord, but more like a father figure. He had captured their hearts and would never let go, no matter what they did, what they said or where they went in life. I wanted that for the

relationships in my life as well. What began as a freedom to be creative ended in a permanent loyalty that crossed emotional boundaries and covered a multitude of sins. I wanted that in my life and was so thankful for this powerful example in my young friend Vikram.

Mona:
Relationships and Love

I have changed most of the names in this book to protect the identity of various people or for other reasons that seemed appropriate to me at the time. Mona, however, deserves the honor of being named. When I think of Mona, my heart fills with love and comfort and joy. I feel embraced by her affection for me. I feel accepted in a way none of my other friendships ever could. I think my deep connection with Mona came initially because Mona knows what it is like to love the people of India so deeply that it becomes her identity. Using that as a jumping off point, our friendship only grew from there. Growing up in a family of five sisters in rural Midwestern Canada, she first journeyed to India in 1987. After losing her twin sister and her father early in life, her family of women clung together with a voracity that rooted in her a passion for women's issues, freedom and equality. She came to India at a time long before globalization revitalized the infrastructure of the nation. Therefore, she learned not only to live, but to love a life of ultra-simplicity which established deeply into her psyche an inability to indulge in even the most basic of luxuries. Her own humble family beginnings prepared her for a life of joyfully-embraced minimalism. She dressed Indian, cooked Indian, ate Indian, drove Indian, slept Indian, spoke Indian, and

altogether lived Indian. It didn't take long before she was truly more Indian than she was Canadian.

How we ever became friends really is quite a mystery. I remember first being introduced to Mona over email by my leaders. She was returning to India after a long hiatus. I had been in India for about five or maybe seven years at that time and I remember feeling jealous that another foreigner was going to be coming to India and was being so quickly accepted into the inner circle of leadership. She was going to be based in Bangalore, so I wouldn't actually meet her personally, but she was going to be a part of my world. I instantly felt contempt for her, my ugly competitive streak rearing its vicious head once again. Ultimately, things didn't work out for her and the role she was playing in Bangalore, so she was asked to move to Hyderabad. What would that be like? She knew everyone and everything about the ministry. Her history was long and well-established. She served with the ministry in its "glory days", something I had missed out on despite my wholehearted commitment now. I would no longer be the senior-most international. Worry gripped my soul.

But any animosity I held for her vanished immediately the moment I met her. Despite the fact that we were nearly opposites in every way, I felt drawn to Mona almost instantly. I was married; she was single. I enjoyed modern conveniences; she reveled in a poverty mindset. I dressed in western clothes; she never left the house without her dupatta. I maintained contact with my home culture via the internet; she had left everything behind. I was a disaster when it came to relationships; Mona was a relational specialist. Nevertheless, we had been prepared for one another. She was a lovely person with a friendly and welcoming character. I was ashamed of myself for thinking ill of her and being threatened

by her mere existence. I had so much to learn from her and was excited to know her more deeply.

What I initially and naively thought would be a source of competition for me (her knowledge of India), actually became one of the things that drew us together. Because Mona understood India, she and I could talk on a different level than any of the other foreigners working with us. She had adapted to the culture as I had and knew what it took to be resilient. She thought only positively of the culture and did not have the same negative, critical outlook so many others had. I had longed to talk with someone who could see the positive points of Indian culture and how it contributed progressively to the world. Until that point, however, no one was willing or able to view things through a constructive lens. With Mona, though, things were different. Sure, we both had our challenging days with the culture which was so opposite from our own shared North American home cultures. But our struggles were never met with disdain for the nation's people whom we had grown to adore, perhaps because of (and not despite) all the distinct differences that confronted us almost every day. This embracing of the people, their culture and their worldview was a source of refreshment and joy for me after wishing my international colleagues could see India and her precious people as I did. Mona's love for India overflowed into every part of her life. People could see how much she loved them. They loved her back. They showed this love by feeding her and inviting her to family gatherings. They included her in their prayers and gifted her saris with regularity. She was a part of them and she was valued. I was jealous of her connection with the Indian people, but it gave me something to which I could aspire. Mona was a relational champion and I admired that.

Mona was also my age. What a remarkable difference this made to me. We were in the same life stage. Although we had experienced different things throughout our lifetimes thus far, we had indeed experienced things. We had lived and loved and lost and survived. We both carried a perspective that comes only with age and a life well-lived. I had been craving this kind of friendship for years. Many of the other foreigners who settled in to work with us were young, single, 20-somethings who were enthusiastic and happy to be serving overseas, but did not have the life experience nor the commitment to India that made connecting with them possible for me. I was different, unique, unlike anyone I had ever met. Most of the young people viewed me as someone who was older and out of touch with their reality. Perhaps I was. "You'll never understand us," they claimed. Perhaps I wouldn't.

But time spent with "my Mona," as she came to be known to me, was meaningful and filled with perspective. The conversations were sweet and on a whole different level. They ranged from the superficial to the serious. We talked about everything from clothing to cultural norms to spirituality. We loved to drink coffee together: me straight up black, her with the tiniest splash of milk. We spent coffee breaks in the office savoring small pieces of chocolate and dreaming up things we would cook together if we ever had the time. Every Saturday morning we would venture out into the city in my shiny red Volkswagen, winding our way through the crowded Indian roads while belting out songs at the top of our voices that played on the radio. When we grocery shopped, I filled up my cart with imported goods, while she bought a few Indian vegetables and occasionally splurged on some "Kraft Dinner" (mac and cheese) or freshly baked bread. We thought of all the places in India and around the world to which

we would like to travel when we won the lottery. We cried together, but laughed together so much more. We talked each other through the trials and tribulations we faced. Mona taught me about managing relationships with greater finesse and I like to think I helped her become a more effective administrator and leader. Whenever I needed prayer support, my first call was to Mona. Actually, she's still my first call and my best prayer partner. She was a faithful prayer warrior and usually when she prayed, God answered. Her connection to the divine seemed to be just that deep.

Author and poet John O'Donohue describes my friendship with Mona perfectly in his concept of the "Anam Cara" or "Soul Friend". He says this:

> "In the Celtic tradition, there is a beautiful understanding of love and friendship. One of the fascinating ideas here is the idea of soul-love; the old Gaelic term for this is *anam cara*. *Anam* is the Gaelic word for soul and *cara* is the word for friend. So *anam cara* in the Celtic world was the "soul friend." In the early Celtic church, a person who acted as a teacher, companion, or spiritual guide was called an *anam cara*. It originally referred to someone to whom you confessed, revealing the hidden intimacies of your life. With the *anam cara* you could share your inner-most self, your mind and your heart. This friendship was an act of recognition and belonging. When you had an *anam cara*, your friendship cut across all convention, morality, and category. You were joined in an ancient and eternal way with the "friend of your soul."

The Celtic understanding did not set limitations of space or time on the soul. "

Truly, Mona is my "soul friend", my "anam cara". Although today we live half a world apart, and I don't know if I'll ever actually see her again this side of heaven, I know that our friendship spans the miles between us and will stand the test of time. Mona taught me what a loving relationship could be like. She taught me what it meant to love and accept and grow. She taught me to ask questions and wait for the answers. She taught me that relationships take effort and that the effort is worth it. She showed me that relationships produce results. I am thankful for Mona and wish everyone could have a friend as dear to them as she is to me. Although we don't do life together any more, I am grateful for the years we had together and long for the day when we can sit together drinking coffee, eating chocolate and laughing together once again.

Joseph:
Leadership and Grace

The other name I've not changed in this book is this one: Joseph. Or should I say Most Rev. Dr. Joseph D'souza, Archbishop of the Good Shepherd Church of India. But to me, he's just Joseph. There are few others worthy to be named as he is.

I still remember the first day I met him. I had no idea who I was meeting. It was 1998 and we had just made the decision that we were definitely moving back to India to live and work, and someone suggested we go to Hyderabad to meet Joseph D'souza. They suggested we could work with him and his organization.

They were known for partnering with foreigners and giving them meaningful roles. Maybe we could be the next ones. So, as Americans generally do, we threw protocol to the wind, called up his office and made an appointment. Miraculously, we would later find out, he was in town and agreed to meet with us.

We walked in to the tiny office in a non-descript office building on the campus of the Hyderabad headquarters and sat with him and his second-in-charge. He didn't even ask us about ourselves. He simply began describing what kind of roles he needed from international workers at that time. God probably chuckled because He had hand-crafted those roles for us. Marketing and Discipleship. A perfect match. The whole meeting lasted probably 20 minutes and was not filled with any extraneous conversation. There was no "getting to know you" time. We didn't learn anything about Joseph at that time, didn't make a personal connection. He wanted us involved, though. He saw God's call on our lives, just as boldly as we felt we had heard it. It was confirmed, we were coming back to India and this was the start of a now life-long relationship with our professional mentor, friend, spiritual director and father figure that changed our lives in remarkable ways.

Joseph was our Indian leader. Actually, he was everyone's leader. Since 1989, he had been the leader of the entire ministry that we had moved to India to serve. For this reason, we thought we wouldn't have much contact with him. We were wrong. He took me, particularly, under his wing and used every opportunity possible to teach and train me in ministry, in leadership and in Christian life and belief. He was an extreme learner. He taught me what it meant to crave knowledge and to go after it myself. He recommended books and authors. Constantly forwarded articles

and interviews. He encouraged me to challenge traditional evangelical thinking and to own my own faith rather than just accepting the conditioning I'd been taught my whole Christian life. His thoughts were often controversial, but ultimately they were Spirit-led and escorted me into a way of thinking that allowed questions and uncertainty as a good, healthy and acceptable way of life.

People who would come after me sought Joseph out as a mentor, whether that be a culture mentor or a professional one. They saw the influence he had in my life and they wanted it in their life as well. However, they expected that his mentorship would take the form of a formal program in which he would take the initiative to mentor them. That's not how it worked. He taught me to be a learner which meant I had to take the initiative. I learned very quickly that if I wanted to learn anything from him, it would have to come from me. He was happy to teach, but he was more likely to just walk through life with me rather than create a formalized six-month program. This did not sit well with most people. They left disappointed. I wished they could have just held on longer and learned to initiate and be patient. They couldn't. That made me sad for them. They were truly missing so much.

What may have been most remarkable in his leadership style, however, was how much trust he put in me. He wouldn't give me a list of tasks to complete. He would give me a concept to implement and a general direction in which he would want me to go. Then he would set me free and allow me to create my own way forward. He valued the progress and the journey I would take in accomplishing every step along the way. This was something new for me and another thing that did not sit well with others. It took me some time to learn that he was not going to give me the

kind of linear feedback I had been conditioned to expect. Once I learned his style, our ebb and flow became seamless. I needed less and less direction to understand what he wanted and accomplish what he intended. I became one of his key confidential leaders. I was his chief ghostwriter. He asked my opinion even when I was still a young woman learning her way in the ministry and professional world. He took time to explain things when I had questions and almost always would take my calls. He would call me from the far-flung reaches of the planet when he had free moments in airports just to update me on his travels and fill me in on whatever meetings he had just taken. He shared the joys of fundraising, and shared the trials of international leadership. If he had something that absolutely had to get done, I was his first call. He trusted me to get it done. I could have felt pressured by those demands, but I felt honored to be chosen instead.

Now don't get the wrong idea. It might seem that business always came first and that his demands were unreasonable. However, that was not the case. He always asked about the family, wanted to hear how Kevin and the kids were doing. He had high expectations, but was always gracious if things didn't go as planned. My favorite saying of his was, "Don't worry, nothing bad will happen." And truly, when he said it, I believed that it would be so! He also set high, likely unreachable goals, but then always caveated them by saying, "Even if we can reach half that goal, it will be great." He knew what it meant to reach for the skies, but was firmly grounded in reality at the same time. He allowed me to work hours that suited my family schedule and trusted me to just get the job done. We worked hard and we worked long some days, but other days we didn't work at all, taking the time needed to recover and refresh for the inevitable heavy days ahead. I learned

so much grace from him. Both professionally and in relationships. Time and time again we would be dealing with a personnel issue in our leadership meetings and I would want to act with what I felt was the most justice, the most deserved action. Most often, that was some form of punishment or consequence for the offender. He, however, would take a softer approach, promoting an approach of grace before anything else. And, wouldn't you know it, he was almost always right.

I am so thankful for Joseph's presence in my life. Even after I left India, he is still a major force for good for me. Whenever he comes to the US, he makes sure to see us. He still calls us from airports around the world just to say "hi" and update us on the latest happenings in India or elsewhere. He includes me on strategy discussions and still trusts me to get the most urgent things done. My life is fully enriched and changed forever because of his influence, encouragement, and love.

HEART STORIES…
PART TWO

Our son Clark was the first white baby ever born in the maternity hospital we chose in Hyderabad. It was about an hour's drive through the thick city traffic from our house, but we faithfully went for our appointments all throughout my pregnancy and felt confident that this was the best place for us to give birth. It was run by a Catholic family, which meant there were crosses and pictures of Jesus on most of the walls, something completely unseen in the rest of Hindu-majority India. It brought me a sense of comfort, despite the spectacle we were as foreigners in an overcrowded healthcare facility.

Clark was born safely and we brought him home, completely unaware of how to care for him. I had read as many books as I could get my hands on, but I had no real maternal instincts. I just knew I had to keep him alive. I didn't have the help of nearby relatives or girlfriends, and our Indian friends felt that their input would be so culturally different that they simply didn't offer it. I was completely on my own to mother this child into a healthy future. I remember standing over his makeshift crib, watching to make sure he was still breathing while he slept. I was not a natural at bathing him or dressing him or any of the things that all those perfect moms out there seem to do so easily. But I did my best and he stayed alive and continued to grow and mature, happy to see us and receive our unconditional love. I considered that 100% success.

In Indian culture, healthy babies that are born and survive are not a guarantee, especially among the urban poor and the impoverished rural communities. Deteriorated living conditions put infants at risk for all kinds of diseases that could kill them. Many families delay naming their babies for months to make sure

the child is going to live long enough to warrant receiving a name. If the baby lives to be a year old, they rejoice. In fact, the baby's first birthday is cause for great celebration. They throw a party that is so big, all other future parties (if indeed they have them) pale in comparison. They want everyone to know that their child has lived. And so they commemorate that fact with a grand affair. If that child happens to be a boy? Well, then, all the better. Male children were valued more highly than female children. A son's first birthday party was almost as important as his wedding. Even the poor families would spend huge amounts of money to make sure everyone knows their child is alive.

As Clark's first birthday approached, we had been living in India for about four years and we felt like we were adapting to the culture quite well. We felt like participating in the ritual of celebrating our son's first birthday in a big way would be a way to honor the customs of this nation, as well as treat our friends to a delicious meal and a fun time. We decided to invite everyone we knew, have a huge buffet of food, and have a short program dedicating Clark to the Lord. Everyone was excited when they got the invitations. We had them professionally printed because it was cheap, easy, and everyone else issued invitations like that for their events. Our friends in America couldn't believe we were pulling out all the stops for a child's birthday party, but we felt like this was what we truly wanted to do.

We put up a huge event tent in the empty lot across from our house. The caterers came and started cooking vats of hot and spicy chicken biryani. We set up a sound system, tables and chairs, and a small stage. We brought Clark's high chair from our kitchen. We dressed Clark in a fancy, traditional Indian outfit which his chubby little body barely fit into. I donned a new, green sari, and

146

Kevin also dressed in traditional Indian dress. We were thrilled to be doing this. Our friends arrived in great anticipation and they were not disappointed. They enjoyed the food and the desserts we provided. They loved watching Clark dig into the smash cake I had ordered. (That was one American tradition I had retained!) We sent all the children in attendance home with a goodie bag, and had small "tiffin boxes" engraved for all the adults to take with them as a memento of the event. Everyone left with smiles on their faces, shaking our hands gleefully. We were so delighted to have shared this time with them.

At the end of the night, I learned that I had ordered too much food and there was a lot left. Migrant workers from the neighborhood had gathered on the fringes of our event to see what the "white people" had been doing. And so, with joy, I had the caterers pack up all the extra food and distribute it to the curious laborers who were delighted to be sent home with a care package. It was as if the whole local community had now been able to celebrate Clark's one year of living.

What a great night it was. Clark, of course, has no memory of this, but we do. We felt as if we had truly immersed ourselves into an important part of Indian culture and our Indian friends had appreciated the effort we made to show them we cared. We began to feel accepted and as if we really were going to thrive in this land that we loved. Two years later when our daughter Claire had her first birthday party, we celebrated with equivalent grandeur. We wanted to make a statement that even though she was a girl, we valued her equally. Our friends quickly came to see how much we loved our children, how much we were going to do our best to raise them, and how much we were looking forward to blending

the American and Indian cultures as parents who wanted to give their children the world's very best.

❀❀❀❀

Fifth Grade is never an easy time. Young ones transition from childhood to adolescence. Changing bodies, changing hormones, changing friends. I remember when I was in fifth grade. I experienced the first betrayal and hurt from a "friend" during that rocky year. I was devastated when she said mean things to the other girls behind my back. That would be the beginning of a lifetime of insecurity in relationships for me. Something of which I could never let go. Up until I moved to India, I thought the problems I faced as a middle class American young woman were so serious. But then I began to meet people who were truly in need. People like 10-year-old Rajneesh.

It was in this difficult transition time of late grade school that we met young Rajneesh, a fifth grader at one of our schools in North India. We had visited his school on one of our many trips to North India where we loved to spend time learning about the differing cultures of the North, eating their less spicy food, enjoying their tribally-influenced dances, and hearing our own children speak the North Indian languages with ease. When we met Rajneesh and began to learn his story, we discovered that he had been learning about helping others in their time of need.

Rajneesh and the children at this school established specifically for the poor, marginalized and outcast members of the community were often the recipients of practical, physical help. They live an impoverished life and suffer from the seemingly unbreakable chains of caste-based oppression. It is a miracle that

they are allowed to attend school and have the opportunity to hope for a brighter future for themselves and for their families. When the children first entered the school, they had no dreams to chase. But now that they feel accepted and embraced by their compassionate teachers, they can dream of being doctors and engineers and teachers. They can now envision light where before there was only darkness.

Despite their generally downcast upbringings and their continued need for material provisions, the teacher of Rajneesh's fifth grade class felt it was important that the moral lesson of helping others was something even poor children should have a chance to learn and begin to apply to their young lives. She told them stories over and over of people helping others and the powerful impact this altruism had on transforming society. While she was hopeful that this lesson would be carried with the children on into adulthood, she never imagined her students would at this young age and with their lack of resources begin to help others right now. What a thrill it was for her to learn that this was happening.

Rajneesh comes from a destitute family. The family barely had enough to eat, but always found a way to send Rajneesh to school. They valued education and knew that their sacrifice now would help them in the future. Unfortunately, Rajneesh began missing school because he was ashamed that in his impoverished state, he could not afford to buy the required sports shoes and socks for gym class. He feared he would be teased, that he would ruin his normal school shoes, and that his sports performance would suffer. He was distraught at all these possibilities and chose instead to stay home from school rather than face what he deemed would be certain humiliation. His parents allowed this

because his shame was their shame. They could not provide for him and did not know what else to do.

Eventually, Rajneesh's classmates discovered the truth behind his absences. Four young boys in his grade, also from desperately poor families, took it upon themselves to remedy the situation. They wanted to help. They didn't want their friend to miss out on the joys of being at school. They needed him on their sports team! So, they found a way to collect money, one Rupee at a time, from students, teachers, and community members. Who could possibly resist this story of love, compassion and altruism? They collected enough to buy the required footwear and gifted the items to Rajneesh with great pride. Rajneesh was overcome with emotion and with gratitude. The boys embraced, all in tears, knowing that they were bonded for life through this act of kindness. Rajneesh immediately donned his new shoes and socks and beat them all at a friendly yet fierce game of soccer. They were all thrilled.

This entire episode was an amazing experience for Rajneesh and his friends, but also for the teachers and the community at large. The teachers at this school know that the example they set and the values they teach are often completely foreign to the children and their family members. It is a new worldview for them to grasp in terms of equality, love, compassion and self-worth. However, once they get a taste of what life can be when lived in this new way, there is no turning back. They want more of this kind of life. They want to bring excellence and a new humanity to everyone around. They know for certain that the lessons being learned in that school are ones that will follow the students for life and will bring permanent positive change to the entire village for generations to come.

❀❀ ❀❀

Choosing to give birth to children and raise them in another culture was both an easy decision for us to make and a slightly controversial one. Kevin and I were newlyweds when we moved to India and so the question was a natural one for many people to ask us: When are you going to have children? And, are you going to have them in India? Our answer was always a wholehearted YES. We were going to give birth to the children in India. It was an easy answer for us because we lived in an urban center where there were modern hospitals and a wealth of the world's best doctors. We were heavily privileged in that our American dollars and American health insurance allowed us access to the best that Indian healthcare had to offer. What came after their birth, however, the actual raising of them, would prove more challenging.

We had so many decisions to make concerning how we were going to raise our children. Would we raise them to be more heavily influenced by our American culture? Or would we immerse them deeply in Indian culture and allow our Indian friends to inspire our parenting? Ultimately, we decided that we wanted our children to know and love Indian culture as we did, but that our home would be a safe haven where American norms were more common. We ate mostly American food, had American furnishings, watched American TV shows, and celebrated American holidays. However, the kids went to all-Indian schools, attended an all-Indian-led church and Sunday School, ate at Indian restaurants, and visited many, many places across the nation of India to learn about the culture and history of the land that we loved.

One of the things we felt was most important for us to teach to Clark and Claire from an early age was the prevalence of poverty in India. Our lifestyle was definitely different from that of impoverished people and the kids attended a school full of wealthy, upper class Indian children. Their friends at school lived in huge houses, had multiple high-end sports cars, and threw birthday parties that were held at five-star hotels and catered by celebrity chefs. Sure, the kids enjoyed partaking of those luxuries from time to time. However, they knew that our lifestyle was different. They knew that we cared for people in need. They knew that we spent the money that we had in practical, economical ways. Moreover, we wanted to develop within their young hearts a love for and a sense of genuine empathy for those who were truly suffering. It was our deep desire for them to be more than simply thankful for what they had. It would be easy to be thankful for our material comforts and then just look the other way when they saw someone who had nothing. No, we knew they were capable of more. We wanted our kids to be aware of their privilege, but then seek to build others up, fight for equity when possible, and always pursue the restoration of dignity to those from whom it had been taken. We wanted them to use the power they had to always battle for good in this world that is so consumed by evil.

One of the ways we were able to bring these lessons into the spotlight and hope to instill them into our kids' lives was by visiting the family of Good Shepherd Schools which were raised up during our tenure in India. These were schools specifically created for the poor, marginalized and outcast of India, those who had been traditionally forbidden from receiving an education. Over the course of 20 years, we saw 27,000 children enter these schools, starting in the earliest of grades. They learned the English

language, excelled in the maths and sciences, and eventually graduated, going on to become doctors, engineers, teachers and public servants. These schools brought full transformation to every village in which they were placed. They were centers of good and light and hope and love.

Bringing Clark and Claire into these classrooms where children sat on dirt floors, did their lessons with chalk and a slate, and ate only rice for lunch, was more than a cultural experience. It was a lesson in God showing up in the neediest of places. It was a hands-on lesson in love and compassion. It showed our children from ages 4 and 6 onward that they were no different than these children who also loved to play and draw and eat sweets. Clark sat next to a boy his age and held hands while they sang a sweet elementary age song together. Claire danced in the playground with girls her age, squealing with joy as they touched each others' hair and drew pictures in the dirt. They had the same smiles, the same laughs, and the same love for their teachers' embrace. Despite the differing color of their skin and their diverse socio-economic backgrounds, there really was so little differentiating these children who only saw the similarities as they played together in true happiness.

As parents living and raising children cross-culturally, we knew that we would face some great challenges. However, exposing our children to some of the greatest poverty in the world really didn't end up being a challenge. It turned out to be a blessing. Today, as they attend American high school in a wealthy, white, privileged, non-diversified school, they are drawn to those who face trial after trial in life. They are drawn to students of color. They are drawn to those who come from broken homes. They are compelled to listen to and love those who have the deepest of

needs. I believe Clark and Claire learned this while in India, even though they probably didn't even know they were learning it. It became a part of who they are. I believe they learned this during their formative years when they were confronted with India's poor and were empowered to make a difference not only through material assistance, but also through emotional and spiritual support.

What joy this brings to our hearts as parents. We are so thankful. So thankful.

❈ ❈ ❈ ❈

We lived in four different homes during our 20 years in India. First, a simple one-floor duplex. Second, a two-story independent home. Third, a sixth-floor penthouse apartment. Fourth, our favorite, another two-story, four bedroom independent home. Each place we lived held special purpose and unique memories for us. Each home had its challenges, each its distinctive character. There was the teeny-tiny kitchen of the duplex. The unexpected move from the second home. The joy of community living at the penthouse. The extraordinary and unexpected gift of God's provision at that last, favorite place. We were thankful for each room, each kitchen, each "yard", each neighbor. God truly blessed us with meaningful places to live.

That penthouse apartment was certainly a unique place to live. It was one of those things that Kevin likes to call "Good from afar, but far from good." It had many good features, but many not-so-good features as well. There was no air conditioning. It had an elevator, but that elevator didn't work very often. It didn't have running water most of the time. We had frequent power outages

and no generator. Did I mention the elevator didn't always work?? But it also had a beautiful balcony that overlooked the city and the airport. It had enough space for our children, who were very young at the time, to run and play. It had a separate office area so our work life could be as separate from our home life as possible. It had a guest room where we hosted guests and interns. We were generally happy there.

On the day we moved in, we noticed that the apartment also had what's called a "Puja Room". This is a very common thing in Indian homes, especially homes built by Hindus. This is a small closet or room in which they put all their Hindu idols and worship implements. They will conduct their daily worship rituals in that area, consecrating their day to their god(s). They use that room/area to burn incense or break a coconut, hang dried mango leaves or squeeze a lime. It is a holy place for Hindus and an important part of any devout Hindu's home.

In this particular puja room, the builder and owner of the apartment had hung tiles with the pictures of about a dozen Hindu gods on the walls in a neat row. We didn't know which Hindu god his family worshiped. Perhaps he was simply covering his bases and honoring as many as he could in the space that allowed. Smart man, I guess! It was very neatly done and I'm sure he was so pleased with how it turned out. The area given for this purpose was spacious and I know that most Hindu families would be so happy to have so much room in which to practice their faith on a daily basis.

We, however, are Christians. Christians with young, impressionable children. And having pictures of Hindu gods in our home concerned us. Not greatly, but it did concern us. We knew in our hearts and in our heads that our God, Jehovah, is

greater than all other gods. But that didn't mean we wanted pictures of those gods in our home. We discussed at length what to do about this. It really was a mental dilemma for us. We asked some of our Indian friends what to do. Finally, we decided. We would ask him to please remove the tiled pictures. We figured the worst that could happen was that he would say no. We could live with that. We would pray and cover ourselves in the power of the Holy Spirit.

The next time the owner of the apartment came to sign the final papers, we humbly asked him to remove the tiles with the pictures of the Hindu gods. We explained that this was not our Christian tradition to have these in our home and we would love it if he could simply take them down. To our delight, he did not take offense at our request. Instead, he launched into a bit of a philosophical negotiation.

"You worship Jesus, right? Why don't I just add a picture of Jesus to the collection?"

We smiled. What a great idea he must have thought that was. So accommodating. We weren't sure how much we wanted to engage with him on this topic. We were pretty sure he wasn't going to be open to a clear and accurate presentation of the Good News as we believed it. However, Kevin decided to have a little bit of fun, as Kevin often does.

"Ah, I see," Kevin started. "So you pray to all the gods?"

"Yes," the owner said. "That way I can be confident one of them will answer when I call."

"But," Kevin challenged, "What if all the gods think one of the other gods is going to answer you and in the end none of them does?"

The apartment owner took a step back, looked at Kevin, and smiled. Ah, he hadn't thought of it that way before. He chuckled and told us just to cover up the tiles if we didn't like them. So that's what we did.

Living in India was always a surprise. We learned something new every day and, even more, learned new things from interacting with her people every time we talked to someone new. Such joy we got from those interactions. It didn't matter that the apartment owner remained a Hindu and carried on with his life. We were something new for him to contend with. We asked him questions he had never before considered. We treated him with respect. That's what mattered.

And yes, we made that Puja Room into a storage area where we kept extra toiletries and the kids' old school projects and we kinda forgot those Hindu god tiles were even there. Our God does indeed reign supreme.

158

PART THREE:
EMBRACING
UNCERTAINTY

CHAPTER NINE

I have had a number of people in my life that I considered mentors. Some of them were more formal than others, but the thing they all had in common was that they intentionally poured into my life during a season in which I really needed it. During our time in India, Joseph D'souza was certainly one of those people. I was so thankful for Joseph D'souza's influence in my life. Our relationship was one of encouragement, but it was also one of challenge. Because he was so committed to learning, his views were constantly evolving and he was also committed to bringing those under his leadership along with him in his evolution of thought and belief. As a young woman from a staunchly conservative background, this type of thought processing was almost impossible for me at first. I had never been taught to question or think for myself. There were social and intellectual and spiritual concepts that were new to me and which pushed my thoughts to their limits. For many years it really was too much. But as my own thinking matured, it became easier to read the books he was reading and write about the topics about which he was writing. It was exciting for me to see breakthroughs in myself as I grew older. I have always thought of myself as intellectually inferior to most people, and so I can still remember the day I realized my thoughts had gone beyond those of one of my early mentors. Whoa, what a realization. Humbling and exciting all at once.

One of the great things I learned during this time of self-exploration and learning was the embracing of uncertainty. Over the years, I had learned on countless occasions that living overseas required going beyond any exercise in flexibility that we had ever experienced. Our entire cross-cultural preparation prior to moving abroad had stressed over and over again to keep an open mind, be flexible, and be willing to change. However, nothing could adequately prepare us for what we would encounter in India. In fact, it would take years for us to understand completely that what we were facing was not merely the need for flexibility, but instead the need to accept ambiguity and uncertainty in our everyday lives. Ambiguity is not something we Americans are used to. We like plans. We like schedules. We like to know what to expect. In fact, although so many people say, "I have no expectations" when it comes to new experiences, in fact their expectations run deep. Those expectations rise to the surface when they are not met, when disappointment appears seemingly out of nowhere, ready and willing to ruin any situation and cause distress in the emotions of its owner.

Five years after we had come to India, our organization began opening schools for Dalit children. The Dalits, or "untouchables" as they've been historically called, are those who are at the bottom of the Hindu caste system. They are considered so unworthy that they are not even a member of any caste. They face oppression and discrimination on a daily basis and have no real hope of escaping their fate. In 2001, we had the distinct privilege of attending a massive rally in India's capital city New Delhi where several hundred thousand Dalit people gathered together under threat of death to jointly declare that they were breaking free from Hinduism and its discriminatory caste system to enthusiastically

embrace other religious ideologies. It was amazing to see people come from all across the nation, proud to be Indians, but longing for a different life, a life that would guarantee them freedom and equality. On that night, they cried out to the Christian leaders who were present there to educate their children and free their women. They knew that their children, if educated, could go on to change the nation and change the world. Joseph D'souza was there that night and he eagerly accepted that challenge on behalf of Indian Christians. Our organization immediately started opening schools for Dalit children and other poor, marginalized and outcast youth. Our schools were filled with the love of Jesus and the Christian worldview of compassion, equality and freedom. Today, thousands of young people have graduated from those schools and are doctors, engineers, public servants and teachers. They are indeed changing India and changing the world.

At the start, however, we were a simple bunch of Christian workers who loved Jesus and were doing their best to open educational institutions. To say the schools were a little rough going at first would be an understatement. So, to help us along this journey, we invited teachers and other educators from around the world to come consult with our staff members to make the schools the best they could be. These good-hearted professionals would prepare loads of lesson plans, activities, special events and manuals to give to our teachers and students during their time with us. They had planned everything down to the minute and were so excited to contribute to this extremely worthy cause. However, their enthusiasm was usually muted as quickly as it had been roused as soon as they reported for duty. The schools may or may not have been in session that day and there would be no advance notice if school had been cancelled. Somehow all the

teachers and staff knew, but our international educators had not been notified. Many times teachers had not been informed of the consultants' arrival and were not prepared, nor were they available to meet with them. In some cases, some teachers refused to meet with the foreign volunteers because it was emotionally shameful for them to admit that they needed help. As Indian teachers, they were required to get not only a bachelor's degree, but also at least two, if not three master's degrees to be qualified to teach. Many of the visiting teachers had inferior education in their opinion.

These things took the visiting teachers by surprise. They had been willing to be flexible on start times or even the order in which they taught their subjects. But the seemingly chaotic workplace environment into which they were placed was, to them, unacceptable. They were facing an environment of ambiguity and uncertainty and they were not prepared for it. They didn't know how to process this and had no personal, internal resources with which to think about their emotions surrounding all that was happening. Therefore, time and time again, our volunteers went away from us frustrated, disappointed, and with a negative overall view of the work and ministry that we were doing. They had expected one thing and got another. They had anticipated a good, rewarding experience, and that didn't happen. They thought they would make a difference in the lives of so many Indian teachers and educators and they left feeling like they didn't accomplish anything at all. More than once I had upset and angry visitors in my office raising their voice with me expressing their frustrations and letting me know all the things that served as obstructions to them accomplishing their goals for their trip to India. Let's just say we didn't have a lot of repeat visitors.

Once some time had passed and I learned that it was ambiguity that we and others were facing, a whole new world of understanding opened up for me. This new interaction with ambiguity exposed a whole new brand of cultural understanding for me. I felt liberated. It no longer mattered to me if I understood what was happening. I knew that eventually I might understand and that was enough. If I never understood that was okay, too. I realized that sometimes there are things about cultures we will never understand and that's just the way God has created them. That's just the way God has created all of life. In fact, our relationship with God is like that, too. We can never understand everything about our holy, immaculate, all-knowing, ever-present God and we never will. And yet we serve and worship Him. Or at least we say we do. Just because we don't understand something doesn't make it wrong or unacceptable. It is good for us to practice living with uncertainty. It stretches our ability to understand and accept. It broadens our ability to love even when we don't comprehend what is happening or who someone is. Loving someone when you don't know everything about them is a divine gift to that person. Trusting them enough to care about them and accept them without first investigating them and making them prove themselves to you is what Jesus would do and what we should do as well. Being willing to be wrong about someone is a delightful quality that breeds relationships that will last, despite what society tries to convince us will actually happen. Why not, then, do that with a whole culture of people who have a worldview that is so enormously different from ours and perhaps even beyond our comprehension?

Although I was beginning to understand, this was still a troubling paradigm shift for most of the western world that values

certainty to embrace. In fact, we as a culture value certainty so much that uncertainty or ambiguity is often viewed as wrong or sinful or dishonest instead of simply as different. We stand high on our puritanical moral ground, judging those we may not understand and imposing our standards on cultures that are not at all based on Judeo-Christian worldviews. As my love for India grew, and as my understanding of her began to blossom (slowly, but surely), my defensiveness also flourished when what I determined to be imperialistic invaders imposed their cultural norms on an unsuspecting 1.3 billion souls. (I do realize how harsh that sounds! My views have become more compassionate over time, but there were many years where my fierce loyalty to India and her beloved people caused me to hurt the feelings of one too many good-hearted newcomers.) As I learned, and as I watched people struggle, there were several parts of Indian culture that were particularly challenging when it came to this issue of uncertainty. Truth telling was one of them. In some ways, it all began with a head bobble.

One of the most characteristic things about Indian culture is the head bobble. When you ask an Indian a question, they will shake, nod and bob their head simultaneously as if their head were anchored to a ball bearing at the base of their neck. It is a curious movement, one which foreigners try to imitate, generally without success. What is even more mystifying, however, is the meaning of the head bobble. For many, it means "Yes". For others, it means "No". I began to learn, however, that it could also perhaps mean, "I heard that you are speaking to me and I'm not quite ready to answer you yet." For those who thought the head bobble meant "Yes", it could be quite disconcerting when their dear Indian friend did not follow through with whatever they had supposedly

agreed to do just moments before. In fact, my experience with "Yes" went beyond just the head bobble. I found that when asking my Indian friends a question, if I really wanted to get the correct answer, I would ask them three times.

> Q1: Would you like to come to dinner?
> "Yes" – meaning "I heard that you are speaking."
>
> Q2: Would you like to come to dinner?
> "Yes" – meaning "I understand the question."
>
> Q3: Would you like to come to dinner?
> "Yes" – meaning "Yes, I will come!"

My constant and repetitive asking of questions became quite a joke, but many people eventually got my point. I knew the way to find out the truth. It just took a little more probing. However, those who didn't know this secret felt that lying was endemic in the Indian culture. They thought it was impossible to learn what an Indian actually thought because it seemed that Indians told foreigners what they thought they wanted to hear. This created an enormous amount of uncertainty in the minds of visitors to the sub-continent, wondering if anything they heard was true, and questioning the morality of an entire nation of people.

Another cultural creator of uncertainty was the Indian aversion to putting things in writing. This could be something as formal as a contract, or as simple as an email. Their belief was that once something was in writing, it was permanent, binding, and they would be ultimately fully responsible for its outcome. This was difficult for many people who were raised in a Hindu

worldview that was steeped in the ideal of "karma": what you do today will affect you tomorrow and in the life to come. Being held responsible for something was incredibly serious. The result? Even simple emails don't get written. Receipts are hard to come by. School certificates are only issued by the highest of education authorities. To the non-Indian trying to communicate with an Indian or negotiate a business deal? This causes frustration and suspicion. Weeks would go by between emails. Then when an email did come, it would not have any of the required information. To someone steeped in western culture, this conveyed an apparent incompetence that hurt relationships and did nothing to bridge cultural gaps. Misunderstandings flourished and the sense of uncertainty was heightened. Could the Indians be trusted? There was heavy doubt.

These are just two examples of how the culture we experienced in India could breed uncertainty and mistrust with those who didn't understand it. It took us a long time to truly figure out what was going on in these and other situations. (And we are still learning!) During our time of exploration, we felt an enormous amount of discomfort because we loved the Indian people and we wanted the best for them, but how could lying and incompetence be the best? It took humility on our part and an open mind willing to embrace the unknown before we would see that what we as Americans believed was "wrong" was indeed simply different and part of this beautiful and diverse culture we called our home. The uncertainty of not understanding the culture for so many years was devastating to us. It affected us emotionally and spiritually. What we learned quickly was how much brainpower it was going to take to process this complex world we had chosen. We began to realize that we had not been trained to

deal with complexity, that we as a culture in general are not bred to mitigate complex situations with grace. We like things simple. We like the easy path. We like things straightforward and clear and concise. India was far from any of those things. And so in uncertainty we would choose to live.

In fact, our mere living in India itself was subject to enormous uncertainty. Immigration is a huge issue in our country today. There is no end to the debates about what we should do with and how we should treat those who have crossed our American borders with or without their legal paperwork in hand. We have a unique perspective on this issue because of our many years spent living as guests in a foreign land. We were acutely aware that we were indeed guests of the Indian government. We had valid visas and had entered the country legally, but our tenure was at the mercy of the local officials. They had every right to remove us from the country at their whim. We had no rights, no recourse, no argument. We lived for 20 years with this constant uncertainty and ever-present awareness. We did everything within our control to obey the laws of the land, to pay our taxes, to comply with immigration regulations, to run our business well, and to be friendly and fair to everyone we encountered. At the same time, we varied our routes when we traveled, hired a security guard for our house, installed security cameras, and left the country with regularity. In fact, at most times we retained only a moderate amount of clothing and household goods and were ready to pack up our belongings into our limited number of suitcases and flee the country at a moment's notice. We explained that to people from time to time and they thought we were a little crazy. Ironically, that's what happened. (More on that later.)

Despite what happened in the end, however, there came a point where we simply accepted the fact that we were going to live in a state of ambiguity. It didn't feel good to feel nervous most of the time. It didn't feel good to wonder if we'd make it through immigration or get turned back at the border. It didn't feel good to see a policeman, curious if we'd be detained. But we didn't base our beliefs on our feelings. We accepted the fact that God had placed us in India and He would keep us there for as long as He wanted us there, and then, at the right time, He would remove us. We clung to the confidence that we were safely kept in His hand and that no force of evil or outside enemy could harm us, even in our vulnerable physical state. We exchanged our American craving for certainty for a faith in God that allowed us to question and doubt while at the same time being certain in the Only Thing that is truly certain in all of life and ministry. That's how we made it through. It was intentional. It did not happen by accident. Every day we once again placed our selves and our trust in God, the only One Whose opinion mattered and the One Who we knew made all the decisions with regard to our future. Ultimately, we were not afraid.

We did our best to convince other foreigners to live as we did, but I don't think we were very good teachers. Or maybe we weren't very good examples. I don't know. We never cracked the code of passing on the acceptance of uncertainty to others. I suppose it is something that every individual must come to achieve on their own, in their own time and in their own way. We all have different experiences and differing worldviews, despite a similar cultural upbringing. Our personalities and temperaments also tend to dictate how we will respond to what seem like crisis situations. What a pity, though, because if there is anything I wish

I could pass on to others, it would indeed be the ability to accept and operate in the midst of ambiguity. The ability to embrace ambiguity and live within it when required was another key component in the growth of resilience in my life. I was able to keep going when things were uncertain. I was able to overcome doubts and insecurities because I had made a conscious choice to do it. And because of that I was resilient in the most undefined and ever-changing of situations. I always wanted that for others! What a relief it would be for people to release their need for certainty and see all that God can do when we truly live in faith.

CHAPTER TEN

Watching God work is one of the most exciting things about the Christian life. Usually what makes it so exciting is the fact that He does the unexpected. Just when we think we've got God figured out, He does exactly the opposite of what we thought He was going to do. And of course it turns out better than we could have ever imagined. God thrives in the midst of our uncertainty. That's why we are called to a life of faith. We have all gone through seasons of uncertainty. Perhaps we don't know what the future holds regarding our job. Perhaps we don't know what will happen in our relationships or marriage. Perhaps we don't know how our children will thrive as adults. Life is uncertain. That is a given. There is no way to avoid the ambiguity and insecurity that life throws our way. We can prepare ourselves for every variable, and still be surprised at what happens in the course of our daily lives. This is where living a life of faith begins to be real for us. We may say that we have faith, but that faith isn't really tested until we don't know what tomorrow is going to bring and there is no way for us as humans to fix it. We love to be in control. We love to have all the information. We love to have plans and backup plans and insurance for when our plans and backup plans don't work out. But the uncertainty that is guaranteed to us in life requires that we live in such a way that we can find resilience in the darkest of days, when our sight is limited, when our understanding is

incomplete. It seems that only when we come to the point when we realize that we ourselves are inadequate for the task of living can we truly begin to see what God may have planned for us.

I remember So. Many. Days. of uncertainty in my life, especially my life in India. Before we went to India, we were all packed and ready to go, support raised, quit our jobs, moved out of our apartment, and then our Indian leaders told us we should come two months later than we had originally anticipated. This uncertainty generated feelings of disappointment and made us wonder if we were even wanted. The email came through and we wondered if it had all been a hoax. Had we gone through all the preparation only to be let down and our life upended?

When we finally arrived in India, nothing went according to our plan. Nothing went according to our schedule. We were left so many days wondering what would happen next, when we would go on excursions, what work we would do, if we would have an office, or if anyone really wanted us to join the team. We labored onward, knowing that God had a plan, but our feelings ranged from excitement to disillusionment, wondering what the heck was going on.

When we made our first trip to Language School, we didn't know if we had a room reserved at the guest house, we didn't know where the language school was, we didn't know how to get a textbook, and we didn't know how to pay our fees! We felt especially hopeless because we were far in the north of India in an unfamiliar place with unfamiliar people, and no access to internet or phone. We had been in India for six months already and thought we were "over" culture shock. However, a new level of uncertainty gripped our hearts as we settled in to our new hill station home.

When a tsunami hit southern India the day after Christmas in 2004, we were certain that we wouldn't be involved in the relief efforts. However, phone calls from all over the world began pouring in to my home office on the top floor of the apartment building we lived in at the time. Funds were racing into the organization's bank account with high expectations that we would save people's lives, rebuild their homes, and provide a livelihood for those whose incomes had been surreptitiously removed with one giant wave from the Indian Ocean. How would we do this? Why were people calling me? We didn't even have any staff in place! People were relying on us to do what needed to be done, but we didn't know how any of it would happen.

When my dear elderly colleague got sick with cancer and decided to remain in India, we lived in a constant state of uncertainty regarding his health. He was certain that he wanted to allow Indians to treat him and serve all his remaining days in this land that he loved. However, those of us around him didn't know what would happen during this season of medical care. Ultimately, when the Lord took him home after his battle with disease, we didn't know the process for dealing with death in a foreign country. We had to ask questions and navigate this previously unknown territory all the while feeling fear and all the expectations of the family on our shoulders.

Eventually, when Kevin was refused entry to the country at the Indian immigration counter and when I was told to leave the country by the chief of police because someone had filed false complaints of misdeeds we had supposedly committed, we faced three months of uncertainty regarding our future in India, our home, our children's education, the fate of our beloved pet dog Fiona, and our future involvement with the ministry in general.

We didn't know from day to day whether I'd be escorted out of the country or thrown in jail because of my refusal to leave the country. We didn't know if our children would be kidnapped and held for ransom by those who held such animosity towards us and had spread vicious slander against us. We knew that God was in control, but we had no idea what He was doing.

We lived with unusually high levels of uncertainty and ambiguity and insecurity for 20 years. It became a way of life. But what also became a way of life was resilience. I had grown up a child, a teen and a young adult of resilience, but now as a grown up woman my ability to be resilient was put to the test… and it held true. Through all the uncertainty, I made it through. I survived. I thrived. In fact, I think I began to crave uncertainty. I loved the freedom of not making plans. I loved the ability to change my mind at the last minute. I loved the fact that my commitments were loose and provisional. What initially caused me great anxiety soon became a way of life. In fact, it was a way of life that began to shape me as a person and shape the way I lived my life even when I returned to my home culture. I had leaned in to the uncertainty and found that I loved it.

You see, leaning in to the uncertainty of life breeds resilience. Leaning in breeds resilience not only in personal life, but also in professional life, in education and in ministry. Leaning in to uncertainty rather than avoiding it allows us to learn. More broadly, as we've talked about before, a culture of learning is essential to maximizing all that uncertainty and ambiguity have to offer. Cultivating a culture of learning at home, at work and at church creates a level of faith that allows space for this ambiguity, uncertainty, and, in general, lack of timely knowledge. Our western culture values certainty, permanence and guarantees. The

professional and political worlds demand these things for sure. I have had the joy, though, of working my entire professional life in the religious non-profit sector, something that is a different beast all in itself. Christian ministry, volunteerism and church work are not neat and clean. In fact, there is a certain beauty in the clutter and confusion that sometimes comes with the territory of doing God's work. Decisions take time. Plans and strategies don't crystalize overnight. Funding isn't there for even the best of ideas. Volunteers generally can't be "fired" and sometimes plague us with their demands and haughty attitudes. Implementing the best of ideas is sometimes met with opposition, discouragement and resistance. Being a learner in the uncertainty, however, allows for all of this disorder. Being a learner who enthusiastically endures ambiguity realizes that there is so much to be learned along the journey of creating something meaningful for the people of Jesus.

In the resulting chaos, therefore, as people who value learning and process, we must find a way to manage our emotions and intellect when things are not presented to us clearly and concretely as we would prefer. Ambiguity offers all of us the chance to have meaningful conversation, whether it's related to the task at hand, or whether it's regarding our feelings about the present lack of assuredness. Some of us will never feel comfortable in ambiguous circumstances, but we don't have to have surety to have success. I imagine the disciples of Jesus rarely understood clearly what Jesus was doing! They likely dealt with a massive amount of uncertainty every day. Yet, their ministry was overwhelmingly effective because their commitment to learn from the Savior was strong. Likewise, if we are able to manage ourselves as learners when ambiguity inevitably arises, we will be able to deepen our learning

and understanding of the ministry, as well as develop our relationship with those whom we serve alongside.

Relationships are indeed the key. Embracing uncertainty in planning and in scheduling and in life in general allows us the space we need to put relationships first. How many times in India were we waiting for something to happen and therefore had the opportunity to talk to someone new or deepen our relationship with an acquaintance or casual friend? If we had adhered to our plan, stuck to our schedule, the relationships would have suffered. Jesus put relationships first. He was the first one to take an extra moment in the midst of a busy agenda to talk to someone who needed healing. He was the one who spent time He likely didn't have with the poor and marginalized of society. He was the one who took time away from His packed-out travel itineraries to spend time in prayer away from the crowds and His disciples. After all, we were created for relationship. Many times, though, we sacrifice our relationships in an effort to guarantee ourselves the certainty that comes with a schedule, the confidence that comes with being on time, or the assurance that comes with a strategy efficiently executed. Sure, those are all good things. However, relationships with one another are better. God has remarkable things planned for our interactions with others if we are willing to embrace the ambiguity that comes with change and pour our lives into people rather than plans. People are hurting and in need. They are desperate for someone to listen to them. They need friends who put them first over the demands of everyday life. They crave someone who can see them, hear them, and know them intimately.

It is the desire to be seen, heard and known that requires those of us who are leaders, or those of us who have had more life

experiences to use our wisdom well. We know from experience that life is uncertain. Many times, we become cynical or impatient with younger ones who are experiencing that uncertainty for the first time. This happened to me multiple times while I was in India. After I had lived there for a number of years, after I had gone through the various stages of culture shock and cultural adaptation, I became used to the uncertainty and ambiguity that we inevitably faced. When new people would come, initially I would simply tell them to expect uncertainty and then I would expect them to cope with it and be able to thrive! That was not exercising wisdom on my part. Everyone must experience life in order to understand it. Therefore, I needed to exercise "Wisdom with Compassion" (thank you, Cynthia Bourgeault) with the many dear folks who came through India with enthusiasm and beautiful naivety. Yes, I knew the way forward, but I had to lead first with compassion. My first job was to listen to them, to hear their hearts and be a constant source of safety for them in a time that felt incredibly insecure to them. I eventually learned this valuable leadership lesson and was able to be what people needed me to be. Empathy was key. I reserved judgment and withheld my opinions, having learned that nothing I could offer would be of assistance until each unique individual was ready for what God had in store for them.

This is how all ministry is. Service to God needs leaders who are willing to take a back seat while people figure things out on their own. The only sure thing in life overseas and in ministry (in life, too!) is that there will be uncertainty. We have to learn about it on our own and with our own tribe. Life lessons cannot be commanded in this regard, nor do they follow a strict timeline. God allows people to grow as and when they are ready. He never

forces growth. Neither should we. On their own, our friends and colleagues must learn to embrace uncertainty, learn to accept it, love it, and operate within it. It will be complex and messy and full of trial and error. I can all but guarantee we won't like this process! We won't like the effort it takes to move through a life of complexity. But the lessons learned in the process will be well worth the effort and will teach us all critical lessons that cannot be learned in any other way.

There are certainly things we can do to make the uncertainty feel better. My opinion, though, is that these coping mechanisms are generally only a Band-Aid ® solution to the larger problem of simply enduring and embracing ambiguity. Nothing can replace time and experience. However, we as a society, in our desire for the concrete and the permanent and the certain, have done our best to create ways in which the blow of the unknown can be lessened. These are not sure-fire solutions that will solve every problem related to the uncertainty of life. However, these few attempts at lessening the sting of uncertainty's pain will be helpful in getting us through the toughest of times until a sense of true understanding has a chance to settle in.

First, we can mitigate the uncomfortable feelings of uncertainty through timely and proactive communication. As a leader of hundreds of people in my lifetime, most of whom I led in a cross-cultural setting, I learned that communication is the balm of a myriad of ambiguity-related hurts. I learned, this, of course, because I failed at communicating over and over again. I am an introvert by nature, and so communication for me is not natural. I much prefer sending an email or a text message to someone, communicating with a written word, rather than a verbal word. However, that was not the way most of the people

under my leadership needed me to communicate. They required me to spend time face to face with them, no matter how awkward the situation, talking through the trouble they were facing, bringing them safety through in-person conversations and security through my listening ear. They needed me to reach out to them and not simply "be available" in case they needed me. I failed to learn that people in crisis refuse to reach out for help. It is not within them. They cannot bring themselves to do it. The uncertainty has paralyzed them and they need for their leader to notice them, realize their paralysis and take the initiative to bring them healing and restoration in their time of severe insecurity. I didn't do this. This was a major failing of my leadership. I was thankful to have eventually seen my inadequacy in this area and I have been working on making improvements. I feel sorry for all of those I led to whom I did not give what they required of me. Proactive communication in a timely manner is the covering we all need which will not necessarily bring certainty, but it will bring comfort and an assuredness of support during times that feel unbalanced and unstable.

Learning about others is another way to make sense of the world and bring feelings of security during ambiguous times. When activities or events are uncertain, we often look for someone to blame. This was vastly prevalent in our work in India. Whenever something did not go to plan, we sought after the person we could approach to figure out what was happening and why things didn't turn out in the way we had expected. We wanted to hold that person accountable. Most often, when confronted, that person didn't give us the answers we wanted. They did not measure up to our own expectations, nor our own standards for how programs should be run or how ministry should be

conducted. Inevitably, we would (erroneously) assign a value judgment to their character. This was not right. Instead, had we taken the time to learn more about that person and how they respond to stress, how they operate, how they think, and their own personal leadership style, our own emotions would have been mitigated and our judgment could have been withheld. Our own culture has developed so many ways for us to explore the personalities of those with whom we interact. Personality and leadership inventories like the Meyers Briggs, Strengthsfinder, and the Enneagram are popular and helpful. People want to know why what they encounter with others might be happening. They have a longing for meaning. These tests help to provide some of that meaning. And yet, they are not a perfect substitute for leaning in to uncertainty and letting time and experience be our ultimate guide.

Finally, and probably the most helpful coping mechanism when dealing with ambiguity and uncertainty whether at home or in some other culture, is changing our own viewpoint. It's likely the most helpful, but also the most difficult. It is not an easy task to change our thinking about the world. It is not easy to change the way we view others and view the things that are happening all around us. However, if we are in some way able to take a step back, see the bigger picture, realize that there are factors at play that are bigger than ourselves, then we are more likely to be able to live at peace in turbulent times. There came a time while we were living in India that our own personal physical safety became compromised due some people who were threatening our organization. Our Indian leadership suggested we install security cameras both outside and inside our house. We initially met this suggestion with fear and with indignation. We felt it was both an

invasion to our privacy, as well as an extreme step. Surely, we thought, no one would go to the audacious step of harming us. But we knew that submitting to the authority of our leadership was the wise thing to do. We installed the cameras and changed our view of the situation. We embraced the uncertainty of our own physical safety and recognized the security that having our home on video surveillance could bring. We had to remember that living in faith is hope in things unseen and hope in things not understood. We didn't know what was going to happen to us and we didn't understand how we could move forward in safety, but we surrendered to the uncertainty knowing we were in God's hands.

Being in God's hands is certainly the safest and most confident place we can be. I'll never forget, however, when the thing I started to become most uncertain about was my own relationship with God. That was something new for me and something which I began to realize so many people struggle with. It was a new journey God would take me on, one which would lead me to new levels of resiliency I never thought possible.

CHAPTER ELEVEN

I've mentioned before that I grew up in a conservative religious household. We loved Jesus, we loved church, and I didn't know any other kind of life other than one of dedication to God and service to Him. I am thankful for that upbringing which taught me all about the scriptures and all about living a life of morality that served me very well. This belief system was all I knew. It was what carried me through my childhood, teen years and into young adulthood. I felt as if I was 100% certain from an early age of everything I believed about God and how He operated. I was absolutely positive that I knew both my eternal fate, the eternal fate of those who believed as I did, and the eternal fate of those who did not believe as I did. There were no doubts in my mind. In fact, I was taught that doubt was something I should not have. Doubt was a failing. Poor Doubting Thomas. He was looked-down-upon as a lesser disciple. He should have simply believed in Jesus without having to see! But no, he had to see and touch in order to believe. What a shame.

I landed in India with all of these faith certainties firmly in place. Frankly, I thought I knew everything there was to know about God and the Bible and the Christian faith. I was ready to counsel anyone who needed spiritual counseling. I had an enormous amount of confidence. Or, perhaps I should call it arrogance. I was not at all expecting what would happen. I was not expecting a full overhaul of my faith that would leave me with

lots of questions that needed answers and lots of my own personal doubts about what was true and what was false. About what was important to conclude upon and what could be left open for discussion. About who had a genuine relationship with Jesus Christ and who was missing the mark. In the end, I realized that my own judgmental spirit was in need of a complete overhaul and that uncertainty in my relationship with God was perhaps one of the most unsettling things I would ever experience. As I began to embrace uncertainty in my own physical and emotional life while living in a foreign culture, I clung to my perceived spiritual certainty. Eventually, even that produced unexpected ambiguity which threw me for a loop.

Two months after we arrived in India, in December 1998, the worst persecution unleashed against Christians ever recorded in India broke out on a national level. Churches were burned, pastors were beaten, nuns were raped, and Australian missionary Graham Staines and his two young sons were martyred. The nation and the world were stunned by these heinous hate crimes, but the Christian leadership in India were not fully surprised. For several years, Christians had been responding to an extraordinary response by India's low caste, poor and marginalized people to Jesus. Christians were reaching out with love and compassion to these millions of people who had been rejected from the Hindu caste system for thousands of years. As a result, these forgotten people were being empowered and were finding a life of hope as never before. Not surprisingly, this drew the ire of upper caste society against the Christians for upsetting the social norms and persecution broke out. Nonetheless, Christians persisted and the Christian Church began to grow.

I remember so distinctly sitting in the office of Joseph D'souza in mid-1999 when he received a phone call. The few of us who were with him chatted idly while he took the call, a seemingly normal interaction taking place. When he concluded the call, we asked who he had talked to. He replied that it had been one of our leaders in North India. Apparently, a group of 10,000 low caste people in a village there had chosen to follow Jesus on their own. They had heard about Jesus from some neighboring Christians, didn't know much about Him, but knew they wanted to embrace the Christian faith. These 10,000 people now needed discipleship and were asking our organization to help. Of course we would help, Joseph replied matter-of-factly. This was not an unusual phone call during this time period. 10,000 here, 6,000 there. People were turning en masse to Jesus freely and they needed help in learning more about their newfound faith. They knew only that God loved them and considered them equal to all other people. That in itself was ground-breaking information for them. They wanted this God in their lives immediately. They were ready to dedicate themselves wholeheartedly to Jesus Christ. These were exciting times and seemed to be just the start of something huge.

We were so privileged to be in India during these remarkable times in the Church's history. We saw the beginning of the Good Shepherd Church of India, a fully indigenous group of churches that almost accidentally established 1,500 churches in its first few years of operation. We were pleased to walk alongside their pastors and priests, train their administrators, and encourage their people. The majority of the people in those churches were women and people from the lower sectors of society, all of whom faced tremendous oppression. For them, Christ brought not only hope

for a positive future, but also confidence and dignity for a better today. We were thrilled to see God's Kingdom being built here on earth among these dear ones who not only received the spiritual teaching and growth they desired, but also community transformation in the form of education, healthcare, economic development, leadership training, and human trafficking prevention. What started out as a fledgling few churches and good-hearted Indian Christian workers trying to be professional, ended in a massive Church movement and education system that touched the lives of 14 million people by the time we left the country after 20 years of service.

What was remarkable about our time with the Good Shepherd Churches, however, was that there was so much freedom in choosing how these new believers and freshly formed congregations were going to "do church". There was no pressure or expectation for them to conform to a denominational prescription. There was no foreign influence pressuring them to comply to a set of cultural norms. So, as the church began to grow, and the need for structure and consistency in theology and teaching became more and more important, the church leadership took several years to study the Scriptures and to glean from Church history all that would be best for this church movement of marginalized peoples. What did they need? How was God most relevant to them? What made the Christian faith something they wanted to embrace? There were so many options to consider and so many good ways of doing church. Ultimately, after seven years of research and prayer and good discussion, my Indian colleagues who had formed the Good Shepherd Church of India settled on doing church in the Anglican tradition. This left me unsettled.

I had grown up somehow believing that any of the church traditions that used "Form" in addition to "Word" were somehow using their rituals and ceremonies as an addition to their faith. That their personal belief in Jesus was not sufficient for salvation. I also believed that the appointment of Bishops and Priests and Archbishops and Deacons was no longer what the Bible called for with regard to church leadership. In addition, I had been conditioned to believe that women should not be ordained, and that drinking wine for communion was sinful. I remember praying so hard as a young girl for those of my friends who went to Catholic Church as children. If only they could truly come to Christ! The truth? My view of Anglicanism, Catholicism and all types of traditional church was limited, ill-informed, and just plain wrong. I didn't know that at the time, however, and I started to get worried about this ministry that I had given my life to. Was it all going to come crashing down? How would I explain all this to the partners and donors who had committed themselves to our work? How would I explain this to our own prayer partners? But first? How would I explain this to myself and come to some kind of understanding? I was shaken to my core and plagued with a level of spiritual uncertainty that I'd never before encountered. However, God had something special in store for me that I never would have experienced if I had continued in my comfortable convictions.

While this is not a book about Anglicanism (although if you don't know about Anglicanism, I encourage you to study it and its people!), it was through my embracing of the Anglican traditions that I also began to embrace the reality that our relationship with God is full of uncertainty, and that that is okay. When my leaders announced that we would start following the Anglican tradition, I

knew their decision had come from God, was best for the poor, outcast people we were reaching, and that it was time for me to get on board with it. For me, this meant reading and doing research. So I got every book I could about Anglicanism. I read about the traditions of the Anglican faith. How they do church, what their structure is like, why they follow a liturgical worship pattern, how their church calendar benefits the body of Christ. I wanted to know everything there was to know. Even in my newly realized uncertainty, I was desperate for something certain to hold on to. I learned about the Eucharist and about incense and about bells and about confession and about the historical prayers. Through all this learning I found that there was so much meaning and richness. There was a depth of spiritual understanding and genuine relationship with God that I had never before considered.

And then I started interacting with Anglicanism's people. Let me tell you... they were some of the most loving people I had ever met. They were open and accepting and forgiving. They wanted to know me and my background. They loved their faith and traditions, while at the same time loving the culture around them and loving their neighbors more than themselves. They were compassionate and wanted to serve. The priests in the parishes, in addition to the bishops and the archbishops, were well-loved by the parishioners because it was obvious that the church leadership cared for the people genuinely. They knew their people's names and life situations. They prayed for them and called on them at home. They took up special offerings and helped people in the community in practical ways. They were quick to bless and slow to judge. What a change this was for me. This all-pervasive love that the Anglican Church displayed was remarkable and stunning and attractive. I wanted this for the Good Shepherd Church. I wanted

this for the poor, marginalized and outcast of India. I wanted this in my life and the life of my own children.

My first experience attending an Anglican church service was in one of America's Anglican cathedrals and the Archbishop was presiding. I had met him previously when he visited India. When he visited India, we rolled out the red carpet of hospitality for him. There were garlands and shawls and sweets and fancy hotels and air-conditioned cars and special foods. You name it, we provided it for him. He, however, was an authentically humble man who shared with us his touching testimony. He didn't require all the pomp and circumstance and even insisted we call him by his first name rather than the traditional "Your Grace". (We refused.) I spent quite a lot of time with the Archbishop during his visit to India escorting him from meetings to meals and driving him from place to place. However, he was busy talking to others and he travels the world widely and meets so, so many people. That morning when I was at his church, I walked respectfully to the front of the church to receive the Eucharist and as he approached me, he smiled and said, "This is His Body Given for you, Leah." He remembered my name! How was that possible, I thought? To me, this reflected all of Anglicanism's love for God and love for others. This was something I had never even considered trying to know or to learn. But now God was blessing me with it.

I thought I had known it all. I thought I had the answer to all of life's spiritual questions. I thought I was crystal clear on what the Bible said about everything. I had no doubts. And then God intervened. He loved me so much to introduce uncertainty into my life. He took me to India to teach me something I never, ever would have considered had I continued living in America. He allowed me to be a casual by-stander while He built an amazing

church movement that transformed the lives of millions of people who didn't need certainty to embrace Him. In fact, many of those who chose to follow Christ initially out of their Hindu or other religious background didn't really know what it meant to be a Christian. They simply knew that the Christian God would give them hope. And so they believed. There were no in-depth apologetics to overcome first. There were no weeks of Bible study first. There were no classes that ultimately led to their choice to follow Christ. They were uncertain about all things except one fact: God wanted a relationship with them. So they jumped. They accepted Him. And now it was time for them to build their Church and love on one another with this love that only Jesus can bring. They didn't know what to do next. They didn't know how to grow in their faith. They didn't know anything about becoming a mature Christian. They just knew they wanted Jesus. Today that movement is sweeping across the country and is changing India from within. And it was all born out of uncertainty and ambiguity.

What I had never realized until I saw this great movement of God among the poor and marginalized of India was that my desire for certainty in my faith was holding me back. It had prevented me from acknowledging that God is actually a mystery. Sure, we always said that "God works in mysterious ways", but in reality, I would come up with a reason for every single one of God's actions in my life and the lives of others. I think I even was so bold to think that I had a special connection to God; that He would tell me His reasons for acting and that I was to be His messenger to others. I thought perhaps I was bringing people hope by easing their uncertainty in difficult times. In reality, I was simply proving my arrogance. We cannot know what God is doing. We don't need to know why He is acting. It's not our job to know

why He is acting. It's our job to love Him and to love others. That's it. He will act in His time and in His way and we get to sit as spectators on the sidelines and marvel at His goodness, even in the midst of trouble. Our entire belief system is based on FAITH which means we are supposed to accept the unseen; receive the unknown. Unfortunately, we are not there. But we can take steps in that direction.

My desire for certainty also prevented me from loving people who either believed differently than I believed or who did not live up to the standards that I had set based on my own interpretation of scriptures and general faith principles. In fact, I think actually I never learned to love. I had learned many valuable and meaningful things in my Christian upbringing, but how to love others was never one of them. For that I hold on to so much regret. I judged people so harshly. If they had questions about their faith, I rebuked them. Even as a young child I would scorn those who questioned whether or not the Bible was true. As a young 20-something, people began questioning the authenticity of the Old Testament and I was livid! Of course it's true! It's the Word of God! I would beat them over the head with my prideful certainty. I would never take the time to listen to them, to hear their doubts and to acknowledge that they were having trouble reconciling God's loving character with the God of the Old Testament who seemed vengeful and merciless. Their "fight or flight" instincts were kicking in because they were facing uncertainty about God and about scripture. They needed my love and listening ear. Not my judgment and condemnation. Alas.

As I finally began to embrace uncertainty with regard to my faith and with regard to my beliefs about God and His character, a whole new world of relationship opened up to me. Sure, I had

grown so much in this area in my physical and emotional life, but now it was time for similar growth in my spirit and soul. I began to notice that my newfound openness broadened my perspective about God and reality. It helped me, above all, to love others more deeply. It grew my empathy quotient multi-fold. As I saw people through a filter of love rather than judgment, I could feel what they were feeling. I understood them more deeply. I was able to relate to them in ways I'd never been able to relate before. Soon, bridges of trust were built and people were willing to share with me their concerns, knowing that I would love them no matter what they told me. I was able to bring people hope in their times of uncertainty rather than simply trying to fix their problems and giving them a false sense of confidence that would last only a few short minutes. Hope is more pervasive than certainty and can last through all our seasons of life. Certainty is based on circumstances and is not something upon which we can rely. However, despite the fact that God is a mystery and we may never fully understand Him this side of Heaven, we can be certain in His love for us and we can extend that love to others. Our ability to embrace the mystery of God wholeheartedly will build in us a long-lasting spiritual resilience that conquers fear and gives us what we need to love one another unconditionally and do God's good work in this uncertain life.

HEART STORIES...
PART THREE

Food is such a huge part of my life. I love to buy food, look at food, handle food, cook food and eat food. I love to express my creativity through my cooking. I love to feed people and watch them eat food I have cooked for them. I even find cleaning up after cooking and serving a meal somewhat satisfying. (Although I will never turn down someone's offer to wash the dishes for me!) Food is a part of every celebration in our family, a part of every major event. Food is a part of every gathering, every meeting, and every casual time of discussion together with a dear friend. Yes, it's true. My life basically revolves around food.

It follows naturally, then, that I spent a lot of time in India learning to cook with Indian ingredients, learning to cook Indian dishes, and learning to cook American meals that my Indian friends might like. Although I was never very good at forming relationships or inviting people for a meal, it was always in my heart to do so. When it did happen, I was thrilled to have people to the house and get the opportunity to feed them. I prepared the menu days in advance, joyfully bought the required ingredients, and began cooking with enough time to have the kitchen all cleaned up before the guests arrived. When they came, the table would be set and we'd be all ready to eat.

That, of course, would be where I made my cultural error.

Time after time, I would escort guests into our home, direct them to the table and fill them with all the food that I'd cooked for them. We'd have lovely conversation over the dinner table and they would "ooo" and "aaah" over the delicious dishes that I had prepared. (Unless, of course, I had cooked Indian food, at which point they would say it was good, "For an American". Sigh.) But then, as soon as the meal was over and we would want to move to

the living room for a cup of coffee and more conversation, our guests would instead move to the door, put on their shoes, and start to leave. What was happening? Did we offend them? Were we bad hosts? Time after time we were left questioning what in the world had happened. Apparently we were slow learners.

What we weren't noticing in every other time we had eaten dinner at someone's home or at an event at the church or at our organization's headquarters was that in the Indian culture, people do not eat immediately upon arrival. In fact, the eating is the last thing people do before leaving. We would go to birthday parties that started at 6:00pm and included dinner, but the dinner wouldn't be served until 9:00pm. We would go to a housewarming party that promised a meal, but there was a two-hour ceremony dedicating the home to the Lord first. We would arrive on time to a dinner invitation to someone's home and they wouldn't have even started cooking the food yet. We would sit talking for an hour and then the wife would excuse herself to begin prepping the meal. Most times we were irritated and hungry and a little confused. Why couldn't people eat earlier and according to our time table?! (Obviously, our stomachs ruled our lives!)

What we almost refused to learn, however, was that the actual eating is not the featured part of any event that included a meal. The gathering for talking and sharing and being together as friends and family is the main event. The spending time connecting with one another is the point. Only after a good amount of time spent together is completed do the hosts invite you to come to the table and enjoy the food they have cooked. In fact, there might not be conversation during the meal because, well, it would be rude to talk with your mouth full! And the woman of the house would be busy serving the food and running back and forth from the

kitchen. When the meal was finished, it would be time to go. No after dinner lingering. No final cup of coffee. It would be late and people would need to get to bed.

All that time when we had been feeding people immediately upon their arrival at our house, we had been unknowingly signaling to our guests that we just wanted a short time together by serving the meal first. It wasn't until our very last year of living in India that we finally understood what to do. (As I said, slow learners. We felt so accomplished, in an ashamed way, when we finally figured it out.) Food was never the point. Relationship was the point. This was a major cultural shift for us. Not necessarily a shift away from American culture, but definitely a shift away from "Kadwell Culture". But it was one that we were happy to make. By that time we valued relationship and were ready and willing to do what it took to build deep friendships with people that would last a lifetime.

❉ ❉ ❉ ❉

For two or three years at the beginning of our time in India, I taught English to first-year students in our organization's Bachelor of Theology program. I was qualified to teach these courses not because I had my teaching degree, but simply because I spoke English. I did the best I could to prepare for these classes and drew upon everything I could remember from high school English to help me develop some sort of meaningful curriculum. I wish I had had some training in English as a Foreign Language, but I did not. I just did the best I could with what I had.

My students were ages 18-25, came from rural villages around India, and spoke absolutely no English. They were often fluent in

more than one of the many Indian languages, but not in English. Because of the isolated nature of the villages from which they came, many had not even heard English spoken, let alone had any framework for how to speak English themselves. Needless to say, I had my work cut out for me. Most days I would teach my lessons (in English, of course) and wonder how much of anything I was saying they were understanding. From the looks of their homework, they weren't understanding much. I longed to get through to them somehow.

More than just teaching English, though, I looked at these English classes as a way to build relationships with these young people and do some fun and meaningful youth ministry among them. I was fresh from America at that point where I had been doing youth ministry for a few years and was eager to get back to the type of work that had been dear to my heart. I wanted to get to know the students, hear their hearts, and help them to grow in their relationship with Jesus. Before and after class I would do my best to somehow connect with the students despite our language barrier. Our broken conversations showed them that I cared, even if we couldn't communicate clearly.

To try to make English class fun, I would incorporate games into the lesson plans to try to help the learning stick in these students' brains. Let's just say that some games were more academic than others. Most of them were competitions of some sort, relay races that required them to know certain parts of speech before the next person could take their turn. The students found this type of teaching interesting and exciting. Their cheers and laughter would fill the room as the game went on. Their smiles were infectious and I enjoyed watching them have some fun in the midst of their otherwise hectic study program. They

would always ask me, "What game will we play today?" in their broken English. It was nice to be liked.

My most "famous" (or infamous?) game, however, was one that took things probably a step too far. Class was held in our organization's main auditorium. It had theater seating and a cement floor. I did the best I could to run my games around this awkward setup. There wasn't much room, but there seemed to be enough at the front of the auditorium for what I had in mind. This game required students to come to the whiteboard, take their turn as individuals to answer a question in writing, and then, along with their teammates, create a human pyramid. The first team to complete their human pyramid after answering all the questions correctly would win.

I had intended for the students to create this human pyramid by kneeling down on the ground, and then kneeling on the backs of one another into formation. However, the English language not being the students' strong point, they misunderstood the instructions. Instead of kneeling, they began standing upright onto each other's shoulders. All of my attempts to direct them otherwise failed as they became so excited to build their pyramids. The formations quickly became very tall, very unstable pyramids. One team realized what was happening and didn't even try to build their pyramid to the maximum height. The other team, however, was determined to win. They built the pyramid four levels high so that the person on top was touching the ceiling of the auditorium. I couldn't believe my eyes! And that's when things took a turn for the worse.

It was as if everything was moving in slow motion. The pyramid came tumbling down. The fellow on top began to fall and hit the cement floor with a huge crash. Thankfully he broke his

fall with his hands and not his head. However, he got up in obvious pain, holding his arm. Yes, that's right, he had broken his arm. In English class. Not on the cricket field. Not wrestling with his friends. He broke his arm in English class. I couldn't believe it. I felt so bad. I quit playing that game, and most other games after that day.

I don't know if the students remember anything about nouns, verbs and sentence structure from my English classes. But I'm 100% certain that they remember the day someone broke their arm in my class. Hopefully they also remember how sorry I was and that I cared for them all deeply. Today most of them are graduates of our program and do speak English with some level of mastery. I'm proud of all of them for their persistence and look forward to the day when I hear reports of their good accomplishments for the Kingdom.

❀❀❀❀

"Just ask Leah. She can do it."

This became a familiar phrase heard during my time in India. This was not with regard to my willingness to complete administrative tasks or organize schedules or run events. That would have been natural and easy for me to do and well within my gifting. I love to create order from disorder and check things off my to-do lists.

But, no. This request was something very different indeed.

Whenever any kind of awkward topic of conversation arose or challenging seminar topic was on the schedule, my Indian colleagues turned to me to tackle it head on. I guess I had gained a reputation for being fearless and bold. "Get the American girl to

do it. She'll do anything!" (I'm not sure if that's good or bad...) I had become known for saying the words that other women were afraid to say. I had developed a method of choosing gentle words for topics that reflected the harsh realities of life. And so, with a lot of prayer, I agreed on many occasions to tackle these oftentimes taboo topics.

As a newlywed 25-year-old, I spoke to young single women about the details of sex within marriage and the physical uniqueness of the male body.

As a young woman in her late 20s, I spoke to a group of 50 pastor's wives in Northern India about how women can also have pleasure in the marital sexual relationship.

In my 30s, I took questions and answers from a room of 300 women leaders on the physical abuse that women face in marriage and what they should do when their husband beats them, knowing that in Indian culture there is no recourse for a woman. She must simply pray and wait for God to intervene in her husband's heart.

On many occasions, I taught young women about to get married on the various options for birth control and family planning.

I instructed young women on how to stay clean and fresh during their monthly menstruation time.

I answered questions from women trying to conceive children on the best time to conceive, how to know if they were pregnant, and when to approach the doctor if they felt there was a fertility problem.

I spoke with unmarried women in their 30s who were longing for a husband and encouraged them to continue praying and waiting instead of taking matters into their own hands. I

encouraged them to honor their parents wishes and to honor the norms and culture of their family.

I never let people use my American culture as an excuse for me to give them "permission" to do something that would dishonor Indian culture. I always pointed them back to their parents, their family, and the culture of their own hometown. There were many times, especially with teenagers or young adults, when they would want to be able to say "Sister Leah says…." to their parents or elders as a means of using my authority to get their way in some divisive situation. However, I was grateful to be able to discern what was happening and would challenge them on this and direct them back to the people in their lives who held true authority.

In all of these situations, I felt incredibly awkward. I had to steel myself every time I had to talk about sex or marriage or any of the other topics we don't generally talk about. I had to be so careful not to mix my American opinions into the conversation. I had to defer whenever possible to my Indian friends and colleagues and hope that they would instead answer the tough questions. When they wouldn't, I would pray that God would give me wisdom in my answers. I feel that most times He did and I am so thankful.

I will never forget the time, however, that there were no answers for a dear sister in North India who came to me in tears at a women's meeting. She was desperate to have a child and had tried everything to conceive. She and her husband were doing everything right. She had seen doctors and taken medications. But still there was no child. She came to me hoping that I would give her some kind of magic advice that would produce the child in her womb. Instead, I told her I had no answers. She would just have

to continue praying and waiting. That day I placed my hands on her, prayed, and then sent her off with God's blessing.

Three years later I saw the same woman at another similar women's meeting. This time she was holding a toddler in her arms. Her smile was so broad and bright. She had the child she had prayed for. It was a miracle and she was so thankful to God for his provision in her life.

It is that kind of miracle that propelled me onward in having the awkward conversations. It is remembering that being willing to say things others were too scared to say could make a tangible difference in the lives of so many people that helped me to persist when I was embarrassed or didn't quite know how to approach the most delicate of topics. That woman holding that toddler was a delightful reward for all the awkwardness. God gave that to me as a special reminder that He is in every moment of our lives, even the uncomfortable ones that make us tongue-tied.

❀❀❀❀

The clock on the wall read 2:00am. I was exhausted, trying to keep my eyes open. I was so thankful it was almost time. Almost time for what, you ask? It was one of my favorite times of the year. It was mid-December and the temperatures had finally dropped. We were able to wear light sweaters in the mornings and evenings. We were able to put the blankets on the beds at night. We had decorated the house with all our Christmas decorations. For us this meant multiple Christmas trees, garlands, and a huge amount of sparkling decorations and lights. Everything felt warm and cozy and comfortable. My spirits were high and it was a delight to be at home.

All of a sudden we could hear a gentle rumbling and some conversation start to come down our street. "They're coming!" I shouted to the rest of the family. Clark and Claire had gone to sleep, so I roused them from their beds. We all ran to throw the front doors open as we heard the clapping begin and drum start to beat. And then the singing rang out.

The Christmas Carolers were here.

Yes, that's right. At 2:00am, our church's Christmas carolers had arrived at our house. Every year, for one week, the church sends out the church youth group to sing carols at every church member's house. They visit 20-25 homes every night for a week. They sing 3-4 songs, then pray for the family, eat some snacks, all before moving on to the next home. The first song they sing every year upon entering the house was Joy to the World, and the last song after prayer was always, interestingly, Feliz Navidad. (I was always amazed to hear our Indian friends singing a Spanish-language song.) They would have a guitar player or two with them to keep them on tune. There would be dancing and someone would always dress up as Santa wearing a Santa mask with white skin. (Why couldn't Santa have Indian skin?)

Usually, they tried to arrange their schedule so they could walk from house to house in one neighborhood, but sometimes the homes were far apart and they had to drive in the church's big blue van. They would start their night at 8:00pm and go on until 3:00am or 4:00am. It was insane. I went with them one year and it was a grueling, yet joyful undertaking. Everyone greets them with so much enthusiasm and with so much food! Families would serve chips and cakes and lots of Sprite or Orange Fanta. By the end of the night it's almost impossible to sing one more note or eat one

more bite. But the excitement of the Christmas season keeps them going and they are so pleased to do it. It really is their duty.

Because of my love for cooking and feeding people, after their first couple years of visits, I began a tradition. I asked the carolers to please make my house either the first house they would come to or the last house they would come to. (Honestly, I always hoped I would be the first house so I wouldn't have to stay up until the wee hours of the morning!) I would prepare for them a special feast of food that they would especially enjoy. I learned that they loved to have "Non-Veg" (meat!) and my specially baked American cakes. So that's what I made for them. I would set out a buffet table full of chicken and cookies and cakes and fudge. The carolers would come, sing their songs, pray for us, and then descend upon the table of food like a cloud of locusts. When they left, there wasn't a scrap of food left. They would stay longer at our house so they could enjoy the food and have a great time of laughter, love and fellowship together with us and one another. If they weren't hungry enough to eat all the food, I prepared special To-Go bags for them and they took the food home to their families.

One year, Kevin's parents were with us for Christmas and for this unique caroling event. We had told them what was about to happen, but I think they didn't quite believe us. Watching them watch the young people completely overtake our house and eat all that food in a matter of just a few minutes was a joyful sight indeed. Their eyes were wide and when the carolers left, they were left speechless. They'd never seen anything like it in their lives. They still talk about the experience to this day.

Of all the things I miss about India, the carolers are definitely in the top ten. It is one of the truly Indian experiences that we

don't have here in America. Sometimes I wish we could start that tradition with our friends. We tell people about it often. We get the same stunned and amazed looks every time we tell the story. But we look back with such fond memories and know that every year the young people will be singing enthusiastically and eating lots and lots of special Christmas treats, hopefully remembering with fondness the good times we had together so many years ago.

EPILOGUE

Our 20 years living, working and learning in India came to a traumatic end. Despite our love for this precious nation, we were eventually the victims of some vicious slander and unfounded accusations that made their way to the highest levels of the Indian government and resulted in our forced removal from the country. Kevin was refused entry to India in late January 2017 when he was returning from an international trip. I was waiting in the airport Arrivals area for him when he called me from a holding cell where he was being interrogated. The officials put him back on the same plane on which he had just arrived and sent him off. He eventually made his way to the US where he took shelter while we figured out what we were going to do.

Early the next morning after the children had gone to school, the police bashed their wooden stick on my front gate, demanded both my attention and my passport, and served me with deportation papers. I told them I had no intention of leaving the country. I explained to the stern looking men that my children were in school and there was no way I could pull them out of school and remove them from the country. This began a three-month fight that included me denying the unfounded accusations against us, and petitioning for the right to stay in the country both with local city officials, as well as with New Delhi-based officials in India's Home Ministry Office. Everyone I met with said some version of, "Madam, if it were up to me you could stay. But you'll have to talk to my supervisor." Despite their seemingly false assurances, they tried everything to convince me to leave. One official even said, "Madam, don't worry about your children. They can stay in India and finish school. But you have to go." Sigh.

Kevin's mom came after a couple weeks to help me manage the house and the kids. What a lifesaver. When Clark finished school in early March 2017, he and Grandma flew home to the US, leaving me and Claire to finish out her school year. My mom arrived in early April 2017 to stay with us for up to a month until Claire finished all her final exams. She would, however, stay only three days.

After three months of uncertainty, petitions, changed plans, and separation as a family, the police finally put their foot down and demanded that I leave. They issued a written warrant for my arrest if I didn't leave within 48 hours. Claire had finished enough of her schooling so we felt it was best that we leave. I packed up a couple of suitcases of clothes, but otherwise left the house completely untouched, hoping we would be able to return to settle our affairs later. Unfortunately that never happened. Our final days in our home in Hyderabad were our final days in India. It was a tragedy to us. Life would never be the same.

After an emotional flight, we landed in America. Tired, worn out, emotionally exhausted, and with faces that were tear-stained. But, we survived. No, scratch that. We thrived. On April 5, 2017, we were re-united as a family in the Minneapolis, St. Paul International Airport. I had left India from Delhi. Claire and my mom had left from Hyderabad and we met up in Dubai. Kevin and Clark were waiting for us in the baggage claim as we came down the stairs from USA immigration. Kevin had grown his beard out, refusing to shave it until we were all safely together once again. The four of us embraced in a big bear hug, happy to be together after months of ambiguity and feeling oh so insecure. The only thing that was certain was that we were a family and that we were now together, ready to begin a new life in our "home"

culture. Of course it didn't feel like our home culture. It felt cold (literally and figuratively) and foreign and unfamiliar. We stayed with my mom in her tiny two-bedroom apartment for six months while we figured out what to do. It was an apartment that we'd stayed in many times before during the previous two decades, but this time we entered it with a certain permanency, a certain inevitability. We continued conversation with India as they dealt with the impact of our departure. Our roles were handed over to others who tried to do them. Our emails slowly started to dwindle. Even in the first few days after our departure, it became apparent that we were no longer a part of the community to which we had given our lives. The emotions were overwhelming, yet unavoidable. Our Indian home was looked after by my Mona. She would stay there for the next six months until we gave her instructions on closing it down. She dealt with our bills and our possessions and all the details of our everyday life that we could no longer handle personally. What a champion she was. Our dog Fiona went to a lovely farm on the outskirts of town until we could send for her. She loved the farm and they treated her like a queen, but we couldn't wait to bring her to be with us.

We didn't know upon our arrival in the USA if we would be headed back to India or whether the USA was now our permanent home. We weren't sure what our roles in the ministry would be. We weren't sure where we would live. We weren't sure if we needed a house or an apartment. We weren't sure if we would need our own car. We weren't sure where we would go to church or who our friends would be. We weren't sure where our kids would go to school. We had so many questions and no answers. Every single person we met asked us what we were going to do. We had no answers for them. We had no answers because we

were mentally and emotionally broken. We had been forced from the only home we had ever known in our adult lives; the only home our children had ever known. Everything was uncertain. Everything was up in the air. And at the same time, every possibility stood before us. We could live anywhere we wanted to live. All things were open to us. We had decisions to make and we actually felt like we were in control of our future. Although the temptation to feel like victims was certainly an easy one to embrace, we chose to embrace a spirit of freedom and saw all the options open to us as a blessing. Within a month of landing in the USA we took off on a two-month road trip around America. It would be a time of prayer and fasting and research and huddling together as a family to make the decisions we needed to make for our future. We traveled to 42 states, plus Canada and Barbados. It was an excellent time for us, one we will never forget. God spoke to us, comforted us, and bonded us together as a family, four people who had shared time together overseas and had experiences together that no one else would ever have. We were uniquely connected.

After our road trip we bought a house in Minneapolis, registered the kids for school, dug in to ministry at Grace Church in Roseville, Minnesota, and began our jobs as professional fundraisers. We would remain connected to God's work in India even though we were based in America. We began to feel that the Lord had intentionally pulled us out of India so that we could work more effectively for the people of India being based in America than we could being based in India. It took about a year for us to realize that we were not doing God's "second best". For that first year in the US, we were plagued with a cloud of depression that we tried to shake, but it was relentless. But then

one day, God revealed to us that, no, our relocation to America was HIS BEST for our lives. It was His ultimate best, His first best for us. We were not on the "B" team. Us being based in America is what He wanted for us at this moment in time and that to be in India would not be right. We oftentimes began to laugh as the pain of our departure from India began to wane and we saw God's hand so very clearly in our lives. We recalled so many times during our time in India when we saw other international workers conflicted about whether they should stay in India or leave, struggling to have a clear word from the Lord about their future. We remember praying, "God please make it totally clear to us when we are to leave India. Just rip us out of this country when it's time." And oh boy, did He do just that. God is remarkable.

Today as we do life in America, we do so with all the experiences that we were privileged to have in India. We do life with the knowledge that we gained. We do life with the maturity we developed through all those years. But I think the most valuable thing we gained from our entire India experience, including the call to India, our training, our cultural adaptation, our time spent building relationships, and all that uncertainty we went through, was the personal resilience we built, something that can never be taken away from us. We learned that we can get through almost any tough time. We learned that even though people don't like us, we will still survive. We learned that even though we fail in some jobs we are given to do, we will still survive. We learned that even when life doesn't go as we expect it to go, we will still survive. Our capacity to recover quickly from life's difficulties is so valuable. It is a capacity that allows us to thrive personally, but it also allows us to care for others who need help. It allows us to remain calm in times of crisis. It allows us to

make decisions when the options are plenty and often confusing. This resilience allows us to overcome obstacles in life and in ministry and in our kids' lives and in our marriage. Resilience gives us emotional strength when life gets hard. We can remember that our history has proven to us that no matter what happens, God will be with us, we will survive and life will go on. We are so, so thankful.

Our time in India has forever changed us. No, not only changed us. It has formed us. It has shaped us. It has made us into the people we are today. We move forward as people who have India as a radical and tangible part of us. The people of India made an indelible mark on our lives that will never be removed, never be forgotten. God used India and her people to transform us into better people, better spouses, better parents, better friends, more resilient servants of God. We are so thankful and look forward to the day when we are reunited with our friends on Indian soil once again.

A WORD OF THANKS

I can't believe I have written this book.

I am so thankful for the chance to have done it at all. It really is a dream come true. I want to thank all those who encouraged me to write about my experiences. I want to thank all those who told me that I have a gift for writing and that they like to read what I write. That gave me the courage to write and the confidence to actually put this all down on paper.

Thank you to all those who agreed to read the manuscript before it was completed and gave me valuable feedback to make it better. I thought for sure that all the feedback would be negative. But you were all so kind to me and I am forever grateful for your good help with this project.: Heidi D., Heidi T., Nicole R., Mom, Darla B., Amanda T., Tina D., Ron S., Shannon S., Debbie B., Barbie G., Doug K., Joy V., Heidi J., Steve L., Debbie G., John N., Amy F., Scott G., Lisa H., Aunt Mary, and Barb C.

Thank you to Jacque Cork for designing the cover of my book. You are an artist! Thank you for being a great colleague, but an even better friend..

Tammy Brice? You're amazing! Thank you for making me look my best. I can't wait to have you take my photo again and again.

Thank you to the nation of India for all the lessons you taught me. I hope I can visit you again one day soon.

Thank you to the Good Shepherd Church of India for loving us so well.

Thank you to the COVID-19 global pandemic for creating margin in my schedule that allowed me the time to dedicate to write.

Thank you to my family for living all these experiences with me and learning all about resilience at the same time. Oh, and for putting up with all my crazy nicknames and singing and propensity to give away all our possessions. Oops.

Thank you most of all to God for loving me, making me resilient, and teaching me about grace a little more every day.

32811516R00137